The List

Joanna Bolouri

The List

Quercus

New York • London

Quercus

New York • London

© 2013 by Joanna Bolouri
First published in the United States by Quercus in 2015

ISBN 978-1-62365-994-3

Library of Congress Control Number: 2014954171

Distributed in the United States and Canada by
Hachette Book Group
1290 Avenue of the Americas
New York, NY 10104

This book is a work of fiction. Names, characters, institutions, places, and events are either the product of the author's imagination or are used fictitiously. Any resemblance to actual persons—living or dead—events, or locales is entirely coincidental.

Manufactured in the United States

10 9 8 7 6 5 4 3 2 1

www.quercus.com

*For Nicola, who
has been making me
laugh for 25 years*

JANUARY

Saturday, January 1

I emerged from my bed like Nosferatu about an hour ago with a mouth like a stable floor. Since the minibar has been cleaned out and I cannot find one cup in this entire hotel room, I've been forced to drink water directly from the bathroom tap. Fuck, I'm so hungover my face feels like it belongs to someone else. Lucy is still asleep on the other bed and I refuse to get dressed and venture out where there are people with eyes who will judge me.

For once the hangover was worth it, as last night's party was amazing! Every year we all stay at the Sapphire Hotel (overpriced, trendy, and slap-bang in the middle of the city center) to bring in the bells and every year I'm surprised they haven't banned us yet. The others had already checked in by the time Lucy and I arrived at half past three. We took the elevator to our floor, dragging our needlessly large suit-cases behind us as we searched for Room 413. I've worked with Lucy for two years and she's never on time for any-thing. "I bet the others are pissed already," said Lucy, "and screwing. I bet they're all covered in Moët and wearing each other's underwear."

Finally, we found our room and I fumbled with the key card in the door. "Jesus, is that all you ever think about? Anyway, we're only half an hour late. Hazel's most likely pricing the minibar, Kevin will be ready for a pint, and Oliver's probably—"

"Getting head off that Spanish girl," Lucy interrupted. "What's her name again?"

"Pedra. I've only met her once and called her Pedro by accident."

She threw her coat on the bed near the window and turned on the television as I started to unpack, wondering why the hell I'd brought four pairs of shoes.

"Are you wearing your green dress?" I asked, looking at the plain black one I'd brought.

"Yup. Although with my red hair, I look like a *Riverdance* reject."

I left her, mid–Irish jig, and went for a shower, excited about the evening ahead and thinking about last year's party: when Lucy got so drunk she fell asleep in the elevator and Oliver hid behind my bedroom door and scared me so badly I wet myself.

My train of thought was interrupted by a knock on the door and a familiar Dublin accent.

"Phoebe, I'm coming in. Put your cock away."

I grabbed the towel and wrapped it around me just as Oliver appeared from behind the door.

"Fuckssake, Oliver!" I shrieked, turning away from him. "Give a girl some privacy! Go and peek at Pedro's tits."

"It's Pedra, and I'm not here to see your tits, impressive as they are. I'm here to tell you that dinner is at seven p.m., and there was something else but Lucy's Irish dancing has distracted me and made me homesick for crazy redheads."

"Fine, I'll see you when I'm dressed. Go and annoy someone else."

An hour and two glasses of wine later, Lucy and I were still getting ready. The plan, every year, was to try to stay relatively sober until midnight, but generally we'd all be hammered by the time the bells chimed for New Year and do shots until we all fell over. I knew this year would be no different. "At least you don't have Alex with you," said Lucy, pulling on her tights. "That man bored the shit out of everyone last year, going on about his damn job. He's a physiotherapist, not a fucking wizard."

"I know."

"I mean, sleeping with his boss all that time, and he had the nerve to bring her into the conversation—"

"Enough!" I shouted. "Don't kill my buzz talking about that dickhead. It's over now. I just need to concentrate on finding someone who isn't a total prick."

"Don't set the bar too high." Lucy laughed. "And besides, it's not a new boyfriend you need, Phoebe, it's a screw! Sex makes everything better."

"My sex life is fine, thank you very much. What I need is another drink."

We met Hazel and Kevin at the bar before dinner. They had already thrown half a bottle of Champagne down their necks. Hazel saw me eyeing up the bottle.

"We have no child for the night. I intend to get shit-faced."

"Hey, I'm not judging. I celebrate the fact I have no child every night," I replied.

Hazel looked amazing in her pastel-pink evening dress. She'd swept her blond hair up into a high ponytail decorated with tiny diamantés. Her husband, Kevin, was in his kilt and looked very handsome. They always looked so effortlessly groomed that I felt a tad thrown together in my black wrap dress, red heels, and the same hairstyle I'd had since 1995.

"Oliver and Pedra not down yet?"

"From the way those two were slobbering over each other in the lobby, I'd be surprised if they've left the bedroom." Kevin laughed and then paused, obviously trying to picture this in his head.

A flustered-looking waiter ushered us into the main hall, where we all sat around beautifully decorated tables covered in white linen with green-and-red centerpieces. There must have been around a hundred tartan-clad guests and the atmosphere was electric. There were tables of hipsters wearing jaunty hats, ready to Instagram photos of their meal as soon as it arrived, the obligatory table of young lads who were pissed before the meal even arrived, and the occasional middle-aged couple who weren't quite sure what to make of the whole thing. The meal itself was traditional Scottish: steak pie, haggis, and some sort of tofu extravaganza for the vegetarians.

"That cutlery is immense," said Lucy, lifting a silver spoon up to her face. "I'd like these in my house."

"Steal it then," I joked, but then I saw the look on her face.

"Hey, klepto! Do not steal it. They made you pay for that robe last year, remember?"

"Yeah, but they don't allocate cutlery to room numbers. That was a schoolboy error on my part."

Ten minutes later, Oliver swaggered in with a cheeky grin on his face, followed by Pedra, a woman so beautiful I wanted to punch her in the face and then myself. "Finally! Did you two get lost?" I asked, knowing full well that wasn't the case.

"No," Pedra answered quite seriously.

"I'm starving," Oliver announced, stealing the bread roll Lucy was buttering. "When's the food?"

"You better replace that with something carby in five seconds, Webb, or I won't be responsible for my actions," Lucy growled.

"You never are." Oliver smirked, dropping another roll onto her plate. "A toast, please!" He raised his glass and we all followed. "To my good friends: Hazel and Kevin, who completely ruin my theory that all marriages are a sham; Lucy, the kind of woman my mother warned me about; Phoebe, my oldest and funniest friend; and finally to my lovely girlfriend, Pedra; I apologize in advance—this will get messy . . . oh, and not forgetting the new friends we will make and quickly lose this evening by being terrible human beings. Let's fucking do this."

We ate, we laughed, we danced, by midnight my shoes were lying under a table, I'd been outside for seventeen thousand cigarettes, and I was starting to get the "I'm going to be alone forever" New Year's blues when the slower songs came on. Thankfully Hazel spotted this and was able to pull me back off the ledge.

"You thinking about Alex?"

"Yeah. I think I still miss him."

"Nah, you miss the idea of him. The man you thought he was."

"The man I hoped he'd be."

"Exactly!"

"He was charming in the beginning."

"So was Ted Bundy," she quipped.

"I always thought Bundy would be a good name for a dog."

"Focus, Phoebe."

"Ugh, look, maybe I didn't try hard enough either. He did have moments when he was quite loving and tender. Maybe I—"

"Maybe you didn't, Phoebe, who knows, but you didn't screw around and he did! Alex was cheating on you for four months. That's four months' worth of lies for you and his mistress! That's not an endearing quality in any man."

I knocked back my tequila. "Why do I always gravitate toward assholes? I'll never find anyone good."

"You'll find someone new. Perhaps you need to go for someone who isn't your normal type."

"Like a woman?"

"No. I mean someone you'd never usually consider, but, most importantly, someone who deserves you."

"YES!" I shouted, startling a nearby man in an ill-fitting kilt. "This year I'm going to find someone. Someone different. Someone brilliant!"

"You can do whatever you want. This is going to be your year, girl. Start living it. Now come dance before we all turn into pumpkins."

And so here I am, the first day of my brand-new year, and all I have to show for it so far is a hangover, a new zit on my chin, and a handbag full of Lucy's stolen cutlery. I'm going back to bed.

Sunday, January 2

Today I have decided to make my New Year's resolutions and become a better, more useful person instantly. But instead of the usual—lose weight, make money, unfollow everyone on Twitter who uses freakin' chat acronyms—I've decided to ask myself one question: if I could do last year again, what would I do differently? Every year I make the same lame resolutions, yet nothing really changes, and I end up wondering why I bothered. So, this year, the plan is to choose just one thing and actually get off my ass and do something about it. The question is, what? I've been brooding over where it went wrong with Alex, but the more I think about it the more I realize it was never right in the first place, even before he pissed off with Miss Tits. (I should really grow up and call her Susan, but that doesn't quite convey the level of my disdain.) The first night we met, I was so grateful that this tall, handsome man had shown interest in me I bought every round of drinks and thrust my phone number into his hand at the end of the evening. I didn't hear from him again until two agonizing weeks later. I realize now that even that was significant. He kept me at arm's length for our entire relationship, occasionally pulling me in to give me a glimpse of what a funny, sensitive person he could be, but only when he chose to. So while I wanted to be swept off my feet, in reality I was just tripped up occasionally. That bastard has a PhD in manipulation, and I swear if you looked up "fucker" in the dictionary, there would be a photo of him, holding my heart, and possibly my severed head, looking victorious and doing a little jig. I could never quite live up to his expectations . . . I wasn't educated enough or groomed enough or impressive enough. I just wasn't enough. I wasted four years with someone who was completely underwhelmed to be with me. That's the real kick in the vag. What a waste of time.

I spent over five hundred pounds on therapy in the last year with a forty-something-year-old American therapist called Pam Potter, whose name makes her sound like a garden gnome, but who happily listens to me bitch and whine in exchange for fifty pounds an hour (she was marginally cheaper than the psychologists with real names) and then says, "I hear what you're saying, Phoebe." The fact she had two working ears leads me to believe this was true, but not entirely helpful. However, it did help me come to the conclusions that (a) I am still angry about the whole Alex thing, and (b) although I wasn't completely blameless in our relationship, I did deserve better. No, I do deserve better. This year, I have to get Alex out of my system once and for all.

Monday, January 3

It was Pam Potter's idea that I keep a diary. Apparently this whole "writing down my feelings" lark should be therapeutic, but it just feels weird.

I haven't kept a diary since I was a fifteen-year-old loner with an ear cuff and a mono-brow. Back then my diary was hidden under my mattress and contained 13,000 different swearwords to describe my parents, along with some angst-ridden poetry about a boy in my class who never spoke and wore eyeliner. As it is, I still like boys who wear eyeliner, but I'm less inclined to insult my parents these days, except for when they send me those organic chocolates I hate at Christmas.

Despite it being a holiday, I had my first monthly session of the year with Pam this evening. She'd dyed her hair brown over Christmas and looked remarkably like Tina Fey.

"How was the New Year for you? In our last session you mentioned you were still struggling with your breakup. Has that changed?"

"God, no. I feel as if all I do is think about him . . . or moan about him . . . or just miss him. Recently I am seeing things more clearly, though."

"In what way?"

"I threw myself into that relationship headfirst. I'll be the first to admit that I was lonely, and when he showed interest in me I clung on to him. I might have been needy, but he was worse—he was lazy. He was too lazy to end it so instead he just kept me there until someone better could replace me. He couldn't even be bothered to have his affair somewhere private. I remember when I caught them in our bed. OUR FUCKING BED!"

Pam just nodded, but I'm certain that if she wasn't being paid to sit through this story for the millionth time she'd have happily drop-kicked me out the office window.

I could feel myself shaking as I visualized the moment I caught Alex. I'd arrived home early from a concert that had been canceled at the last minute. I came in and threw my jacket on the couch and watched it fall on top of a bra I didn't own. It was bright pink and about three cup sizes bigger than mine. The moaning from the bedroom gave me the answer to a question I hadn't even had time to ask myself. "I walked into the room and stood there like an idiot. I couldn't even speak. He just shrugged and said, 'This was bound to happen. You knew things weren't right between us.' I stayed with Hazel until I found my own place. She's been very supportive. All my friends have."

"Good. That's important. But it's been almost a year, Phoebe. How do you feel you can move on from here? You've expressed the desire to on several occasions."

"I've been thinking about New Year resolutions. I need to change the way I think, otherwise I'm going to be stuck in this cycle forever. I'm going to change. I'm just not sure how yet."

After my session with Pam, I called Oliver to tell him my plans. I could practically hear him rolling his eyes at me.

"You don't need to make a list of stupid resolutions you'll never keep, Phoebe. Remember last year you were going to start running?"

"I did start running. I totally ran. And anyway, I'm just making one resolution this year, one that matters."

"You ran once 'round the park and then you vomited in a hedge, Phoebe. That doesn't count. You need to stop being so uptight and planning things. You never used to be like this. You used to be fun and carefree! We used to get pissed and you'd tell me all your secrets and we'd dance to really shit pop music at five a.m. Now you're like the anti-Phoebe."

So much for the support of my friends. "I got a little lost," I said quietly. "You know it's taken me a while to get back on track after I split with Alex."

"I know that, but I suggest it's time you start getting found. And laid. You need to get your groove back."

"Jesus, you sound just like Lucy. You two are obsessed."

"You sound repressed."

"I'm going now. Save your sex advice for Pedro. I have plans to make. Talk later."

Trust him to piss all over my chips. He knows nothing.

Tuesday, January 4

Back at work today after my New Year break and I immediately wanted to set myself on fire. I've been working at this newspaper for three years, and approximately three weeks have been enjoyable. After running screaming from high school at seventeen, advertising sales was pretty much the only job for which my supposedly winning personality was more important than my qualifications. This was just as well, as I scraped a C in English and had a master's in forgery after faking my mother's handwriting on sick notes throughout my final year. I'm surprised they didn't have some sort of fun run to raise money for my recovery. The trouble with my job is that I'm meant to be good with people. Charming, even. Be interested in what they have to say and make them trust me, nay, LOVE ME to the point that they name their first child after me and then leave the kid out of their will because they love me more. But in fact I suck at small talk, I hate it, and if someone doesn't want to take advertising space that's fine with me; I honestly couldn't care less. That last statement perfectly sums up my attitude toward my job: *I couldn't care less.* But I do my best to talk a good enough game and sell my soul on a daily basis because I need to pay the rent. We share office space with ten other companies, most of which are in the financial sector, so I often have to share the elevator with ball bags who wear ridiculous ties and talk about numbers and golf. On the upside, the location is brilliant: a two-minute walk from the train station and upstairs from a pub and a sandwich shop, where I'm found most mornings buying coffee and toast. The sales floor is mostly open-plan, and my desk is unfortunately directly in front of my boss Frank's office, giving him a perfect view of what

I'm doing all day (which is usually nothing). Most of the other staff have pictures of their family on their desks, but my "unkempt shambles that I call a workspace" (Frank's words) is decorated with a picture of a cat with a watermelon on its head, mostly obscured by empty coffee cups and aspirin packets. Today's regular morning meeting was painless enough—lots of encouragement from said boss, who is the most horrendous blowhard to have ever walked the Earth, which no one paid any attention to. Then I caught up on four hundred e-mails that had arrived over Christmas and the skeleton staff had ignored. Lucy arrived late as usual, stuffing her face with a breakfast bagel and swigging coffee from her glittery flask. "You all right, my lovely?" she shouted over. "Recovered yet?"

"Yeah, I'm fine; you want to have dinner tonight? Sushi?"

"I can't. I already have plans."

"New fella?"

"Old fella. That guy I was seeing last year, the one with that yappy dog I hated."

"You said you'd never date anyone with dogs again. What changed?"

"His dog died."

I am 43 percent 97 percent sure that Lucy had nothing to do with that dog's demise. Lucy, like Oliver, is a serial dater. When I first started at the *Post* she was dating two men at the same time and this seemed perfectly acceptable to her. She's like the Pied Piper with men; they follow her wherever she goes and she has no intentions of becoming tied down anytime soon.

"The dating part is the fun part. After you start all that living-together nonsense it becomes a drag, so I prefer to keep things simple. I love the 'getting to know you' part."

I, on the other hand, have never been very good at dating, and the "getting to know you" part scares the shit out of
me. I've had five dates in my entire life, and all of them ended
up in some sort of relationship. There was Chris—my first
boyfriend at school, which lasted precisely six months, until
he went to university in Manchester; Adam with the exceptionally large penis, whom I dated for five months before he
decided he'd rather piss off and join the Air Force than be stuck
in Glasgow with me; Joseph, who only lasted three months
as he had issues with intimacy and being shit in bed; James,
whom I dated for a year, but who was profoundly annoying
and had a crippling phobia of baked beans; and finally Alex,
who turned out to be the biggest mistake of my life. Even
though it's been nearly a year since we split, the thought of
having to find someone new continues to be frightening and
I don't see me rushing out to meet anyone anytime soon.

Thursday, January 6

Alex has been on my mind a lot today, but I've had her in my
head too, with her bouncing curls and bouncing tits, held
up by her giant pink bra. I imagine it's never easy when you
find out someone has cheated on you, but when you actually catch them screwing in your bed, it's a tough image to
erase from your mind. I could never figure out what he saw
in her, but as always, Lucy's on hand to offer some insight.

"I'll tell you what he saw in her!" she bellowed down the
phone. "He saw his damn mother. It's his Oedipus complex.
His father's dead, isn't he? Says it all."

"His father's very much alive, but excellent theory. Anyway, how was your dog-free date?"

"Horrible. He talked about the dog, showed me pictures
of the dog, and as his life is so empty he's thinking of getting

hamsters. What is he—an eight-year-old girl? I'll be fucked if I'm dating a grown man who keeps rodents. Right, I must dash, but please try not to dwell on Alex too much. You'll drive yourself crazy."

Three hours later and I'm still dwelling. I have so many unanswered questions, which I know I'll never get answers to. Even if I confronted Alex, I doubt I'd be happy with, or even believe, a word that came out of his mouth. I still have feelings for him—that much is clear. I just don't know whether it's love or a need for closure. I think Oliver is wrong; I shouldn't be trying to find "the old Phoebe." Even I don't recognize the old me anymore. Perhaps Oliver still sees me as that seventeen-year-old who used to smoke grass in his bedroom and sneak into clubs with him on weekends. But I haven't been that girl for a long time. I think instead I should be embracing the arrival of a "new Phoebe." One who is successful and liberated and brave and who doesn't refer to herself in the third person. Oliver texted me on his way home from work.

Tomorrow night: me, you, Jack Daniel's and the Human League.

He's either trying to cheer me up or he's dumped his girlfriend.

Friday, January 7

Kelly, who works on the health-and-beauty section, is a strange fish. No one (except Frank, I guess) has any idea how old she is. She dresses like a woman in her twenties, but has the leathery face of someone twice that age who's also spent the past twenty years asleep in a sunbed. She can be difficult to work with, as she doesn't bother hiding her contempt for the rest of us, choosing instead to express it through scowling, tantrums, and passive-aggressive cuntery. This morning was no different.

"If you're going to borrow my pen, Brian, I'd appreciate it if you put it back exactly where you found it. How am I supposed to write down information when you've taken my fucking pen?"

Kelly hates Brian, and Brian feels the same about her. He works on the recruitment section and although he's good at his job, he's a mouthy, arrogant little shitbag, known throughout the office for his sexist views and love of large-breasted women. We seem to get on well enough, but I assume that's partly because I have big tits. Brian looked at the nondescript pen in his hand. "You could buy another pen and then you'd have a spare. I'm sure these babies come in packs of ten."

"Not the point. The point is, keep your hands off my shit and get your own pen. Now, give me that one back."

"You're serious, aren't you?" He laughed.

"Of course I am. Give me it back."

He stood up, shaking his head. Then he got up, put the pen up his left nostril and left it hanging there as he approached Kelly's desk.

"I'm sorry I took your important pen, Kelly. Here. Take it."

"What a disgusting child you are!" she exclaimed, and promptly slapped the pen out of his nose and onto the floor. I was still laughing as she stormed past my desk straight into Frank's office. Shrugging, Brian picked up the pen and put it back on her desk. These people are not normal.

Oliver arrived a little after seven this evening with a huge duffel bag and a bottle of bourbon.

"Moving in?" I inquired, closing the door behind him.

"No, I'm off to Edinburgh for work tomorrow afternoon, didn't want to leave this in the car. I'm crashing on your couch tonight though. I intend to get wasted."

He handed me the bottle and produced a Best of the '80s CD from his bag. "You pour, I'll stick this on. If you're not dancing by track six, we can no longer be friends."

By track five ("Kids in America") I was pouring my second drink and shuffling on the kitchen tiles in my pink slippers. By the end of the CD we were both hammered and deep in conversation.

"You're like my brother."

"What the fuck? Don't say that! That's just weird."

"No, I mean, you're like my family. You're more than just my friend."

"Yeah, but your brother? You can't like your brother."

"What? I don't like you! You think everyone likes you."

"That's because they do. I'm awesome."

"No, I'm awesome. You're just handsome."

"You are awesome and also handsome, Miss Henderson."

"Am I? Do you like me?"

"Nope."

"Ha-ha, fuck off."

By five a.m. I'd gone to bed leaving awesome Oliver asleep on the couch. Maybe I do like him a teeny bit, but I'm not telling him that.

Saturday, January 8

I didn't surface until four this afternoon, and Oliver had already left for Edinburgh. I thought about doing something productive, but decided that watching *Dexter* and eating teacakes was a far better way to waste an entire day. It's now eleven p.m., I'm wide-awake, and I'm horny. Stupidly so. Hangover horns are brutal. I'm also still thinking about stupid freakin' Alex and ways to get him out of my system. Maybe Oliver and Lucy have a point? I haven't had sex since we broke up, and now I'm turning into some raging hormone who tweets her desires because she has no one to pounce on. When I think about it, my sex life has always been a bit hit and miss. People go on and freakin' on about how fantastic sex is, and although I've enjoyed it, it's like watching the second *Matrix* film—parts of it were good, but it didn't exactly blow me away. But I've never had sex just for me; it's always been about the other person. Maybe it's time to start taking care of me for once. If I focus on me, I won't have time to think about that dickhead, will I? Maybe the best way to get over him is to get over my hang-ups. The old Phoebe, the one who loves Alex, is a timid, sexually inhibited doormat. If I get rid of her, there won't be any need for him. That's it! That's what I'm going to change, what I'm going to do differently this year. That's going to be my one resolution: I'm going to improve my sex life!

There are loads of things I've always wanted to try—I'm going to take matters into my own hands and find out what all the fuss is about.

Wednesday, January 12

My apartment really needs some sort of makeover, but I have neither the funds nor the motivation to do anything about it. It's a tiny one-bedroom shoebox, approximately one-eighth of the flat I shared with Alex. It has an open-plan kitchen/living room, which means everything I cook makes the entire flat smell for days, and walls made from tracing paper. I can hear the old lady upstairs coughing at night, so God knows what she's heard me doing. There's a small garden at the front where flowers go to die, and if I ever manage to move, I'll be throwing a lit match behind me as I go.

Lucy came over after dinner tonight and promptly threw herself down on the couch face-first.

"Evening, Lucy. Um . . . why are you wearing cropped pants in January? Has winter not arrived on your planet yet?"

"Style knows no seasonal restraints," she said, her voice muffled by the faded blue cushions on my couch. "I've come to reclaim what is rightfully mine. Give me back my straighteners."

"They're in my room. Feeling rough?"

There was a groaning sound, followed by another unidentified one, which could have been a fart. "Ugh. Your neighbors were all hanging around outside, wearing velour and drinking. Why do you live in this dump?"

"It's all I can afford. Besides, I'm at work, I hardly see them."

"They're probably wondering where you go during the day. Speaking of which, I don't want to go back to work on Monday. Can you break both my legs, but do it in a way that won't hurt?"

"No," I replied, not looking up from my magazine, "I'd be bored without you there."

"This isn't about you. What's happening, anyway?"

"You need to help me with my sex life."

She started to dry-hump the couch.

"I'm serious! I haven't had sex since Alex."

"What? I thought you said your sex life was fine? A WHOLE YEAR? What's the matter with you?"

"Nothing! I want to have sex, but I just can't face more awful sex where I fake it and then have to pretend he's just done something amazing. I want it to actually BE amazing! You can help me with this; how can I change things?"

Lucy wasn't speaking now. Or humping. She turned over to face me, pushing her red hair out of her eyes.

"I can't believe you're still faking it in your thirties! Are you secretly one of those women who'd prefer to eat an entire chocolate Easter egg than have sex?"

"Ha-ha, NO!" I insisted. "I love sex—it's just never been that great. I mean, I'm sure not every guy I've slept with has been awful—"

"Joseph?"

"Oh Christ, yeah, he was awful."

"But why the hell are you faking?" she asked, looking genuinely confused.

"I think that if I make sure the guy has a good time and make him think he's brilliant in bed, he'll keep seeing me and maybe it'll get better. I mean, I'm not a prude—there's a million things I've always wanted to try but I've never had the guts to, or even a partner who's been sexually adventurous enough. Alex wasn't an adventurous person; he was the freakin' missionary king. Jesus, I don't even know where to begin. But I've been thinking about the one thing I want to change this year and that's it: I want to change my sex life. I want to explore every sordid fantasy that comes into my head!"

I really wanted to tell her the other reason behind all this, but I knew she'd only sigh with frustration if she found out Alex had anything to do with it.

Lucy sprang into life. "You should make a list!"

"A list of what? Ways to fill my time while I'm waiting for my virginity to grow back?"

"You know, like those lists you get online of 'Twenty Things You Should Do Before You Die' or 'Ten Places to Visit Before You Have Kids and They Just Ruin It Completely.'

Well, you should make your own list—a list of sex challenges. I'll help you. Oh, this could be fun."

So we threw on some music and the rest of this evening was spent drinking wine, creating my list, and occasionally stopping to sing at each other as loudly as possible. Our Eminem-Dido duet was particularly impressive. There are some things that never made it onto the list, mainly because they were stupid, like banging movie stars from the '90s. Much as I like Christian Slater and Johnny Depp, I'm not risking a restraining order finding out if they'd be up for it now. In the end, this is what we came up with:

THE LIST

1. **Talking dirty**. I suck at this.
2. **Masturbation**. I am BRILLIANT at this, but still, practice makes perfect and I'm very curious about female ejaculation.
3. **Younger men**. I say "men," but one will do.
4. **Anal**. This could go horribly, HORRIBLY wrong.
5. **Role play**. I get to dress up.
6. **Sex outside**. I want to do it in the great outdoors. Or even a reasonably sized garden.
7. **Group sex**. Threesome and/or another couple. No bukkake—yucky.
8. **Sex with a complete stranger**. Like a one-night stand but without all the painful small talk beforehand, or afterward.
9. **Bondage**. No furry handcuffs though.
10. **Voyeurism**. Consensual, obviously. I'm not going to peek in windows.

The main rule is "no bareback," but I've also come up with a small list of things that are out of the question. Even though I consider myself an open-minded kind of gal, everyone has their limits and these are mine:

1. **Anything to do with feet.** I hate feet. They're ugly, hard-skin-covered monstrosities that should be kept away from my face at all times. I'd never dream of sticking my toe in someone's mouth, but perhaps it's because I have horrific little trotters.

2. **Pissing/Shitting.** WHY GOD WHY? Someone explain this to me. Waste is not sexy; not my own and certainly not someone else's. I can honestly say that I would never piss on anyone, even if they were on fire or had been stung by a satanic jellyfish. I won't even pee in the shower, so this is never going to happen.

3. **Fisting.** Childbirth in reverse? I'm sure it has its own merits, but I don't intend to find out. A particularly large cock can leave me feeling violated, so I'm sure some guy's fist would be the end of me.

4. **Animals.** As a teenager I saw a video clip of a woman giving a horse a blow job. I kept hoping it would kick her in the face. It didn't.

5. **Facials.** I find the whole idea totally degrading but I understand it's more for the guy than the girl (obviously). That said, I really don't want the image of my face covered in spunk embedded in some guy's mind for all eternity. The only time I've ever come close is when I was seventeen and gave my boyfriend a hand job on his couch. It was just unfortunate aiming on his part and my eye caught the majority of it. Temporary blindness and a feeling of mortification followed,

while he giggled and almost patted himself on the back with his own cock.

Lucy is far more forgiving when it comes to facials. "I think it's a territorial thing. I'd prefer that to him pissing in the corner of the room." Fair enough. There are undoubtedly a million more things I won't or can't do, but until then my line has been drawn with a big black marker. "Right, I'm off," said Lucy, pulling on her coat, "but before I go there is one thing you should think about. Something we seem to have overlooked. A minor detail, but pretty crucial."

"What? What have we forgotten?"

"Someone for you to do these challenges with. Oh, and my straighteners."

Thursday, January 13

Unfortunately a busy sales office is not what I need when all I can focus on is sex, or rather whom I'm going to recruit to help me in my quest. Lucy arrived at half nine and got straight on the phone to me.

"Morning, lovely! Had any more thoughts on who you could ask to be your fuck buddy then?"

"Not yet. Slow down. This scares the hell out of me! I know you're used to all this but I'm not. I've never slept with someone I wasn't dating. What if I panic and can't go through with it? This is a very real possibility."

Lucy's always been more adventurous than me and used to have her own blog detailing her abundant bangs and rating them. Perhaps she's right, though—maybe the trick is to avoid conversation and just grunt at each other before you, well, grunt at each other. I do have a problem with it only being physical though. For me, sex is about more than just physical attraction, and I'm not particularly into the idea of banging people I don't like. Where's the fun in that? I can barely make small talk with someone I'm not keen on, let alone let them have access to my vagina. I want someone I can connect with mentally, too; not necessarily emotionally, but knowing we're at least on approximately the same wavelength is important. While I should have been working I started making a list of possible participants.

From: Phoebe Henderson
To: Lucy Jacobs
Subject: Men

OK, I've come up with a list of guys I think might be up for this—please review and comment.

Brian—Yes, I know he's a prick but he's single and good-looking.

Paul—He's back from New York now.

Oliver—He'd obviously be my last resort and I doubt he'd even say yes but he's hot, and from what I've heard through walls, he seems to know what he's doing. Also, is he still seeing that Pedra girl? I can't remember.

xx

From: Lucy Jacobs
To: Phoebe Henderson
Subject: Re: Men

See comments.

Brian —Yes, I know he's a prick but he's single and good-looking. *Agreed, but he's younger, a total lad and would definitely tell the entire office.*

Paul—He's back from New York now. *Maybe . . . He is fit but I don't find him sexy. This isn't about me though, is it?*

Oliver—He'd obviously be my last resort and I doubt he'd even say yes but he's hot, and from what I've heard through walls, he seems to know what he's doing. Also, is he still seeing that Pedra girl? I can't remember. *I have no idea, but you have been friends with Oliver for sixteen years—even asking him to do this might ruin your friend-ship. Tread carefully with this one. Wait. Actually, if you guys stop being friends I can sleep with him, so forget what I said. PICK HIM!*

From: Phoebe Henderson
To: Lucy Jacobs
Subject: Re: Men

You are not allowed to sleep with Oliver regardless. He's one of my best friends and you have a tendency to make men cry. I guess since Brian is sitting four feet away I could start with him. I'm going to have to find a way to approach the subject without just blurting it out and then watching him either knock me back or die laughing. Any ideas? Hair looks great today btw.

From: Lucy Jacobs
To: Phoebe Henderson
Subject: Re: Men

Does it? Thanks. Unless "great" actually means "frizzy," in which case, up yours. Good point—there's nothing worse than watch-ing someone try to squirm their way out of something. Get him drunk and deny it all if it goes tits up.

So I've arranged a boozy lunch with Brian on Monday. I'm praying this doesn't backfire.

Saturday, January 15

I had a dream last night where I was sitting in the pub with Hazel, and Miss Tits walked in. I promptly pulled her outside by her bra straps and proceeded to beat her to death using my kung-fu moves. I'm excellent at dream-world kung fu.

I got up early to catch up on housework, but approximately seven minutes after starting I remembered that housework is astoundingly boring and stopped again. This interlude was followed by showering, eating, and a quick call from Oliver.

"Want to go to the cinema tonight?"

"What's on? I'm not going to see some superhero shit with you, Oliver."

"They're showing *The Breakfast Club* at the GFT."

"Really? I love that film! NO, DAD, WHAT ABOUT YOU?"

"Phoebe, I'm not letting you come if you just shout random quotes from it all evening."

"Will milk be made available to us?"

"Forget it, I'll go with someone else."

"Ha-ha-haa, nooo, I'm sorry. No more. I'd love to go."

"OK, it starts at eight. I'll meet you there."

He was standing outside smoking as I walked over. A group of girls behind him were looking over and giggling, clearly talking about how fit he was. Their stares of lust for him quickly became looks of hatred for me as I hugged him hello. As I watched him smoke his cigarette I remembered the "Hey, smoke up, Johnny" line from the film—the film I'd promised not to quote from. I pursed my lips.

He noticed. "You're dying to say it, aren't you?" He laughed.

"Hmm? Say what? I wasn't going to say anything," I lied, when in fact at that moment my need to say it was greater than my need to breathe.

He purposefully took long draws, smiling slyly as he did. It was torture, but my resolve was strong. HE WOULDN'T BREAK ME. If I just stopped thinking about it, the urge would pass and . . .

"HEY, SMOKE UP, JOHNNY!" I yelled in his face as he took the final draw from his cigarette, then proceeded to march into the cinema, leaving his group of admirers laughing, and me cursing myself for not being able to control my own geeky behavior.

Afterward, Oliver dropped me off and I've been back here for fifteen minutes with no one to quote the film to. Dammit. Luckily Twitter is full of geeks just like me.

Monday, January 17

After the morning sales meeting, Marion announced that she was taking her maternity leave a week earlier than planned, her reason being: "I am too fat and too tired for this shit." Frank agreed that she could finish at the end of the day and then we all watched him panic because he'd obviously forgotten to even bother looking for someone to cover her section. I reminded Brian that we were having lunch and went to fix my makeup in the bathroom so as to give my potential sex helper one less reason to say no.

We trudged downstairs, ordered food, and started to chat. Within about fifteen minutes I got a sinking feeling in the pit of my stomach. I knew it wouldn't work. He most definitely wasn't the one. I tentatively approached the subject of sex (which he was more than happy to get into) but then listened, openmouthed, as he bragged about his latest "conquest," who apparently was useless in bed and had no tits, followed by a story of when he forwarded a sex text from a girl at university to all his friends for a laugh. "It was dead funny; you should have seen her face." Bah. Lucy was right. This guy would tell the office, his friends, their friends, and the guy who sells *The Big Issue* outside Boots. Probably his mum, too. Not the discreet, mature setup I have in mind. I changed the subject to something less salacious, finished my sandwich, and told him he was a prick. He thought I was joking. I spent the rest of the afternoon drawing little hangman stick figures of Brian and putting nooses around their necks.

I went to see Hazel after work. She'd been visiting family in London since New Year to show off her new baby, Grace, who, as far as babies go, is disgustingly cute. The walk over was freezing, and lethal due to the ice on the sidewalks. I despise January. It's slippery and cold and I spend most of it with a broken ass after spectacular public falls. Hazel welcomed me with a high-pitched squeal and ushered me into the kitchen, where she'd laid out mince pies and mulled wine. Her house is so impressive: hardwood floors, massive rooms, and a huge garden with a hammock between two tall trees in the center (which I've drunkenly fallen out of more times than I care to remember). Her place is comfortable; it feels like a family home. When I come here I'm reminded of how much I hate my apartment.

"This is why I love you," I said, sitting down at the table and grabbing a pie. "So how was the trip? Did you have fun?"

She handed me a glass. "It was great. Kevin's family are loaded. They have a freakin' hot tub. I pretty much lived in there. I only came out to feed Grace and eat scones. Anyway, Grace is asleep with Kevin and I need a drink. How are you? You've coped well with your first holiday season without Alex."

"Yeah, I'm OK. Don't get me wrong, I've thought about him, but I've decided it's time to get him out of my system once and for all. Fuck, it's all I ever talk about these days . . . with Lucy, with Oliver, with Pam Potter, and now you. When will it end?"

"He's just a habit you have to break. Like smoking. Or that time we both went to the gym three times in one month."

"I like smoking and a month's free gym membership can't really be classed as a habit, can it? Although, without it you'd never have met Kevin."

"Ah, yes. In a sea of six-packs I chose to fall in love with the fat fella on the treadmill. His stamina was incredible. Still is." She grinned.

"I have no idea what to say to that."

She poured some more wine. "It took me two years and a tequila drip to get over Jon. I was thirty-four when I divorced him and was married to Kevin by thirty-seven. Life goes on."

"There were never any marriage plans with us. Alex made it clear from the start he didn't want to. I guess I just went along with it, in case he changed his mind about the whole thing."

Hazel paused for a moment, chewing on a mince pie, and I knew she was thinking about Jon. She'd been divorced for two years when we met and she rarely speaks about him, but what I do know is that Jon was a doctor who'd been struck off for inappropriate conduct with a seventeen-year-old patient. "Do you think of Jon often?" I asked, wondering if I should have kept my mouth shut, but she laughed into her glass.

"Sometimes I do, but never fondly. To be honest, the divorce settlement allowed me to stop working for that ad agency and set up from home, so I have that to be thankful for."

"Yeah, but now I have no reason to visit your office and pretend we're discussing clients. Jon made my day longer, so that's another reason you can hate him."

She clinked my glass. "I don't need another reason, but I'm taking it. Do you realize it's been three years since you first came into my office? I wish I'd known you before you were with Alex. I'd have been more use in helping you back to your old self."

"God, everyone wants me to go back to the 'old' me. The old me can fuck off. I plan to become a brand-new woman."

I detailed my plan for sexual liberation, listing what I wanted to try, but quietly in case Kevin overheard. Hazel listened with a massive smile on her face.

"Goddamn! You're so brave. At the moment my sex life is nonexistent. We grab the occasional quickie while Grace sleeps, but I think my vagina is still traumatized after giving birth. But you'd better tell me everything you get up to. Maybe you'll inspire me."

"I'm hoping to inspire myself. I just want to move on from Alex."

"Fuck him. You're already a year down the road; it'll get easier. You'll be fine. Trust me."

Of course I'll be fine. I'll have to be—the alternative is too bleak to contemplate.

Tuesday, January 18

While walking up Hope Street on my way into work this morning, I saw Alex. Self-righteous, annoying, but still handsome Alex. I must remember *never* to date someone who works in a nearby office, let alone live with them. It would have been easier if it had just been him on his own, but oh no, it had to be him and Miss Tits getting into her flashy car. If I could have run away without being spotted, I'd have gladly kicked off my shoes and bolted, but I might as well have been holding a banner with OVER HERE! painted in neon letters, as they both spotted me simultaneously. I could almost feel the cross hairs from Miss Tits appearing on my forehead as if I were some kind of enemy target. She stole *my* boyfriend, not the other way around.

There was no conversation, just an awkward nod of acknowledgment on his part. I did my best to stare straight ahead, when in hindsight I should have karate-chopped them both into oncoming traffic. Alex broke my heart with that woman and they haven't even had the decency to die in some random "evil couple eaten by pandas" incident, or at least leave the country. Sometimes, when I think about the whole thing, I imagine myself on one of those weird documentaries about female killers, with a dramatic voice-over intoning: "THEY BROKE HER HEART . . . SO SHE BROKE THEIR NECKS." I got into the office and ran into the toilets. I didn't even hear Lucy come in. I swear that girl moves as if she's on casters. "What's up? You're not being sick, are you? You're on your own if you are—I'm allergic to vomit."

"I just saw Alex and that woman outside. I feel like throwing up, believe me. I saw them and it was like being punched in the face and the stomach at the same time. They looked fucking . . . happy."

After hearing Lucy call him every swearword ever invented (and some I hadn't heard before, including "asshat"), I felt better.

Wednesday, January 19

I arrived into work this morning to discover a new fella sitting at Marion's old desk. Distractingly attractive. So attractive, in fact, I want to sound a klaxon to show my appreciation every time he walks past my desk. A quick introduction later I discovered his name is Stuart. I watched Lucy drool over him before e-mailing me.

From: Lucy Jacobs
To: Phoebe Henderson
Subject: Yum

He is gorgeous. I might be in love. I'm going to find out his address, break in and watch him sleep. You should add him to your list. I don't even have a list but he's on mine.

From: Phoebe Henderson
To: Lucy Jacobs
Subject: Re: Yum

Yeah, good idea. "Welcome to the company, Stuart. I know you've only been here 13 seconds but do you feel like having meaning-less but discreet sex with me? Well?"

Reminded that I'd better be getting on with my search, I called the next possibility on my list, Paul, and arranged to see him this evening. I never usually like blond guys, but there's something very endearing about him. He used to work at the *Post* before he went back to university to study economics, and we've kept in touch since he left. He's a lovely guy, but nothing has ever happened between us and I've always secretly wondered why. We rarely discuss dating, or sex, or anything really, other than friends, music, and how many drugs he'd taken the previous weekend and how many I hadn't. He's been in New York for the past six months and is back in Glasgow to sign papers on an apartment he's just bought and to arrange his moving-in date.

10 p.m. Just back from seeing Paul. We sat in his parents' house and had tea (not ideal when probing for clues as to whether he'd be up for sex).

"How does it feel to be home?" I asked, looking around his bedroom. "Jesus, Paul, have your parents kept this room exactly the same since you left home?"

"Pretty much." He grinned. "Although there used to be a signed Celtic photo on the back wall. My dad's probably nabbed that for his shed. It feels weird actually—so much has happened since I was last here."

"Tell me about it. Like, I've been forced to go to the cinema alone, as 'horror films are for dickheads with no imagination.'"

"Lucy?"

"Who else? Everyone is excited to see you though. Oliver says you've to call him for footie practice."

"What's been happening with you?"

"Boring as usual," I lied. "I've been filling my time with work, American TV shows, and very little else. I'd much rather hear what you've been up to."

"Lots of sex," he said confidently. "It's been wicked."

"You lucky shit. Was it the Scottish accent? How many women did you sleep with?"

"Um, none," he said, smiling. "Actually, I came out in New York. I met a guy."

"Came out where? Wait. What? WHAT? Oh. Shit! I had no idea!"

"Yeah, it's taken me a while, but it's out there now. Mum's cool but Dad's not handling it too well. He keeps asking me if I like to dress in women's clothes and watch *Glee*."

I decided not to tell him the real reason I had wanted to see him. His news was much more worthy than mine. There's a horror double-bill showing at the cinema next week, so I'll tell him about my plan for the year then. Anyway, I've crossed him off the list of candidates and finally closed the "Why didn't we ever sleep together" file and moved it to the "Because I'm not a man" section. Two down, and only Oliver left to go. This might be a huge mistake.

Thursday, January 20

I invited Oliver out for a drink this evening and of course he said yes. Not because it's me; purely because the guy never refuses a pint. I sat waiting for him for fifteen minutes, worrying he'd somehow magically worked out what I was after and fled the country, but he finally arrived. As he walked into the pub, for a second he looked just like that sixteen-year-old boy who'd joined my high school in sixth year. I remembered being bewitched by his smile and that mop of black curly hair and how we'd become friends so quickly, much to the disgust of every other girl in school who fancied the ass off him. He'd never laid a finger on me, but we knew all the gory details of each other's early fumblings. Normally it was easy to talk about sex with Oliver, but tonight I was nervous.

Oliver wandered back from the bar carrying an elaborate cocktail and a pint of Guinness.

"What the hell is that?" I asked, staring at the blue monstrosity he put in front of me.

"It's called a Moody Blue. I have no idea what's in it, but you'll look like a prick drinking it."

"I make anything look good," I lied, taking a sip and trying not to gag at the overly sweet concoction. "Fucking hell, this tastes like armpit."

"And your lips are now stained blue. Well worth the two quid."

He pulled off his scarf and looked toward the bar, winking at a girl standing beside a short, overweight man in a parka.

"Behave yourself. Whatever would Pedra think?" I asked, rubbing my blue lips on a napkin.

"I dunno. I'm not seeing her anymore."

"Oh, there's a surprise. What happened? Did you buy her an armpit cocktail too?"

"Nah, she asked me to meet her parents. Why the fuck would I want to do that? I don't even want to see my own parents."

"Your parents are lovely. Normal. I think you were adopted, or a huge mistake at the very least. I pity them."

"Ouch. What's your excuse then? Your parents left the country to avoid you."

"A girl's abandonment issues are her own business. I'm going to get a proper drink."

Three gins later I'd finally summoned up the courage to tell him the real reason I'd asked to meet up. "So . . . you know my resolution idea to change one thing? Don't look at me blankly—I told you after New Year. Anyway, I've decided what it is."

"I do remember, and it'd better not be taking up Zumba or some fitness shit again."

"No, I've decided I'm going to improve my sex life."

"OK. That sounds like a very good plan, but how exactly? Are you going to take classes or something?"

"No. I've made a list of everything I've always wanted to try. And I'm going to work through it. Simple, eh?"

"A list?" he asked, suddenly becoming interested. "What's on it?"

"Just . . . stuff."

"Tell me."

"No."

There was no way I was telling him until he agreed to help me. Otherwise he'd never stop asking me if I'd taken it up the ass yet.

"Fine, but knowing you, it's probably having sex with the lights off or kissing with your mouth open or not showering first—"

"You make me sound fucking frigid. I'll have you know it's quite dirty."

"Doubtful." He laughed. "I pity the poor chap who's going to have to endure this. Who's your new fella then?"

I looked back at him and smiled.

He smiled back and raised his glass to his mouth. Two seconds later the penny had dropped. He put his pint down, never taking his eyes off me. "Wait. You want me to help you?"

"Yes."

"With sex stuff?"

"Yes."

"The man you claim not to like."

"Well, um—"

"But that means that we'd have to—"

"Yes."

He stared at the table and I sat there, wishing I were dead. After what seemed like an eternity he spoke.

"Fuck, Phoebe! I wasn't expecting this. Jesus, it's a big ask. Do you realize exactly what it would mean? I'm actually upset that you'd think this was appropriate. Quite frankly, I feel used."

"What? Shit! I'm sorry. I'm really sorry. I just . . ."

Then I noticed the smirk on his face.

"You're fucking with me, aren't you?"

"Yep."

"So you'll help me?"

"'Course I will, stupid. Another drink?"

And Bingo was his fucking name-o! The hunt is over and I have secured my very first sex partner, my friend Oliver. My best friend. Is this really a good idea? Oh fucking hell.

"I'll come over tomorrow night," he said as he got into his taxi. "We'll see how we get on and you can tell me what the fuck is on this list of yours."

"Get on"? That means sex, doesn't it? Oh God, now I feel sick. On the way home from the pub I panicked: the girls he usually screws are gorgeous. I look like I've been drawn with an Etch A Sketch, but he must find me sexually attractive in some way—surely? Or is it the NSA sex that's the attractive part? In theory it's ideal—no wondering if he'll call the next day, no game playing, no distracting butterflies in my stomach to turn me into a blabbering wreck—just sex. But I'm also very aware that no one has seen me naked since Alex. When you're in a relationship, little things like stretch marks or zits on your bottom don't matter, but when you're just screwing, do they make a difference? Will one look at my cellulite be cause for reconsideration? Will he decide sex is out of the question when I lie down and my boobs flop sideways and disappear into my armpits?

I called Lucy.

"He agreed? Goddamn, good for you! Thank God for that. For a moment I thought I was going to have to strap on and help out. You're a lucky cow—I demand to know everything afterward."

"I'm nervous. You've seen the kind of women he dates—they have no extra body fat."

"Oh, shut up. If those women were so perfect, he'd still be sleeping with them. Don't be nervous about that; be nervous that he'll be bad in bed and then you'll have to reject him, thus ruining your friendship and any mental images I have of him. And I have a lot. In my head he's quite the thruster."

"You're going to hell."

Friday, January 21

5 p.m. Took a half day at work and I've spent a ridiculous amount of time preparing for this; John Hurt probably spent less time in makeup while filming *The Elephant Man*. There was skin to be scrubbed, eyebrows to be plucked, toenails to be painted, and of course legs to be shaved; no one wants to fuck a yeti.

7:00 p.m. I'm ready and I'm nervous. Been trying to distract myself by flirting with some man called @granted77 on Twitter. I love how the Internet is always ready with random men to take my mind off reality.

7:45 p.m. I have a voice in my head, telling me, "Relax, it's just sex," like the trailer from *The Last House on the Left*, where you're told, "To avoid fainting, keep telling yourself it's only a movie!" It's not working. I want to vomit. There's a part of me wishing he'd get hit by a car on the way over, or something less painful, and fatal.

Saturday, January 22

Last night Oliver arrived at 8:30 and pounced on me. Literally. It took me by surprise, as I was ready to make coffee and discuss our imminent sex in a sensible, adult fashion, but before I knew it my lipstick was smudged and my hair messed up. He had me up against the wall, on the hall floor, and then finally on the bed, where I think I dislocated my hip. But in a good way. My neurotic body-image crisis was pointless as he couldn't have been more enthusiastic. For once I didn't care how many folds my belly had or that my hair was sticking straight up, and the weirdest thing was: it wasn't weird. Well, maybe a tad odd at the beginning, because I automatically compared his penis to Alex's, and although Oliver isn't huge in length, the girth is extremely impressive, to the point where I feared my mouth would resemble a victim from *The Ring* after I'd given him a blow job. He also took time with me and didn't just grab my tits and call it foreplay, one of Alex's favorite tricks—honestly he might as well have made honking noises; it was ridiculous.

Oliver is also very vocal, which I love. I like noisy sex, and despite not being particularly "verbal," I'm pretty loud, and it's nice to hear some sort of agreement instead of wondering whether he's lost in the moment or has nodded off. Afterward we sat in bed and managed to have a mostly grown-up chat about the list and all the things I want to try, and he didn't have a problem with any of them; he even elaborated on a couple.

"This wasn't what I was expecting. You're rather filthy. The role play—I definitely want to try some domination. Nothing too weird, but I'm never submissive. Might be interesting. . . ."

"This stuff doesn't faze you at all, does it?"

"Nah, why should it? It's only sex."

"I have no idea if I'll actually have the nerve to do all of this. Sleeping with you was nerve-racking enough! Let's promise that things won't get weird between us, OK?"

"It'll be fine, Phoebe. Stop worrying. Don't overthink it. Oh, and I have no problem with watching you with someone else. A girl would be preferable. Just saying. . . ."

"You'll have me running a bisexual dungeon by the end of this. Anything else?"

"Yes," he said, running his hand down my thigh, "we're doing that again."

He left sharpish after the second round and it was then I fully realized that this was definitely just a friendly arrangement for him; he kissed me on the cheek, just as he always does. There was no lingering kiss good-bye, no hand-holding, just a peck on the cheek and some joke about me needing a shave. The passion had gone, and we were back to being friends. This is something I'll have to get my head around, as I'll admit it brought me back down to Earth with a thud.

Sunday, January 23

Oliver and I had sex again this evening. I've gone from having no sex at all to having ALL THE SEX in a very short space of time. I'm awesome. I cannot wait until we actually start my list.

The first time we banged in my bed, which was polite and sweet really. Then I walked out of my room, naked, to get some water and he followed me into the kitchen, where we did it over the worktops. I was unsettled for a second when I found myself face-down in toast crumbs, but then he started whispering delicious obscenities in my ear. I tried to return the favor, but failed miserably: "Fucking prick."

"What?"

"Erm, nothing. Carry on."

How embarrassing. I need some help with this. Perhaps now is a good time to embrace my first challenge: talking dirty.

Monday, January 24

Hazel and Grace were shopping in town today so I met them at lunchtime for a quick bite, which for me was half a grilled cheese and a large glass of wine.

"What are you up to tonight?" Hazel asked, giving Grace a crust to gnaw on.

"To hell with it. I'll probably end up having a bath and watching *EastEnders*."

"Oh, good. Then you can come to the gym with me instead."

I stared at Hazel for a second and then laughed. "Piss off; you know how much I hate the gym and I got my period this morning. My cramp says no."

"But we used to have fun when we went."

"No, you used to have fun; I was always on the verge of having a stroke."

"But I'm carrying a lot of baby weight—"

"Put her down, then! Ha, look! INSTANTLY ten pounds lighter! You look exactly the same as you've always done, and sometimes this makes it difficult for me to like you."

"Fine then, but if you change your mind, there's a yoga class on at eight."

"Yoga? Don't you remember what happened when I took that yoga class last year?"

She was already laughing. "That poor woman who farted, she must have been mortified."

I was now mildly hysterical. "It wasn't just the fart, it was the length of it. It was like a trombone solo."

"I think you might be the first person to be thrown out of a yoga class for laughing."

I tried to compose myself. "This is the very reason I won't go back. Even the thought of it makes me wet myself. I wouldn't last two minutes before they forcibly removed me from the sports center."

Hazel pulled Grace's jacket on and started packing away her things. "Fine, I'll go myself, but please be aware that you are a terrible friend for making me do this alone."

"You'll have the last laugh when you're all fit and toned and I'm so fat I'm being airlifted out of my apartment for some Channel 5 documentary. Shit, is that the time? I'd better run."

I kissed them both good-bye and ran in my heels back to the office like a champ. Who needs the gym?

Tuesday, January 25

"Pillow talk" has always conjured up images of Doris Day wearing a nightdress up to her eyebrows waiting to be prodded by her gay male costar. Like so many things in life, it's something I briefly considered becoming a world champion at, but the crippling fear of making a complete fool of myself stopped me. Mostly, I just moan louder to compensate, throwing in a couple of oh-yeahs for effect, and generally keep my mouth shut.

I think talking dirty requires a certain amount of sexual confidence, which in the past I've been seriously lacking in, as I've never considered myself particularly sexy. When I stop to analyze my sex with Alex I find myself dissecting everything I've said or done and it makes me cringe. I don't have long, flowing locks of gorgeous hair to flick over my shoulder or hold up while I'm on top like some *Playboy* bimbo; I have thick, straight hair which tends to fall in front of my face, making me look like something from a Japanese horror film that's about to crawl out of the television. I even tried out my "sex face" in front of the mirror, but found I looked more like someone who'd just been asked to do some complex long division than a viable sexual prospect. Shit. Combine that with my inability to comfortably express my desires and forcefully demand to have my ass smacked, and I feel rather deflated. It doesn't help that dirty talk always seems so contrived to me, like a God-awful porn film with some slap bass ready to kick in when a zipper gets pulled down. When I try to imitate it I find myself hurling abuse in the throes of passion, as if I have porn Tourette's. I have to get more comfortable with this. I discussed it with Lucy at lunchtime.

"The trick is not to make it sound forced. There's no point shouting, 'OH GOD, YES, YOU DIRTY BASTARD!' when he's kissing you gently or brushing the hair from your face. You'll just startle him." I looked around, aware of how loudly she'd said that, and saw the canteen staff laughing. "You just have to get used to saying the words to another person. You can't expect it to come naturally right away if you're not used to it. It's like learning a foreign language. A really dirty one. Like French. Do you want to practice on me?"

"I'd rather die."

"What about chat rooms then?" said Lucy. "You should go online and cyber some fellas. That would be good practice."

It sounds like a good idea, but I'm scared I'll only find a dongle-charged world full of socially retarded lonely losers, all looking for other equally lonely losers to masturbate with, or husbands crying out that their wife doesn't understand them and they need some sort of escapism. Normal, happy people don't go online. Do they?

Wednesday, January 26

My boss Frank is obsessed with his new piece of "art," which he hung in pride of place in his office this morning. It looks like someone painted it for a dare. He'd been going on about what an important piece of work it is and how expensive it was, so when he went for lunch Stuart nipped into his office and turned it upside down. Frank left at half five and still hadn't noticed. Genius. We then all took bets on how long it would stay like that. I also noticed Stuart's bottom for the first time today. How slow of me but, my word, it's quite perfect. Unfortunately he caught me noticing too. I blame my hormones. Not just for this.

This evening I began my first challenge by joining a site called Highland Flings, armed with a false name, fake picture, and a 36DD imaginary chest. I can't believe I've sunk this low already.

I'm trying to be discerning in my choices, but it's tricky. The majority of profiles are from people who obviously didn't win any grammar competitions at school, and I can't bear the thought of having to read sentences with badly placed apostrophes all glaring at me, just waiting to be corrected. The messages come through surprisingly quickly. So far, some have tried the whole "getting to know you" shit, while others just get straight to the point and begin conversations with: "How big are your tits?" or the obligatory: "What are you wearing?"

"I AM WEARING SOME CLOTHES, YOU CUNT! MAKE THE FUCKING EFFORT!" I didn't say that, obviously. I don't know if I can do this.

Luckily a call from Mum distracted me from throwing my laptop out of the window.

"Hello, Phoebe, how are you?"

"Good, Mum. How are you and Dad?"

My parents used to call every week when they lived in Glasgow. When my dad sold off his chain of hippie tearooms and they emigrated to Canada, the calls became less frequent and were replaced by random gifts of utter shit and postcards from their latest vacation destination.

"We're going on safari, darling. Last-minute deal to Kenya. Heading off in about an hour so just thought I'd call before we're in the middle of nowhere."

"You can use your cell in Kenya, Mum. It isn't the moon."

"Your father's decided we're not taking phones. He also decided we're not taking gin, but I vetoed that immediately. Everything OK with you?"

"Yeah, everything's great . . . nothing new here . . . same old. Have fun! Tell Dad I said hi, and don't get mauled by anything!"

"Only your father, dear. Oh, don't make that groaning sound, Phoebe—your father and I didn't conceive you by holding hands. Lighten up. Anyway, we're off. Take care!"

"Bye, Mum. Speak soon."

It doesn't matter how old I get, knowing my parents had sex in order to conceive me will never get any less distressing. If I wasn't an only child, I'd swear they've done it more than once.

Thursday, January 27

Frank wasn't in the office so I got to use his parking space today. Hurrah! No public transport for me. I got stuck on the motorway for forty-five minutes on the way home, but totally worth it as I got to sing along loudly to the *Rocky Horror Picture Show* soundtrack without fear of being heard. Tim Curry dressed as Frank-N-Furter gives me the horn.

I made pasta for dinner and opened a bottle of red wine before logging back onto Highland Flings. I tried to ignore my initial "What the hell am I doing?" thoughts and repress the overwhelming urge to send back an array of jokey, sarcastic responses and instead focus on why I'm doing this. I know I'll have to try it on Oliver at some point and it has to at least be smirk-free and somewhat believable. So far it's only been brief e-mail/messenger flirting, but I'm getting more confident and I'm finally managing not to turn everything into a great big joke.

I told Oliver about my training regimen and he thought it was hysterical.

"You can't do this! You're too nice!"

"No, I'm not. I can be filthy, GODDAMMIT!"

"Phoebe, you called me a fucker while we were screwing and then texted me on the way home to make sure I knew you didn't really mean it. You're the kind of girl who might be able to tell me you want to suck my cock, but not how you'd actually do it."

He's right. I hate it when he's right.

Friday, January 28

Work today was a complete washout. I don't want to be there at the best of times, and I am so distracted by my project. Several times I was close to shouting: "FUCK YOUR TARGETS, FRANK—TELL ME IF I'M USING TOO MANY ADJECTIVES WHILE PRETENDING TO GIVE YOU HEAD."

After work I made my way to see Pam Potter for our next session. She always looks dead pleased to see me and has a great big smile, like the Cheshire Cat. I keep expecting her to slowly vanish mid-conversation. For some reason it doesn't seem right just calling her "Pam"; it sounds too normal, which she isn't. Every mug in her office is animal-shaped, which isn't surprising, as her organic coffee smells like dung. I was in need of a session, given my emotional state after running into Alex last week.

"Do you think it was seeing Alex that upset you, or the fact he was with his new girlfriend?"

"Both. It was like a great big slap in the face and I felt so vulnerable. It was a reminder of everything I've been trying to forget."

"You have to remember that the part of your life with Alex is over, Phoebe, but accept that you will be reminded of it every now and again, and that's OK. It's difficult to move on until you've made peace with your past. Are you using your free time productively?"

I could have told her about my list but I wasn't ready for that conversation. Perhaps ironically, the one person who was being paid to hear my innermost secrets was the one person I wasn't willing to tell. "Yeah, I guess so. I mean, I spend a lot of time with friends; I'm not sitting at home obsessing over Alex. Well, not as much as I used to. I don't really have any hobbies. Is that what you're talking about? Shit, should I have a hobby?!"

She smiled. "Relax. Look at this time in your life as the beginning of your new chapter. You cannot rewrite what's already been written but you can determine where the story goes from here and you can choose which characters to keep or kill off. Metaphorically speaking, of course."

I left her office feeling a bit like a character in a "Choose your own adventure" book: "To allow yourself to forget Alex and begin to heal, turn to page 9 . . . To run Alex over with a tank, turn to page 12."

"To find a new therapist who also moonlights as a hit man, turn to page 87."

Later I got chatting to my first fella online. Bradley is a writer, twenty-six, with long hair, skinny, and strangely attractive in an eccentric, Russell Brand kind of way. He approached me with a quirky "Let's discuss philosophy and Leonard Cohen over imaginary champagne and truffles," but pretty quickly his urge to appear interesting and cultured was overtaken by an even greater urge to discuss his fantasy of watching me have sex with another woman. Testosterone will always kick intellect's ass when it comes down to it. All I had to do with this guy was describe how my faux lesbian action was turning me on:

"I'm getting so hot thinking about this . . ." (Wasn't.)

Then, "I'd lick her nipples slowly while you watched . . ." (Really? Would I? WOULD I?)

I couldn't tell him that I was only blowing smoke up his ass and wasn't genuinely getting turned on by any of this, and I realized how unconvincing it must have been, claiming to be playing with all kinds of toys, in all kinds of positions, while dancing the flamenco during orgasm. What was I typing with? My feet? Second up for cybering was Bill, who got me to watch him masturbating on webcam while I typed in detail what I'd do to him. He was a good-looking guy—brown, messy hair, a nice face, yet another man who was wafer freakin' thin—but from what I could make out, had an incredibly small cock. A few times he stood up in front of the webcam to proudly show me his erection, and I had to peer into the screen. It disappeared when he wrapped his hand around it, and he had pretty little girl hands so I couldn't even put it down to his having big bear paws. I mean, I prefer a medium-sized cock to some ten-inch monster doing me damage, but this was the smallest penis I'd ever seen. I'm grateful I wasn't in front of the camera; I'd have looked awkward, made an inappropriate joke, and then blurted out an apology while he logged off.

Saturday, January 29

Oliver came over this afternoon and brought me lunch: a half-eaten pizza and a bottle of Irn-Bru.

"Oh, that's very sweet," I said, opening up the box. "Hmm, what's on this pizza? It looks weird."

"Dunno, I found it in a bin."

"Oh fuck off. Now I don't know if you're kidding or not."

"'Course I am. It's ham and sweet corn with sweet chili peppers. It's nice, but you'll have to eat some too in order to cancel out my chili-pepper breath."

I ate the rest, carefully studying his face in case it revealed that he did actually find it in a bin. I don't trust boys.

We sat on the couch and I put *Arrested Development* on. I had planned to have a lazy afternoon and send Oliver out for more pizza later, but he had other ideas. Halfway through the opening credits, he stood up and began to unbutton his black shirt. He's very aware of how good he looks naked and I think he knows I enjoy watching him undress. He didn't take his eyes off me as he stripped. "Horny?" he asked.

"I am now."

"How's that dirty talk coming along?" he asked, pulling me in close to him and making me feel how hard he was.

"Um, good. I think. It's interesting; you know . . . I'm feeling more confident," I bluffed as he pushed back my hair and whispered in my ear, "Go on then. Tell me what you're going to do to me."

So much for confidence; I started to blush.

"I'm going to suck your cock," I blurted out quickly.

"OK . . . tell me more about that. . . ." He was now kissing my neck.

"Erm, I'm going to lick it and then blow you."

I could feel him starting to laugh.

"Blow me? Lick IT? Really? You do know there's no actual blowing involved, don't you? Have you done this before?"

I started to laugh too. "Oh God, I've put you off now, haven't I? You distracted me with the neck kissing!"

He pulled down his pants. "Does this look like you've put me off?" he asked, grinning. "Don't stress—some people just can't talk dirty. Maybe this should just be something I do, and you stick to listening."

"You just say this shit to wind me up, don't you?"

"Normally, yes, but not in this case. I genuinely don't think you can do it."

I felt determined to prove him wrong. After we had sex he showered while I made us a cup of tea. We sat on the couch and I watched him inhale a sandwich he found at the back of my refrigerator.

"You're either starving or in a hurry. Which is it?" I asked as he pushed his crusts to the side of the plate like a four-year-old.

"Both. I said I'd meet Dave for a pint, although I'd much rather take you back to bed."

"Tough," I gargled through a mouthful of tea. "I have things to do. I'll text you later."

I ushered him out the door and poured myself a gin and tonic to steady my nerves for what I was about to do. I'd decided it was time for desperate measures. It was phone-sex time. The whole concept of phone sex is hilarious. Firstly, you call up and leave a message for the male callers: "Hi I'm [insert false name here] and I'm feeling lonely tonight." *hang up and place head in hands*

If any guys are interested they will then send you a message in return. Usually along the lines of: "Hi, I'm [insert false macho name here] and I'm a really 'genuine' but horny guy, looking for a horny lady." *hang up and put hand down pants*

All going well, you can connect and chat about the weather, soccer, crisis in the Middle East, or engage in some dirty phone sex from the comfort of your own couch/car/shed.

It took me seventeen attempts and a lot of wine before I finally plucked up the courage to speak to someone. Seventeen. Eventually I connected with some random guy from London, who said he was just back from the gym (at 1:30 a.m.—do me a favor), all hot and sweaty and looking for a dirty chat. That's exactly what he got. I was so determined to prove Oliver wrong, I turned into a sexy, panting filth monster. I eloquently described what I'd do to him and he jacked off down the phone for at least ten minutes. When he came I did a victory wiggle like I'd just progressed to the next level on *X Factor*, then hung up. I'm happy to be the porn-speak queen of Glasgow, but I'm calling time on this now. People are weird.

Sunday, January 30

This morning all I wanted to do was lie in bed and read the papers, but instead I agreed to meet Hazel for brunch because I am an awesome friend and also because it was her treat.

She drove us to a little country pub that served giant pots of tea and the most amazing Eggs Benedict I have ever had. I actually felt sad when I'd finished eating them.

"Thanks for coming today; I just had to get out of the house for a bit. Don't get me wrong—Kevin is brilliant with Grace, and when he's on his own with her he copes like a pro, but when I'm there it's like he forgets how to think for himself. She cries—he passes her to me; I'm in the shower—he appears two seconds later so she can watch Mummy. Then she sees me and wants a cuddle and I have to get out, dripping everywhere, and I JUST WANT TO HAVE A FUCKING SHOWER ALONE. PEOPLE NEED TO WASH THEIR HAIR!"

"Have you spoken to him about it?" I asked, pouring her more tea and trying not to giggle at her outburst.

"No. I don't want him to think I'm a cow or that I feel he's not pulling his weight or that, God forbid, I don't want to spend time with my daughter. I love my kid; I just need ten minutes to wash my hair without an audience."

"Then say that to him. You're the most diplomatic person I know; you'll find the right words. Either that or just lock the bathroom door when you go in."

She looked at me like I'd just cured cancer. "GAH! Lock the door! Why didn't I think of that?"

Oliver came over straight from work this evening, and when he arrived he produced a bunch of flowers. Before I could say, "I appreciate the thought but we're not dating so what the hell are you playing at?" he laughed in my face and said, "Don't panic; it's not a romantic gesture. My boss was being a complete witch today so I nicked them off her desk on the way home. It's more of an 'up-yours' to her than anything else." He collapsed on the couch. "You know, I was thinking about this dirty-talk thing. It doesn't matter if you can't do it; most women can't anyway—don't feel bad about it. I'm sure you'll manage the other challenges."

I began to smile. "Take off your pants," I demanded.

Then I took off my skirt and tights, pulled my panties to one side and slid down on him. Hard.

I whispered in his ear, "I am going to fuck you slowly and take every inch of you, until you're begging me to let you come. Can you feel how wet I am already?"

He raised one eyebrow (man, I love it when he does that) and said, "Good God, Phoebe! Keep talking like that and I think I'll keep you."

So I did.

Monday, January 31

I had the dentist at three this afternoon so I cheerfully left work early, only to have a giant needle shoved into my gums and my tooth drilled by a man who had unusually large nostrils. I'd rather have stayed at work.

9:40 p.m. My mouth is now quite sore so I've taken to bed in a dramatic fashion and had enough codeine to knock out a horse.

10:30 p.m. I have checked the front door is locked three times now. I have either developed OCD or those painkillers are way too strong and have caused short-term memory loss.

11:00 p.m. I'm still wide-awake but mentally exhausted. It's been a busy month. I've successfully acquired a new friend with benefits and engaged in some outrageously filthy talk with complete strangers. Alex still hasn't spontaneously combusted, which is perhaps the only downside, but on the upside, I'm now a lot more comfortable being obscene and Oliver loves the fact that this polite, professional girl with lovely manners can open her mouth and make sailors run screaming from a pub. I can happily tell Oliver exactly what I intend to do to him, even with something in my mouth. I have skills now. The talking-dirty challenge was excruciating at times, but I'm pretty happy with the outcome, and I'd say the list has got off to a good start.

FEBRUARY

Tuesday, February 1

Oliver's been coming over to my house more and more frequently and tonight he turned up without warning after soccer practice, covered in sweat. Without saying a word he went into my kitchen, drank a pint of water in one go, then turned on the shower and dragged me in.

Sex in a shower cubicle is great—confined space and nothing but wall to lean against. Sex in a shower-over-bathtub setup, however, is something completely different. "I'll buy you another shower curtain tomorrow, Phoebe. That one was moldy anyway."

It was also the first time he'd seen me up close without my makeup on or hair done and I could see him staring at me for a second while I was drying off. If that doesn't put him off me I'll be surprised. My mum once said something that's stayed with me forever: "I remember your dad telling me that the first time he saw me without makeup, he thought he'd woken up next to a man."

Christ, I bear more than a passing resemblance to my mother. I wonder if they offer airbrushing on the NHS.

Wednesday, February 2

In the morning meeting Frank announced that Marion had given birth to a baby boy called Harry, who weighed nine pounds nine ounces, and both were doing well.

"I don't think she'll come back," remarked Kelly. "She's a nice woman but she hated it here and she never did any real work."

"Thanks for your input, Kelly." Frank scowled. "Now can we please make sure Lucy gets your call sheets by the end of the day? She has enough to do without chasing you lot for paperwork."

"I'd hardly call Lucy overworked—" began Kelly, before Frank told her to "zip it" and we were all sent back to our desks.

"Don't you ever get tired of running people down, Kelly?" I asked as she sat down at her desk. "Marion's just given birth and you're bitching about her. It's not cool."

"I'm just speaking the truth," she said with a shrug. "If anyone has a problem with that—tough. I'm here to do my job, not make friends."

"Then be quiet and do your job, Kelly!" Frank shouted across from his office. "You're giving me a headache."

Kelly might be a bitch, but she's right about Marion. There's no way she'd choose to come back to this lunatic asylum. With some free time on my hands tonight, I started to think about the next challenge, which doesn't require Oliver's help, or anyone else's for that matter: masturbation.

The subject of masturbation is one I've always enthused about and I've never been one of those "Who? Me? Never. I don't need to. Shut up . . ." women who you know are either lying or desperately unhinged from sexual frustration. I guess it comes from being raised by parents who are very open about sex. For me it's a given, but for some women it can be like having a poo; it's common knowledge that we do it but we like to pretend we don't. Like somehow the feminine mystique we've worked so hard to maintain would instantly disappear if the secret ever got out.

We use our genitalia to insult people: he's a dick, a pussy, an ass, and so on, and we call each other "jack-offs" to denote how idiotic we are. We're also taught as children not to touch or play with ourselves, usually accompanied by a stern look that says, *If you do that, no one will like you*— giving us a big healthy dose of shame and introducing the hellish fear of getting caught with our hands anywhere near our bottoms. But I've never subscribed to any of that crap.

So now to think of something new I can do during masturbation. New sex toys, perhaps?

Thursday, February 3

I've been having increasingly odd dreams since my sex life returned, including one last night involving a man made of wood. He was Dutch (as most wooden men are, obviously) and we went at it in a forest. Creepy but weirdly arousing. I would have looked it up in my dream book, but it's pointless because my dream book interprets everything as death, even smiling kittens.

I've decided that I'm going sex-toy shopping this weekend. In fact I'm going shopping for a wooden man. I'd ask Lucy and Hazel if they want to come along, except I know the answer to that already.

Saturday, February 5

Today I met the girls for some lunch at my favorite Japanese restaurant, Ichiban, on Queen Street. Lucy was late as usual. Hazel met me inside and we ordered beers while glancing at the menu. "Where's Grace today?" I asked.

"Kevin's taking her to Hamleys so I have the whole afternoon free. Are we still going to Ann Summers?"

"Yes, we're going to the grown-up toy shop. Much more fun."

Lucy arrived as the waitress brought our drinks. She ordered some sake and sat down beside me on the long wooden bench.

"God, I'm starving. Fuck the chopsticks; I'm going to eat like a man with ten hands. HAZEL! Did you get Botox?"

"NO!" Hazel said, frowning. Only her face didn't move. We both stared at her. "Fine, I did. Spur-of-the-moment decision. It hurt like hell. Never again."

"You're going to end up like that woman who's had so much cosmetic surgery she looks like a lion." I grinned.

"I am not!" She laughed, pulling apart her chopsticks. "I'm turning forty next year. Call it part of my midlife crisis. Now, let's eat. I'm aging rapidly as we speak."

After lunch we walked to Sauchiehall Street for a rather expensive jaunt around Ann Summers. I buy most of my sex toys on the Internet rather than in Ms. Summers's shops because it's usually cheaper, but as I feel like a walking hormone recently, there's no way I could wait a week for delivery and then greet the postman, red-faced, hoping there was no mention of my purchase on the packaging. Thankfully, BigfakecocksforPhoebe.com are usually very discreet.

The men in my life have had varying attitudes toward sex toys, but most have felt intimidated. Trying to explain to them that toys are to use as well as, and sometimes during, sex, rather than instead of, is a tough one. Sex for me is definitely about skin on skin, which will always be more of a turn-on than some plastic phallic oddity buzzing uncontrollably, but the orgasms from sex toys are freakin' amazing and it's FUN, DAMMIT!

The last time I went shopping for sex toys with a guy, I ended up talking to myself while he stared at the floor, looking awkward, shuffling his feet like a child, and occasionally saying, "I don't care."

Hazel is fairly conservative when it comes to sex toys—she just likes the buzzing action, nothing inserted or too "out there." As she'd mentioned to me before, she's had issues with her sex life since she gave birth.

"I'm scared it still looks like a horror film down there. I don't want Kevin to look at my vagina in case there's a Jabberwocky staring back, so I'm starting small."

Lucy and I are quite alike, although she prefers the outrageous ones. I'm happy with a simple rabbit but she buys the double-penetrating, action-packed, G-spot stimulators and pretty much anything that looks like it might make your eyes roll to the back of your head and reduce you to a blubbering wreck. She's always first in line for new sex toys.

"I wonder if they sell 'fucking machines'? You know, like a Sybian? I want one of those. I don't care how much they cost—I'll pay it up for the rest of my life." The sales assistants in these sorts of shops are brilliant. They're all mellow and thinking, Yeah, you've just bought enough lube to fit a truck in there, you big PERVERT! but they never raise a pierced eyebrow, or look like they give a shit that you have £150 worth of anal beads in your basket. So on Lucy's advice I've become the proud owner of something that looks like a medieval torture device, a G-spot vibrator, and, after a text to Oliver, he now possesses a cock ring with a dolphin on it. I've decided to call it Flipper just to annoy him.

Monday, February 7

I've never properly used toys with a partner, so tonight was exciting. The cock ring lasted about ten minutes before Oliver decided it was too distracting and whipped it off. He was then more than happy to operate the machinery while I lay on my stomach, giving muffled instructions with my face in the pillow. He didn't flinch at the thought of using toys with me, but when he went near my asshole, I flinched. Literally.

"What's wrong?" he asked. "I thought anal was on your list?"

"It is, but I'm going to need some notice before we go there," I said, looking over my shoulder, now very much aware of my exposed bottom.

"Ah, OK." He shrugged. "We can try it another time then. You'll like it. It's no big deal."

"No big deal? Oh really? I'll try to shove Flipper up your rectum and see how laid-back you are about it."

"Stop calling it Flipper. Did you know you have a giant zit-thing on your ass?"

"It's not a zit, it's a mole. It's been there for years."

"It looks weird. It's really big. I think it has a hair growing out of it."

"WHAT? Right, you're about one comment away from never being allowed access to my ass ever again."

"It's like looking into the round, featureless face of a witch. OK, I'll stop."

Tuesday, February 8

I'm trying to put the anal discussion out of my head for a while. I am curious, but that little gem is definitely one that I have to be completely ready for, in every respect. For once I don't have to soul-search for the reason why I'm hesitant to do this, and that would be because of the poo. Christ, Oliver put his pinky up there last night and I nearly had a heart attack. What am I going to be like when he puts his penis up there?

I was in a rush this morning, so I didn't have time to buy cigarettes on the way to work. I cadged one off Stuart on our coffee break and while we chatted all I could think was, *I wonder what you'd be like in bed. I wonder if you're hairy. Would you hold me down or be polite about the whole thing?* Basically I didn't listen to a word he said. While I ate lunch I thought about Stuart looking good, but by then he was looking good on top of me. And he was naked. It was a fun pastime, but I fear this man and his tight bottom might have possessed me. I made a doctor's appointment for tomorrow to see about my moley ass. Now I'm obsessed, and keep trying to catch sight of it in the mirror like a cat chasing its tail.

Wednesday, February 9

I left work early for my doctor's appointment and after much poking and prodding he's decided to remove it, so I have to go back on Friday. Finally the obscure red thing on my bottom shall be gone. He doesn't think it's anything nasty or even interesting—which is good.

Hazel offered to come with me, but I'd have to sit and stare at her while she screws up her face and goes green at the sight of a scalpel, and quite honestly I can do without that.

Thursday, February 10

Lucy has a new man, a twenty-one-year-old "musician" called Sam who leads a double life as a shelf stacker in her local supermarket. Lucy has the ability to attract and conquer men even while pursuing mundane tasks like shopping. It seems he'd gone out of his way to find her an undamaged tin of pineapple and it was love at first sight. I say love; Lucy falls in and out of love very quickly. Her last boyfriend lasted three months until she decided one morning that he looked like a lizard and it was all off. The guy before that—Robert, I think—was dumped when she found out he owned a Michael Bolton album. "Can you imagine what other little dirty secrets he's been hiding from me?"

Lucy loves being in love, or the idea of it anyway. She's always in a relationship or with a fuck buddy until someone better comes along. For an independent woman, her need to be attached is quite staggering. She's a bit like Oliver in that respect—neither of them wants to be without someone, but they both won't commit to anything long-term. I know that Oliver would rather grate his own ball sac than get married. She also insists on dating younger men: "I love being Mrs. Robinson. I wouldn't fuck Dustin Hoffman, though."

Work plodded on as usual. Frank still hasn't noticed his picture is upside down because he's a self-absorbed prick. I pity the woman who ends up with him. Speaking of which, it feels like love is in the air—I could hear Stuart whispering on his cell to some mystery woman during his cigarette break earlier. *Stop that, you handsome phone-whisperer.*

Friday, February 11

Ouch. That was nippy. The mole was removed by Dr. Jekyll and his lovely nurse, Mary "Scissorhands" Reilly. They were very rushed and he started to cut before the anesthetic had kicked in.

"ARGH!"

"You can't feel that, can you?"

"Uh-huh. What? Am I not supposed to?"

(Ignores my question) "We'll use some more local anesthetic, then."

He reckons it's scar tissue.

"Do you remember sitting on something sharp? Like some glass?"

"No."

"Are you sure?"

I thought of every drunken tumble I could remember.

"No."

Apparently it was deeper than he first thought and I got four stitches. So the ugly red mole has been removed, leaving me with an ugly red scar. I don't know which is worse, but my dreams of a blemish-free booty have been dashed forever.

Oliver came 'round just to see it. I felt like a freak show.

"Oh, you poor thing! Does it hurt?"

"Yes."

"Would it hurt if I bent you over the couch?"

"I'm guessing yes."

"Can I see it?"

"Piss off, Oliver, it'll be disgusting and weeping and covered in death."

Even the sight of a bloody bandage and stitches doesn't curb that boy's sexual enthusiasm.

Saturday, February 12

Went over to Oliver's apartment this evening, and even though I've been to his place many times it never fails to impress me, which, given that I live in a hovel, isn't surprising. It's very big, with a marble fireplace, high ceilings, and a view right into other people's windows, which has provided us both with many hours of amusement. His bedroom is also bigger than my entire flat. He makes shitloads of money working in IT, which he spends at an alarming rate. "Hey, Phoebe, are we sleeping with other people?" he asked as I got dressed to go home.

"I'm not," I replied, "but I'm only sleeping with you because I couldn't find anyone else, remember? We're not dating so there's no reason we shouldn't, is there?"

"That's what I thought, but I wanted to check. There's a girl I'm into and I feel like banging her."

"Ah, always the hopeless romantic, eh? Don't let me stop you. You can bang whoever you want, but if you give me any weird diseases, I'll kill you."

But I felt miffed for a second that he wanted to bang someone else. Wasn't I enough for him? I'm not jealous, but we're barely weeks into our agreement and he's already thinking of moving on. Dammit, this is what I always do: assume it's because I'm not good enough. So instead I focused on how I'd jump Stuart, given half a chance, and that had no bearing on Oliver, or how good he was in bed, and it all made sense. So why am I still annoyed about it?

Sunday, February 13

Well, my unconventional sex dream suitors have returned. Last night I had the filthiest dream about Stephen Fry. He had great big hands like shovels and whispered the most eloquent filth I've ever heard.

"Oh, I've had him!" said Lucy at lunch. "Well, in my head, of course. My most recent one was Gordon Ramsay. I woke up halfway through shouting, 'YES, CHEF!' My best was with Noel Fielding, who banged me in an elevator. I still get shivers thinking about that."

I wish she'd shut up.

Monday, February 14

The best thing about February is that the snow has finally started to melt and the worst thing is freakin' St. Valentine's Day. Out of all the saints, he's the one I hate the most. It's the biggest con since fake tan and yet people still insist on doing it. Every year when I've been single I know that I'm not going to receive an oversized, ridiculously expensive bunch of flowers, or chocolate hearts, or even a card, but every year there's still a tiny part of me that foolishly hopes someone out there is desperately in love with me and will finally make some sort of gesture. It never happens. I've never been properly romanced—well, not the romance that Hollywood vomits all over everyone, making us feel like lesser human beings because we know that no one will ever frantically run barefoot to an airport to stop us from taking that job in New York. Alex's biggest gesture was whisking me off to Rome for my thirtieth. I say "whisking," but it was more of a limp stir. He paid forty pounds for cheap flights and I had to get the hotel. That was where he told me he loved me for the first time. On our first Valentine's Day together I bought him a card and a CD and he bought me nothing. From then on it was just an unspoken rule that this was something we didn't do. But although I don't really buy into the whole thing, part of me really wished that he'd make some sort of silly gesture just because he loved me.

Nearly all the girls in the office got flowers; even Lucy got a bunch from her music man, which thrilled her to the point of shrieking at the delivery girl. I just smiled and tried not to notice the pitying looks that were being thrown my way from the office Botanic Gardens.

So this year was no exception and I know that tomorrow I'll remember why I've sworn off relationships, but tonight I'm desperately missing something I've never had: someone who gives a shit.

Tuesday, February 15

Stupid Valentine's Day. I had a think about things on the way to work this morning and have come to a pretty obvious realization. In previous relationships I've always been a total doormat, making myself completely available and always afraid to rock the boat. Of course no one has ever fought for me; I didn't give them any reason to. I'm positively bleeding self-awareness these days and grateful I don't have to worry about this crap any longer.

Work was still brimming with unimaginative bouquets of red roses, but it was back to business as usual. Stuart is still being secretive about his girlfriend and I saw him shuffling off to the toilets with a funny walk after a lengthy conversation with her at lunchtime. It must have been hot. I'm going to put his phone in the bin when he's not looking.

Wednesday, February 16

Oh, look, Alex outside his work having a cigarette at the same time as me. Is he doing it on purpose? That man spent most of our relationship moaning at me to stop smoking after he quit and now he's started again. Ha, maybe he's finally realized he's screwing someone who should be in a museum and the stress is too much. He looked good though. Really good.

The trouble is, no matter how much I hate him (and I do), every time I see him I still get a knot in my stomach and for a minute I miss him. I still remember how much I adored him. Then I remember how it felt when he cheated on me and it disappears pretty quickly. I know I loved him, but I can't quite remember why anymore . . . so why won't the feeling go away?

He can spot me from his office window directly across the street. She converted some old office space into a physiotherapy clinic, which pretty quickly attracted a large client base of soccer players and sporty types. I once visited his office. It's much fancier than mine—loads of state-of-the-art machinery and oak paneling.

The fact that our offices are on the same street and directly face each other used to be "cute" when we were together; we could wave at each other from the window, have our ciggy breaks together, and meet up after work, but now that we hate each other it's just plain creepy. In the future I'm going to have to adopt a cunning disguise, if he's going to come down to smoke whenever I do. I bet that while I was waving at him in his office last year, SHE was under the desk giving him a tit-job. The beasts.

Thursday, February 17

I managed to have my smoke breaks without catching sight of Miss Tits or Alex today. Of course, when I don't see him I wonder what he's doing, and when I do catch sight of him I'm praying he'll set himself on fire with his own cigarette.

Lucy came into work today covered in love bites, barely hidden underneath a white polo neck.

"I know! Don't say a word," she shouted over when she saw my face. Freakin' love bites. At my age!"

From: Lucy Jacobs
To: Phoebe Henderson
Subject: I feel like a dick

Any girl I've snogged has never hung off my neck like a fucking fruit bat, so why do guys feel the need to? Maybe it's an owner-ship thing, like a branding. I didn't even notice him doing it until it was too late. I now stink of toothpaste, which, by the way, doesn't help to get rid of hickeys AT ALL. I might as well just have covered them in your Auntie Pat's jam.

So Lucy's snogged girls and, more remarkably, I have an Auntie Pat! I don't. Was it a euphemism?

Friday, February 18

Back to my challenges, and the only thing I haven't man-aged to master in terms of masturbation is female ejacula-tion. It's more elusive than the G-spot, according to some people. I've only witnessed the phenomenon in porn films, where it basically looks like the woman is urinating over some poor sod and passing it off as an explosive, screaming orgasm. The more I've read about it, and watched it (mostly with a look of bewilderment), the more curious I've become. I'm willing to try most things on my quest, but if it turns out to be nothing more than a pissing contest, I'm not participating.

"Making a woman squirt is about the horniest thing you'll ever do," said Oliver, before admitting he's never actually managed it—it's at the top of his to-do list.

My G-spot might have eluded many men in the past, but I know it's there and I'm willing to become best friends with it. So, with this in mind, I've Googled everything I can think of regarding female ejaculation, from where it actually comes from to how it's successfully done. In theory, it's all about pressure, build-up, and release—simple enough, right? Wrong. I've been at it for about three hours now (admittedly an enjoyable three hours) but nothing. Not even a dribble. I'm beginning to think my initial bullshit theory is correct. This is far from simple and now I'm exhausted with a crampy, clawlike hand.

Saturday, February 19

It's getting annoying now. There should be a formula for it, like shampooing your hair: *lather, rinse, repeat.* Various websites and books have simply advised that some women can do it and others can't, but I'm not having any of that. One piece of advice that made me slightly dubious about the whole thing was: "You might feel the urge to pee but just keep going." What? Keep going? But what about the pee? FOR THE LOVE OF GOD, WHAT ABOUT THE PEE?

I fear that the only thing I might successfully accomplish is adult bed-wetting.

Sunday, February 20

I lay in bed until one today and I'm still tired, which means my period is on its way like one of the horsemen of the Apocalypse. I'm also horny as hell, another sure sign.

I don't mind having sex near the end of my period and I've never been out with a guy who finds it a problem—they didn't care that I occasionally looked like prom-night Carrie after sex.

I remember reading somewhere that "sex during your period is one of the great taboos," which I think is utter crap. You either do it or you don't; end of story. Unless you're a fifteen-year-old boy it's not a big deal to most guys, and it takes a lot more than a little blood to stop them getting laid. If roles were reversed, I certainly wouldn't give a shit. At the moment I feel like a sexual kettle that's forever at the boiling point, wishing that someone would just flick my damn switch.

Monday, February 21

Mondays are distinctly depressing when you've done sod-all at the weekend. I did less than that, which didn't stop me consuming gazillions of calories. The horseman arrived as predicted so I've called in sick and all I want to do is glue a hot water bottle to my stomach and make snarling noises. I feel like having a hysterectomy and renting out the empty space to struggling artists. I'm lucky though—my periods last only four days. Lucy gets hers every three weeks and they last about seven years. I joined in with the usual Monday moaners on Twitter to proclaim my hatred for everything and instantly received a direct message from @granted77:

> **What are you doing?**
> I'm in bed
> **So does that mean you're naked?**
> Yes but in no mood to flirt with someone whose avatar is a cartoon dog
> **Shame. I think you're hot.**
> I'm not feeling well enough to continue this, but I'll keep that in mind

7 p.m. I slept all day. This is amazing. I'm like that Van Winkle dude. I'm going to make some tea and watch a film.

12:45 a.m. I thought watching *Paranormal Activity* would be a great idea. I was wrong. I'm now convinced that something is going to drag me out of bed by my foot. It could totally happen. THAT SHIT IS REAL. Ugh, this is why I shouldn't live alone.

Tuesday, February 22

I called in sick again today. I do feck-all anyway—it's just a matter of time before I'm found out and sacked, so the company won't suffer if I'm not there clock-watching.

I spent the morning watching *Dexter* and found myself thinking that if he were a real person I'd happily overlook the fact he's a serial killer if it meant I got to share a bed with Mr. "check out my blood samples" Morgan. In fact, scrap that, I think I actually want to *be* Dexter. While lying in bed was nice, I began to wonder how I could use my day more productively than fantasizing about a fictional character or murdering "Cosmic Love" with my awful, AWFUL singing. The whole squirting challenge is starting to feel more like work than play. I even tried pretending I didn't care and then attacking myself with my vibrator to see if a surprise ninja move worked. It didn't. So I gave up and e-mailed Lucy—I knew she'd be bored stiff without me.

From: Phoebe Henderson
To: Lucy Jacobs
Subject: Piss or pleasure?

How's it going? Thought I'd pick your brains about the ejaculation challenge as I'm beginning to think that it's either nonsense and those women are just pissing or my vagina doesn't work properly. Oh, and I love Dexter more than you. P x

From: Lucy Jacobs
To: Phoebe Henderson
Subject: Re: Piss or pleasure?

Hey! I'm all right but completely BORED. Frank is walking the floor like Herr Asshole so I take it you guys haven't made your targets yet. Dexter is FINE—I can accept coming second to him, it's understandable. Just keep trying, it'll happen, and believe me, it's not piss, otherwise my bedroom would smell like a nursing home.

From: Phoebe Henderson
To: Lucy Jacobs
Subject: Re: Piss or pleasure?

You're my hero.

Friday, February 25

Stuart's phone girlfriend came to meet him after work today. She's called Laura. He seems smitten. She looks like Paris Hilton and therefore the complete opposite of me: blond, skinny, small boobs, and an obvious passion for designer clothes and hair extensions. If that's the kind of girl he goes for, I can rule out ever getting him into bed. *Hey, Stuart, how about me then? I'm so pale my veins look like a road map and I can guarantee my bottom will have a least two zits on it. Possibly more—my underwear is nylon.* What a catch.

I saw Pam at half five tonight. We talked about Valentine's Day and how although I hated the concept, I was still pretty miffed no one fancied me enough to send a card. I told her how I'd seen Alex outside his office and how I obviously still wasn't comfortable looking at his stupid handsome face and just generally rehashed a million issues we'd already been over.

"This seems to have been a tough month for you, emotionally. Do you think you might still be focusing too much on the past? I suggest finding something new to concentrate on. A new interest? Some kind of challenge, perhaps?"

"Oh, I'm way ahead of you there," I replied.

Saturday, February 26

Since starting my list, I've been thinking about sex a lot, more than I ever have before. What I've noticed is the range of people that pop into my head when I'm feeling frisky. When I was younger, it used to be the pretty boys with great bodies and winning smiles, someone my mother would approve of, husband material. More recently it's been guys who perhaps aren't as pretty, or as toned, or even as respectable, who are getting it mentally. Tall men. Especially tall men. Vince Vaughn, Zachary Levi, Jason Segel, Eric Bana—you know, men who would never look twice at me but could easily see over the top of my head to spot the hot girl on the other side of the room. If I spot a musician with eyeliner or black nail polish, their image gets locked away, along with the handsome geeky guy in glasses who works in marketing and the overweight guy with the big hands who regularly serves me in Tesco. I've never been able to visualize someone else while I'm actually screwing, only when I'm masturbating. It's always seemed dishonest and well, kind of tricky. I think men are more capable of that than women, as Neanderthal Brian from work once pointed out: "If you're pissed and horny, it doesn't really matter. Doggy-style and lights off solves the problem of having to look an ugly girl in the face."

Ugh. Cannot believe I considered sleeping with him.

Sunday, February 27

Annoyingly I haven't yet been able to fully complete my masturbation challenge. Ejaculation is still eluding me, and so I've moved on to the next one: group sex, or, more specifically, a threesome. It might be some time away though, as Oliver has decided to go skiing with his friends for a week. The cockiness of it! Here I am waiting for some three-way action and he'd rather get pissed and fall off a mountain somewhere.

Lucy has asked me to go and see her boyfriend's new band on Saturday. "It'll be a laugh—there'll be cheap booze and they're actually really good."

Translated this means: "I have to go or he'll think I don't care, and I'll be bored shitless if you don't come along."

I've never been crazy about seeing unsigned bands; the gigs tend to be full of noisy boys and their noisy friends who've been forced to buy a ticket. Of course, I agreed to go; I'm not doing anything else and I really need to make up for my atrociously quiet past weekend. Lucy, of course, was thrilled.

"Hurrah! He has some nice friends, you know. And isn't sex with a younger man on your list?"

"No offense, but your boyfriend is twenty-one. What the hell would I do with a twenty-one-year-old?"

"Whatever you like." She grinned.

"I was thinking more twenty-eight or twenty-nine."

"Oh, for God's sake, try to be more adventurous, woman!"

The much younger men I slept with when I was also much younger were useless. Lots of fumbling, rubbing three inches above where they should, and assuming that almost fisting me would be a turn-on. I'm sure a lot of younger men are wonderful in bed, but I don't think I have the patience to find out. I'm trying to take my sex life to the next level, not regress back to when I was seventeen. But maybe she's right. I said MAYBE.

Monday, February 28

"You're wrong about much younger men," Lucy announced at work this morning.

"And how do you know I'm wrong?"

"Because I'm right. . . . In any case, you're meeting one of Sam's band mates, Richard, tonight. It's all been arranged. He's seen your picture and thinks you're a fox. Be at the Box for eight p.m.," she said.

"What are you, my pimp? If he thinks I'm a fox then he's obviously crazy. Why are you setting me up with someone who's clearly unstable?"

"He's very attractive. Looks like that guy from that film you liked."

"Jesus, Lucy, that narrows it down. Who? Jason Bateman? Peter Sellers? Simon Pegg?"

"No. Thingy. Vince Vaughn."

I doubt that. I suspect Lucy is trying to lure me there under false pretenses, fully aware of my knee-trembling lust for Vince Vaughn. It's a cheap trick.

MARCH

Tuesday, March 1

I was totally unconvinced but nevertheless curious about Lucy's "meet" and so, wearing my best underwear (under my clothes obviously), I made my way to the pub, hoping there was enough Jack Daniel's on the premises to make everyone more attractive, including me. But I should learn to trust Lucy more. I spotted her at the back of the pub, sitting with her boyfriend and Richard, who had his back to me. When he turned around he looked exactly like a younger, messier, but just as tall version of Vince Vaughn. I went red and gave Lucy a huge "I owe you big-time" smile.

The evening went well, but even though I could have straddled him right there and then purely for looking so hot, my initial fears were confirmed when I realized we had very little in common. He drank pints of cider like they were soft drinks, showed me three YouTube videos of Batman parodies and found it hysterical that I was born in the '70s.

"Did you wear flares and love ABBA?"

"I was two."

"But the '70s, man, that's so funny. Were you a hippie or a disco chick?"

"I WAS TWO! When were you born?"

"1990."

I was twelve when he was born. TWELVE. "Well, that's like me asking if you were a New Kids on the Block fan."

"Who?"

"Forget it."

I like my men to challenge me, and the only thing he would have challenged me to was a game of tennis on his roommate's Wii. Fortunately the more drunk I got the more endearing he became, and I still had my mind firmly on completing the challenge of sleeping with a younger man. So when he uttered the words "You're totally hot for your age," it was only a short time before we ended up back at the apartment he shared with his friend John: a nice place but with a surprising number of scatter cushions for two straight guys.

Anyway, we started messing around. The kissing was great, but he was overeager and I constantly had to give him slow-down signals. At that point, I didn't feel confident that this was going to be anything other than mediocre sex but, to his credit, he went down on me as soon as my underwear came off and actually seemed to know what he was doing. Or so I thought. He stopped halfway through and announced he had a confession to make: "I can't find your clit."

"Eh? What do you mean you can't find it? Your tongue was just on it."

"Was that your clit?!"

". . ."

After that I then went down on him . . . for about twenty seconds before I became aware he was going to come and decided to let him fuck me instead of having to gracefully wobble off to the bathroom and spit. His cock was huge and had a slight curve to it which rang my G-spot bells.

The sex was good, but I got the feeling he was nervously trying to work through some mental checklist. I think someone told all teenage boys in high school that foreplay involves touching all the good bits, but as soon as you actually penetrate a woman you must forget that these bits exist and JUST THRUST LIKE YOUR LIFE DEPENDS ON IT, LADS! He had explored every area—my breasts, my thighs, my neck, and even my ears, but as soon as he was inside, that was all forgotten and I was left to stare at his concentrating face. Even his beard appeared to be concentrating.

"Lick my nipples."

"I did."

"There isn't a lickage limit, you know. Anyway, it makes me wet."

"Oh. Sorry."

"Don't worry, you don't need to apologize."

"Sorry."

After all the fun I'd been having with Oliver, my expectations were high, but I know it's unfair of me to expect someone to get it right first time or know exactly what I want. Anyway, it wasn't all bad—when Richard stopped acting so nervous I caught glimpses of a guy who'd be pretty fabulous in bed. If this had been Lucy she'd have turned into a drill sergeant, screaming, "ASSUME THE POSITION, SOLDIER!" after a shaky start or some misplaced tongue action. Also on the plus side, approximately two minutes after we'd banged, he was ready and willing to go again. After the third time, my vagina had made it painfully clear it couldn't take any more. Then he started boring me with talk of music and an oh-so-hilarious incident that occurred during an "awesome" gig with his friend "Speedy" the previous weekend, resulting in them both throwing up at his nan's house. I must have resembled the Road Runner with the speed I took off at into the night.

So I can cross the younger-man challenge off the list, and it actually wasn't bad. Richard was very enthusiastic about my body, almost to the point where I had to check there wasn't someone else with "winning tits" in the bed beside me. I felt sexy with him, and being in control made me feel powerful: strong like bull. I like the new me.

We exchanged numbers and maybe I'll give him a call sometime. He might not rock my world, but I might be willing to let him rock my bed. A girl has needs, after all.

Wednesday, March 2

The commute to work was extra-dull this morning as the train got stuck outside Central for twenty-five minutes and I didn't have my iPod to distract me. But I perked up slightly when I noticed a man in a sharp suit across from me cross his legs to reveal a pair of Hannah Montana socks and perfectly smooth legs. While I waited for the train to move, I decided he must be called Xavier. Xavier had a wife called Shirley and six children who all played the piano together at the same time. He worked in a publishing house by day, but by night ran an underground Disney rave night where everyone got off their tits and danced to Miley Cyrus and hardcore remixes of "Step in Time" from *Mary Poppins*. My dreams were shattered when he pulled out his phone and called in late to the office.

"Hi, Nicola, it's Alistair. The train's delayed but I shouldn't be long. OK, just tell Mrs. Harris I'll be there shortly and give her some property schedules to look at while she waits. Cheers. Bye."

And with that the imaginary Xavier died in a terrible tractor accident. In space.

Later that day Oliver texted me about the anal challenge for about the billionth time from the ski slopes, obviously pissed:

Your ass is ging to get a lot of attenttion when I get bck.

Not until you learn to spell, it won't.

Despite his idiotic text, I'm sort of excited. Bum fun never happened with previous boyfriends. I remember discussing it with Alex, but he made a yuck face and carried on with his plans for vaginal domination. Now that I'm single again, everywhere I go it's an anal frenzy. Lucy even buys home enema kits so she doesn't have to deal with any poo fiasco and apparently has anal more frequently than regular sex. I can't help laughing uncontrollably when she mentions her occasional "ring sting." Hazel is convinced that no women genuinely like it—they just say they do to please their partner, like big old Stepford idiots.

To be honest, I'm still unclear about what pleasure I'd actually get from it. There was one drunken incident at nineteen with Adam where it was sneakily attempted but quickly cut short with me screaming "OUCH!" and giving him a dead leg, so I'm aware that there might be some pain involved, but there must be something in it? Surely not all women grimace, bite down, and bear it just to please their fellas?

Thursday, March 3

During a particularly quiet moment in the office today, Lucy yelled at the top of her voice, "Richard was asking after you. You going to see him again?"

Thankfully the rest of the conversation took place over the telephone, like normal people.

"I haven't decided. I don't want him to get any ideas," I replied.

"If you screw his brains out the poor guy is definitely going to get ideas. He likes you. He told Sam. Oh, and he also said you give the best head. Ever. Even Sam got hard hearing about it. I drew the line when he wanted to tell me about it."

"Oh fuck off. Boys are weird. What's his basis for comparison—some eighteen-year-old? Of course he'll think that," I muttered, slightly embarrassed but secretly delighted.

"Well, don't break his heart, dear; remember he's just a baby."

Exactly. Oliver and I have fantastic sex because there are no hearts involved and our friendship was there in the first place. The burning question of the day however is: do I really give good head? I'll have to wait until Oliver's back and ask him. He'll tell me the truth; he has no reason not to, well . . . except to continue getting head, obviously.

Friday, March 4

I'm horny. I woke up this morning and have been climbing the walls ever since. I'm just having one of those days when no amount of hand work will satisfy me, I need flesh on flesh, hands on my ass, and someone's mouth on mine.

It's getting ridiculous; I can't even eat a banana normally. I did think about calling Richard for a quickie after work but soon changed my mind; I need my no-strings savior who is probably off banging some girl called Heidi on a ski lift. I'm still no further forward in my quest to ejaculate, either. Maybe I needed specialized training and Bond-style gadgets. Lucy texted me this evening to tell me that she's having a small dinner party for her birthday on the twentieth and that she wants a spa voucher instead of the usual crap I buy her. I would be hurt if it wasn't true.

Saturday, March 5

Against my better judgment I ended up at Sam's gig with Lucy, feeling weird about seeing Richard again but eager to take advantage of the cheap drink offers. The gig was in a bar at the student end of Sauchiehall Street, where everyone is out to get hammered or laid, or preferably both. Determined not to give Richard the wrong impression, I wore baggy jeans, sneakers, and a granddad top. Lucy of course wore a short dress and knee-high boots, which made me look even dowdier, but for once I was glad; I didn't want to look like I'd made any sort of effort. I headed for the bar and ordered a shot of tequila and two rum-and-Cokes while scouring the room for signs of Richard. I found him setting up onstage and, dammit, he looked great: jeans, white shirt, and skinny black tie *and* he'd shaved his beard. He waved at me casually, then continued tuning his guitar while I made my way to a booth and sat down with Lucy.

"He looks fit, Phoebe. You sure you won't go there again?"

I knocked back my tequila and glanced over at him. "Another couple of these and I won't be sure of anything."

After the gig (loose definition, it was a bunch of twenty-year-olds mimicking early Blink-182 and failing miserably), I was drunk but still just able to hold a conversation. Even so, I was genuinely surprised when Richard cornered me outside the toilets and felt me up. After that, we left everyone at the pub and went back to his place again. After a couple of glasses of wine at his apartment, things got interesting. This time around he was very gentle, took his time, and when he found the special spot I have on my neck with his mouth, my clothes fell to a crumpled heap on his floor. I love the fact that most men have a body part they favor: with Oliver it's my bottom, Stuart at work always stares at my legs, and Richard is like a chubby kid at a chocolate factory when it comes to my breasts. I left right afterward; I don't want him thinking I'm his girlfriend and I hope he understands that. I did meet his roommate on the way out (well-built, boyishly handsome, and covered in tattoos) and walked to the nearby taxi rank with wobbly legs and a secret smile, wondering if said roommate would be up for a threesome. Am I now incapable of even seeing a member of the opposite sex without immediately rating him for sex potential?

Monday, March 7

Oliver is back, thank the lord for that. I made him get his ass over here pronto this evening and practically mounted him in the hallway. The session with Richard on Saturday only seems to have fueled my raging libido and after a marathon session, we lay in bed.

"Do I give good head?" I asked, while trying to uncramp my toes.

"No. You give fucking GREAT head," he replied, lighting a cigarette. "It's honestly remarkable! You have this two-handed, tongue-and-lips combination thing you do. You should teach that shit—you'd be loaded."

"Are you messing with me now? Is it just average but you're frightened if you tell me that I'll sulk and never go down on you again?"

"Jesus, take a compliment. You give exceptional head. Your reverse cowgirl needs some work, but apart from that I'm happy."

I was tempted to argue the cowgirl case, but he has a point. I've never been that comfortable doing it. I always feel off balance and it's definitely a good thing that my back is turned so he can't see the look of sheer concentration on my face. I'm sure sometimes my tongue sticks out when I'm really focusing.

Friday, March 11

I arranged this morning off work in order to go underwear shopping. I have two sets of "sexy time" lingerie, which have recently been through the wash approximately seventy-five times and are on the verge of disintegrating. I did my best to ignore my sensible side, which just wanted to buy reasonably priced black-and-white sets and opted instead for some overpriced red ones, electric-blue ones, and a black corset-and-suspender set, all of which I hope will make Oliver hard before I've even put them on. After all, it's only fair. If he turned up wearing worn-out Y-fronts all the time I'd be less than impressed. I arrived back at work, armed with carrier bags that I made sure to hide in my locked drawer—the last time Lucy bought underwear and left the bags lying around, she came back into the office to find everyone modeling at least one item. Even me.

I ignored the client messages waiting for me and called Oliver instead.

"I bought new underwear."

"Shit. Did you? Anything in blue?"

"Maybe. We can try that anal thing tonight. Let's just get it over with."

"Fuckin' hell, Phoebe, I'm not giving you a root canal."

"I'm sure that's less invasive."

"You'll love it. I'll be over around nine."

By the time he arrived I'd "prepared" myself with an enema kit. I felt nauseous. Did I really think I was going to shit all over the floor? What the hell am I, an elephant? I was actually more worried about getting poo everywhere than any sort of pain element, but Oliver had promised to stop if it hurt.

I wore my new blue underwear.

He couldn't stop grinning. "You look amazing! And we're doing anal! This is the best night ever!"

"Oh fuck. I'm nervous."

"Look, Phoebs, we don't have to do this if you don't want to."

"I do. We do. I'm fed up with wondering what it's like. This is an integral part of my sexual metamorphosis."

"Let's have a drink first. Maybe a Valium? Some ketamine?"

"Oliver! You're making it worse!"

Half an hour and a strong Jack and Coke later, I was ready. Oliver returned from the bathroom and put a towel down on the floor.

Jesus! I thought. HOW MESSY IS THIS GOING TO GET? quickly followed by, THAT'S MY BEST TOWEL!

I was pretty sure I knew what was going to follow: fore-play, finger work, lots of lube, and then me shouting and making an ouchy face. I braced myself.

But it was not what I imagined at all.

We started messing around and, as ever, I was good to go as soon as Oliver kissed my neck, but then he made me bend down on all fours and disappeared behind me. Startled, I glanced over my shoulder to see him lubing up his fingers with a slight smirk on his face.

It felt odd as he started, not unpleasant, but definitely odd. I must have clenched up because he started to massage my breasts with his other hand, while slowly circling my clit with his thumb. It worked. Before I knew it there were two fingers in there and I suddenly felt a huge wave of arousal wash over me. After that, it took a while for him to get fully inside me: lots of me telling him to slow the fuck down! and serious amounts of lube, but once we started and I finally got over the fact that it felt like I had to use the toilet, I was hooked. The feeling is hard to describe but it was definitely enjoyable.

It was also perhaps the most submissive thing I've ever done. I could hardly move and the whole experience was overwhelming. I'm so glad that I picked someone I knew wouldn't abuse the obvious amount of power it gave him and who understood it wasn't an area you just take a run at. Oliver was gentle, made sure I was happy with everything, and was extremely vocal about how "fucking hot" he found the whole thing. As did I.

He stayed over and we did it until we both couldn't move anymore. Anal + vibrator = OOFT! That's all I have to say about today. Oliver and I should have been doing this daily since high school. So this challenge was a huge success. I'm a complete convert. Big-time.

Monday, March 14

After work the girls and I went to get our nails done at a new salon on Byres Road. I'd arranged some free advertising in the paper in exchange for the manicures and the promise that they'd never mention it to my boss. Lucy and I met Hazel outside, then took our seats at the nail bar, sipping free Prosecco and choosing our colors.

"Black," I decided, dismissing the array of pastels displayed in front of me.

I could feel Hazel staring at me. "Stop being so emo, Phoebe. I thought this was the new you."

"OK, tell you what: I'll get whatever color you think, if YOU get the black, Hazel."

Lucy laughed. "Hazel with black nails? Jesus, whatever would the yummy mummies think? You'd be thrown out of the mother-and-baby class."

"Black just isn't me," Hazel replied coolly, running her hand through her blond hair. "Kevin would hate it, but I couldn't care less what those idiot mothers think."

"Prove it then." I held up her usual shade of pearly pink and swapped it with the black I'd already chosen. "You do it and so will I."

We left the salon forty-five minutes later: Lucy with her usual red, me with nails by Barbie, and Hazel with black talons that looked incredible.

I got a text from her half an hour ago:

So Kevin likes my nails. A lot. Who'd have thought it?

This might sound like the lamest dare ever made, but getting Hazel to be even a wee bit rock-and-roll is worth walking around with nails like marshmallows for the next two weeks.

Tuesday, March 15

So with anal very successfully achieved it's on to the next challenge on my list: role play. A program I saw on TV tonight gave me a few ideas. A couple had hired a company to help them play out their "abduction" fantasy: guy gets jumped by dudes in balaclavas who shout at him loudly, then he gets bundled into a van and taken to a remote house, where his captor (i.e., wife) is waiting, dressed as a terrifying but sexy dominatrix. I have to say, the whole idea is pretty cool and I was impressed they'd actually hired outside help. I've never participated in any kind of role play before, mainly because it has always struck me as something for bored married couples. Well, except for a really sketchy French maid's outfit I bought over the Internet once, which looked *très* ridiculous and soon found its way into the bin (not least because Adam, the guy I was seeing, actually let me clean his bedroom before we had sex, which I refuse to believe was just to "help me stay in character"). I'll call Oliver tomorrow and discuss what we should do. I BET he says "hooker," the little shit.

Wednesday, March 16

I work with the strangest group of people, and if it wasn't for Lucy I'm sure I'd have killed at least one of them by now. As it's a sales environment, they're all obsessed with the team bonus, which can only be achieved when we hit target. Of course, this only applies to the sales team, so admin extraordinaire Lucy doesn't give a shit and frequently offers to make them all a big cup of SHUT THE FUCK UP. The thing is, they never want to buy anything interesting with the extra money. For Brian it's always something new and decidedly boring for his car, and I can see Kelly already planning her next fake-tanning session with Jennifer; a woman who "totally doesn't streak you so is worth the £40." (I could see everyone eyeing up her streaky legs and making a mental note to avoid Jennifer and her tanning gun like the plague.) The worst of them all is Frank, who is clearly an idiot but a very clever one. He gets paid big wads of cash to do sod-all and then buys stuff with it. Not content with his upside-down artwork, he came blazing into the office today with a new piece of bling, which makes all other bling weep uncontrollably and want to try harder. "It's a one-off, you know," said Frank, waving his wrist around the office like a magician. "Only one like it."

Lucy grabbed his arm to take a closer look: "My, my. You have your initials on there and everything. That. Is. Special."

The sad thing is, the majority of people in the office, even Stuart, were actually impressed, but I'll forgive him one tiny mistake because I love him.

From: Lucy Jacobs
To: Phoebe Henderson
Subject: Tick Tock

That watch makes me want to stab Frank in the face, but strangely I find him sexy today. Shame he's such a prick as I totally would. He looks like David Duchovny. Ever noticed that?

From: Phoebe Henderson
To: Lucy Jacobs
Subject: Re: Tick Tock

I wish that last email had a "dislike" button.

From: Lucy Jacobs
To: Phoebe Henderson
Subject: Re: Tick Tock

Remember my birthday dinner on Sunday. Can you bring some
wine with you? Thanks love x

Shit, I had totally forgotten. I must buy her that spa voucher.
How do I manage to have any friends at all?

Thursday, March 17

I left the office in record time this evening and zoomed
home to get ready for the first role play I had planned with
Oliver. We've decided on three scenarios, and the first is
based on the very common university student/lecturer
scenario: Mr. Webb and Miss Henderson having a one-to-
one tutorial, which inevitably ends up in some serious and
somewhat illicit sex. A no-nonsense prim-and-proper student arrived at Oliver's apartment, complete with a folder
full of essays (well, actually just a couple of magazines I'd
been reading on the train), dressed casually in jeans with
suitably provocative underwear hidden underneath.

"Hello, Phoebe. Are you ready for our session?" were
the first words "Mr. Webb" uttered as he opened his door,
dressed in a suit with his hair all disheveled.

Fuck me, Oliver had made the effort.

We sat down, and as we stared across the kitchen table at each other I remembered something important: I hadn't planned this part. Shit. I had been so excited about playing out this fantasy that I'd overlooked a vital detail: how the hell do we actually act this out? My improv skills are sketchy to say the least, and I could almost hear myself being heckled with "Ooh, matron!" as I racked my brains trying to avoid anything that sounded like a Robin Askwith or Sid James line.

Oliver, on the other hand, had obviously put some thought into it, and just as I was about to panic he reached for something under the table.

"I've got some material for you to look over, Miss Henderson. You can let me know if you need anything explained in more detail."

He handed me three porn magazines and sat back.

I started to browse through them, pleased that they weren't "barely legal" or "gummy granny" mags and felt my cheeks go red, not so much because I was embarrassed but because this was starting to be the hottest thing I'd ever done in my life.

I undid some buttons on my cardigan, showing a glimpse of the red balcony bra I'd bought. He'd told me before that red underwear gets him hard, and I intended to find out just how true that was. I made him wait for a few minutes, studying the magazines, licking my lips and feeling his gaze fixed upon my mouth.

"I don't understand this," I said, sliding the magazine across the table. "Can you explain exactly how this works?"

He put on his glasses to look at the page I'd turned to and I started to ache. A handsome man in glasses has the same effect on me as red underwear does on Oliver. As he stood up to walk behind my chair, the bulge in his pants told me everything I needed to know, so I undid another couple of buttons. He leaned in and his breath on my neck made me tingle all over.

"This is a complex position, Miss Henderson," he whispered in my ear. "I could explain it to you or I could show you."

He slid one hand inside my bra and I could hear him undoing his belt with the other. I was so turned on I forgot to be sensible, abandoned my character, and turned around, pulling him in toward the kitchen table. He had my jeans off in record time but I made him keep his shirt and tie on. Oh, and his glasses.

My preconceived notion that role play is only for couples who've become bored with their sex lives has been totally overturned. I was still horny as I stood in the shower afterward. To say it was a success would be an understatement.

"I can't believe you have porn magazines. I mean, the Internet is full of free stuff. Why would you buy those?" I asked, stepping out of the shower and beginning to dry myself.

"I've had them for years. They might be collector's items one day."

"In what universe? The one where people collect old porn mags covered in Irish DNA? If you shone a UV light on those magazines it'd look like a crime scene."

"Fair point."

I made us some tea and we took it back to bed. I stayed over; it was too cozy to go home. Today was a good day.

Saturday, March 19

I was shopping for wine for Lucy's party tomorrow when I bumped into Alex AGAIN. What a feckin' disaster. Everything was fine at first: he was handsome, I got butterflies in my stomach, and I even felt grateful when he was nice to me. I mean, really? It's like I've learned nothing. We began flirting (I'm such an idiot) and then Miss Tits appeared 'round the corner with a box of wine wedged between her breasts.

"Oh. Phoebe." She looked uncomfortable.

"Brilliant," I sighed under my breath. "There's no show without Punch, eh? I'm glad to see this charade is still being played out."

As I started to walk away, Miss Tits shouted, "We're getting married, Phoebe! End of the year. Get over it."

I could feel my face flushing and I swung around to face Alex again.

"Married?! Oh, what an idiot I am! So one minute you're all flirty with me and the next you're GETTING MARRIED? To THAT? So telling me you didn't see the need for marriage was yet another lie? What, are you going to live happily ever after with that giant box of wine and her giant tits?"

"HANG ON A MINUTE!" she shouted, looking as if she were about to spontaneously combust.

"Hang on for what? So you can sleep with my boyfriend? Oh, wait, YOU ALREADY DID THAT!"

"Let's go, Lexy," she said, placing her hand in his while he stood there enjoying the carnage.

"LEXY? Oh Christ, there's a pet name and everything. How about CUNTY? That seems more appropriate."

As they rushed off grumbling I took the piss out of her age and wine choice by telling her that her box of wine was best served in "nineteen fucking seventy." It was not my finest hour. I'm not sure whether I was angry or surprised or just annoyed with myself for letting my guard down with him. For a second while we were chatting I missed him, I really missed him. What the fuck is the matter with me?

Sunday, March 20

I arrived at Lucy's house at around eight for her birthday dinner with Paul and Hazel. Oliver had to work so I gave her a bottle of Champagne on his behalf. She lives half an hour away from me in a house that her grandparents left her, on a tiny little estate that is quiet, pretty, and very classy. The house is a two-bedroom bungalow with a massive living/dining room and a bathroom with a whirlpool bath. It's no wonder she's always late for everything; I'd be in no hurry to leave either. Sam was there to wish her happy birthday, but had to go to band practice. He swaggered off before we ate and, thankfully, there was no mention of Richard. Lucy loved her spa voucher and dinner was delicious. As a birthday gift Paul had paid a local Mexican restaurant to prepare a small feast for us. Paul and Lucy have a strange relationship. They also became friends when he worked at the *Post* but became much closer than Paul and I ever did. They're rather like siblings—they love each other to death but pick on each other constantly.

After dessert we had coffee and I shared my earlier encounter with Alex and Miss Tits, hoping someone would make me feel better about it.

"If he wants to bang someone a hundred years older than him, he's an idiot," announced Lucy.

"Well, you're banging someone a hundred years younger. I'm going to start calling you Humbert," Paul commented.

"Stop being mean to me on my birthday, you gaylord."

This went on until we started on the vodka and Hazel passed out in the toilet.

I'm home now and the question that's still gnawing away at my heart isn't why is he marrying her . . . It's why didn't he want to marry me?

I am not coping with this well at all. PAM POTTER, WHERE ARE YOU?

Wednesday, March 23

I called Pam first thing this morning demanding an appointment and she agreed to fit me in after her last session at six. It's now just after three and I've been thinking about Alex and THAT WOMAN all day . . . and their wedding . . . and their future children . . . and generally just making myself ill over the whole matter. I want to talk to Lucy or Hazel about how I'm feeling, but I'm aware there's only so much whining they can take before they lose the plot with me for being so pathetic. God knows I'm angry enough at myself.

8 p.m. My session with Pam went well. It was such a relief to just vomit out all the crap that's been festering away inside my head. Highlights included:

(On Alex)

Pam: Why are you so angry that he's getting married?

Me: He always said he'd never get married. Now I know it's that he just didn't want to get married to me. I feel like a fool.

(On this diary)

Pam: We discussed keeping a journal last year. Have you made an effort to do that?

Me: Yes. Oh yes. Lots of writing. I'm keeping a note of everything. Although the content is mostly sexual. It's like the Secret Diary of Estrogen Mole. (She didn't laugh.)

(On sex)

Me: I don't know why my sex life is so important now.

Pam: I think the question should be why you didn't think your sex life was important then?

Good point. I feel a lot better having had a rant to someone other than my friends. At least Pam didn't start a fight and call me a gaylord. But at the end of the session she told me she's going to visit her family in Florida for a few weeks so I'll have to bore someone else with my troubles while she's gone.

Thursday, March 24

This month seems to be going from bad to worse. Just when I thought it couldn't get any more abysmal, something happened today which made me wish I'd never embarked on this freakin' list of freakin' challenges. While Frank was out for a meeting, I decided, in my infinite wisdom, that I would use his office to give Oliver a surprise sex call at work. Only Frank came back, didn't he? He came back and just as I was uttering the words "I'm going to take your cock in my mouth—" Frank took the receiver out of my hand, said, "Indeed you are not," and hung up.

I have to go in first thing tomorrow for a meeting and I want to vomit. Of course, Oliver thinks this is hysterical and doesn't appreciate that my boss has no sense of humor.

"He's a guy, Phoebe—he'll be laughing about this with his wife."

"He's divorced."

"OK, then he'll be jacking it while thinking about you putting his—"

"ARGHH. Shut up!"

"Look, I've met your boss. He's an uptight knob. This is probably the most exciting thing that's ever happened to him."

"So you don't think he'll sack me?"

"Well, I didn't say that . . ."

"Oh God. I'm totally getting fired."

Friday, March 25

This morning I snuck furtively into the office only to discover that Frank wasn't in, which meant I was able to relax for exactly half an hour before he rang and told me we'd have our meeting on Monday morning instead. Asshole. I now have the whole weekend to cry and job-hunt. I spent the rest of the afternoon taking too many cigarette breaks and flirting on Twitter with @granted77. He's changed his picture to one of his face and he's rather attractive. I'm now at home, pacing up and down my living room, wondering if I should learn a trade.

Monday, March 28

I sat meekly in the morning meeting, wishing Frank would suddenly have a fatal heart attack and I'd be off the hook. Afterward I crept into his office for my inevitable humiliation and sacking. Or so I thought.

"We seem to have a problem, Phoebe. You used my office for personal calls and from what I overheard it wasn't a family emergency."

"Oh, come on, it wasn't that bad." I tried to remember exactly what I'd said. "How much did you hear?"

98   **Joanna Bolouri**

"Enough, Phoebe, I heard enough. From your e-mails I'm also aware that your mind hasn't been on the job for a while. These challenges of yours seem more important than giving a hundred percent to your job, which is what you're paid to do."

The sneaky bastard. "YOU READ MY E-MAILS? THAT'S—"

He shushed me. He actually shushed me! "Do you want to keep your job, Phoebe?"

"Of course I do! Look, I'm sorry. It was . . . unprofessional."

"With a poor reference from this company, chances of finding anything else in the current market are pretty slim."

"I get it, Frank. I've apologized. What more do you want?"

He paused for a moment and began shuffling some papers on his desk. He seemed flustered.

"Well . . . I . . ."

"Put me on probation, anything."

"There is one thing that, um . . ."

He started typing on his keyboard, staring at his computer screen, which wasn't switched on.

"What thing? Jesus, Frank! Just tell me what I have to do to keep my job."

He remained silent and my nerves began to get the better of me. I could feel my bottom lip trembling. I stood up to leave and he motioned me to wait before replying: "Add me to your list."

"What did you say?" I asked in disbelief.

"Let's just say things aren't going so well for me . . . with the ladies. Perhaps you can give me a few lessons, I can't get past a third date, I—"

Totally weird. "I'm not sure I'm the best person to be sharing this with. . . ."

"Look, bottom line: if you help me out, I won't take this any further."

We both stared at each other for a minute in some sort of bizarre Mexican standoff. I was furious.

"Help you out? Fuck off, Frank! I'm not sleeping with you; I'd rather get fired. This is blackmail."

"I didn't say I'd sleep with you. God no. You're heavier than I'd normally go for anyway. Just some direction. I must be doing something wrong and I feel you're the girl to help me find out what that is. You just think about it, and let me know tomorrow."

So I'm thinking about it. He's already sent me two e-mails and I can tell that he's actually kind of desperate. Could I even consider this? Could I turn this pretentious twat into someone worth dating? At the moment I'm so angry with him I want to violently pluck out my own eyelashes.

Tuesday, March 29

So I caved. After considering the alternative, which involves signing on at the job center and having to make up excuses as to why I'd been sacked, I've decided to help Frank out. It seems I now have an additional challenge to add to the list, which keeps me in a job I hate but need and has helped me take my mind off Alex and Bridezilla. It hasn't taken my mind off Stuart and his tight butt, though. He e-mailed me this afternoon:

From: Stuart Sinclair
To: Phoebe Henderson
Subject: Afternoon

Nice Legs. Back to work then.

From: Phoebe Henderson
To: Stuart Sinclair
Subject: Re: Afternoon.

Oh, you're for it.

Wednesday, March 30

Back to business and the next role play will involve me being a prostitute and Oliver my punter. That little gem was all his idea. And not the *Belle de Jour*, tea and crumpets, "why don't you have a lovely shower?" type of call girl, oh no. *That* would have been way too civilized. Oliver wants me dressed like a dirty girl: high heels, miniskirt, fishnets, and every other stereotypical item of clothing you'd see in a bad film involving streetwalkers, pimps, and two maverick detectives on a stakeout. Actually, most of his fantasy role-play suggestions involved really clichéd scenarios like doctors and nurses, someone coming 'round to fix the remote control, or something equally lame, but it's only fair that he gets one of his choices in this particular challenge too. "Just be dirty and don't cry if I'm mean to you."

I have a horrible feeling I'm going to end up looking like an '80s drag queen. If any money changes hands, I'm fucking keeping it.

Thursday, March 31

"What the hell? This office smells like gravy," I announced as I walked in this morning.

Brian looked up from his desk and raised his coffee mug. "Bovril," he declared triumphantly. "What's wrong, don't you like something meaty in the morning?"

"Oh, please, it's too early for innuendo, Brian, and that stuff reeks."

"I'm nearly finished. You'd be useless at a soccer match—we drink gallons of it."

"Yet another reason to avoid sport."

He shrugged and carried on drinking it while I made gagging noises from the other side of the room. Knob.

The day dragged. I drank about twenty cups of tea and pissed about on Twitter. I practically ran out of the office at five, desperate to get home and have a lazy evening, but when I got to the station my train home was delayed. Fucking typical. I sat in Burger King for forty-five minutes, nursing a milkshake and fries and contemplating what an odd month it's been. I've banged a younger guy, lost my anal cherry, done my first proper role play, and somehow agreed to make my boss more datable to avoid being sacked. I'm exhausted. This is shaping up to be an interesting year.

APRIL

Friday, April 1

Richard texted me at six this morning, telling me he wants to see me again. I politely but firmly replied no, thank you. What would be the point in that? I already have a fuck buddy.

Saturday, April 2

Scottish weather is the worst. It rained so hard today that there was nothing to do but sit around in my robe talking shit on Twitter, watching YouTube videos and eating biscuits. I've been horny as hell and started sending Oliver pictures of my breasts, mainly because I knew he was stuck at work all day and it amused me to think of him getting an erection at an inappropriate time. Women have it easy in that respect—we can be completely aroused and no one will ever know. Richard texted me AGAIN, after I told him already I'm not interested. I've ignored him. Jesus, man, take the hint!

From: Oliver Webb
To: Phoebe Henderson
Subject: Bored

Nice tits. More please.

From: Phoebe Henderson
To: Oliver Webb
Subject: Re: Bored

You *must* be bored. There's an internet full of tits much more impressive than mine. Anyway you shouldn't be looking at tits. God is watching.

Oh, I watched that porn film you left here. Well, parts of it. Didn't really do it for me, there was too much rimming, and he kept his socks on. Rimming with socks on is never a turn-on.

When do you finish?

From: Oliver Webb
To: Phoebe Henderson
Subject: Re: Bored

Rimming with socks on? That's what I'm going to call the first Native American child we adopt.

I'm on till 10, then I'm going out with a girl called Sandra who thinks I'm charming. She's right, of course. Well, if you're not going to send me any more boobs I'm not going to send you a picture of my cock.

From: Phoebe Henderson
To: Oliver Webb
Subject: Re: Bored

Good. I've just eaten. Fine, go and play with Sandra then, but that's an unimaginative name and she won't send you boobs pics like I do. Don't say I didn't warn you.

So given that Oliver's going to be spending all evening and probably tomorrow morning with Sandra Dullname, the hooker role play will have to wait.

Next up is sex outside. I've always fantasized about it—I'm not talking about going so far as dogging, but the thought of being watched or even caught sends a naughty shiver up my spine.

The majority of my sex life hasn't been especially adventurous: mainly on my back in bed, nice and safe, away from prying eyes and risk free. I blame myself for this. It would be easy to say that my partners have all been sexual bores, but for all I know they might have been up for skydiving sex or bungee humping but I never inquired. I do remember once asking Alex if he'd be into using sex toys and he looked at me like I'd just pissed in his favorite sneakers. Now that I think about it, I'm quite stunned that I've been waiting for permission from someone else to go after what I want, whatever that is. I know I want an element of risk but, more important, I want some freakin' excitement! Like movie sex, where pretty people who are hot for each other get it on in exciting, risqué places and no one goes to prison. I've come close a couple of times, once giving head to my ex-boyfriend James behind a restaurant. It lasted about ten seconds though, as we had chosen to hide behind some large bins; there's nothing like the whiff of rotting food to kill the mood. The second time was when I fumbled around in a phone box with Alex early on in our relationship. It was cramped, smelled of piss, and he was hardly Superman.

The more I think about it the more excited I get, imagining all sorts of debauched outdoor activities, so I've decided that this is definitely happening. I'll just have to make it clear to Oliver that I don't mean hiking off into the wilderness or camping—I'm many things, but I'm not THAT kind of girl. I texted him to let him know I was ready to do this.

Yo. AL FRESCO SEX. Let's do it. Call me or text me ASAP

I hope Miss Dullname looks at his phone.

Sunday, April 3

I called Mum earlier to wish her a happy birthday. I gave her Amazon vouchers, as I had absolutely no idea what she likes.

"Thank you, darling! Your dad got me tickets to see Muse. Apparently they're doing some sort of benefit show."

"MUSE? You're sixty! When did you start liking Muse?"

"Since I heard 'Plug in Baby.' Amazing band. I'm sixty, Phoebe; that's not ancient."

"I know, I'm just surprised. I thought you'd be going to see Cat Stevens or some other crumbly hippie."

"Maybe twenty years ago, but he's called Yusuf now and far too godly for my liking. Anyway, I have to run. We're going for a swim. Bye, darling, and thanks for the vouchers!"

Fucking Muse? My parents will never stop surprising me. I called Oliver twice and it went straight to voice mail. He hasn't responded to my texts, either. Where the hell is he?

Monday, April 4

Oliver still wasn't returning my calls, despite my having left several "ravage me in a car park goddammmiitt!" voice mails on his cell today. So I gave up and went out for drinks after work with Stuart. Oh, how I've longed for this day! He's the only sales guy I've ever met who's also a decent human being. Also, he has the most perfect mouth and nervously bites his lip every so often, which drives me insane. Seriously. It took all my strength and willpower not to leap across the desk, grab his tie, and lick his face. But sleeping with people you work with is always a tricky area that requires discretion—mainly in case it's God-awful or they think I'm fat and tell everyone.

We had been flirting all day, and when it came time to go home we both took our time packing up until the office was empty. "What you up to now?" asked Stuart, switching off his PC.

"Nothing much," I replied casually. "Drink?"

"Yeah," he said with a smile, "definitely." We went to the pub downstairs, ordered some shots, and sat squashed together at a table in the corner. Our initial shoptalk turned into a drinking game of Truth or Dare. Yes, it's all innocent fun, until someone's dared to see just how wet he can get me underneath the table. A challenge he accepted, by the way. It got to near closing time and the sexual tension became too much. "Want to get out of here?" he asked, and it suddenly hit me that Oliver wasn't the only one who could help me with my next challenge. We both practically ran out the door, wishing we were wearing invisible sex cloaks and could just screw right there in the street, but we ended up in an alleyway behind a club, me with my tights around my ankles, grabbing on to a jaggy wire fence. I could hear people passing by the entrance to the alley, myriad voices and laughter. It was thrilling knowing that we could have been spotted or even watched. "I can't believe we're doing this," Stuart panted partway in. "I've wanted to bang you for ages."

"Likewise," I groaned. "Now, do it harder."

It was exciting, passionate, and absolutely freezing. I felt incredibly sexy and very, very naughty. Once I'd got my head around the situation, all I could think was, He likes me! like some love-struck teenager. I could have happily carried on for hours, but when it was over we got our clothes in order and kissed for a couple of minutes before deciding it was time to head off. Then, with a vow of discretion and a good-bye look that lasted a little too long, we parted company. For once I cannot wait to get to work tomorrow. I texted Oliver before bed:

Where are you? Are you dead? Let me know.

Tuesday, April 5

It wasn't at all awkward at work with Stuart and I didn't come into an office full of giggling gossips, which was a relief. We exchanged a few e-mails, complimenting each other on our session, but he managed to ruin it all by saying, "I have a girlfriend, you know. I can't do this again."

Spoilsport. I finally tracked down Oliver. He'd been in Brighton at a conference, which pretty much meant one hour of tech talk and twenty hours of cocaine and Jack Daniel's abuse.

"It was deadly. I slept with two sisters."

"Please tell me it wasn't at the same time."

"God no, Phoebs. One after the other."

"Yes. That makes it much better. What about Sandra?"

"You were right. She wouldn't sleep with me on the first date, and it was a shit date anyway. All she did was talk about her freakin' cat. Nice ass though."

In return I told him about Stuart from work and for a second he seemed put out. Hardly fair given that he's been off humping an entire family, but his response was, "I thought I was helping you out with this stuff. I thought we were doing another role play first."

"You were away with the incest twins; I couldn't get hold of you. We'll still do the role play—there's no specific order to this, Oliver. Besides, this is about me becoming the master of my sexual universe. Be pleased for me!"

"I know. I am! I was just looking forward to it, that's all. Well, we're doing it outside too. I'll pick you up after work tomorrow."

Wednesday, April 6

Oliver was waiting for me as arranged and I caught him getting a look at Stuart as he walked down the road. "I thought you didn't like really short hair," he muttered.

We drove for about forty minutes and barely spoke for the entire journey. We eventually got off the motorway and headed up some dirty country lane leading to God knows where. Oliver stopped the car, checked his face in the mirror, got out, and then walked around and opened my door. He was acting strangely, and I started to get a sinking feeling in my stomach, like he was about to kill me or something.

I started to speak but it's hard to talk when someone has suddenly pressed their mouth firmly up against yours. I gave up and gave in.

We maneuvered around to the front of the car and he pulled down my tights and underwear. I say "pulled"; it was more of a ripping action, which would have been sexier had I not been wearing industrial-strength panties and tights. With some help they were flung into a nearby hedge and I was flipped over and banged on the hood of the car, quite dramatically. While it was obvious he wanted me, I could tell he was mostly trying to out-screw Stuart so he could then jump up and down in front of me shouting, "I'M THE WINNER, I'M THE FUCKING WINNER!" In the midst of it, as he was kissing my neck, he moved his mouth to my ear and said, "It's never this good with anyone else, is it?"

I answered truthfully: "No. It isn't."

After we'd finished he kissed me and offered to help look for my panties. We found them but they had already been explored and conquered by some small animals so I gladly abandoned them. "You want to stay at mine tonight? I can take you home to get some new panties first."

"Nah, I have to get home. I want to do girlie things like paint my nails and cover my face in mud. Besides, I'm exhausted. This was fun though."

So he drove me home, where I fell into bed, grinning to myself and feeling a tad tender. The sex-outside challenge has definitely been my favorite so far and was even better than I expected. I'm not sure if it was the danger element, Stuart's lip biting, or Oliver's competitive humping that thrilled me the most, but I intend to make this a regular event. I hope to God I don't end up on some "Caught Banging on CCTV" website.

Thursday, April 7

"Are you free tonight, Phoebe? Let me take you on a date."

There are certain sentences you never want to hear your boss say, and that is one of them.

"Hang on a second, Romeo! I made it clear that—" but before I could finish my sentence more words flew out of that hole in his face.

"Well, it's not a proper date, obviously, but recently I've been struggling and I don't know why. I'm getting really fed up, and you did promise you'd help me."

"You're making me help you. This is feeling more and more like blackmail, Frank. But fine. We'll go straight from work, separately. I'm not having Maureen in admin whip herself into a frenzy when she sees us leaving together. And you're paying."

I had arranged to meet Frank in a cozy Italian restaurant *waaayyy* across town. I was sitting at the bar waiting for him when Oliver called.

"You want to grab something to eat? I'm starving and—"

"Sorry, Oliver, I'm already out on a date. Well, a fake date. With Frank. I'll explain later."

This was met with a silence long enough to make me uncomfortable.

"Come around later if you want. You can eat me!" I quipped.

My attempt at a joke fell flat, as did Oliver's tone.

"No, it's fine. I'll see you later."

He hung up on me and I felt pissed off. What does he expect? That I'll be there at his freakin' beck and call? Then in lumbered Frank looking flustered and still wearing that stupid watch. We sat down at a table and the waitress brought over some menus. The date had officially begun.

"Our soup tonight is minestrone. Can I get you some drinks?"

"I'll have a glass of dry white wine," Frank replied, taking off his suit jacket. "Large."

"Just make it a bottle," I added, watching him mentally undress the waitress. "We'll need it."

She walked away, completely unaware she'd just been added to Frank's spank bank. A few minutes later she returned with the wine and took our orders—mushroom ravioli for me and some sort of fishy risotto for Frank. "So, did you get that half-page ad sold?" Frank began, pouring himself some wine.

"No work talk, Frank. It's boring. Wow me with your chat."

"My chat?"

"Your conversation, y'know, your witty repartee."

Ten minutes later I knew exactly what the problem was, and when we'd finished eating I decided to nip it in the bud.

"Frank, do you know that you're the worst company on a date ever? And when I say 'ever,' what I actually mean is 'EVER'!"

He looked genuinely confused. "So far you've turned around twice mid-conversation to look at that waitress's backside, you've poured yourself wine without offering me any, you've managed to turn two separate conversations into really dull anecdotes about buying expensive shit—speaking of which, your watch is idiotic—"

"Jesus, Phoebe, you don't have to be so blunt about it! I knew something like this would happen," he said with a sniff. "You see, Phoebe, there are two types of people in this world: people like you, and people like me."

"What 'narcissist' and 'blackmailed'? You might be right," I said, rolling my eyes. "And that very statement you've just made is the reason women would rather stay at home and self-harm than go out with you. Remember that."

He wasn't happy.

"Look, you asked me to help you. Stop being such a big baby. I'm going to write all this down and e-mail it to you in the morning. My advice is to STOP DATING until you've worked on this, but first step is to get rid of that freakin' watch—it's hideous."

The one thing I didn't mention was that, despite his lack of social skills, he smelled amazing, like vanilla, and it reminded me of cake and . . . *STOP IT, Phoebe! Under no circumstances will you nibble your boss.*

Friday, April 8

I got into the office bang on nine a.m., caramel latte in hand, eyes shielded from the bright-yellow cardigan Kelly was wearing. The very second I sat down my phone rang; it was Frank.

"Good morning, Phoebe."

"Morning."

"Regarding last night, I would appreciate your feedback ASAP." He pronounced it Ay-sap. I couldn't let him get away with that.

"You do know that ASAP isn't actually a word? You're supposed to spell out each letter. It's not like—"

"Oh, stop being a smartass. And get on with it. And then get that half-page sold."

He hung up and I opened my e-mail and answered thirteen terribly unimportant messages before getting around to e-mailing him. When I did, I kept it short and sweet.

From: Phoebe Henderson
To: Frank McCallum
Subject: Further to our meeting

Frank,

Further to our meeting yesterday, here are some pointers I think would definitely help you with your problem:

1. Unless you are a rapper, stop wearing bling, you maniac.
2. Consider for a moment that there are many women in the world who do not give a fuck how much things cost or, indeed, how much you've paid for them.
3. If you must look at other women's bottoms while on a date, learn how to be subtle for fuck's sake.
4. When your date speaks, let her finish. It's also helpful if your reply doesn't start with "That's the same as when I..." because it isn't anything like something you once did. No, don't argue—it isn't.

Work on this and we'll try it again.

Saturday, April 9

Oliver called this evening, thankfully not in a huff, telling me he was going to Club Noir next Friday with a girl he works with called Simone. I didn't even know he was into burlesque. He says even I'd find her hot, which brings to mind my next challenge: group sex or, more specifically, a threesome. But before I think of starting on this particular challenge, I'll need to consider one question: do I like women? The only answer I've come up with so far is—I'm not sure.

I can appreciate a beautiful woman to the point of becoming quite taken with her, but I can't say I've ever fantasized about ripping her clothes off in the way I've imagined doing to many, many, MANY men, from Jack White to Eddie Izzard and even those two guys off *MasterChef*. I often wonder if they'd be as descriptive in bed as they are with their food. . . . But I digress.

If I'm going to throw myself into this, surely it'd be better if there's a chance I actually wanted to bang both parties? I remember when I was seventeen I kissed a girl. We were completely pissed and unfortunately the whole of my school found out, landing me with a "lesbo" tag that I didn't shake until years later. But there was part of me that secretly loved the fact that my sexuality was seen as ambiguous (mainly because I wanted to be Madonna) and that it pissed off the girls and intrigued the boys. What I do believe is that attraction is something you have no control over, and even though I class myself as straight, I'm open to the possibility that I could enjoy being with women too. If I was completely straight maybe I wouldn't even entertain the idea. No! The point of these challenges is to do things the old me wouldn't, regardless of how much they scare me. Am I just overanalyzing everything? Sex is just sex . . . Right?

Monday, April 11

Frank called me into his office at lunchtime today. He wasn't wearing his watch. Praise the lord.

"So when can we schedule another date? It's rather more urgent, as I met a woman over the weekend and I like her. Vanessa. I mean, she's only a checkout girl but—"

"Christ, listen to yourself, Frank: 'only a checkout girl'—who do you think you are?"

He looked embarrassed. "Well, I do like her and I don't want to mess it up. Are you free tomorrow night?"

"I don't know, I—"

"That's settled then. Off you go."

How did I get myself into this? I'm beginning to think getting fired would have been less hassle. Still, if I can help him impress Vanessa, he'll get off my case so it's worth it.

Tuesday, April 12

We'd arranged to go to an Indian restaurant tonight, as Frank knows the owner and gets a friend's discount. I met him by his car (hidden away in the underground car park) and stayed low in the seat until we'd left the city center.

"My God, Phoebe, are you that embarrassed to be seen with me?"

"I told you, I refuse to be the subject of gossip at work. If anyone saw us together, I'd never hear the end of it."

"Well, I often drop Maureen from accounts home."

"I've never seen that happen."

"No, she lies down on the backseat until we get to the motorway." He chuckled quietly to himself.

"Did you just make a joke? Fucking hell, maybe there's hope for you yet! How long till we get there? I'm starving."

Five minutes later we pulled into a side street and I saw the restaurant. Not much to look at from the outside, but inside it was warm, inviting, and covered in colorful, modern Indian art. The aroma of cumin and saffron reminded me just how hungry I was.

"Frank!" came a voice from the other end of the room. "Glad to see you!"

A handsome Indian waiter appeared and man-hugged Frank. I was stunned that someone genuinely seemed happy to see Frank, let alone make physical contact with him.

He led us to our seats, where there was a bottle of wine waiting. "I'll send someone over in a minute to take your order. Enjoy!"

Frank poured the wine (me first). It was clear he'd been doing his homework.

Astonishingly, I had dinner with a relaxed, bling-free version of Frank, who made jokes, complimented me on my green eyes (without being too cheesy), and personally went to fetch me some water when I ate some curry that made my face melt. After dinner I had to ask him how he'd done it. I mean, he was almost a normal human being.

"When someone so brutally points out your shortcomings, it's hard to ignore them, Phoebe. I don't want to be on my own anymore, simple as that. Being vulnerable isn't something that comes naturally to me, but I'm trying."

"Don't worry, you'll be fine!" And for the first time in the three years I've worked with Frank, I smiled at him. It must have been quite alarming.

Wednesday, April 13

I left work at half five today, and after standing at the taxi rank in the rain for fifteen minutes, I caught a cab to Oliver's place. The rain was pissing down, my feet were killing me, and I think I was probably more excited about getting my shoes off and lying in front of his fire than actually seeing him.

Oliver opened the door to a soggy wet shell of a woman who had a bottle of wine in one hand and her shoes in the other. Half an hour later I was showered, wearing his fluffy robe, and lying in front of the fire listening to Regina Spektor. I want to marry his apartment.

Like a vision of domesticity, Oliver sat across from me on his brown leather couch, reading a newspaper and sipping red wine. "Comfy?" he asked, throwing a glance in my direction.

"Very. This is perfect. Just ignore me if I start purring."

He put his newspaper down. "That's hot. I'm very glad you started these challenges—you're a sexy bitch these days."

"Maybe I always was."

"Yeah, maybe I just didn't notice. So what's next on your list?" He lay back on the couch and his T-shirt rode up a little, revealing his deliciously flat stomach.

"You up for having a threesome?"

W"Have you ever had a threesome?"

Again he nodded.

"Oh, COME ON! Give me some feedback here! What was it like? Was it good?"

He glugged his wine, "It was OK. Bit of a let-down, actually. It felt like someone was always waiting their turn, and unless everyone is totally into it, it's rather pointless. I did get to bang two women though."

"Hang on, I'm confused. So if it wasn't that great, why do it again with me?"

"Didn't you hear me? I get to bang two women."

Fair enough.

He's agreed to "look into it," like some sort of sexual private investigator.

Friday, April 15

I didn't get a chance to ponder my threesome for too long before I got the phone call.

"Phoebs! Remember Simone? The girl from work? She's agreed. The threesome. Are you up for it?"

"What? Yes? NO! It's one thirty in the morning, I'm in bed. I have big hair."

"Don't bother getting dressed, then. We'll be there in half an hour."

"What? Now—" But he'd hung up.

Yes, cool as a cucumber, Oliver had been to the burlesque night and somehow convinced his date to have a threesome. Just like that. Oh shit. I could have killed him, and did in fact plan his demise as I showered, brushed my teeth, hid my pajamas, and stuck some sexy undies on. What the hell was he thinking? And, more important, who the fuck was he bringing? If he brings a beast, they're both leaving, but he won't; she'll be gorgeous and I'll just be the third wheel. Why did I say yes? I still haven't made up my mind about the whole girl-on-girl dilemma, and now the decision has apparently been taken out of my hands. I would have liked to have at least had a peek at her first.

An hour later the doorbell rang and in came Oliver and Simone, looking very pleased with themselves and obviously tipsy from their night out. He was wearing a suit and tie and she was wearing a wiggle dress, complete with amazing red shoes I wanted to try on.

She wasn't a beast thankfully: blond hair, tiny compared to me, and pretty, like a little doll. He stood with his hands around her waist, nuzzling her neck, and I stood there not knowing where the hell to look. To say that the next few minutes were uncomfortable would be an understatement. I think I even offered them tea at one point, but when we finally made it into the bedroom, the kissing started, which was a perfect excuse not to talk anymore. Oliver seemed different somehow with Simone. He was very assertive, almost to the point of domineering, and she played along, doing exactly as she was told. I felt awkward. But, I thought, when in Rome . . .

Oliver and I kissed, Oliver then kissed Simone, and then he said to me sternly, "Kiss her." So we kissed, which I have to say, was very, very nice. The whole thing was a blur after that. There was lots of touching and more kissing, hands were everywhere and I remember lots of questions firing in and out of my mind: would they prefer it if I wasn't here? Does he prefer her body to mine? Should I have shaved it all off? As we all got completely naked, I forgot about my insecurities and actually started to enjoy it. Maybe I was into girls? Maybe this could be the start of something new? But as I went down on Simone my questions were answered with a resounding "NO!" like a big, booming, Brian Blessed voice from above.

The kissing was great. Feeling her body was amazing . . . but as soon as I went south it didn't feel right. I can't explain it, but I didn't enjoy it. I felt like a fumbling teenager who'd never been near a vagina and didn't have a clue where anything was. Sounds odd now when I think about it: I have a vagina and an in-depth working knowledge of where all the good parts are, but with someone else's right there in front of me, I didn't have a clue. Oliver quickly rescued me and we kissed as he fucked her. Afterward I threw on some clothes and sat in the living room while they got dressed. They came through shortly afterward, thanking me for a lovely time and calling a cab to Oliver's. And I was left, face in hands, cringing. Another challenge crossed off the list and the verdict? Completely terrifying and totally out of my comfort zone. I can understand why Oliver thought his previous threesome was a let-down; it felt contrived and my lack of experience with women made me feel like an idiot. So unless I get a Cunnilingus for Dummies handbook pretty soon, I can't see myself rushing to do it again. I guess when there are three of you, someone is always going to feel like the odd one out. Tonight it was me. Perhaps it would be easier with two men?

Saturday, April 16

I woke up to the sound of the phone ringing and for a second thought it might be Oliver announcing he was returning with Simone for round two. Thankfully it was Paul, calling to invite an extremely exhausted me to a gathering at his house tonight. "It's just a wee party for my birthday, nothing fancy, and also an excuse to show off my boyfriend Dan. He's flown over from New York and I'm hoping he won't fly back, so be nice!"

"I'm always nice! It's Lucy you should be warning!"

"Oh, don't worry, she's been well warned. Well, threatened actually. Hazel can't make it and Oliver is busy, but it should be fun! Anyway must dash—see you at eight?"

At six I grabbed something for dinner. In hindsight, garlic bread was not the best idea, but since Paul came out, the only men he introduces me to are gay (apart from one guy he calls "Bald John"), so kissing was definitely off the menu.

I arrived at Paul's new apartment, which is a typical bachelor pad in the city center. Everything is modern, oversized, and very spare apart from the huge Salvador Dalí print on one wall. Over the noise of the chatter, I could just make out Madonna's *Immaculate Collection* coming from the iPod dock. Good choice.

I kissed Paul on the cheek, very conscious of my garlic breath, but hopeful that booze would mask it and make it possible for me to have a conversation with someone from less than ten feet away.

Lucy was already there, carrying around a plate of oddly shaped nibbles. "I made spinach balls. They went a bit wrong." I nodded in agreement and made my way back over to Paul to avoid having to sample them.

"I should have got some more chairs. I hate it when people lean against the wall."

"Who are all these people? I hardly know anyone!"

"They're mainly work colleagues and partners. I didn't expect everyone to show up! I might need to get more booze."

"Well, where is he then? Where's the new fella? I want to meet him!"

"See that guy over by the window talking to that young lad? That's him."

And there, standing beside Paul's new boyfriend, was Richard. I turned around quickly and hissed, "What the hell is he doing here?"

"What? Dan's the reason I'm having this party! What do you think? Hot, eh? His ass is—"

"No. Richard. The one he's talking to. The boy—Richard. I've slept with him. I've been ignoring him! This will be entirely awkward."

I felt a tray of misshapen spinach balls being thrust in between Paul and me.

"Sorry, Phoebe, Sam brought him, but they're heading off soon. Just smile and he'll vanish shortly."

But he didn't vanish shortly. He didn't even vanish when Sam left. He stayed completely visible and followed me around all evening, telling me how he couldn't stop thinking about me and how I wasn't like any other women he knew. Where the fuck did all this come from?

"What the hell is wrong with you?" I asked abruptly after he'd almost followed me into the bathroom.

"I can't stop thinking about you," he gushed. "The way your body felt and how you smelled and I keep replaying it over and over and—"

"Look, Richard, I'm not interested," I snapped. "You're a lovely guy, but you're far too young for me. We had some fun. Let's just leave things the way they are, OK?"

"BUT I WANT TO SEE YOU AGAIN!" he yelled. Christ, he was having a tantrum! I thought he might turn into Rumpelstiltskin and demand my firstborn.

Lucy finally convinced him to go home and I spent the rest of the evening feeling like shit. I had completely, but unintentionally, led this guy on. I'd assumed that because I hadn't given him a second thought, he'd done the same.

I feel like a complete prick.

Sunday, April 17

Lucy called off our lunch date to meet up with Sam, so rather than leave the house I chose to spend the afternoon in bed, drifting in and out of consciousness and playing with my toys. I started to get carried away and then just like that: it happened! I felt like I was going to pee so I kept going, I thrust harder and I came. Loudly and probably shouting, "I AM SPARTA!" due to the fact I was fantasizing about Gerard Butler (I hope to God I didn't). It was astounding. My vibrator looked like it had been run under a tap and the wet patch was mighty impressive. I SQUIRTED! Oh, hooray for me, I'm almost a porn star! Well, apart from the fact that my family still speaks to me and I'll never bleach my anus. I also felt like I'd been punched in the face with a narco-lepsy fist, and fell asleep in record time afterward: right in the wet patch. Masturbation challenge complete and quite frankly I deserve a medal—I worked hard at this one.

I made the mistake of texting Oliver when I woke up and it took him precisely seventeen minutes to arrive at my apartment. I didn't even have time to get dressed before he threw me back down on the bed, romancing me with the words, "Let's get a look at this then."

Despite leaving me with an extremely sore pubic bone after his first attempt, he's now managed to get it down to a fine art. I can see him looking at the sheets afterward thinking, *I did that.*

He left around midnight, grinning to himself. I threw the bedsheets into the washing machine and fell asleep on the couch. Fuck, it makes a right mess.

Wednesday, April 20

I woke up at seven this morning to eight missed calls and a text message, all from Richard:

U R a cold hearted bitch, dont eva contact me again

Eva? Grr. And THEN, halfway through my working day, an e-mail pops up from Alex. Fucking ALEX. I actually held my breath as I read it, because as everyone knows, holding your breath acts as some sort of force field to deflect emo-tionally damaging e-mails.

From: Alex Anderson
To: Phoebe Henderson
Subject: Hi

Phoebe,

Been thinking about you since we met the other day. I feel bad about the way things went and also about the way things ended with us. Can we meet for coffee or something? Or I'll take you for sushi?

A x

A kiss and everything. What the hell is going on? I haven't replied yet. I don't think my work e-mail swearing filter could cope.

Thursday, April 21

Lucy and Sam have broken up because he thinks I'm a dick and she doesn't. Well, that's the way she explained it anyway. For some reason Richard seems to think we had something really special and he's been telling everyone how I dumped him and how he's never going to feel the same about anyone ever again. EVA, EVA, EVA. I certainly know how to pick 'em. I must remember to physically remove the heart of my next sex.

Frank has his date tomorrow night with the checkout girl, Vanessa. He's taking her to some pretentious seafood restaurant near the Clyde, where they serve flaming seahorse or something. We went over things at lunchtime to prepare him.

"OK, Frank, let's run over some possible scenarios. If she compliments something you're wearing..."

"Thank her and don't mention how much it cost."

"Correct. Do not compliment her immediately after, as this will look insincere. Next, if your waitress looks like Cameron Diaz, you will . . ."

"Become aroused. Oh, stop scowling, I'm kidding. I will not leer at her or pay her more attention than Vanessa."

"Good. This also includes when Vanessa goes to the toilet. Don't use that an excuse to smarm all over the hot waitress. Have some respect."

"Anything else?"

"Yes, wear something blue. You suit blue."

"Oh. Do I?" He began to blush a little. "I was expecting you to say something mean there. Blue, huh? Noted."

Friday, April 22

It's the Easter weekend so no work until Tuesday, which couldn't have come at a better time, as my period has arrived and I'm insanely hormonal. I want to laugh, cry, and start a fight all at the same time, but most of all I just want to have sex. Oh, how I want to have sex. Oliver says he doesn't mind that I have my period, but this time I do. I feel about as sexy as a potato. Also, a huge zit has appeared on my face, so between that and my menses misery I'm staying put in my apartment. Frank's date is tonight. I wonder if he'll fuck it up. Bet he does. Bet he forgets everything I've said and just goes on about how much he sold his soul to Satan for. Why am I thinking about Frank when I'm not even in the office? *Behave.*

Tuesday, April 26

I cornered Frank after the morning meeting, desperate to find out how his date went. Purely so I could tell him where he went wrong, of course.

"I think it went all right," he said sheepishly. "Dinner was great and I was the perfect gentleman."

"Did you perv over the waiting staff?"

"No, I didn't find our waiter Sean attractive."

"Ha. OK then, so what's next?"

"Well, Vanessa's agreed to see me again, so that's a good sign. Oh, and she's not just a checkout girl, she actually owns the business but isn't afraid to muck in. Not that it matters, of course."

"So why the long face?" I asked, perching on his desk. "No good-night kiss?"

"We did kiss good night. It was nice."

"So?"

He stared at the wall silently for a moment. "How long has that painting been upside down?"

"I hadn't noticed," I lied. "Answer the question."

"It's delicate. Let's just say I haven't been with anyone in a while. I'm nervous, and if you laugh I'll kill you."

"Ha-ha . . . Oh. Right. I don't think I like where this is going. You want actual sex tips? No chance."

"Oh, come on, Phoebe! Just give me a few pointers— that's all. After overhearing your phone call, I'm sure I could learn a lot."

"Don't push it, Frank. I'm already feeling compromised by this." He looked so pitiful that I finally relented. "OK, I'll see what I can do, but after this you're on your own."

"Deal."

Christ, I'm the one who's supposed to be on a voyage of sexual discovery, not him.

Wednesday, April 27

"You seem to be seeing an awful lot of Frank these days," Oliver remarked when I went over to his place this evening.

"This is the last time. I made him promise."

"Good, I don't like sharing you."

The minute those words came out of his mouth I could see him start to panic. "I mean, do what you like, I'm just being selfish. We're both free agents."

"Ha, you secretly love me and this is driving you insane with jealousy." I laughed.

Oliver laughed too but not very convincingly. I hope he's not getting fed up with me already.

Thursday, April 28

"Is it just me or is Frank being more, well, normal these days?" asked Lucy, who'd decided to come sit on my desk and chat while I was trying to work. "He actually thanked me for something this morning. That never happens."

I shrugged and kept my mouth shut.

"Sounds vile, but I really like him sometimes. When he's not being a dickhead. I had a dream where he—"

"I don't want to hear it! It's going to be like that dream where you banged Christian Bale in my house and made him shout at you like that viral off YouTube. Shit like that stays in my head."

Lucy giggled. "GOOD FOR YOU! Fucking love him. Actually, that's who else Frank reminds me of. Shouty Bale. Big ride that he is."

"Ha! Stop distracting me, I need to get these orders finished."

She hopped off my desk and wandered back to her own, whistling the *Batman* theme tune as she went. I have no idea how I'm going to approach this sex stuff with Frank. What I do know is that Lucy can never know. She'd put me into a cannon and launch me into space.

Friday, April 29

The whole country was given the day off today to celebrate the wedding of Prince William and Kate Middleton. I assumed that, like me, no one actually gave a shit and would use the day off to sleep, but both Lucy and Hazel turned up at eleven that morning, armed with cava and canapés. Lucy was wearing a tiara. I wasn't even dressed.

"We're watching the wedding here," said Lucy, thrusting the booze into my hand. "You have the good TV."

"Seriously?" I asked as they rushed past me into the living room. "You're into this shit?"

"Hell yes!" exclaimed Hazel, turning on BBC One. "Actual princes and princesses? You bet I am."

"I just want to see what everyone's wearing," said Lucy, plonking herself down on the couch. "It'll be all massive, stupid hats and tummy-control panties under dull designer dresses. Someone always looks a fright—I'm here for that show."

"Well, make yourselves at home," I said, shaking my head. "I'm off to shower and tidy up until you both leave and let me get back to bed."

I busied myself with cleaning the apartment, occasionally glancing at the screen when Lucy shrieked with laughter at someone's hat, but not really paying much attention. My attitude lasted until the actual wedding began, when I couldn't resist any longer. Giving in, I plonked myself between Lucy and Hazel, mesmerized by the sheer grandeur of the event. By the time they kissed on the balcony, I was on my third glass of cava, sobbing into a hanky. "She's a real-life princess now!" I sniffed. "I want to be a princess."

"You've certainly changed your tune." Hazel laughed. "She did look beautiful though. Must be odd being on display like that."

"I know!" agreed Lucy. "Imagine that was your life. One minute you're getting pissed in the university bar, the next you're engaged to a prince and getting married in front of the entire world. If she so much as pulls her thong out of her backside in public, it'll be front-page news. I'd hate that."

I took Lucy's tiara off her head and placed it on mine. "I hate being shown what I'll never be. It's depressing. I saw a video on YouTube of that lion hugging the man who'd rescued her and I thought, I'll never even be a lion rescuer. I don't like the thought that my life will always be this unremarkable."

Lucy bit into her canapé and nodded. "I know what you mean. I remember when Obama got sworn in and I was like, 'I'll never be the first black president of the United States!'"

"Fuck you." I laughed. "I'm serious!"

Hazel finally stopped laughing and said, "You've created a list which most women only fantasize about and you're actually doing it. You might not be a princess but you're an inspiration."

I raised my glass. "YEAH, I AM. Here's to screwing my way to a more significant life!"

Around nine Lucy and Hazel finally went home and I fell into bed, still wearing Lucy's tiara.

MAY

Sunday, May 1

11 a.m. I'm still considering the possibility of meeting up with Alex. Maybe it would help me get past all this. The list has shown me that I'm more than capable of change, of taking my destiny into my own hands and calling the shots. Perhaps this would be a good test of how far I've come. And he's offering sushi.

No. That's ridiculous, I'll buy my own sushi and he can go to hell! No amount of maki is worth this much hassle. I half wonder if he still has feelings for me, but the more realistic part of me thinks he's just playing his usual games. Whatever his motives, it seems things can't be going as well for him as I'd imagined. Maybe he's not randomly high-fiving strangers on the street before rushing home to have a laugh with HER at how blissful life is without me in it. Then telling her everything he felt he couldn't share with me because he never loved me the way he loves her. I bet she doesn't know he's e-mailing me. He's keeping her in the dark about this, and I have to admit, I'm finding it rather intriguing.

9 p.m. After giving the matter a lot more thought today in bed, I have decided that I am NOT going to meet Alex, that's a definite. I think. . . . Yes, it is. Despite my fantasy of me sitting there looking hot and him begging for forgiveness, I realize it would be nothing like that. It would inevitably turn into another hollering match, which I can do without. He'd just talk over the top of me in one continuous drone and I'd give up being sensible, or even reasonable, and start swearing. The best thing to do is ignore him. Pam Potter thinks I have a problem staying in control around him. She thinks he manipulated me so badly that I have trouble remembering who I am when he's there. She also thinks she'll one day persuade me to stand in front of her patting my own head while telling myself I'm a great person and that isn't happening. I'm just tired of feeling angry when I see him, so the obvious solution is not to see him. I'd happily tap his freakin' head though.

Monday, May 2

I thought a little Bank Holiday boning might be nice, so I tried to persuade Oliver to come around after he'd finished his soccer game this evening. I wanted to breathe in his man smell while squeezing his thighs, but instead he went out with that Simone girl again. Selfish. He called me on his way there.

"I just remembered something really important. It's my birthday next month. What are you getting me?"

"You're on your way to meet Simon and—"

"Simone."

"Whatever, and all you can think about is your birthday? Poor cow. Maybe I'll get you an 'I ♥ Simone' T-shirt and matching pants?"

"Don't get me something to wear. You're not my mother."

"Anyway, with all the sex we've been having, it must feel like your birthday every month, Oliver."

"Hardly, unless squirting all over my sheets is your idea of a present. Extra laundry is not a gift, Phoebe."

"Stop complaining. I'll see you tomorrow for our next role play."

"Oh yeah. Hooker time! Can I call you a different name? Like Candice? Or Chastity?"

"If you must."

So instead I dragged myself over to Lucy's house, where we ordered a takeaway and made our way through two bottles of wine. By ten I was facedown on her couch with the top button of my pants undone, suffering from naan-bread sweats, while Lucy lay on the floor and finished off the last of the popadoms. "Are you crashing here tonight? I have more wine."

"Nah, I spilled korma on these pants, I'll need to go home."

"I'll give you pants."

"You're a size ten. I haven't been a size ten since high school. I used to have a flat stomach and a space between my thighs, you know. Now I just eat until I can't see my feet."

"You left some black pants here ages ago. And shh, you're gorgeous. Curvy. Like Christina Hendricks. She's a goddess."

"And you're drunk. But I agree I do look exactly like her; it's uncanny. Tell you what—I'll stay for wine if you put your *Mad Men* box set on."

"Oooh. Deal." We watched *Mad Men* until three, when Lucy began snoring loudly and I was forced to retreat to the spare room.

Tuesday, May 3

I went into work with Lucy this morning, which of course meant I was late, wearing the black clubbing pants I'd left in her bedroom last year after a drunken night at the Arches. Classy. Halfway through the afternoon I remembered that Oliver and I had a role-play evening planned and invented a hospital appointment to get away early. Oliver had e-mailed me a picture of the kind of "look" he thought I should go for, which felt more porn star than street-corner prostitute. The picture showed a heavily made-up dark-haired woman with a black miniskirt, stockings, garters, and ridiculously high shoes, similar to the ones I'd bought last year in a fit of optimism but never wore as they killed my feet. I got home, showered, shaved my legs, and blow-dried my hair, then spent twenty-five minutes putting on black eyeliner, 475 coats of mascara, and some bright-red lipstick. I wore a tight black minidress and tried to copy his picture as best I could: red underwear, black fishnet thigh-highs, and garter belt. I carried my high heels as I rushed down to my car in my stocking feet. I hoped to God I wouldn't get spotted, or stopped by the police as my vision was impaired due to the amount of mascara I had clogging up my eyelashes. I must admit, even though I felt like a Halloween reject, I did get into character quickly and got completely turned on at what he might have planned. I climbed the stairs to his apartment and strapped myself into my stupidly high shoes as I rang his buzzer. He opened the door wearing a bathrobe and I thought for a second he'd forgotten. However, looking down at his noticeable erection I guessed that I'd arrived right on time. I hobbled past him and threw my keys down on his hall table (they missed of course and landed in a shoe). Still, not put off by my clumsy entrance, I turned around and uttered the words "What do you want then?" in a startling husky voice even I didn't recognize.

He walked into the living room, dropped his bathrobe and told me to get on my knees. I took my coat off, managed to navigate my way into the living room in my idiot shoes, and gratefully flopped onto my knees. I was halfway through one of my finest blow jobs to date when he pulled my face up to look at him and asked "How much for anal?"

I had to resist the urge to shout, "ONE MILLION DOLLARS!" but just shook my head, horrified that I couldn't remember when I'd last been to the toilet. Suddenly the fun was gone for me and all I could think was that if anything went wrong, I'd stab myself with my own stiletto.

He noticed my worried face and whispered, "Don't worry; if it's messy then it's messy. Just keep going."

He started to fuck me from behind, but for the first time ever it was all very average. Just pounding with the occasional "You filthy whore" thrown in for effect.

I looked over my shoulder. "Not what you had in mind?"

He shrugged and stopped thrusting. "Nope. Not remotely. This was very different in my head."

"Is it me? I look ridiculous, don't I?"

"Nah, you look sexy. In my head this was much seedier and without feeling. That's impossible to do when you're banging your best friend."

"Feeling? Since when did you start feeling?"

"Did I say feeling? I meant chafing. These sheets are really harsh." He moved to the edge of the bed and lit a cigarette. "I cannot believe this has ended with me thinking about thread count."

I took a drag of his cig and ruffled his hair. "You pictured this like porn, didn't you? Never mind. I'm an awful hooker anyway. You're still going to pay me though, right?"

"Not until I've come in your ass."

He asked me to stay over. And I did. We didn't have sex again though, we just talked and cuddled. It seems the second role play was a washout, but I got breakfast in bed so it wasn't all bad. Well, he burned the toast but it's the thought that counts.

Wednesday, May 4

Do you know what happens when you spend so much time having/thinking/writing about sex? Your fish dies, that's what. I came home from Oliver's to find my goldfish floating on the top of a very green, stinky bowl and had to flush him away along with a spider I killed earlier. Is this how serial killers start? No wonder Hazel never asks me to babysit.

Thursday, May 5

Day off from work today and spent the first half of the morning rearranging the furniture in the living room before deciding it looked better the way it was. In the afternoon I went shopping. I bought junk food, red apples, some coasters shaped like daisies, and two bottles of fancy conditioner that were half-price and will look lovely sitting beside the seventeen other bottles I already have.

At half four I had an appointment with Pam, who was finally back from her vacation. She met me at the door, tanned and looking rather like a cowgirl in a checked shirt and jeans.

"Nice vacation?" I politely inquired.

"Sure was, thanks for asking. Take a seat, Phoebe." I sat on my usual purple chair and put my bag at my feet.

"So, how are you? Anything in particular you'd like to talk about today?"

"My boss. Frank."

"Are you having problems at work?" she asked, looking surprised that for once I wasn't talking about Alex.

"No. I'm not sure. Basically he caught me in a compromising position at work and we came to an arrangement to let me keep my job."

"Do you want to tell me what the arrangement is?"

Hell no. I tried to be as vague as I could. I was still mortified I'd agreed to it.

"I help him sort out his personal life. So to speak. It's quite silly really, but I still feel . . . a bit uncomfortable with the whole thing."

She closed her notebook. "I see. Tell me, Phoebe—you say that 'we' came to an arrangement. Was it Frank's arrangement, with his terms, and you agreed to it?"

"Well. Yes." Damn she's good.

"And you're concerned that his position of authority might enable him to manipulate you whenever he feels like it?"

"Yes. I mean, no. I wouldn't let him. He's not that clever."

"But clever enough to use your mistake to his advantage."

"Um . . ."

"Just think about this, Phoebe. Whatever your arrangement is here, it doesn't seem like it's one where you're both equal. Do you think that might cause problems?"

"You're saying I shouldn't trust him."

"I'm saying you should be aware of him. And of yourself. Now, anything else before we end today?"

I thought about all the things that had happened last month: the threesome, sleeping with Stuart, getting rid of Richard, and squirting, but I chose to tell her about Alex e-mailing me wanting to meet. The other events were in my control—I chose to do them—but with Alex I always feel like I have no control over anything.

"Why do you think Alex wants to meet?" asked Pam Potter. "Do you believe that he genuinely wants to make amends for his actions?"

I thought about it for a moment. "He's very manipulative, so I don't believe for a second that it's just about making things right. I get angry that he feels he has the right to continue being in my life in any capacity. I know how he works. He wants something; I just haven't worked out what that is yet."

Half an hour ago, I got another text from him.

I'm not giving up. I just want to chat. Please call me.

I've ignored him again. I don't know what he wants but I have the feeling I'm soon to find out.

Friday, May 6

This afternoon at work, Kelly threw a wobbler when she went to make coffee and found her mug unwashed in the sink. "Stop using my fucking things!" she shouted, holding up an oversized white mug with KELLY printed in red lettering on the side. "It's not hygienic!"

Lucy stared at the mug. "But how do we know it's yours?"

Kelly glared at her. "You're not funny. How would you like it if I used your mug?"

"I don't have a mug. I have a flask."

"Well, your flask then. What if I used your flask?"

"Why would you use my flask when you have your own mug?"

I started to giggle as Frank appeared at the door of his office. "I used your mug, Kelly. Can you please stop disrupting the office and get back to work?"

Kelly sat back down and shoved her mug into her locked drawer, muttering under her breath about the injustice of it all. Frank emerged completely and proceeded to give me a right ear-bashing about some copy for a client that had a typo. Considering the customer sent it directly to production, I felt it was harsh to be blamed for something I had no part in. I followed him back into his office to tell him so.

"THAT FREAKING AD WASN'T—" I shouted, shutting the door behind me.

"Ah, good, you're here. Yes, yes, I know, I just needed an excuse to get you in here. I slept with Vanessa and she said it was good. Just thought you should know," he said with a smirk.

"Yeah, thanks for that, Frank. Although 'good' isn't necessarily a word to get all excited about. 'Phenomenal' is. 'Incredible'—definitely. 'Good' . . . Not so much."

"Well, she wasn't exactly brilliant either, but it was our first time. We both held back somewhat."

I stood up. "Trust me, Frank; if you hadn't held back, you'd have been getting all sorts of praise thrown at you this morning. Next time just go for it. I imagine you're terrible in bed, but if this woman likes you enough to see you naked, then make it worth her while."

"I AM NOT TERRIBLE!" he shouted, rising from his chair and then sinking back into it when the whole office turned around to see what was going on. "I am actually very good, no, GREAT, in bed. I can't imagine you shutting up long enough to be anything other than a hindrance in bed."

"All right, fine, I'm leaving now," I said. "And if you really thought that, then we wouldn't be having this discussion now, would we?"

I sat back down at my desk, annoyed by his comment. He makes me sound horrendous.

From: Phoebe Henderson
To: Frank McCallum
Subject: Me

I am outstanding in bed. So there.

He didn't respond but I could hear him laughing in his office.

Sunday, May 8

As it was such a beautiful day, Oliver and I decided to have lunch in Kelvingrove Park, stopping off at Marks & Spencer first for supplies. "Sushi or sandwiches?" he asked, peering into the chill cabinet.

"I think you already know the answer to that," I replied, looking around at all the Sunday shoppers who obviously would have rather been anywhere else than here.

He grabbed a small box of maki and a larger one of tamago and prawn nigiri. I nodded in approval before heading toward the bakery counter.

Twenty pounds later we were heading toward the park, driving past lots of young men with their tops off. Glasgow is hilarious when the sun comes out. Everyone stops what they're doing and stands for at least ten minutes staring upward, like a scene from *Independence Day*, wondering what that big ball of fire in the sky is. Then they walk around half-naked in the hope of either getting a tan or being beamed up by aliens. Oliver and I were no different. We found a spot near a tree and placed a tartan blanket on the grass. The park was so green, gorgeous and filled with people who were not looking wet and miserable for once.

Oliver poured the miniature bottles of white wine we'd bought and I lay down, using his denim jacket as a pillow, leaving him to unpack the rest of the food and arrange it between us.

"You bought pecan swirls! I can die happy now," he exclaimed, picking the nuts off the top of his pastry.

"Have you come here to die? Why are you eating your dessert first? Have some sushi."

"You're not the boss of me."

"Now, THAT would be an interesting challenge. Shall we do that next?"

"Nah, let's try the swinging," said Oliver, throwing pastry crumbs at a pigeon, "I've always wondered what that would be like, and it technically falls in the category of 'group sex,' right?"

"It does. Although it'll be two women faking it and two men comparing their 'guns' while secretly checking out who's got the bigger cock," I replied. "Are you up for that?"

"Yeah. Totally. Let's fucking do it."

"OK, but I'm a little nervous," I admitted. "I trust you with my life, but what if the guy is too rough? Or he gets weird?"

"I'll be there. If you're uncomfortable, you panic or you just don't want to go through with it, we leave. End of story. But I think it'll be grand . . . and hot."

"Why weren't we like this in high school?" I asked, sitting up and pulling my flowery skirt over my knees. "We could have been skipping fifth period and doing all sorts."

"I was. You were a lesbian back then, remember? Besides, you were too funny to sleep with back then. You were the only one who made my day bearable—I couldn't risk messing that up."

"What? And now you can?"

"This was your idea, remember? And what kind of friend would I be if I didn't help you and your naked body out?"

"You're going to appear on some sort of register one day."

We finished lunch and lay in the sun until it eventually vanished, leaving us with no option but to pack up and head home. "What do you want to do now?" I asked, putting the blanket in the backseat of his car. "It's only half seven."

"We could take a walk," he suggested. "It's still nice out."

We drove back to Oliver's apartment, dumped the car, and started off through the West End. The tree-lined streets were peaceful as we sauntered past stunning townhouses and rows of brand-new, highly polished cars. "I want to live here," I said, sighing at the cozy lights glowing from the windows. "It's so pretty."

"The people who live here are probably in debt up to their eyeballs," he said with a laugh, "Oh, be careful of that hole in the—"

I stumbled straight into a hole in the pavement but Oliver caught me before I fell flat on my ass.

"You OK?"

"Yes. Mortified. But yes."

"Here, link in," he said, placing my arm through his. "It's getting chilly anyway."

It wasn't, but I didn't object. It felt lovely.

Predictably, by nine the rain had reappeared and we ran back to Oliver's apartment, soaked to the skin.

I stripped off in the bathroom and stood there in my white underwear, drying my hair with a hand towel.

He knocked on the door and came in with his robe for me. "I've put the heating on; it's cold in here." He picked up my bra off the floor, offering it to me. "Do you want to wear this or should I just hang it on your nipples?"

Before I could think of a witty reply, he walked over to me and pressed his body against mine and I felt a rush of arousal flood over me.

He pushed me down onto the floor, pulling off my panties and moving his head between my legs. This lasted approximately five seconds before . . .

"You smell weird."

"What? Do I? Oh fuck." I quickly pulled my offending vagina away from him.

"It's all right, we can just—"

"I'm mortified! Look at my red face! We're doing nothing!"

I got dressed and went home, praying to God that I didn't have some awful STD that would leave me foul-smelling and sexless for the rest of my life. There's nothing like being told your snatch stinks to boost your self-esteem. This is the kind of shit schoolboys say to make girls feel insecure, and I know Oliver didn't mean it in that way, but I feel rattled by the whole thing. Perhaps I'm not as confident as I thought.

12:55 a.m. Text from Alex:

I want to see you. Please. I miss you.

WHAT? Oh, today can fuck right off.

Monday, May 9

This morning I had to sit in the doctor's for an hour before answering loads of questions about my sex life and facing the vaginal smear from hell. God, I hate them; there must be a way to make them less uncomfortable—like having them performed by kittens.

"Call on Wednesday—you'll get your results then."

To avoid dwelling on the possible results I've decided to move ahead with planning the swinging challenge. After the threesome with Simone I'm worried it might be a mistake but have reassured myself with the thought that another guy thrown into the equation might even things out. I also felt I had to make sure that Oliver would be happy being all kinds of naked and erect in front of another guy. I took a pizza round to his place this evening to quiz him. He didn't seem to have a problem with it: "As long as there's no sword fighting, I couldn't care less." I held back from telling him that the sight of two naked men up close and sweaty was actually a huge turn-on for me and just smiled instead.

"So what's the attraction then?" he asked, knowing full well.

"You know that thing we watched with the two guys and that redhead? Where she sat on top of one guy and then—"

"Oh. Oh, I see. You want a DP, huh? Oooh yeah," he teased in a terrible American accent, "you want it all ways."

"Absolutely," I agreed with a straight face. I moved closer to him, trying to be seductive. "I want your cock in my mouth while the other guy goes down on me and . . ."

"Best get that whiff seen to then, eh?" He laughed loudly at his own joke, so in return I knocked his pizza on to the floor.

Tuesday, May 10

After work Hazel and I went to get haircuts using some vouchers she'd purchased ages ago and had forgotten about. I was happy to go; my hair was frizzy as hell and it gave me a chance to catch up with her.

"So what's new?" she asked, getting her hair detangled by a grumpy, purple-haired junior called Morven who looked about ready to kill everyone in the salon.

"Erm, not much really. Same old." There was no way I was telling her about my rotten vagina in front of Morven.

"We've just booked a vacation to Greece. Two weeks in the sun, all-inclusive. I cannot wait to lie beside a pool and read some trashy novels."

"Amazing! When do you leave?"

Morven moved on to me before pausing to sigh, "Tea or coffee?" in our direction. The look on her face said that if we made her walk to the kitchen, our drinks would be spat in. We declined and carried on chatting.

"Saturday. Grace will love it. They have some sort of babies' club where giant tigers dance for them."

"I'm so jealous. I want giant tigers to dance for me. I won't get a vacation this year unless I win the lottery."

"You actually have to play the lottery to make that statement, Phoebe."

A tall hairdresser called Patrick appeared to do Hazel's hair and, compared to Morven, he actually seemed happy to be there. Unfortunately my hair was to be managed by

"Eve," whose own hair looked like Kate Bush's after she's finished running up that hill.

"What am I doing for you today then?" Eve asked, staring at me in the mirror.

"Just a tidy-up really. Trim off the ends and my fringe. Nothing too drastic."

"You'd suit short hair."

"Nah, I don't think—"

"You would. You should get something more stylish. This is very '60s. It's not the '60s anymore."

"Thanks, but no. I had short hair once and I looked like a LEGO figure. Y'know, with the clip-on hair that . . ."

She wasn't laughing. She picked up a plastic bottle and started spraying my hair with something that smelled like bubblegum. "Fine." She shrugged, taking a pair of scissors from her belt. "Whatever."

I shot a look of panic at Hazel, who was deep in discussion about her hair needs with Patrick and didn't notice. "Just a trim, Patrick, I like this style. Maybe a bit off the layers." "No problem, Hazel."

Ugh. Fucking typical. This was the worst fucking salon ever.

Forty-five minutes later we were all finished. Despite the fact she had so reluctantly trimmed my hair, Eve did a good job. I might have a defective vagina, but my hair is swishy and awesome.

Wednesday, May 11

After the morning meeting I nipped outside to call the doctor's and get my test results.

"You'll have to come in and discuss them," the receptionist chirped down the phone. "I can give you a five thirty appointment."

"What? Why? Is it serious? What do I have?"

"You'll have to come in and discuss it with the doctor. Shall I book you in?"

"Fine. OK."

I came back into the office and called Lucy. "They won't tell me over the phone. I have to go in at half five. Should I worry?"

"Yes."

"REALLY?"

"No."

"Oh, you're no help. Stop laughing."

"Sorry. They never tell this stuff over the phone. It'll be cool. Relax."

"I'm not going to be able to concentrate on anything now."

"So what? It's only work."

"Fair point."

For the next six hours I tried to distract myself by rearranging my desk, rearranging Lucy's desk, doing fifteen coffee runs, and pretending to be interested when Frank told a story about some cheese.

I took a taxi to the doctor's and thankfully was only kept waiting for a few minutes before I was called in.

"OK, your gonorrhea and chlamydia tests were negative," the doctor told me, "but we did find something: BV."

"Oh God. That's not good. I can't believe it. I'm always careful. What is it?"

"Bacterial vaginosis. It's not an STI. It's when the bacteria inside your vagina become unbalanced."

"My vagina is unbalanced?"

"No, the bacteria are. My advice is not to wash yourself with anything perfumed. Smokers are also more likely to get this, so that's another reason to give up. I'll give you a gel; it'll clear up quickly."

Ten minutes later I was in the chemist waiting for my prescription, feeling very grateful I didn't have some weird STD. When I finally got home, Oliver was waiting for me.

"Well? Are you all right?"

"Yeah. It's BV. A vag thing, NOT a sex thing. I got some gel. It's all good."

"Do I need to get tested?"

"Not unless you have a vagina."

We went upstairs and he made coffee while I pulled off my shoes and lay on the couch. "This has been emotionally draining . . . and embarrassing. You are never getting within smelling distance of my lady parts ever again."

"Yeah, I'm guessing that won't last long. We both enjoy that too much. Anyway, be thankful I told you. A lot of guys would have kept quiet and just laughed about it drunkenly with their friends if you ever dumped them."

I fear this is very true.

He finished his coffee and stood up to leave. "I have soccer now, but I'll be back tomorrow so we can start on the couples challenge."

"Oh, will you now? What if I have plans?"

"Do you?"

"No."

"Shut up then. Tomorrow at eight. See you then."

And so I was left alone to face an evening of gel insertion and crappy TV. I'm so rock-and-roll.

Thursday, May 12

Ugh, I slept in for work this morning and had to run for the train like a fool. Then I was forced to sit beside some guy who reeked of garlic, applying my makeup and getting mascara all over my nose when the train stopped suddenly.

As I walked out of the station I realized I'd forgotten my cigs. I popped into a nearby shop, where I pulled out my purse to pay and found a sanitary towel stuck to it. The cute guy behind the checkout just laughed and said, "Don't worry. That happens to my mum all the time." His mum? Little shit. This was not the best start to my day. Other highlights included falling up the stairs and dribbling coffee down my white top.

I had finished all my work by four so Lucy and I played text games to pass the last hour. The theme was "replace a word in film title with food." We came up with several, including *The Lambshank Redemption, The Evil Bread,* and *Prawn on the Fourth of July* but Lucy triumphed with *9½ Leeks* just as Frank came out and threatened to confiscate my phone. By the time five rolled around I was ready to go home and spend my evening with Oliver.

He came over later as arranged. He brought some beers and we got tipsy while looking for a couple online, as we'd decided the Internet was the easiest and most discreet way to go about finding one. He's totally getting into this. He mentioned that his colleague Gary and his girlfriend could be up for it, but quickly rethought this plan when I reminded him that he'd have to look his friend in the face every day afterward.

"Morning, Oliver.

"Morning, Gary. At some point today I'm going to have flashbacks of you balls-deep in my friend Phoebe. Your sweaty sex face will be imprinted on my memory forever."

"I see your point." He shuddered. "Game over."

In order to get access to the site we had to place our own advert, which read:

O & P. Looking to meet attractive couple under forty-five for discreet fun. No water sports or weird shit.

A couple of minutes later we were registered and good to go.

Browsing swinging sites is like a looking at a car crash. A certain morbid curiosity takes over and you can't help staring. Lots of seemingly "normal" couples all looking to experiment and share sexual encounters with other like-minded people. We tried to take it seriously, but we're the world's most useless, giggling deviants. The webcam chat rooms were completely hysterical, ranging from couples screwing while voyeurs watched to guys who looked like they'd just been released from prison and one guy who sat naked in front of his webcam in a Stormtrooper helmet. There were also a staggering number of middle-aged, rough-looking married couples open to water sports and sex parties—call me old-fashioned, but I will not be diving head-first into that puddle of desperation just yet.

Finding a good-looking, young couple who are discreet, have a sense of humor, and practice safe sex should be simple, right? Fuck me, we might as well have been looking for a banjo-playing unicorn; they just didn't seem to exist. "What about them?" asked Oliver, clicking on a thumbnail. "They look all right."

I read through the advert:

Sue and Duncan. Professional, attractive couple looking to play safely with similar couple. Must be clean, trimmed/shaven and discreet.

"Their ad is better than ours. Yeah, OK." I nodded. "Shall we e-mail them?"

"Their photos are hot. We should put some photos on; we won't get a reply without them."

"Yeah, you're right."

Oliver looked surprised. "Really? I never for a second thought you'd be up for that. Get you."

"I know. I surprise myself sometimes. Just make sure my face isn't in them. Nothing to identify me."

I had barely finished my sentence and Oliver was already stripping off and looking for my camera.

"How should we do it? I'm not spreading my legs and letting you disappear up there with the flash on."

He laughed. "Relax. I've done this before and—"

"Of course you have."

"AND if you don't want your face in them, it's probably easiest if I take them while we're doing doggy."

I got undressed and knelt on all fours on the bed with Oliver behind me. I could hear him fiddling with the camera.

"I feel like an idiot like this," I said impatiently. "Hurry up before I change my mind."

Then I heard the first of many clicks. He took pictures of him inside me, outside me, spanking me, grabbing my tits, coming on me and as soon as he'd finished I grabbed the camera, eager to see what he's taken.

"OH FOR THE LOVE OF FUCK, MY ASS LOOKS HUGE."

"So does my cock." Smug bastard.

"Ugh, I had no idea my asshole looked like that. I need some bleach . . . and it's spotty. Delete these immediately."

"Nope. They're sexy. They're going on the site and then we can e-mail Sue and Duncan."

By the end of the evening, my big fat ass was online and a message was winging its way to Sue and Duncan. We'd also found another couple, J and Y, who weren't quite as attractive as our first choice but their ad made us laugh:

Couple looking to experiment with others. If you look like you should be on a daytime chat show, please don't bother contacting us.

Oliver left at one, taking the memory card with him. "You'll delete these five seconds after I'm gone. I know your game, Henderson."

"What if one day we fall out and you use these against me?" I protested. "What if your camera gets stolen and my pussy ends up on some weird porn site? This could happen."

"Two things: number one—only a lowlife would do something like that; and number two—there are seventeen million vaginas on the Internet. Some even have their own channel on YouTube. No one cares, Phoebe, stop worrying so much. I'll be back tomorrow to continue this; I need to be up at six for work."

And with that he was off, taking my badly lit porn photos with him. After this challenge they're getting deleted off the face of the Earth. Got a DM on Twitter from @granted77 just before I went to sleep, trying to engage in some late-night filth but I didn't reply. I have enough online escapades going on for now.

Friday, May 13

9 p.m. As everyone has plans tonight, I've decided to have a "me" evening. Red wine, horror movies, and as many Doritos as I can fit in my mouth.

9:30 p.m. Found a copy of *Insidious* online, which is meant to be a pretty decent horror, and it stars Patrick Wilson, which is reason enough. YAAS! His face is quite perfect.

11:15 p.m. Patrick Wilson's pretty face cannot make up for the fact that I'm shitting bricks. I don't cope well when there are clearly ghosts in every fucking house that was ever built. Might have to call Oliver to come sleep here.

12:30 a.m. The Doritos are finished and Oliver is refusing to bring more around despite my text pleas:

You want me to bring you snacks round? At this time?

Yes.

Fuck off . . . Oh, hang on. Have you been watching horror films?

Yes.

So basically you're scared and you just don't want to be alone?

Um . . . maybe. Will you come over?

Awww, poor you. Answer is still no. You're right to be scared though, I always had a sense there was something creepy lurking in your house. Sleep well!

Prick.

1:15 a.m. Am watching crappy romantic comedy with Matthew McConaughey. I'd rather go to sleep angry at this terrible movie than scared shitless. Oh dear, the wedding cake is ruined. Good.

Saturday, May 14

I was eating my breakfast when Oliver called me on my cell. "Ghosts didn't kill you then? That's good."

"I didn't get to sleep till four a.m. I think Matthew McConaughey's hairless chest scared them off. Anyway, what's up?"

"That couple we e-mailed want to meet us tonight."

"Which couple?" I asked through a mouthful of cereal, now not sure whether I had the balls to go through with this.

"Sue and Duncan. The good-looking ones. Let's just do it. I'll message them back."

Holy shit! This is happening.

Oliver came over around six and showered while I got ready in my bedroom. "Does this skirt look all right?" I asked, walking into the bathroom. "I think it's a bit short."

"Nah, it's great. You're quite dressy. I'm just wearing a granddad top and jeans."

"No one cares what you wear. You're a boy," I replied, smoothing my skirt over my tummy.

"Nervous?" He smiled.

"Totally. But eager to tackle another challenge. I even did an enema, y'know. In case."

"Too much information. Now, piss off and let me wash."

By seven Oliver and I were ready to go. We got in the car and managed to drive to the end of the road before he got a text:

Sue's being a psycho. 2nite's off. Sorry.

"Oh, that's just brilliant!" I shouted, throwing my hands in the air "Fucking time-wasters."

Oliver put his hand on my lap and started to turn the car around. "I was looking forward to that. Fuck 'em. We'll find someone else."

We plodded back home, feeling very disappointed, and sulked in front of the TV. It's now eleven, Oliver's asleep on the other couch, and I'm finishing off a bottle of wine. Earlier he told me that splitting up with Alex was the best thing I had ever done; for both of us.

How right he is. If I were still with Alex, I'd be asleep and he'd probably be sitting at the dining-room table marking off my calls on the phone bill with a highlighter.

Sunday, May 15

I woke up with Oliver's arm around me and his hairy leg over mine. He must have crept in beside me during the night. The sound of his cell beeping made him stir.

"I'm exhausted," he mumbled. "Can I just stay here and sleep today?"

"Yeah. Lucy's coming over for chili later but I have nothing on until then."

"You have nothing on now," he whispered, moving his hand down my body. "Can I come for dinner too?"

"Sure."

"Good, and now you can stay in bed with me." He moved his hand on to my breast.

"Hold that thought. I need to pee."

While I was in the bathroom, I heard Oliver shout from the bedroom: "It was a text from Sue and Duncan apologizing. They've invited us back next weekend."

"They can piss off."

"Don't be so hasty. You still want to do this challenge, yeah?"

I ran back into bed and pulled the covers over me. "Of course, I just don't like being messed around. I'll think about it. Also, Sue might be horrendous. I'm wary now."

He pulled me in toward him and started kissing my neck. "Enough talk. Move your ass up a little."

He slipped inside me and held me close and we had very sleepy, slow morning sex. When I came, I felt it everywhere.

Lucy arrived at half five for dinner, holding a bunch of lilies and three bottles of ready-to-drink margarita mix. Oliver went to fetch the tequila and some glasses and I took her coat.

"I hope I'm not interrupting anything," she said, smiling, "and I hope you've washed your hands—"

"Stop making mischief." I scowled. "Sit yourself down; dinner's ready."

I carried through my massive white serving dish filled with chili, which took up most of the space on my tiny table. "This is yummy," said Lucy. "My chili is terrible."

"There's a shocker," teased Oliver.

"Oh, behave. You two look like you're going to collapse from exhaustion. I take it 'the list' is going well?"

"Great." Oliver grinned. "Wouldn't you agree, Phoebe?"

I nodded. "I think this is the first time anyone's asked us both about it. How odd."

"Well, I did help you come up with some of the challenges," said Lucy. "What are you doing now?"

"Foursome," I replied solemnly, taking some more salad.

"Phoebs isn't sure she wants to go ahead with the foursome." Oliver laughed. "She's scared the woman will be the Glaswegian Aileen Wuornos."

"I'm not!" I laughed. "I'm just not sure if it'll be any good. And her own partner called her a psycho. Just sayin'.'"

"You have to do it!" exclaimed Lucy. "I've always wanted to know what that's like. Oliver will protect you from the bad lady."

Oh my lord, there's actually something Lucy hasn't done! My competitive side makes me want to go ahead with this for that very reason. "No, I will do it. I haven't come this far just to chicken out. I'm nothing if not determined. Who wants the last taco?"

"Me!" said Oliver, swiping it off the plate. "And it'll be grand. Even if it's terrible, we'll still have fun. We always do."

"Eurgh!" said Lucy. "Don't go getting all smooshy on me now. I'm still eating."

Oliver dropped Lucy home after dinner and went back to his own place. I'm now curled up on the couch listening to the White Stripes, trying to drown out the noise of my neighbor watching television. Her cackle is piercing. She laughs like she's on fire.

Tuesday, May 17

When I was sixteen, my guidance teacher asked me what I wanted to do when I left school. I think I mumbled something about being famous, but at no point did I say that I wanted a job that I hated with a boss who was blackmailing me for sex advice. That wouldn't even have been my backup plan, in case the being-famous idea didn't work out. Still, here I am in exactly that position and I think Frank is enjoying it more than I am.

From: Frank McCallum
To: Phoebe Henderson
Subject: I hate to say it but . . .

You were right. We did it again and I went for it. She was obviously delighted. She gave me a terrible blow job but regardless it went very well. She's even texted me twice telling me so.

From: Phoebe Henderson
To: Frank McCallum
Subject: Re: I hate to say it but . . .

HA! I told you so. Shame about the blow job but I'm sure you can show her where she's going wrong.

Regards,

SMUG Henderson

From: Frank McCallum
To: Phoebe Henderson
Subject: Re: I hate to say it but . . .

Yes, yes. It appears I have something to thank you for. But you're keeping your job so I guess that's thanks enough.

From: Phoebe Henderson
To: Frank McCallum
Subject: Re: I hate to say it but . . .

You always ruin a perfectly nice moment. I hope she bites it off.

I could hear him laughing and then my phone rang.

"I am grateful. Really. She's charming and I'm happy."

"Good for you. Quite frankly you're much nicer than you used to be. She must be good for you."

It seems my work here is done.

Friday, May 20

I must admit I'm stunned at the change in Frank—everyone is. He's most definitely calmed down. I can't remember the last time he mentioned how much he'd paid for something and he's actually funny when he isn't trying so hard to be a twat. Apparently Vanessa has given him a reason to smile and he's really into her. We spoke after work for a while and if he weren't my boss we might have been friends. I can't believe I just said that. He wants to have one last meeting and then he promises he'll drop this. He'd better—I'm not an expert on anything, and I don't see what else I can do, his hair?

Saturday, May 21

Oliver appeared around five, a couple of hours before we were due to rendezvous with Sue and Duncan at their house on the south side of the city. I still had reservations about the whole thing, which I vented to Oliver as I paced around my living room, waiting for it to be time to go.

"He called her a psycho!" I said. "Why would we even think about this again? I'd like to do this with people who like each other and who are preferably in good mental health!"

"The guy was denied a foursome, Phoebe—I can understand where his text rage came from," Oliver replied from the couch. "It doesn't mean that she is one; she's probably very nice. For a psycho."

"Fine, but if she kills us both I'm blaming you."

He turned on the television while I got ready and I stood looking into my wardrobe hoping that the perfect outfit would leap out at me. Either that or a magical world would appear and I could fuck off and have tea with a fawn instead.

Oliver popped his head 'round the door twenty minutes later. "You ready yet?"

I gave him a twirl, feeling very feminine in a flowery tea dress. "This do?"

"God, you look great. I'm almost sorry I have to share you this evening."

"We're really going to do this then?" I asked, touching up my lipstick. "Shit. Let's go before I change my mind."

We made it all the way to the house this time. They lived about a fifteen-minute drive away—a tiny redbrick bungalow with an immaculate front garden covered in gnomes. Seriously, I felt like Gulliver. I knocked on the door and held my breath. Through the frosted glass, the silhouette of a man made his way toward us. Oliver put his hand on my back and whispered, "Here we go."

We were greeted by Duncan, a website designer, very tall and toned through his white T-shirt. He led us into the living room, where we met the psycho, Sue, a very slim mature student who was surprisingly welcoming. She hugged us both and invited us to sit down while Duncan got some wine. I began to relax a little.

"I'm so sorry about last time," she said, kicking off her shoes. "I got a little nervous. I'm glad you agreed to meet us. I hope you don't think me rude."

"Oh, we understand," I replied. "Don't worry, we haven't given it a second thought."

Duncan returned with the wine and sat beside Sue. "Here's to an interesting evening!" he toasted.

Before long I was so lost in conversation I had forgotten why we were there, until Duncan stood up and reached out his hand toward me. Being the clued-up, suave girl that I am, I handed him my glass. He laughed, put it on the table, then took my hand and led me into the bedroom. I followed, completely lost for words and throwing Oliver an "Oh shit" look as we left.

The bedroom was gorgeous, all soft lighting and candles, and I was immediately reassured that at least my bodily flaws wouldn't be scrutinized by two strangers under a fluorescent bulb.

We started to kiss and undress and I didn't feel awkward at all. He absolutely knew what he was doing and I happily let him. I even put the condom on with my mouth and resisted the urge to go, "TA-DA!" like I'd just whipped a tablecloth off and the flowers were still standing. A breakthrough for me.

Then he pushed me down onto the bed and moved my legs apart with his knee. Before I knew it my legs were wrapped around him and he was gently moving inside me, asking if it was OK. It was more than OK. "Harder," I replied. "Fuck me harder."

The bedroom door opened and in walked Oliver and Sue, both naked, with Oliver standing behind her, his hands moving over her body as they watched us. I turned my head to see Oliver, his eyes fixed on mine. Even as he kissed Sue's neck, his gaze never left me.

Within ten minutes we were a big sweaty heap on the bed. Everyone was kissing everyone (not Duncan and Oliver, unfortunately—I think that would have been hot for me and the end of Oliver), and I must say the sight of Oliver going down on Sue while I was being slammed hard by Duncan was incredible. There was a silly voice in my head narrating the whole thing as it happened, like "Oh, look, now I'm kissing a lady" and "Oh, look, now there's two erections pointing directly at me like divining rods" but I carried on, determined not to let a small thing like my own weird internal monologue come between me and hot swinging sex.

The next thing that happened will remain lodged in the filthy part of my memory forever. Duncan lay down on the bed and I climbed on top of him as gracefully as my clumsy nature would allow. We started to have sex and I noticed Oliver walking behind me and heard the noise of the condom wrapper being torn. The next thing I knew he was fingering my ass and then he was inside me and I couldn't move. Or speak. Or breathe. Sue then started to kiss me. Oh yes, I was Queen of the Foursome and it was the most mind-blowing thing I've ever experienced. Completely overwhelming, sometimes uncomfortable, but I didn't feel panicked, or violated, which I had feared I might. Then I got to watch as they both screwed Sue and came on her.

We drove home giggling and very pleased with ourselves. Even laid-back Oliver was shocked at how well things had turned out. "That could have been a disaster!" He laughed as he put on a CD.

"Very true. They could have been crazy, or killed us, or EVEN WORSE, just been really crap in bed. Oh God, not Radiohead, Oliver, that's hardly going to keep us in high spirits."

"Did you like it when I—"

I immediately interrupted. "Put it this way—that will be top of my shower-nozzle masturbation fantasies for a long time to come."

He smiled at me and we drove the rest of the way back in triumphant silence. Another challenge complete. I win at this.

Sunday, May 22

I left Oliver's place and made my way to Central Station this afternoon, only to discover my train had been canceled, but I was in such a good mood I didn't give two hoots. I decided to wait in the station bar and have a quick coffee when I received the worst compliment ever from two neds:

Ned 1: "She looks like Katy Perry."

Ned 2: "Naw, she looks like Katy Perry's maw."

I turned around and scowled.
"It's awright, missus, he'd still gie ye one."
Oh, would he? Oh, how brilliant: Right, big boy, put down your Scampi Fries, whip off those trackie bottoms, turn your cap around backward, and let's go for it.

I vowed to forget it, but I still put on loads of antiaging cream before I got into bed.

Tuesday, May 24

I took Oliver out for a birthday meal this evening, mainly because I knew it would win me sex brownie points afterward. He was working till seven so I met him in town. He looked rough.

"HAPPY BIRTHDAY! You look awful," I said, giving him a hug. "You feeling all right? Your eyes have massive black circles under them."

"Gee, thanks," he replied, running his hand through his rather greasy hair. "Yeah, was a late one last night. Boys from the office took me to a lap-dancing bar. I got hammered. Nothing some food won't fix."

We went to one of those barbecue places where they hurl big chunks of meat and fish onto a grill and you stand there and go "Ooh!" while it cooks. I bought him the novel *Death of a Ladies' Man*, firstly because it's brilliant and sexy but also to remind him what happens to big swingers who hit on the wrong women.

"So tell me about your night," I demanded, watching him stuff three king prawns into his mouth at once. "Did you get a dance?"

"I did. To be honest, I'm not that into lap dancing. The girls are lovely and all, but it's all a bit cold, y'know; soulless."

"But you had a half-naked woman dancing for you. Surely that must have been fun."

"Nah. She smelled a bit sweaty."

"Yuck. That's made me feel quite queasy. I think I've had enough."

We had a fantastic night but it's now three in the morning, I'm sick as a dog and exploding from both ends. Oliver went home shouting, "JESUS CHRIST, PHOEBE, THAT SMELLS LIKE SLURRY!" and if I wasn't so close to death already I'd kill myself through sheer embarrassment. Forget the food poisoning, I wonder how I'll ever be able to face Oliver again after this—if it's not bad enough that he had to endure my BV whiff, now he's privy to my angry bowels.

I feel awful. I would complain to the restaurant, but knowing my luck they'll just offer me a free meal if I go back.

Wednesday, May 25

I was relieved to get a text from Oliver this morning asking if I was feeling better and could I please fumigate the house before he came over to look after me. Hurrah! I'm grateful he's decided to come back, but aware that I'll have to face an evening of endless bowel jokes and ritual humiliation. I called in sick to work and had to speak to Kelly, as Frank hadn't arrived yet.

"Can you tell Frank I'm ill and won't be in today? Ta."

"What's wrong with you?" she asked abruptly.

"Food poisoning."

"Oh really?"

"Yes."

"Seems a little sudden."

"Food poisoning tends to work like that, Kelly."

"You know you'll be expected to be at home all day if we need to get in touch."

"I'll be at home. Tell Frank to phone me if he wants to chat about what a fucking jobsworth you are. Good-bye."

I then crawled under the shower and made plans to set the bathroom on fire before Oliver came over.

Thursday, May 26

I'm feeling much better today. Oliver was so sweet last night; he didn't try to paw me, he made me lots of tea, and he even slept on the couch in case I got unwell again. Nothing to do with the fact I have all the cable channels and there was a late-night boxing match on, obviously.

Friday, May 27

Freakin' Frank thought I called in sick to avoid having our next meeting, or *last* meeting, should I say. It seems the whole world still revolves around him, but he's now convinced that I was indeed ill (apparently his sister had got food poisoning from the same restaurant, so that makes it true). I've agreed to meet with him on Monday to get this over and done with. Then I can get back to some sort of normality.

I also discovered that Hazel is a genius. Her folks have a house in Skye and we're all going to drive up there and have a party for my birthday, which is months away but I don't care! She says the house sleeps up to eight, has a real-life coal fire, and is miles from anywhere so we can shout and bang drums and stuff. Early birthday presents are the besterest.

Tuesday, May 31

My train journey into work this morning consisted of me trying not to scratch a massive, itchy heat spot that has appeared on the inside of my thigh. However, as the train pulled into Central station I gave in and practically clawed through my pants to get at the little fucker. Public displays of scratching are never a good look, but I was desperate.

I managed to convince a car dealership to advertise with us, which seemed to please Frank.

"Well done, we've been trying to get them in for ages. What swung it?"

"A massive discount."

"Good. You can squeeze some money out of someone else to bring your figures up. Can you stay a bit later tonight? I'd like to have a chat."

"Yes, OK, but last one, Frank. You promised. I think I've more than kept up my end of the deal here."

"You have. Last one. Scout's honor."

Everyone left at five and I cunningly pretended to be on the phone so Lucy wouldn't hang around for me or wonder why I wasn't leaving. When the office was clear I walked into Frank's office and sat down.

"Right, what can you possibly need help with now?"

"Well, I was thinking if there was anything else I could do for Vanessa that I'm not already doing."

"What do you mean?"

"Well. Y'know. In bed. Sexually."

"Oh my. 'Sexually.'" I laughed.

"Don't mock me," he said, looking embarrassed. "Oh, I need a drink." And then the shithead produced a bottle of bourbon from his bottom drawer and ran off to get some Coke for me from the vending machine. How could I not have known that was there?

When he returned, I took the can and poured some Coke into my coffee mug. "I don't really know what I can say, Frank. Why don't you go through what you'd normally do in bed, unless it's going to frighten me?"

He knocked his drink back, neat. "We do normal stuff. Probably tame compared to your depraved standards—"

"HEY!"

"But I just want to be sure I'm giving her as much pleasure as possible."

I held out my cup for some bourbon. "Maybe you should be asking Vanessa?"

"Oh, don't be silly. Then she'll think I don't know what I'm doing."

"That's exactly what I'm thinking."

"Behave. Look, I'll go through what I do and if you can respond or advise without being a smartass, I'd appreciate it. Now, drink up."

An hour later we were both smashed. "Hah! For God's sake, Frank. Unless she asks you to bite her, DON'T! No wonder she wasn't impressed. This isn't fucking *Twilight.*"

"Stop swearing. I just wanted to be different. You know when you look at someone and the urge to make love to them takes over and there's nothing you can do about it?

I have that with her, and I really shouldn't say this, but I've imagined that with you, too. A lot." We looked at each other and in the pit of my stomach I knew what was coming. I couldn't stop myself. I don't know if it was the booze or the fact that he'd grown on me over the past few weeks, but at that moment I could tell he wanted me and I felt the same. "Show me how you kiss," I said, looking at him over the top of my cup.

"What? How, I mean—"

I put down my glass and leaned over and then stopped a couple of inches from his face. He smelled of booze and that aftershave I'd noticed before.

"Show me," I whispered.

He leaned in and kissed me. Oh, he kissed me good-style—softly at first, then his hands were on my face and in my hair. I pulled back and we both paused for a minute to get a grip on what was happening. Next minute my top was off, my skirt hitched up and I was straddling him on his swivel chair. He lifted me off his lap, spun me around, and bent me over his desk. Excitedly, I pulled down my underwear as he put a condom on.

Within seconds he was inside me.

It was intense, it was hot, and it felt amazing. We did it over his desk, then on the floor, where our knees sustained dreadful carpet burns. It was intense, it was hot . . . and it was totally WRONG. What the fuck is the matter with me? So, what, now I can't even have a drink with my wretched boss without having to screw him?

"Just as depraved as I'd imagined," he smiled, fastening his pants. "Maybe next time we'll do this somewhere nicer than my office."

"Next time?" I was genuinely surprised that he didn't think this was a one-off. How arrogant. "This was a mistake, Frank. This will cause all sorts of problems," I told him as I clumsily buttoned up my shirt and started searching for my heels, finally finding them under his desk.

"You still haven't answered my question. Anything else you think I can do? From your reaction, I'm guessing no. . . ."

"No, it was fine. I think the best thing you can do for Vanessa is not screw anyone else. I'm going home now."

I ran out of the office and caught a taxi home. For some reason Christian Bale's voice appeared in my head shouting, "So you fucked your boss, Phoebe. OH GOOD! GOOD FOR YOU!"

But to be honest, it wasn't "fine"; it was incredible. That said, the more I think about it the more I realize that Frank probably never had any doubts about how good he was in the sack. I've just been played. Pam Potter was absolutely right; she called this weeks ago. That shithead. Pretending he was naïve about sex, making me think I was in charge when all the while he was seducing me. I could murder him.

JUNE

Wednesday, June 1

"I'm sorry," Frank said when I marched angrily into his office first thing this morning, "But after you asked me to kiss you, I couldn't help myself."

"You absolute fuckbastard. All that nonsense about wanting help and pretending you weren't sure what to do—it was all bullshit, wasn't it? Did you plan this?"

He looked at me. "Keep your voice down. We both wanted last night, Phoebe. Don't act like you hadn't thought about it too."

"We will never speak about this again," I insisted. "Tell Vanessa I said hi." And I left his office and got on with my work.

By seven this evening we'd screwed twice in the staff toilets.

Thursday, June 2

Although banging my boss wasn't on my initial list, I hate to admit it, but it feels exciting. But it shouldn't feel exciting. It should feel icky and vile and degrading and embarrassing.

I mean, it's Frank, for God's sake. Improved or not, this is the man who buys infantile art and wore that ridiculous sparkly watch and thinks he's so much better than every other human being on the planet; the one who, in the past, I've wanted to stab repeatedly with the spoon I keep in my desk for yogurts, and the one who made me come twice on the floor of his office and gives me butterflies now every time I think of him. Whenever he walks past my desk I get flashbacks of him inside me, of his breath on my neck and his hands on my ass, and although there's a huge part of me that wants to kick the shit out of him, the sex is pretty knee-trembling.

A phone call from him earlier made me believe he feels the same.

"Phoebe. Meet me in the station car park tomorrow after work."

"Why?" I asked, knowing full well why.

"Because I'm going to take you back to my place, pour you some Champagne, and make love to you. Properly."

Oooh, "properly." Of course he'd say something totally cheesy like that when I'm surrounded by an office full of people and can't shout at him. It's certainly taken my focus away from Alex, which can only be a good thing, but I have the feeling I'm getting into something that will eventually turn around and bite me on the ass.

Friday, June 3

Why can't I be one of these women who gets excited about rich men? It would make life so much easier. I'd be all: "Look at my boobs! Now, give me some money for something! Anything!" and he'd be like: "You're the best girlfriend EVER. Have some euros!" (Because he'd be French.)

I'm certain it would be very nice living in luxury and having wads of cash thrust at you, but I've always been more interested in a meeting of minds than the contents of someone's wallet. Anyway, after a quick fumble in the car after work Frank and I drove to his apartment—brand-new and undoubtedly worth a fortune. He opened the door to reveal a massive entrance hall with doors leading off it and a very large living room at the end. As expected, the decor was truly misguided. His walls are covered in a bizarre mix of abstract and tribal art, with a zebra-print rug sprawled out on the floor and a chandelier hanging from the living-room ceiling. There were wooden statuettes everywhere, minimalist furniture, and a flat-screen television the size of my bed.

"Champagne?" he asked, taking my coat. "Have a seat."

I sank onto the huge red corner suite and nodded, unable to take my eyes off a luminescent dragon statue glaring at me from the corner of the room.

"So, your apartment is . . . spacious, Frank. You have quite the eclectic taste."

"Yes, I do. I think it's entirely possible to appreciate many forms of art and design at the same time."

"And in the same room."

"You have *Sophie's World* in your desk drawer. I wouldn't expect someone who reads chick-lit to grasp art."

"*Sophie's World* isn't . . ." I began, trying very hard not to laugh. "Never mind. You're right, Frank. I have no insight into your world. Seeing what makes you tick on a personal level really is an eye-opener."

"Indeed. But I don't believe we came here to discuss literature." He took the glass from my hand and placed it on a stained-glass coaster.

"Did we come here to discuss those coasters? Because I really think we should."

"You're a funny wee thing, aren't you?" he said, taking my hand and pulling me to my feet. All I could think was, *You patronizing shit, where's your girlfriend?* but I kept my mouth shut and followed him into the bedroom anyway, dying to see whether he had mirrored ceilings and a couple of tigers roaming around in there. He dimmed the lights and actually tried to romance me, which, given that our previous sessions were all lust-filled and frantic, seemed strange. I expected him to clap his hands and Barry White's voice to start floating out of the lampshade. Instead, to my horror, I heard the opening notes of Celine Dion's "My Heart Will Go On" coming from the stereo.

"No. No. NO. Turn that off!"

"I thought you'd like that song. It's romantic."

"Are you kidding me?! That song makes me want to hurl myself off a boat that's not even sinking. . . ."

"Right."

"Or in water. . . ."

"FINE. I get it, Phoebe. I'll change it."

Celine was replaced with Dean Martin and then he kissed me softly, and stroked my hair, and, to be honest, it was really annoying.

"Stop being so gentle. I don't want to make love, I want to have sex."

"No. This is nicer and you'll—"

"Shut up, Frank. I'm not asking you, I'm telling you."

He stopped dead. Then, grabbing my arms and throwing me down onto the bed, he pulled my underwear to one side and began ramming me hard. Too hard at one point—perhaps I should have been clear that though I wanted sex, I didn't want him to poke a great big cock-sized hole in my kidneys, either. Nonetheless, it was over quickly and I reached for my skirt, hoping he'd just disintegrate.

"I don't know what it is about you, Phoebe Henderson," he said, watching me dress. "You're such a pain in the ass and you swear too much, but there's something about you that I'm drawn to. Until you open your mouth, that is— then I just want to throttle you."

Tuesday, June 7

Drinks with Hazel and Lucy this evening in town. For once Lucy was on time and I was the last to arrive. The bar was busy for a Tuesday evening but I scanned the room and eventually saw them sunk into a brown leather couch near the window. Hazel looked wonderful after her vacation. Her tan was flawless.

They waved me over, Lucy lifting up a glass to indicate she'd already bought me a drink. I hugged Hazel before sitting down.

"You look amazing! The sun has really lightened your hair, and that tan! God, you make me sick."

"I never tan. You're so lucky!" Lucy added, glaring at the freckles on her own arms. "I need to wear total block or I start to fry. So, tell all! Did you have a good time?"

"It was great," Hazel said, taking a sip of her French martini, "I feel so rested. Kevin was wonderful and spent the entire time looking after Grace. Well, when he wasn't throwing himself down water slides. I've taken loads of pictures and will bore you with them some other time. What have I missed here?"

I decided against announcing that I'd been doing Frank since the end of May, opting instead for "Not much. Y'know. The usual."

"What about you, Lucy? Any men worth discussing?"

She grinned, pulling up the bra strap that was making its way down her arm. "Actually, yes. I met a guy who works in the library near my house. I've told him I'll go out with him if he can remove the fines on my overdue books."

"How do you find them?" Hazel asked. "The man who works in my library is over sixty and wears a bow tie. I'd rather just pay my fines."

"You don't have Lucy's magical powers. Another drink?" I asked.

Six cocktails later I was in a taxi, heading to Oliver's for an impromptu, look-how-drunk-I-am booty call.

He answered the door in his bathrobe. "What are you doing here?"

"Oh, that's a nice welcome!" I laughed. "Let me in. I need a pee."

I pushed past him and ran to the bathroom. He followed me in. "If you don't leave now, you're going to see me urinate and that definitely isn't on my list, young man. Go and warm the bed up for me."

"It's already warm. I have someone here, Phoebe. You need to go."

The sound of my peeing made (a very drunk) me start to laugh. "Oh Christ, this is awkward. Who is it? Is it Simone? Can I say hello?"

"No, it's not and, no, you can't. I'll phone you a taxi."

"Who is it then? Tell me. IS IT A MAN? I definitely have to say hello."

"It's just some girl I know. If I'd known you were coming I'd have got rid of her earlier, but we're in the middle of it now, so you have to go."

I made him look the other way while I wiped and pulled up my tights.

"Fine. Go have sex with your mystery man. I'll just grab a cab outside."

As I stood on the pavement waiting for an empty taxi I kept looking up at his bedroom window. I realized that (a) looking up while drunk isn't a good idea, and (b) I felt foolish. Even though he hadn't technically done anything wrong, I still felt rejected. Ugh. What, did I expect him to turf the other woman out into the night just because I'd arrived? Well, yes. Actually I did.

Wednesday, June 8

Last night I had a dream that I bought coffee for people who didn't deserve it.

I had the hangover from hell but I managed to make it into work without throwing up on the train. At tea break, I slipped into the conference room and laid my head on the table, desperate to close my eyes for five minutes. The silence was wonderful until the door swung open, interrupting my nap.

"Phoebe! It's bad enough that you came to work looking like you got dressed in the dark, but this is too much. Pull yourself together."

"Go away, Frank. I'm entitled to fifteen minutes. This is how I choose to spend them."

He closed the door and walked over to me. "I'm serious, Phoebe. I'm still the boss around here."

"That's very true," I replied in a whisper. "But it's hard to take the boss seriously once you've seen his penis. Now stop speaking so loudly. I'll be out in a minute."

"Get a coffee and something to eat and then get back to work. I can't be seen to be doing you any favors here."

I pulled my head up from the desk and headed toward the kitchen to make coffee, passing Kelly, who looked thrilled that I'd been reprimanded by Frank. "That was very undignified, Phoebe. I can see why Frank is angry."

I returned five minutes later drinking a black coffee. From her mug.

By noon I was starving. I'd arranged lunch with Lucy in the canteen—she was surprisingly fresh-faced. I ordered more coffee and a bacon roll and demanded we sit at the back, away from all the noisy people. Again my head made its way downward and onto the table.

Lucy laughed. "I don't think I've ever seen you so hungover. I feel fine, but I only had three cocktails. Those shots you were doing would have floored me."

"I did shots? That might explain things." I took a small bite of my lunch.

"I saw you and Frank earlier. What's going on there then?"

I nearly choked on my roll. "Going on? What do you mean?"

"I mean, he's obviously got it in for you. All those office rants, the way he speaks to you in front of folk—I'd complain. Cheeky shit. Although, saying that, he does have a spring in his step these days. Must be that new girlfriend of his. Poor cow."

Oh thank God, I thought she'd twigged. "Yes, quite. I don't know what his problem is with me, but if he doesn't pack it in I just might complain," I said, desperately trying to think of something to change the subject. "He'll get bored of it soon enough and pick on someone else."

How I wish that were true, but somehow I doubt it. I cannot let Lucy find out about this. I would have no idea how to explain it. Frank might have tricked me into this situation, but I'm hardly blameless and that's the most confusing part. If I can't understand it, how could she possibly begin to?

Thursday, June 9

I called Oliver tonight to apologize for Tuesday. He didn't seem bothered.

"It's fine. Don't worry about it. I'm not."

"So your friend wasn't annoyed?"

"Nah, she just thought you were some crazy girl who needed to use the bathroom. 'Cause that's what I told her."

"Ha, that's fine. I didn't know you were seeing anyone."

"I'm not. She's just someone I know. I mean, you've hardly been around lately, and when you have you seem distracted. And we haven't had sex since before your food poisoning. I thought maybe you'd decided to take a break. Thought you were getting bored with me or the list or something. . . ."

Perhaps Oliver is also feeling a little rejected and I can understand why. I've pretty much dropped off the radar recently. It wasn't intentional, I've just been caught up in the whole Frank business. Still, I couldn't face telling him I'd actually been humping Frank; his ego would never recover.

"Not at all! It's just been work stuff, but I'm still up for the remaining challenges, if you are. We still have three left."

"Absolutely!" I could hear him smiling down the phone. "Just let me know when."

"Now?"

He hung up and was outside my door fifteen minutes later. He pushed me against the living-room wall and we had sex right there. He's asleep in my bed now and looks so peaceful I feel bad that I'm about to wake him up and demand sex again. Once with Oliver is never enough.

Saturday, June 11

It's Hazel's birthday today. She's thirty-nine and not happy about it.

"I didn't even want to do anything," she moaned as we arrived at the restaurant. "Kevin insisted on getting my mum to watch Grace and going through this whole freakin' charade. I don't want to celebrate being closer to forty and my face collapsing."

The first thing we noticed when we walked into the restaurant was a huge "Happy Birthday, Hazel" banner stretched across the entire, balloon-filled main room.

"Oh, forfuckssake." She laughed. "He's hired out the whole place! Why did I agree to this public humiliation?"

"Because you love it really," said Lucy. "You get a night off from Grace, you get to drink booze, which we'll all pay for, eat like a piggy, and then you'll go home and have noisy sex with your husband. What's not to love?"

Kevin walked over and placed a great big kiss on Hazel's pink lips.

"Thank you, darling. Lucy says we get to have noisy sex tonight. Up for it?"

Kevin winked at Lucy. "YOU BET I AM!" He howled.

We left Kevin baying at the moon and took our seats at the table. "He's a good guy, isn't he?" Hazel whispered.

"Of course he is," I replied. "He went from Jack the Lad to Superdad the moment you announced you were pregnant. You got a good one."

The Chinese buffet was tremendous; I must have got up seventy-two times at least and nearly punched someone for the last prawn toast. Kevin bought Hazel a beautiful locket, which made my gift of a photo frame look pitiful but at least I didn't give her a crotchless fishnet catsuit, UNLIKE LUCY. Kevin loved it; Hazel wasn't so sure. "I'm going to look like a seedy superhero in that, Lucy. But cheers." We all left around half eleven and Kevin and Hazel headed to their hotel, Citizen M, for the night. I went there once with Alex and loved it because it was furnished in the style of IKEA meets Star Wars; Alex hated it for the same reason.

Lucy and I wandered down to the taxi rank. "I'm going to ask that librarian out again tomorrow," she mused. "He seems a tad slow on the uptake. Perhaps I didn't make myself clear enough."

We shared a cab home. Lucy shamelessly flirted with the cabdriver to get money off the fare and his phone number. Sometimes I want be her.

Monday, June 13

Today I was bombarded with messages.

From: Alex Anderson
To: Phoebe Henderson
Subject: My email

Did you get my last email? Would really like to get together at
some point. Just to talk.

Then . . .

From: Frank McCallum
To: Phoebe Henderson
Subject: A Question

I can't stop thinking about you. Are you thinking about me?

@granted77 When we gonna hook up then? You know you
want to.

And finally a text from Oliver:

Did you eat my Twix?

OH, STOP WITH ALL THE QUESTIONS! Why don't you all just
put me in an orange jumpsuit and shine a light in my eyes!

Lucy dropped by after *EastEnders*. She'd been to the library
and was pissed off that her librarian man won't go out with
her, or get rid of her £18.75 fine.

"Jesus, how overdue were the books?" I asked.

"Months, maybe years, but that's not the issue here. The
issue is that he won't go out with me. Why the hell not?"

"I have no idea. Maybe you're just not his type?"

"He wears double denim. He has no right to be picky."

"Maybe he knows you'll insult his fashion sense. It's the
self-preservation defense."

"Hmm . . . you know, I don't think the fact I'd borrowed
both *The Bell Jar* and *On the Beach* and kept them for

months helped. Bleak fiction isn't sexy. Perhaps I'll borrow some erotic novels next time I'm in, something like: *The Scoundrel's Mistress* or *The Smoldering Butler*."

"Ah yes: the classics. Get one with a busty wench on the front. Let him know you mean business."

Anyone else would have admitted defeat and moved on. Lucy just sees it as a battle that she'll eventually win. This library guy doesn't stand a chance.

Wednesday, June 15

I was just leaving the office this evening when Frank called me back in.

"Something you need?" I asked.

"Just thought we could have a catch-up. Y'know . . . see how you're doing."

"I'm late for my train now, but apart from that, fine."

"I'm good. I'm taking Vanessa away on vacation. I've just booked it."

"How charming. When do you leave?"

"The twenty-second, back the fifth of July."

"Two whole weeks. It must be serious."

"It's just a leisure break, really. It'll be relaxing."

"Are you taking her miniature golfing?" I teased as he slid his hand up my skirt. "Perhaps fox hunting? Will there be a butler?"

"Yes, Phoebe, very funny, we are indeed going somewhere refined where there will be an opportunity to play golf. Somewhere you would hate. Are you jealous? Vanessa appreciates the nice things in life, but then again she's not the kind of woman who'd let her boss do this . . ." and with that he slid two fingers inside me.

I stopped him. For the first time since starting this whole sexual adventure game I felt cheap. "She obviously has sense then, Frank," I replied, knocking his hand away. "Anyway, if you're away with her, it means you won't be here bothering me. That's good enough."

"Suit yourself," he replied, getting out of his chair, "I'll see you when I get back."

I pulled down my skirt and left his office, very aware of my flushed face. I seem to be drawn to situations I know won't end well. But sometimes knowing how something will end, albeit badly, is less scary than, well, just not knowing.

Thursday, June 16

"How are you, Phoebe?" asked Pam at our session this evening. I began to blurt out the epic saga of Frank and his recent access to my lady parts. Relieved to finally get it all off my chest, I told her everything.

"I think he did start out wanting help with his love life, but then he used that to sleep with me! It appears he was clever after all. I should have listened to you."

"And yet you continue to be involved with him?"

"Ugh, it's crazy. He's such a sneaky little shit, but we have this dynamic now where we're both drawn to each other for reasons unknown."

"What is it that attracts you to Frank, Phoebe? From your comments so far, it sounds as if you don't particularly like him."

"I KNOW!" I exclaimed. "This is what's confusing me! I don't like him!"

"You should think about why you're attracted to him in the first place. Perhaps then things will become clearer."

I did. Nothing happened.

"We'll pick this up next time. I'd suggest reflecting on what you actually gain from your relationship with Frank."

I left her office, still clueless, and made my way home, picking up a curry on the way.

9:20 p.m. I've eaten too much. This is becoming a habit. I can hear my waistband begging for mercy. I can't be bothered to think about Frank tonight. I'm going to watch *The Good Wife* in bed.

10:15 p.m. WHY AM I ATTRACTED TO FRANK? We have nothing in common—he's just like freakin' Alex, all materialistic and superficial and full of shit. There is no logical reason.

12:13 p.m. Oh God, he's exactly like Alex! Is this the reason I'm drawn to him? Fuck! Surely even I'm not that stupid.

4:10 a.m. I am that stupid. I've let another Alex into my life and I haven't even got rid of the first one yet. Dammit. I need to sort this out. Frank has to go.

Friday, June 17

I had just finished my first cup of coffee this morning when Lucy called me from her desk. "So I had my date with the librarian last night."

I looked over and saw her shooing away Kelly, who was trying to talk to her about invoices.

"Fucking hell, you work quickly. How did that happen?"

"I took out *The Story of O* and *Lady Chatterley's Lover.* He made some joke about my borrowing 'softcore porn,' and I told him it was inappropriate for him to comment on my reading choices and that he'd better buy me coffee to say sorry."

"You're outrageous. So how did it go?"

"He was a pompous little prick and it didn't go further than a cappuccino and biscotti. He told me he'd rejected me previously based on the fact I wore too much makeup. He says 'natural women' are usually more intelligent in his experience. He seemed surprised that I had a degree in law and still chose to work in admin."

"Holy shit. Did you kill him? Do you need an alibi?"

"Not at all. I might have 'accidentally' spilled my coffee on his lap and then left him with the bill while he was in the bathroom drying his crotch under the hand dryers. But I'm sure he's still breathing."

"You're going to have to use another library now, aren't you?"

"Yep. Worth it though; he was wearing white jeans. Shit, gotta go—I see Kelly whining to Frank about me."

I turned around to see Frank staring blankly at Kelly, who was reconstructing the whole "shooing" event with elaborate arm flailing. This office is nuts.

Saturday, June 18

This morning Oliver mentioned that he'd been offered a free night in a hotel as a thank-you in return for work he'd done for them and would I like to go with him?

"Hell yes! Where is it?" I asked eagerly. "Does it have a pool?"

"Don't think so. It's only in Edinburgh, but might be nice to disappear somewhere. You know, chill out."

"When can we go?"

"Tonight. Up to it?"

As we drove to Edinburgh he was still being secretive about where we were staying, which made me think it was going to be some sketchy hostel-type place where I'd have to sleep with my eyes open in case Gustaf from Sweden in the top bunk decided to walk in his sleep. How wrong I was. It was the Witchery, one of the most exclusive hotels in Edinburgh, where coincidentally I once hung around outside trying to catch a glimpse of Jack Nicholson when he was staying there. That's six hours of my life I'll never get back.

"Are you serious?" I yelled when we pulled up outside, "We're staying here? I can't go in here—I'm dressed like a tramp!"

Oliver just raised an eyebrow. "Think you're going to be dressed for much longer? I have plans for you."

We checked in and I spent the first five minutes running around like a five-year-old. The rooms—sorry, suites—were all themed like something from a Gothic castle and I pretty much wet my pants.

"What do you think?"

"People actually pay to stay here?" I grinned. "Look at that massive bed. And the fireplace. And the plush carpeting. I mean, seriously, Oliver, what a shit hole."

"Happy?" he laughed.

"No. It doesn't have a pool. Still, I guess I can overlook that, as THIS IS UNBELIEVABLE!" I beamed, running my hand over the velvet cushions. "I pictured us staying in a Travelodge with a painting of a leaf hanging over our mediocre bed. I feel like I'm in a fucking Bram Stoker novel. I've always wanted to stay here! Look! A giant bathtub! Champagne!"

"I've booked us in for dinner tonight," he said. "Did you bring a dress?"

"No, just jogging bottoms and a baseball cap." I smiled, pulling a little black dress out of my suitcase. "This do?"

He looked at it for a second.

"Feel like a bath?"

Later we got ready for dinner and Oliver wore his dark blue suit, something I'm not used to. Handsome doesn't even come close. I could see women eyeing him up as we walked down the stairs into the dining room. "Jesus, you're making quite the impression, Oliver," I whispered. "You look great."

"So do you," he replied with a grin. "Very pretty."

The distinguished-looking waiter sat us in the middle of the room, at a table surrounded by opulent candlesticks, statues and hanging flower displays. I felt quite giddy. We ordered some wine and began reading the menu, trying very hard not to drool. The waiter came back a few minutes later.

"Are you ready to order?"

"Decided what you're having?" asked Oliver.

"No. Unless 'everything' is an option?"

"We'll need a couple more minutes."

I finally decided on scallops to start and Oliver chose haggis. I love haggis. I don't care how it's made or what's in it, it tastes amazing.

"Why didn't I order haggis?" I asked when our starters arrived.

"Because you're completely indecisive and you knew I'd let you try some of mine. Sadly this is too delicious to share, so your plan has failed."

"Give me a bite. I'll give you a scallop."

"I don't like them. You have nothing to bargain with here."

"Ha-ha, stop being a shit and give me some; you're almost finished."

Oliver smiled and handed me his plate. While I finished the tiny amount he had left, he reached over and stabbed his fork into my last two scallops, devouring them.

"I love scallops," he said with his mouth full.

"How is that a fair trade? You gave me a thimbleful of haggis! And you lied."

"I did. I wanted your starter quite badly. I'm not sorry, and I'd do it again."

"Man, you're a devious one. I should have you taken outside and shot."

We ended up sharing our main courses of pork and fish as well, bickering over who got the last hand-cut chip before ordering a second bottle of wine. By the time we'd finished I felt completely full and rather tipsy. Oliver signed the tab and we made our way upstairs to our suite.

We lit the fire and opened the bottle of Jack Daniel's I'd brought. Oliver loosened off his tie and sat beside me, stroking my face. It was nice.

He leaned over and whispered in my ear, "This is pretty romantic, isn't it? The wine, the room . . . it's almost perfect . . . shame I'm here with you."

I started to laugh. "What do you know of romance, you Irish womanizer? You screwed me on the bathroom floor before dinner with your socks on. That's hardly moonlight and roses, now, is it?"

"True. Anyway, fuck romance, I'd much rather spend twenty minutes screwing you on the floor than two hours telling you how strikingly blue your eyes are—"

"They're green."

"Shut up, or how you are the most amazing woman I've ever known. How you make me laugh until my face hurts and I can't picture my life without you."

I just stared at him.

He smirked. "Did you buy that?"

"What? No."

"YES, YOU DID! You totally bought that. Shall we move in together? Do you want to marry me now and have babies, Phoebe? Let's get a dog!"

"Oh, you bastard." An hour later he had me pinned to the bed, my head hanging over the side and was slowly and unromantically going down on me. A most splendid weekend.

Sunday, June 19

We drove back to Glasgow in the afternoon and argued about politics, music, and the fact that I snore like a demon. Oliver dropped me off and I've reluctantly unpacked, feeling refreshed if sore from all the frantic screwing. I'm very glad Oliver agreed to help me out with the challenges, as I'd never have found out how delicious he is in bed. I wonder what we'll do when I've finished my list.

Tuesday, June 21

Lucy's love life seems to be picking up again.

"Remember when we went out to that restaurant karaoke place and there was that fit older guy, David? Well, he asked me out tomorrow night."

"You don't date older men."

"I'll make an exception for him."

"But I thought we were having dinner tomorrow night?"

"We are. He's buying it. I'll eat with you and then have drinks with him. Possibly sex. It'll be a beautiful thing. You don't remember him, do you? Well, you were pissed that night."

"Of course I remember him!"

I had to think hard but eventually I did remember. Ages ago we'd had a staff night out at a speakeasy-themed bar/restaurant called Bugsy. The main attraction, apart from the karaoke, was the gangster-themed cocktails with names like "The Goodfella," "The Bugsy," and, most important, "The Leetle Friend," which tasted of raspberry and got me drunk enough to serenade my colleagues with "The Lady Is a Tramp" on karaoke. How appropriate. I remember briefly chatting to David, mainly about my awful singing, and then demanding a "Henry Hill" before losing both of my shoes.

Hopefully he won't remember me.

Wednesday, June 22

Oh, he remembered me all right. He came over to say hello halfway through dinner this evening and asked twice if I had managed to retain my footwear. I made a sharp exit shortly after eating, leaving Lucy to work her magic.

However, I did notice he was wearing a rather hideous gold "man bracelet" and matching chain. Yuck. That's reason enough not to sleep with someone. She's off work on a training day tomorrow but has promised to come around tomorrow night and tell me everything.

Thursday, June 23

So Frank has officially took off on vacation for two weeks, leaving the lunatics to run the asylum. He left Maureen from accounts in charge, much to Kelly's annoyance.

"She doesn't even work on our floor, for God's sake. What if there's an advertising emergency? Someone from this office should have been given the chance to run things."

"Like you?" Brian laughed.

"And why not? I'd be perfectly capable," she said, checking her nails in front of her monitor.

"You'd be perfectly annoying. Maureen worked in advertising for years before she moved into accounts. Stop being so pissy about it."

"Oh fuck off, Brian."

They continued to argue while everyone else got on with making a shitload of personal phone calls, including me.

"Morning, Oliver. Whatcha doin'?"

"I have the day off. I'm playing football, then going for a massage. What are you doing?"

"Boss is off all week. I'm calling everyone I've ever met to pass the time. I'm bored."

"When's the next challenge? And not another jacking-off one. The ones where I'm involved are much more fun. For me."

"I'll need to check the list, dude, but I'm sure there are plenty more hands-on tasks for you."

"Don't call me dude. You're not a surfer. Anyway, I'm off to football. Don't be thinking about me all sweaty now."

I thought about it. "I hate you," I muttered.

Lucy came 'round this evening, armed with a bottle of red wine to give me the lowdown on her date with David.

"So, how did it go?" I asked, finally managing to uncork the bottle after quite a struggle.

"Not great. He was more nervous than I was, but we hit it off pretty well."

"Sounds promising, but not nearly enough detail."

"Well, a couple of times I had to veer the conversation away from his ex-wife, but he was a gentleman and genuinely looked surprised when I replied, 'Hell yes!' when he finally asked me back to his place for coffee. Anyway, he owns an apartment overlooking the river. Actually, he owns a fucking block of apartments overlooking the river, as well as the restaurant where we first met him, a PR firm, and a bar in London that his ex-wife still runs. KER-CHING! He mentioned this quite casually—I kept hoping he would offer to buy me some boobs."

"So he has money. How was the sex?"

"I made the first move and kissed him. It was all very polite: no tongue, and lips firmly planted on mine. I half expected him to light up a cigarette and call me 'dahling' halfway through."

"Jesus. You still slept with him?"

"I almost didn't. Get this—first thing he said was, 'Don't expect me to go more than once.'"

"What? Was he kidding?"

"Well, I laughed, but his face was so sincere, and he said, 'I mean it. It won't happen.'"

"Oh, in the name of the wee man. Was it awful?"

"Pretty much. Lots of moaning in the wrong places, calling me 'baby,' telling me I was a 'bad girl'—I fucking wish I'd been a drunk girl. We went at it for a while, but he was pretty exhausted afterward."

"Ha, that's awful." I laughed, trying to picture this poor broken man and a very unimpressed Lucy standing over him.

"It IS awful. BUT that wasn't the worst part! As I got dressed, I noticed an A4-sized framed photo of his ex-wife on his bedside table. She had seen the whole fucking thing!"

At which point I laughed for ten minutes straight. It's nice to know Lucy's sex life is as weird as mine.

Friday, June 24

Oliver got a big promotion at work and he's thrilled. I'm really pleased for him, although I wonder why he never even mentioned he was up for it. I tell him everything, even when we get an extra half hour for lunch or if someone in the office sneezes and farts at the same time, but it seems he doesn't like to share with me. We might have to have words about this.

We went out for dinner to celebrate and then back to my place, where we had a marathon session on the PlayStation 2 (I am about a decade behind everyone else).

As I got ready for bed he put his arms around my waist and said, "You've put some weight on, eh? I like that—you're all soft and squashy."

"SHUTUPIAMNOT!" I yelled, frantically pulling a vest top over my head.

"I don't care." He shrugged, getting into bed. "Better than breaking my hand on your ass when I spank you. I'm talking from experience here. Pushing against your cushioned ass is so much better than pushing against a bony one."

I have put on weight though, loads in fact, but I don't like anyone else pointing it out, thank you very much. I'm sitting here singing "Do You Know the Muffin Man?" and thinking it's time for action.

Saturday, June 25

I've started the Atkins Diet, mainly because the only things I had in my fridge this morning were bacon, which was almost out of date, and two sad-looking eggs. After breakfast I went shopping and stocked up on everything meaty, fatty, or eggy. ATKINS IS BRILLIANT! I've had fuck-all carbs, about ten fry-ups, and pretty much just hooked myself up to a cream drip while throwing cheese and fried eggs into my mouth. Apparently I'll get God-awful breath for a while but I'm feeling positive and not at all hungry! Result!

Sunday, June 26

Diet seems to be going well but I'm flagging. I'm three pounds down and living off cooked chickens from the supermarket when what I really want is pasta and garlic bread. Unfortunately the only place I'm noticing any weight loss is my collarbone, but at least it shows there's still bone underneath all my flab. I'm also running out of exciting things to do with eggs—as if there was actually anything exciting you could do with them in the first place—apart from adding them to a big giant cake.

Monday, June 27

Fuck you, Atkins! I cannot face another egg or a chicken or indeed anything that once had, or came from, something with a face. I feel gross. How do people live like this? Celebs lose shitloads of weight on this diet, but I guess they have chefs who cook for them to ensure that every meal doesn't taste like Satan's hoof. So, in conclusion, I hate you, Atkins. You're not brilliant at all; I take it all back. I feel like shit. It's only been three days and I've had enough. For the love of God, someone SHOW ME THE TOASTIES! Oh bread, how I've missed you and how I'm also scared of you now I've been brainwashed by the carbtologists. Maybe I should just stop eating crap, but then where's the fun in that? At lunchtime I met Oliver in the pub. He was already halfway through a pint of lager when I arrived.

"You're drinking already? I'm only here for the food."

"Yes, Mum, I'm having a pint. So you're back on the normal food then? Glad to hear it."

"Yeah, I need to feel satisfied, and do you know what satisfies me?"

"Cock?"

"No, the answer you are looking for is carbs. I was foolish to think I could live without them."

"Dunno why you even tried."

"You said I was getting fat! I blame you for this, Oliver." I said. "I'm now frightened of bread."

"I didn't say you were 'fat,' and now I'm sorry I said anything at all," said Oliver, staring at his sandwich suspiciously. "Jesus, it was meant to be a compliment. I didn't know you'd get all concerned about it. I thought you were one of those women who doesn't care about that stuff."

Has this man ever met me?

"I wouldn't expect you to understand, Oliver, considering you've never dated anyone bigger than a size eight. I keep thinking you're comparing me to them. I'll never be that thin."

"Yes, I've slept with thin women, Phoebe, I'm not going to apologize for it. But your body is great; sure you have a belly and your boobs are massive, but why do you think I've been sleeping with you for so long?"

"Because I asked you to?"

"Wrong. Because when we're having sex it's fucking fantastic, and do you know what? I'd take a belly over a protruding rib cage any day. If you're unhappy with your body, do something about it; if not, eat your fucking bread and enjoy it. I couldn't care less."

As I left Oliver and walked back to work I realized that I believed him and his annoying truth-telling. Clearly it was me who had the problem. Not him. Say to a fella that he's put on weight and he'll just shrug it off and rub his belly in the mirror. Say it to a woman and all she'll hear is, "You're a failure. You're hideous." It's ridiculous. I'm ridiculous. The world isn't going to stop turning if I'm a bit overweight. Fuck it.

Thursday, June 30

"I'm getting sent to train new staff at the head office tomorrow afternoon," Oliver casually announced this evening.

"Oh, that's cool, how long for?" I asked, lighting a cigarette.

"Just a month. It's in Chicago. I fly out in the morning."

I swallowed my smoke and spluttered for a second, "A month? CHICAGO? BUT . . . BUT—"

"But what?" replied Oliver, smiling. "I'm sure you can find someone else to keep you company. You don't seem to have a problem in that respect."

"Of course I can," I said, smoking furiously. "I'm just surprised by your announcement, that's all."

"You could always just put things on hold until I get back."

I thought about this for about a quarter of a second. "Yeah, I'll just sit here and wait for your return. Light a candle . . . maybe write some poetry . . . I KNOW, I could put on a nightdress and wander around the moors, yelling Oliv—"

"I get the picture," he interrupted. "Don't be a dick about it." He walked into the kitchen and I heard him open a beer.

"Are you sulking, Mr. Webb?" There was no reply.

"See, in nursery school, were you one of those kids who didn't play well with other children?"

Still no reply.

"OK, I'm going if you're going to get all hormonal on me."

He walked back through to the living room and handed me a beer. "Have this before you go. Sorry, my head's just full of work stuff. I'll text you before I leave tomorrow."

I left feeling rather annoyed. Why the fuck didn't he tell me he was going, and why is he the one in the huff when I'm the one who's going to be left without a fuck buddy for four freakin' weeks? He really can be a selfish prick sometimes.

JULY

Friday, July 1

Oliver is now winging his way across the world for the whole month of July, leaving me buddy-less and in serious danger of doing Frank again. I grabbed a vanilla latte and a croissant on the way to the office, relieved that Frank was still on vacation, and I'd have some breathing space to work out what the hell I think I'm playing at. Truth is, I have no idea. Since I started this, I'm like a woman possessed. Is this how sex addicts feel? These days, life without sex is like a nail without varnish: bare and pretty much unforgivable, so I've decided to carry on without Oliver. After all, I've come so far in just six months and I really feel like I'm making up for lost time. My next challenge should be simple enough and one I'd have to do minus Oliver even if he were around. Sex with a stranger. No real names, no messy connections— just sex. After my disaster with Richard, I'm not taking my chances with any getting-to-know-you shit.

With Frank on vacation, the office was relatively relaxed. Lucy and I took an extra half hour for lunch, which was noticed by Kelly, who threatened to tell Frank on his return.

"You can't just do what you like, you know!" she boomed with her hands on her hips.

"Yes, we can," replied Lucy, "and so can you. Tell Frank if you want to; you're mistaking me for someone who gives a fuck."

Brian started applauding, told Kelly to "grow up," and then announced he was off to the shops to buy sweets for everyone. Brian the sexist moron has redeemed himself!

Saturday, July 2

I thought I'd have heard from Oliver by now, even just an e-mail to say he'd arrived, but I've had nothing. Meh, he's probably still sulking for no reason. Anyway, I have far more important things to worry about, like how I'm going to do this next challenge. I think it'd be easy enough to pick someone up in a bar or club but then I'd have to spend the evening looking for potential sex partners, making small talk, drinking too much and having to deal with the whole "I'll call you" nonsense afterward while waiting for my taxi. It all sounds too much like hard work. Also, I don't want to invite anyone back to my house as I don't need them remembering where I live and stalking me or shimmying up my path for a booty call at three a.m., thinking I'll be pleased to see them. I think the problem will be not finding someone to sleep with, but rather finding someone attractive, discreet, and, more important, who wouldn't decide I'd look better tied up in the trunk of his car. I've placed an online ad that reads:

> **Female, 30s, looking to meet attractive man for NSA encounter. Must practice safe sex and be discreet.**

What I really wanted to write was: "*Woman wants man for NSA sex. Please don't kill me.*" I intend to proceed with caution on this one.

4:50 p.m. Hazel popped over this afternoon with some muffins she'd been given by a client.

"They irritate my stomach. Might be the bran. You have them."

"Thank you for giving me something that gives you the runs, Hazel. Yummy."

I made her a quick coffee before she left to meet Kevin and Grace at some soft-play center in town. "Kevin has to do that stuff. I hate those places. They're full of other people's children. Want to come over later? I have sushi."

"Tempting as that is, I need a night of couch-laying, film-watching, and a couple of vodkas, I think. I feel like I need to unwind alone."

"That's cool," she replied, pouring herself more coffee. "You've been drinking quite a lot recently. Booze makes you fat, you know. And depressed."

"I have, haven't I? And there was me blaming the carbs. Maybe I'm drinking because I'm fat."

"You're drinking because you're bored, and shut up, you're hardly obese. You've just gained a few pounds. Now don't go getting pissed this evening just because you're missing Oliver," she said, smirking.

"I'm not missing him, and I have no intentions of getting pissed."

8 p.m. I will not watch any horror films. I will watch something meaningful and thought-provoking. This vodka is really strong.

9:05 p.m. Just started watching *Black Swan*. This should be good.

9:55 p.m. This is not good.

10:19 p.m. This can fuck off.

11:15 p.m. I'm watching *ZOMBIELAND*!

1:30 a.m. VODKA! VODKA!

2:15 a.m. I miss Oliver.

Sunday, July 3

I got up at four in the afternoon. Then I lay back down again. I got up again at seven, made some cheese on toast, and checked my e-mails to see if anyone had responded to my advert: twenty-six replies. Blimey! However, twenty-five of them contained "cock shots" with no indication of what the rest of the person actually looks like. I can't make a decision based on a webcam photo of a penis—I don't like a penis; I like the face and body it's attached to. The other one (which had no photo) was sent by a man who was "60 years young and everything still works." That's the same age as my dad.

This won't do. This won't freakin' do at all. I've e-mailed Oliver. It's much more fun when he's around. It's nice knowing that, whatever I do, he doesn't judge me, and I think that's why we've stayed friends for so long. Most people would have chased me with sticks toward some sort of drowning pond by now. How the hell am I going to cope without him?

This is going to be a long month. I have some vacation days to take from work, so perhaps now is a good time. I can't afford to actually go anywhere, but a week pottering around at home sounds like it might do the trick.

Monday, July 4

We're having a girls' night on Friday. Dancing and cheap booze. You know, just once I'd actually liked to get pissed on expensive booze. God, if I said that in front of Frank he'd be thrilled. Speaking of Frank, I put my vacation request sheet on his desk so he can sign it off on his return. I wonder how his vacation with Vanessa went. I bet he romanced her with Champagne and a box of Milk Tray by the fireside. I hope they melted. The chocolates—not Frank and Vanessa. Scrap that, I hope they melted too. Perhaps they had some sort of log cabin, surrounded by woods? And bears. BIG GIANT HUNGRY BEARS! Are there any bears in Scotland? I've just checked. There are no bears in Scotland. Disappointing.

Tuesday, July 5

As I'd finished my work for the afternoon I decided to go on Twitter, where there was a message waiting for me.

@granted77 You ignoring me? I'm free next week. Let's meet up.

I was about to reply when Lucy appeared with a coffee and pulled a chair over. She peered at my screen.

"I'm bored. What are we doing? Who is he?"

"Oi, nosy! Guy on Twitter. Wants to meet up."

"Ooh, like a date? Or just random sex he can tweet about later."

"I don't really know him, so sex would . . ." I stopped midsentence. If this had been a cartoon, a lightbulb would have appeared above my head.

"Sex would what?" demanded Lucy. "Tell me!"

"Sex would mean I could tick off challenge number eight. It's perfect. Why didn't I think of that?"

"You did. Just there."

"Yes, but you inspired me. I'm going to tell him it's on like Donkey Kong."

"That's just weird, but you're right. I am an inspiration."

I've sent him a message back telling him I'll meet him. It's perhaps not the completely anonymous deal I had in mind, given that I know what he looks like and we've spoken on Twitter, but after those replies to my advert, it's about as close to a stranger as I'm willing to go. This would mean another challenge down and it's only July! I'm way ahead of myself. I could come up with another thousand.

Wednesday, July 6

I got into the office this morning to hear Frank boring everyone with tales of his vacation. I overheard talk of fancy hotels and oysters, and although I clamped on my phone earpiece to block him out at that point, I imagine the great adventurer took a trip on a magic carpet and killed a fucking dragon while he was there.

From: Frank McCallum
To: Phoebe Henderson
Subject: Pleased to see me?

I'm back. It was great. Your vacation request has been grudgingly approved—going anywhere nice?

I thought about you . . . a lot. I need to get you out of my system. This isn't good for anyone involved.

From: Phoebe Henderson
To: Frank McCallum
Subject: Re: Pleased to see me?

You don't pay me enough to afford somewhere nice. You're right, this isn't good for anyone, so here's an idea—let's not do this anymore. Problem solved.

From: Frank McCallum
To: Phoebe Henderson
Subject: Re: Pleased to see me?

Fine with me.

I didn't reply and he hasn't e-mailed again. This made me feel relieved and, for some reason, annoyed.

9 p.m. I've decided to catch up on my reading and not be led astray by crazy boys and my hormones. I'm in bed, snuggled up with *The Time Traveler's Wife,* and so far it's one of the best things I've read in ages. Whatever happened to romance? Two people realizing they can't live without each other and kissing properly.

11 p.m. Gosh I've missed reading. I could spend all day lost in someone else's imagination. I love reading.

12 a.m. I can't put this book down. I've made coffee and will sacrifice sleep in order to see it through. My life is an uninspiring sham.

3 a.m. I'm completely distraught. Henry died. Reading is stupid.

Friday, July 8

I was so exhausted at work today I pretended to be ill and came home. Frank didn't seem too convinced, so I told him disgusting fake tales of menstrual blood and clotting, and he almost booted me out of his office. I've had a nap and am now looking forward to a night with the girls, foot-loose and man-free. Frank didn't mention anything about us so perhaps things will get back to normal. The annoying thing is, even if we go back to ignoring each other and keeping things work-related, there will be that small matter of having seen each other all shades of naked.

Still haven't heard from Oliver, but he's probably already hooked up with some gorgeous American stick insect called Brandy or Clammy and they're off feeling each other up at fun-filled baseball games while eating six-foot-long hot dogs suggestively.

Anyway, screw him—I have a night of dancing and general shenanigans with Lucy to look forward to.

Saturday, July 9

Last night was fun—I hadn't been dancing in ages.

I went to Lucy's house to get ready as her shower is much better than mine and her straighteners don't burn the ends of my hair, unlike my cheap ones.

"I'm wearing my biker boots and that minidress with the floaty skirt," Lucy announced.

"So we're not going anywhere fancy then?" I laughed. "Just as well, I'm wearing my jeans and Converse. I'm not in the mood for sore feet."

"Cool. I feel like somewhere with rock music and tattooed women. I'll be damned if I'm surrounded by men who are all wearing the same shirt from Topman. Glass of wine before we go?"

I pulled my favorite black top with the sheer sleeves over my head and replied with a muffled "Yes," knowing full well that one glass would quickly become more.

A bottle of Chardonnay later, we caught a taxi to the Cathouse, home to aging rockers, emo kids, and everyone in-between. We danced, drank, drank some more, and, as I found out, seven hundred gin and tonics turns me into a complete idiot. Younger men seem to gravitate toward me these days—it's unreal.

At one point during the night a twentysomething guy, who was completely pissed and hobbling with one shoe hanging off his foot, decided he'd chat me up: "Want to see how far I can kick my shoe?"

Quite far, as it happens. Best chat-up line I've ever heard.

Shoe Boy was full of drunken compliments, but I stuck to my resolve, and even hearing "You have the most amazing body" didn't make me drag him home, and the fact that he said it seventy-five times didn't make it true. We did have a kiss outside and I swear he giggled when he touched my boob. Men closer to my age never hit on me anymore. It seems that men in their twenties want an older woman but men in their thirties want someone in their twenties. But after the disaster with Richard, I think I'd like to play with someone my own age now.

Sadly the night didn't end as planned, as Lucy went home with the dirtiest man in the world, and not in a good way. We ended up back at his place (I have no idea what his name was), where I passed out on his couch. I woke up at seven a.m. to the sound of them screwing, and when I finally managed to focus I wanted to run away screaming from the shithole we'd ended up in. The place was filthy. Actually, that doesn't even come close to describing the squalor this fella lived in. The floor was covered in cigarette ash and dirt, every piece of cutlery and crockery he owned was covered in old food and mold and I half expected to hear a voice say "ZUULLL" when I opened the fridge. How the hell can anyone live like that? "He didn't have any sheets on his bed," said Lucy in the taxi on the way home. "Christ, when did I stoop this low?"

She made me promise never to mention it again and spent the rest of the journey with her head in her hands, mumbling about celibacy and convents. I now realize that Lucy is just as messed-up as I am and, if I'm honest, I'm just so glad it wasn't me waking up on a bare mattress and staring at the man directly responsible for the next plague outbreak.

Sunday, July 10

I met Hazel and Lucy for lunch at Blackfriars Pub in the Merchant City. "How was Friday night?" asked Hazel. "Wish I could have come but the Cathouse isn't really my scene. Everyone just seems a little grubby."

"It was, erm, fine," said Lucy, glancing at me. "Tell Hazel about your man with the shoe, Phoebs."

Hazel laughed as I recounted my Shoe Boy adventure. "And you didn't pull him, Phoebe? He sounds sweet."

"He was," I replied. "I just don't want another younger guy. I don't get why younger men are so keen on older women."

"Young boys have always had a thing for older women. We're experienced and we're more comfortable with our bodies. It's quite flattering really."

"Younger men are also more grateful," added Lucy, cramming a cheeseburger into her mouth. "I mean, they understand how lucky they are to be touching a boob; of course they're going to be overenthusiastic."

"I'm too old to have my boobs giggled at," I mumbled, wishing I'd got a cheeseburger instead of pasta. "Oliver never giggles at my boobs. Or tells lies about my body."

Hazel was already on her second gin. "Maybe you do have an 'amazing body, dude.'" She laughed. "Men don't see what we see. They see lady bumps and round bottoms. We just see excess fat."

"Why don't you just go out with Oliver?" suggested Lucy, "God knows you see enough of him anyway."

"Oliver as a boyfriend? God no. He's terrible at relationships, as am I. Having a relationship would ruin everything. We're fine as we are."

I saw Lucy and Hazel glance at each other.

Lucy smirked. "Whatever you say, Phoebe."

Monday, July 11

With Oliver away, Frank and I apparently over, and no ridiculous younger men around, I did nothing at work today except look at Stuart's bottom. Then I sent Lucy e-mails about Stuart's bottom. Then I sent Stuart e-mails about his bottom, and when there was nothing left to say I watched a pigeon look stupid on the building across the road. Frank also noticed my lack of enthusiasm in the workplace.

From: Frank McCallum
To: Phoebe Henderson
Subject: A request

Phoebe, I know you stop for a week on Friday but do some work, please.

I ignored him.

From: Frank McCallum
To: Phoebe Henderson
Subject: Re: A request

Don't make me bring you in here, Phoebe.

From: Phoebe Henderson
To: Frank McCallum
Subject: Re: A request

What for exactly? We're not doing that anymore, or had you forgotten?

From: Frank McCallum
To: Phoebe Henderson
Subject: Re: A request

I hadn't forgotten, quite the opposite. I'm sitting in here watching you chew your pen, and if I stood up right now my erection would knock over that pigeon you've been watching for the past ten minutes. I'm taking you home.

So Frank dropped me home and we had sex again. Why can't we end this? It's driving me crazy. "Head office would have a fit if they found out about this," he grunted while on top of me. I rolled onto my side and he spooned me.

"No shit," I moaned (I love that position). "We need to stop this. It's crazy."

He flipped me onto my stomach.

"Let's cool it then. It's been fun, but [speeds up thrusting] . . . Dammit, Phoebe, it's so good I could do this all day long." The rest of the conversation had to wait as he made me come and I was speechless.

Afterward we both agreed that was the last time. I don't even like him that much and I'm pretty sure he feels the same. "No hard feelings?" he said to me as he left, and amazingly I resisted the urge to use the word "hard" in a filthy reply.

"Of course not. It's best that this ends. I hate you anyway."

He laughed. "I hate you too."

Tuesday, July 12

The most interesting part of today was when a woman turned up to meet Frank in the office, whom he formally introduced as Vanessa. Ah, the elusive Vanessa. At least she exists. She was well dressed, late thirties, pretty, very thin, and he kissed her in front of the staff—they all giggled like ten-year-olds. The happy couple then left hand-in-hand and Frank didn't meet my eye as they passed my desk. I think this was his way of making our "end" official. He looked really happy, and I feel relieved. Things were much simpler when he was just the annoying boss I hated and not the slightly less infuriating man I've now grown quite fond of. I genuinely hope it goes well for them.

Wednesday, July 13

Alex was waiting for me after work today. What an utter bastard. He hasn't done that since we dated and I never thought he'd have the nerve. He stood there bold as brass smoking a cigarette, watching me walk through the doors, knowing I wouldn't be able to leg it without him spotting me. If they had been revolving doors, I'd have kept spinning and gone back upstairs.

"Fucking hell! What do you want, Alex?"

"Just to talk, Phoebe. You won't reply to my e-mails."

"Doesn't that indicate that I don't want to talk to you?" I said, turning to walk away.

"Are you seeing anyone?"

"That's none of your business."

"That's a no then. Look, I have some things I need to say. Please. Just dinner or something?" he pleaded, walking after me.

"NO!" I shouted, stopping dead in my tracks. "I'm not interested. Go away."

He walked off shaking his head and I did the same. Who the hell does he think he is? Why is he asking me if I'm seeing anyone? He knows that if I were, I would have answered yes to rub his face in it. Damn him.

Friday, July 15

First day of my vacation! A whole week to do nothing and I intend to do exactly that, AND I finally got an e-mail from Oliver! I love you, Internet.

From: Oliver Webb
To: Phoebe Henderson
Subject: HELLO!

What have you been up to then? I'm stuck here training a bunch of 20-year-olds, all male and all annoyingly chipper. One girl in marketing who looks about fourteen asked me out for a drink and I had to check her company file to make sure she was over twenty-one. I considered it for a second but thought it wise to keep my cock in my pocket where work is concerned. Anyway, email me back with tales of your sexual misadventures as I'm horny as hell. You're going to bear the brunt of this when I get home—I hope you realize that.

I didn't receive it until the early hours so I'll get back to him tomorrow. It's made me really happy and so I'm going to bed before anything happens to kill my buzz.

Saturday, July 16

I got my eyebrows threaded and my nails done, as tonight was date night with stranger @granted77, who is called Scott when he's not on Twitter. We met in town first for drinks as I wanted to be completely sure I wanted to sleep with him and also check for signs of weirdness.

I felt incredibly nervous as I walked into the bar. This wasn't just taking someone random home after a drunken night; this was a premeditated, soberly planned hookup and there I was on my own in a bar wearing my fuck-me boots and skinny jeans. It felt like the scariest challenge I'd attempted so far.

I looked around the bar for a face that resembled the one I'd seen on Twitter, but the place was so crowded I couldn't find him. It was like a bizarre game of Where's Waldo? and in the end I decided to let him find me and sat down. I saw the barman walk over and rummaged in my bag for my purse.

"What can I get you?"

"Gin and bitter lemon, please. No ice."

"No problem. And then back to mine after?"

"Pardon?" I stopped searching my bag and looked up to see the tiny Twitter head in real life, smiling back at me. He looked exactly like his photos: my height, hipster glasses, and short blond hair.

"Scott? It's you! You work here?"

"I'm the manager. My shift finished half an hour ago, but we're busy so I thought I'd help out till you got here. Slice?"

"Pardon?"

"Of lemon."

"Oh, ha," I laughed, completely thrown by what was happening. "Please."

He handed me my drink and pushed my money away. "On the house. Give me five and I'll be right with you."

I took my drink and breathed a huge sigh of relief. He was a normal guy with a normal job, and from first impressions I fancied him.

He came and sat down beside me. "So here we are," he said, knocking back his whisky. "I assume you're still up for this."

"Gosh, you're subtle," I laughed, "but yes. I am."

"Good. Finish up then. I have no intention of spending the rest of the night at my work, getting too pissed to screw you. And believe me, I want to screw you. Let's go."

I was speechless. I downed the rest of my drink and was dragged by the hand outside. We flagged down a cab.

Scott lived on the ground floor of a traditional tenement apartment in Shawlands, an area known for its beautiful park, broke students, and frustratingly limited parking spaces.

We were barely into the hallway of his apartment when he began to kiss me. I responded and he took off my jacket, moving me toward the pitch-black living room.

"You've done this before, I take it?" I asked as he fumbled for the lamp switch.

"'Course. Isn't this what Twitter is for?" He switched the lamp on to reveal an exceptionally messy living room. I was tempted to ask if he'd been burgled but thought it wiser not to make fun of the strange man I was about to sleep with.

"I dunno. First time for me."

"Let's make it memorable, then, shall we?"

I've never seen a man get naked so quickly. I barely had my jeans unbuttoned and he was already standing there, erect and ready to go. I started to unzip my boots.

"I want you bent over that couch wearing those boots. Take off your jeans but leave the boots on."

He got busy with the stereo while I removed my boots, took off my jeans, scowled at the mark they'd left on my stomach and then put my boots back on, but eventually I was ready. I turned around, grabbed the couch and braced myself. Then he banged me from behind while Led Zeppelin played loudly on his stereo. It wasn't great. He pretty much thrust in time to each song, even singing along with "Kashmir." All I could think was, I hope "When the Levee Breaks" doesn't come on. I don't want this to ruin that song for me. When "Moby Dick" came on it was game over. To stop myself from laughing, I just started to moan really loudly and clenched to encourage him to come. Afterward I thought, Thank fuck that challenge is over. I'd thought it would be dangerous and sexy and hot. It wasn't. It was a huge letdown.

"Well, that was fun," he said, watching me put my jeans back on. "God bless Twitter."

"Indeed," I replied, determined to delete my Twitter account as soon as I got home. "Can you call me a taxi? I have to get back."

1:25 a.m. I arrived home a couple of hours ago, showered, and now I'm in bed removing certain Led Zeppelin tracks from iTunes. It's odd—I've just completed a challenge on my list and I'm not even vaguely excited. I'm done now with the solo items and all that remains is bondage, voyeurism, and a final role play that I have to wait for Oliver to do with me. I don't like it when Oliver's not involved; it's much less fun high-fiving yourself.

Sunday, July 17

I've been sitting here listening to the Flaming Lips in some sort of melancholic trance today, but of course Alex seems to creep into my head when I'm feeling at odds with myself. Ever since he showed up outside work, I've had him in the back of my mind.

I really hate the fact that Alex knows I'm single; he'll take that as a sign that I'm not over him. Maybe I'm not, and it's possible I won't ever be until I let someone new in. I have no intention of falling in love, but maybe having someone around will get him to finally back off. He'll be less likely to pursue me if he knows I have a big strong man on hand to fend off his unwanted attention. And I guess the idea of having someone in my life isn't as unappealing as it once was . . . Shit, I think I've convinced myself here. Am I ready to start dating again?

Wednesday, July 20

From: Phoebe Henderson
To: Oliver Webb
Subject: Re: HELLO!

Dear Oli, (Yes, you hate it when I call you that, but you're too far away for me to care) Things I have done:

1. I read a lot of words on some pages. This would be a book.
2. I slept with someone off Twitter, so the sleeping-with-a-stranger challenge is now complete. It was so crap that now I've now deleted my Twitter account. Stephen Fry was never going to follow me back anyway. Please bring me home presents. Lots of them, not like that time you went to Canada and brought me back NOTHING, claiming you didn't think I'd be bothered. I am bothered about presents, let's be very clear on this matter. I'm almost at the end of these freakin' challenges so now I'll have to find something else to do. I think I'm going to start dating again. Is this the worst idea ever?

Hurry back. My vagina misses you.

From: Oliver Webb
To: Phoebe Henderson
Subject: Re: HELLO!

You've been busy. I've been stuck in a training room all day, accompanied by one woman who was incredibly hot and unfortunately married. I've considered just jacking myself off into oblivion. It's been nice knowing you. Dating? You want a boyfriend? Really think anyone is crazy enough to go out with you, weirdy? I know the way your big ears poke through your hair makes me go all funny, but I doubt anyone else would want to date a real-life pixie. Good luck though. I'll sit on the porch with my shotgun when your suitors come a-callin'.

I miss your vagina too. Probably more than I miss you, which isn't much.

From: Phoebe Henderson
To: Oliver Webb
Subject: Re: HELLO!

Shut up. I'm a catch. I can play backgammon and I have 100% positive feedback on eBay. These are important qualities. They would have to be bed-head tolerant, mind you. You TOTALLY miss me because no one will play with your penis over there. My ears rock.

Friday, July 22

I noticed a salon deal online this morning: full-body massage for fifteen quid, so I called and managed to get an appointment for noon.

From the outside, Beauty by Betty looked remarkably like a pensioners' hair salon, squashed between a pound store and a bakery. As I walked in, I noticed how tiny the place was. There was a couch, a front desk, a shelf with beauty products, and one, somewhat menacing, large gray sliding door at the back.

I smiled at the dark-haired woman behind the desk, who stopped reading her magazine and stood up. "Hi. Do you have an appointment?"

"Yes, for twelve. Phoebe Henderson."

"Oh, yes, Phoebe. I'm Betty. You'll be with me this afternoon."

She took my jacket and walked me the ten steps to the gray door. "Just through here." It was the most unwelcoming door I'd ever seen and reminded me of one I'd seen at the back of a butcher's shop when I was little. What the fuck was behind it? I suddenly envisioned it being pulled open and me getting clubbed over the head by Leatherface in his manky apron. She opened the door and I was faced with a surprisingly luxurious therapy room: dimly lit with scented candles and hanging fairy lights. "Wow," I said, admiring the fresh flowers in the corner. "This is beautiful!"

She asked me some general health questions and then left me to undress to the sound of pan pipes. "Just press the buzzer when you're ready."

As I got undressed I was already feeling more relaxed than I had in ages. I lay on the table and covered myself with a white sheet before pressing the buzzer next to me.

She came in and began. I remember her massaging my legs and arms, but when she got to my back I must have passed out as the next thing I remember is waking up in a tiny little patch of my own drool. I apologized but she just laughed.

"Don't be silly, it's very common. Do you have sinus problems?"

"Oh God, was I snoring?"

"Yes. We do Hopi ear candling here. You might have an ear-wax buildup. It'll help."

So for an additional £10 she stuck beeswax tubes in my ears and set them on fire. The sensation was actually very relaxing, like a fizzing in my ear, but as I had a candle burning into my skull, I thought better of having another nap.

When she'd finished both sides she offered to show me the mountain of ear wax that had been sucked out of my ears, but I declined because YUCK. Despite the snoring, I left the salon feeling refreshed, calm, and like a normal human being again.

This evening was spent on the Internet, reading about Zionism, how to bleed my radiators, and looking at old photographs of Christian Slater, which took me back to being fifteen, when I used to practically mount the posters of him I had on my wall while hating boys my own age. At that age I never doubted for a second that I'd find the man of my dreams and live happily ever after. I never doubted I'd be happy. Seventeen years later I doubt it every single day. I think I've been brokenhearted for so long I've forgotten how to function properly. Oliver was right; I am weird. Not "let me see the contents of your sandwich" or "look at my giant leg" weird, just a tad unconventional. I'll just have to hope that someone out there finds me endearing.

"Of course they will, silly!" said Lucy when I phoned her, "You're now sexually emancipated warrior-girl. You can have anyone you want."

"Sure, I'm better in bed, so these challenges will either prove very useful or give me ridiculously high expectations. What if I feel cheated when my next boyfriend refuses to have sex while hanging off a cliff, just because I decide I want to try it?"

"Stop worrying. There are plenty of men who're just as adventurous as you are. Oliver isn't the only one. You'll be fighting them off."

"And where am I expected to meet all these men? It's like a meat market when we go out to bars; everyone's just looking for sex."

"Online! If a guy spends money on a dating site, surely he's looking for more than just sex? Everyone's doing it these days."

"My, that's logical. You could be right."

I like the sound of this. Internet dating it is. This could be fun!

Sunday, July 24

Internet dating is truly frightening. For the first time I'm putting up real photographs, giving real details about myself, and hoping that I don't sound like a twat. Hazel helped me pick some pictures:

"You look nice in this one."

"Piss off. I look like a horse."

"A happy horse though."

"Oh great. How about I put: 'Horse-faced girl would like to meet man with ridiculously curly hair, for fun conversation and deep and meaningful sex. Must be accepting of my outrageous bed head, stupid friends, and recent sex partner who will make fun of you regardless.'"

"I'd reply to that."

"Ugh. Fetch me seventeen cats and a subscription to *Spinster Weekly*. This is going to be tough."

Monday, July 25

Back to work today, and I had a mountain of e-mails to go through and calls to return. I'm starting to regret not taking two weeks off instead. Two of the e-mails were from Alex, who obviously didn't know I was on vacation, and I deleted them without reading, otherwise I'd have been tempted to reply, "GET IT RIGHT UP YOU, FUCKFACE" in 72pt Comic Sans.

Stopped off and got a pizza on the way home and settled down in front of the laptop, eager to browse through all the profiles of single, professional men in my area who are obviously too busy saving lives or hand-rearing kittens to have found a girlfriend the normal way.

10 p.m. Jesus, it's slim pickings on these dating sites! For the money they charge I want Josh Groban and his magnificent hair to be on there. Strangely enough, the profiles I saw before joining seem to have disappeared and been replaced with men who think it's a good idea to stand proudly in front of their cars, like they've just invented a time machine. And why do so many of them put "If you want to know about me, just ask"? That's just lazy! They're meant to be wooing me with their charm and wit, not leaving me to do all the freakin' work. Saying that, the last wooing I was privy to was when my dad dressed as a ghost one Halloween.

Tuesday, July 26

The messages from suitable bachelors have begun trickling in. . . .

> Hello Phoebe, you've received a message from **John**!
>
> Hi. My names John and I liked the look of yo pic. Nice mouth. Mail me bak.

Nope.

> Hello Phoebe, you've received a message from **Paul**!
>
> I've never done this before but I thought what the hell you only live once and I'm shy until you get to know me but then I'm not. I also have better pictures but not on this computer. I'm into gaming and soccer and gadgets and wearing my black leather coat when I am out.

What computer would that be then? How many computers do you have, Neo, and why is one reserved for pictures, hopefully showing a full set of teeth?

This is getting ridiculous.

Wednesday, July 27

Frank was hovering around our desks this afternoon, trying to motivate us to make target by offering a bottle of wine for each ad sold. Thirteen ads later, he called time on his costly mistake and shuffled off to the supermarket.

While he was out I checked my e-mails and was thrilled to see that someone decent e-mailed me. I say "decent"; he can spell—which is a start.

> Hello! I'm Alan. This is the part where I try to appear cool and fail miserably, so I'll be quick. I'd love to meet for drinks/dinner/coffee and embarrass myself in person if you're free any night this week?

As I clicked on his profile I prepared myself for him to have a face like a Hobbit's foot, but surprisingly he's handsome, with only a hint of beard. It seems I found a good one! I e-mailed him back to tell him I'm free on Sunday before sending Lucy his picture to show off.

She phoned right away. "His picture looks Photoshopped. He's not real. He's far too symmetrical."

"What? That must be him. Why on Earth would anyone agree to meet, knowing they've put a fake picture up?"

"Maybe he hopes his personality will be enough to make you forget he's a big fake-faced liar."

"Go away. I love him."

Saturday, July 30

I received another e-mail from Alan, saying how much he's looking forward to our date tomorrow. I called Lucy for advice on what to wear.

"Wear that red flowery skirt. The one I borrowed ages ago and got toothpaste on."

"That doesn't fit me anymore and we both know that wasn't toothpaste."

"Ha. Fine. The dark blue dress with the white collar, then. You look pretty in that. Where is Mr. Symmetrical taking you?"

"Red Onion. Apparently he's gluten-intolerant and they have a special menu. I'm not complaining; their seafood is amazing."

"Gluten intolerance isn't real and neither is his face."

"Shh. I'm really excited—this is a much more normal way to pass the time than looking at cock photos and planning my next challenge."

"I dunno, there's a lot to be said for looking at—"

"I'm going now."

"OK, have fun and just remember not to feed him any bread."

"He's not a duck. Thanks for your help. Speak soon."

I'm a tad nervous. I hope neither of us is disappointed.

Sunday, July 31

6 p.m. Half an hour in the shower was longer than I intended but that still leaves ninety minutes—plenty of time to get ready for the date with my new husband.

6:30 p.m. I pour a gin and have a cigarette, then dry my hair. Lots of volume needed so I dry it upside down and emerge looking like I've been assaulted. So then I need to spend twenty minutes flattening it, followed by a further ten minutes back-combing and wishing for baldness.

7 p.m. Half an hour to go and I lay out my outfit. The only question when deciding on clothes is "Will he want to bang me if I wear this?" I then ponder if men really think they have any say in whether they get sex on a date. If I'm going to sleep with him, then all underwear must match and of course be clean. If not, then it doesn't matter a jot and I won't even shave my legs. I then remember I haven't actually shaved my legs. I decide to at least give myself the option to sleep with Alan and grab my razor. I take off my robe and became aware of my alarmingly untidy pubic region. The song "Monster" by the Automatic starts playing in my head.

7:10 p.m. I grab hair-removal lotion and as there's no time for any sort of landscaping I decide to get rid of the lot and shave my legs while it's working. One leg done and my lady parts are starting to nip. Nippy I can handle, but halfway through the second leg, I'm in the shower, shouting "FOR THE LOVE OF GOD GET THIS FUCKING STUFF OFF ME!"

7:15 p.m. Fifteen minutes to go and I've given my bits third-degree burns and can't sit down.

7:25 p.m. I've canceled with Alan and I'm sitting on some frozen veg. Veggies for my vag. Oh God, I'm never going to find a boyfriend.

I had to lie to Alan and say I'd suddenly become unwell and I hoped we could reschedule. Obviously he thought I'd changed my mind, and although he pretended to be fine about the whole thing, I imagined him drawing a Hitler mustache on my profile picture and moving on to someone else.

Oliver texted to say he was home early (hooray!) but seemed miffed that I had planned a date for the evening of his return. I wouldn't be able to do anything with him anyway given my current disability. I can't even sit on the couch properly, never mind anything else. God, this stings like crazy. Who the hell decided that it was more attractive for women to be hairless? I don't remember being asked. One minute we all have *The Joy of Sex*–style bushes and the next we're hair-free and sticking freakin' jewels and glitter all over our asses. I despair.

AUGUST

Monday, August 1

I've rearranged my date with Alan for tomorrow. Of course I didn't tell him what had actually happened, but luckily my downstairs disaster area feels a million times better. I swear I'd rather be bushy than attempt that again. Oliver's coming over on Wednesday—apparently he's bringing me a present. It had better not be his penis—I'm not sure I could stand being prodded or poked down there just yet. I thought he was going to start convulsing he laughed so hard down the phone when I told him.

"Ha-ha, have you got a little bandage on it?"

"Shut it and tell me tales of Chicago," I said, quickly changing the subject.

"Hmm. Was all right. Mostly work, although I did meet a woman there."

"There are lots of women in Chicago, I'd imagine. Be specific."

"Her name is Ruth, she's a model from London and she's coming up to see me in a couple of days."

"A model, huh? From London? Did you have beautiful-people sex then?"

"No, she was heading home the day after we met, but we really hit it off. Been doing the sexting thing for a while now."

"Spare me those details. So she's flying up from London? This is quite sudden, isn't it?"

"Not really. You're dating, why shouldn't I?"

"Fair point. Actually, this could work out well. Maybe we can double-date and—"

"Not a chance. I'm keeping her to myself. Right, I'm going now, still jet-lagged."

Click.

Hmph. Why did he have to mention she was a model? I'm telling him one of my dates is something really impressive like a spaceman. Or Jesus.

Tuesday, August 2

I took a taxi home after work to give myself plenty of time to get ready for my second attempt at a date with Alan. The plan was still the same: wear the blue dress, meet for dinner at Red Onion and be charmingly irresistible to the man with the perfectly proportioned face.

I arrived at the restaurant and Alan was waiting for me outside, nervously shuffling his feet in his brown loafers. At first I wasn't entirely sure it was him; this guy was almost bald compared to the man in the photo and his face was a lot thinner. I recognized his perfect teeth when he smiled, but it quickly became apparent that the photo he'd put on his profile was at least ten years old. This guy was in his late forties. I mean, why would you do that if you actually intend to meet up with someone in a place that has working lights? Why don't I listen to my friends?

Desperately trying not to look like a shallow bastard, I kissed him hello on the cheek and followed him into the restaurant, determined to have a nice evening regardless.

We were seated in the mezzanine and ordered drinks while we looked over the menu. The restaurant was dimly lit, cozy, and just busy enough to give it some atmosphere.

"Sea bass is excellent here," I said with a smile. "Any thoughts on what you're having?"

"Steak and skinny fries." He nodded, rolling up the sleeves on his black shirt. "You look lovely this evening."

"Thank you." I blushed. "How kind. You also scrub up well." And he did. Sure he might have been older than I expected, but by the time the food arrived and we began to eat, I began to think maybe not all was lost. That's when I glanced at his plate: his full, pathetically picked at, main-course-filled plate.

"Something wrong with your food?"

"Erm, no, it's nice. Very nice, I just have a small problem with food."

"But you ordered off the gluten-free menu. . . ."

"I did. It's not just that."

"No? That's intriguing." I laughed. "Tell me."

He frowned at me with his old face. "Basically I used to be fat, so I don't like eating in front of people . . . or eating in general. I just thought I'd get this out of the way right now."

He had suddenly become very intense and was staring at me, waiting for a response. I just looked at him . . . and then at the floor . . . and then at his plate.

"Wow . . . right . . . So are you going to finish that then?"

So while I ate his fries and waited for God's big Monty Python foot to squash me, I wondered why you'd take someone out for dinner on a first date when you have a food phobia? AND SHARE THIS INFORMATION WITH THAT PERSON?

Luckily I managed to finish the rest of my meal without any further phobias or traumatic childhood events emerging, but for me the date was well and truly over.

"Feel like a drink somewhere?" he asked, pulling on his leather jacket.

"I can't, I'm afraid," I lied. "I have to be up early. But thanks for a lovely meal. Was great meeting you."

"So, what, that's it?" He laughed in disbelief. "Can I see you again?"

"Probably not. You're a nice guy but I don't see this going anywhere, Alan. Sorry."

"It's because I said I used to be fat, isn't it?"

"Erm, no. It's just—"

"Oh, save it. You women are all the fucking same," he snapped. "Bitches, the lot of you. I'm out of here. Hope you enjoyed your meal."

Stunned, I watched him walk away, but not without shouting, "ACTUALLY, I ENJOYED YOUR MEAL MORE, YOU FUCKING ODDBALL!" I then realized shouting at an unstable man in the street probably wasn't a good idea and ran up an alley to hide.

I had a text conversation with Lucy on the taxi ride home.

Disaster. Guy was a fruitloop. It WAS his face however. In 2002.

LOL. Never mind. I told you internet dating was a bad idea.

If you use LOL again, we're going to have words. AND THIS WAS YOUR IDEA.

Oh yeah. Never mind eh? One down, 20k unhinged users to go. You're getting closer to your soulmate. I can feel it.

Ugh, at least I get to see Oliver tomorrow. Damn I've missed him.

Wednesday, August 3

Oliver brought me presents from Chicago. Wise move. A big present, which was a bag filled with stolen hotel stuff, and a smaller bag, which contained a blindfold and a pair of wrist restraints. "Nice to see that even when you're on the other side of the world, you're still invested in helping me. That's commitment."

"Well, bondage is still on the list, isn't it?" He grinned. "Unless you're finished with me now you want a boyfriend who'll be bad in bed but put up with your singing."

"What about Ruth? I doubt she'll be too happy with our arrangement."

"I doubt I'll tell her."

"Good, because I intend to see this thing through to the end. And you love my vocal stylings; they're what get you out of my apartment in the morning. Bondage is on, baby! And we still have another role play as well—any ideas?"

"I'll think about it, but right now I haven't had sex in a month, so I advise you to remove your jeans this instant before I explode. I warn you. It's going to be brutal."

So I did and I thought at one point he was going to devour me. It was like his last meal on death row. He threw my legs over his shoulders and went so deep I could hardly breathe, but it didn't last long. The second time lasted almost an hour though.

Thursday, August 4

Hugo Beale, the advertising director from London, flew up to Glasgow to meet with Frank today, which meant everyone was on their best behavior, including Lucy, who made it into work early for once. "That man scares me. He smiles at you but you know that behind the smile he's planning to have you killed."

It was true. He's a tall, thin man, well dressed and charismatic, who has nevertheless been given the nickname "Satan" by his staff in London, whom he scares and bewitches in equal measure.

He arrived at half past eleven, briefly taking the time to thank each of us for our tiny contribution to the *Post*'s vast empire before disappearing with Frank for lunch at Malmaison.

"I wonder why he's here," said Kelly, making sure they'd gone before taking her nail file out of her drawer. "Maybe Frank's getting the chop."

Lucy shook her head. "It'll be redundancy talk. Seventeen sales executives were laid off last month in Manchester."

The whole office stared at her. "I'm kidding!" she laughed. "Relax. Manchester doesn't even have seventeen sales staff. It's just his usual yearly meet with the regional managers."

Stuart started to laugh, much to Kelly's annoyance. "That wasn't funny, Lucy. You're playing with people's lives here. People who—"

"Need people?"

"What?" asked Kelly, bewildered.

"Are the luckiest people, in the world . . . Sing with me. . . ."

By this time I was in tears at Lucy's Barbra Streisand impersonation and Kelly had stormed out of the office in her usual dramatic fashion. Lucy bowed and returned to her computer like nothing had happened. I really need to watch *Funny Girl* again.

Frank and Hugo returned two hours later with wine for everyone and a "keep up the good work" motivational speech given by Hugo, who more than likely didn't know any of our names and was obviously desperate to get back to That London.

After Hugo left, I heard Lucy and Frank arguing in his office just before half five. Every year Lucy books a last-minute vacation on her own—a week of sun, sea, and her iPod. It's like her little ritual. This year she's chosen Greece, but Frank wouldn't sign her vacation form because it was short notice.

"Frank, no one is off next week, I've checked the vacation board."

"That may be, but you're a separate department from sales. I need time to organize someone to do the admin."

"We had this discussion last year when I went to France and the year before that when I booked last minute to Rome. Maureen takes over the figures and Kelly runs the reports. I DO THIS EVERY YEAR."

"Well, not this year," he replied stubbornly.

"I've already booked it. I'm going."

"Then I'll have no choice but to fire you," he said, rising from his chair indignantly.

"You said that last year. But fine. Fire me."

"What?"

"I said, 'Fire me.' If it's less hassle for you to find some-one, interview them, hire them, and train them than it is to let me take my annual leave, then go for it." She folded her arms and began tapping her fingers on her forearm.

He sat back down. "You said that last year, didn't you?"

"I've marked my days on the board. See you in a week."

She left his office and walked past my desk, giving me a little wink. I wanted to climb up onto my desk and applaud her, but I'm not as brave as she is, and the last time Frank threatened to fire me we ended up screwing, so I sat quietly and got ready to leave work.

When I got home I checked my e-mails and scary Alan had emailed me twice; the first included "fat" pictures of himself to show me his weight loss and in the second he asked me out again. Neither e-mail had an apology for his psychotic outburst. I sent a polite but firm 'I'm not inter-ested but thanks anyway, you nut case.' And why on Earth would I want to see his before-and-after weight-loss pic-tures? Maybe it sounds a tad harsh, but give me a fucking break.

Saturday, August 6

"Are you awake? Let's do something today."

"Oliver?" I mumbled, looking at my bedside clock, "it's eight a.m. Why are you calling me in the middle of the night?"

"It's a beautiful, warm, sunny day, grumpy ass. Let's go out. I'll pick you up in an hour."

Two hours later we were stuck in traffic, heading toward the seaside. "Jesus fuck," said Oliver, banging his fists on the steering wheel. "Did everyone in Scotland decide to come here today?"

"Looks like it," I answered, turning on the radio. "Ooh, I love this song."

"Since when did you start liking Girls Aloud?"

"Since they did this song."

"Fine, have it on; just don't sing."

"Why not?"

"Two reasons: one—I hate this song; two—you sing in the key of pish."

"How dare you. I have singing skills. There's obviously something very wrong with your ears. And taste in music. How can you hate this song? That's like hating happiness."

Twenty minutes later we arrived at the beach and found a place to park. I stepped out of the car and breathed in the sea air, which instantly took me back to beach visits with my parents when I was a kid.

"God, I haven't been here for years. I remember eating ice cream and writing my name in the sand when I was about seven. I made a sand castle and put a dead crab in the wee moat around it."

"How chilling."

"Shut up. I didn't kill it."

"The beaches in Dublin were great. My auntie lived close to Dollymount and I'd spend weekends there with my cousins before we moved to Glasgow. We played football constantly."

"Sounds nice. I'd love to go to Dublin one day."

"I'll take you with me next time I go back. We can stay with Megan—I remember when she visited last year; you spent more time with her than I did."

"I love your sister. She's so pretty. Are there any ugly people in your family, Oliver?"

"Yeah, my cousin Colin is a bit unfortunate-looking, though I think he might have been adopted. Funny as hell though, and has a huge knob so he still gets the women."

I placed my bright-blue towel on the sand and sat down. "God, this is bliss," I said, closing my eyes and turning my face toward the delightfully warm sun. Oliver sat beside me and kicked off his sneakers.

"What are you smiling at?" he asked.

"The sun. On my face. It makes me happy."

"You're fucking adorable. I'm going paddling."

"We're in Scotland. The water will be subzero, regardless of how sunny it is."

"Yeah, I know, but you have to go paddling. It's the law of the beach!" he proclaimed, opening some sandwiches. "Here, I brought you chicken and sweet corn."

"My favorite. You are lovely."

"I know. You eat—I'm going in the water."

He rolled his jeans up to his knees and walked away across the sand toward the sea. I began eating, watching families play with their children and glaring at the seagulls already circling like vultures for my sandwich crusts. This day was perfect. Looking across to the water's edge, I saw Oliver take out his phone and start texting, smiling to himself. My mood suddenly changed. I felt my temper rise and thought to myself angrily, He's texting that Ruth woman. We've only been here five fucking minutes and he's already making other plans.

Then I felt my own phone vibrate in my pocket:

The water's freezing. Get your ass over here and warm me up.

I got up and walked toward him, carefully avoiding broken shells until I was ankle-deep in cold, calm seawater.

"Arghh! I cannot believe you made me come in here. My feet are numb!"

"Me mum always said that saltwater was good for the feet." He smiled. "And the soul. Draws out all the bad energy or something."

"That sounds like something my mum would say." I laughed. "Must be something about being born in the '50s that turns you—"

My inane observations were cut short as Oliver suddenly placed his hand on the back of my neck, pulled me in, and kissed me. It was firm at first but then became so slow and soft I felt my entire body tingle with pleasure. I moved my hand up to his face and kissed him back with an urgency I couldn't explain. Usually kissing Oliver was reserved for pre-sex buildup, but this time it felt different. There was no groping or expectation; it was just two people standing in the sea, making out under a bright-blue sky, totally unaware that nearby the seagulls had shat all over their nice clean towels.

By six the weather finally remembered that it was Scotland and began to turn chilly. I smiled to myself as Oliver wrapped his hooded top around me without even asking if I was cold. We gathered our things together and walked leisurely back to the car, past quaint gift shops, bed and breakfasts, and cafés.

"Ice cream!" I exclaimed, spotting a large 99 poster in a cafe window. "Wait here."

I ran in and purchased two cones from an elderly woman who expertly operated the Mr. Whippy machine, despite quite obviously not being able to see two inches in front of her.

"Two pounds, son," she said, holding out the cones.

Son? I thought about protesting but the ice cream was already starting to drip, so I took the cones and made my escape.

"If you drip that in my car, you're in trouble," said Oliver, taking his cone and licking the side.

"What if I drip it on my breasts?" I asked, staring at his tongue.

"Then you're definitely in trouble," he said, raising one eyebrow. "You're coming home with me. It's decided."

"Good. I'm horny now. Drive quickly."

He started the car and we began the journey home. We were almost back in Glasgow when he suddenly yelled, "FUCK! I completely forgot Ruth's flying up tonight! I'm supposed to collect her at the airport at eleven."

I felt like I'd just been punched in the face. I'd been having such a perfect day.

"Well, that sucks." I pouted. "But it's fine." It wasn't fine.

"If she wasn't flying up, I'd cancel on her, but I can't now. That would be a shitty thing to do and—"

"Honestly, it's OK. I have a million things to do anyway. We'll do it another time."

He dropped me home and I went inside, still peeved that I'd been dropped for Ruth.

As those "million things" I had to do didn't technically exist, I slipped out of my clothes and into a yellow romper and slumped down on the couch. As I turned on the TV and flicked through endless channels of crap, I wanted to scream with frustration. It was then that I vowed I'd never be left alone on a Saturday night again, dressed like a giant toddler.

Sunday, August 7

I've joined a new and freakin'-expensive, seemingly-filled-with-hot-men dating site. I've only joined for a month, though; even I'm not stupid enough to hang around on one of these sites for six months in the hope that someday my prince will log on. Still, after only a few hours I've already arranged two dates. Hazel seemed puzzled by this when she came 'round for coffee with Grace.

"You've arranged them on consecutive days? Why?"

"Because I'm determined not to mess about with this and I had nothing planned for Friday and Saturday night anyway. Might as well use my time productively, don't you think?"

"I suppose so. What happened to dating one man at a time? Where's the excitement? Where's the romance?" she asked, giving Grace a plastic spoon and cup to play with.

"I'm not looking for excitement and romance, Hazel, I'm looking for a boyfriend. Those things never last anyway—that's if they even exist in the first place. I just want someone I like to spend time with."

"And keep Alex off your back too?" She smiled. "I'm sure Oliver would be happy to oblige there."

"He would but he's dating a model. Anyway, Alex knows Oliver and I are just friends. He needs to know I've both physically and mentally moved on."

Hazel moved Grace onto the floor to let her play. "I think Alex would be less likely to annoy you if he found out you were sleeping with Oliver. I'd imagine Oliver's quite intimidating to most men."

"It wouldn't work. Alex wouldn't believe for a second that someone like Oliver would sleep with me. He'd know it was a lie."

"Um. Phoebs?" she said. "It isn't a lie. You are sleeping with him."

"Yes, but not for real. He's only helping me out with my list. He's doing me a favor."

Hazel looked sad. "Phoebe, this is real. Your lack of self-worth astonishes me sometimes. Oliver is more than happy to be sleeping with you; it isn't some sort of pity fuck." She quickly glanced at Grace to make sure the F-word hadn't made her daughter spontaneously combust. "I think it's great that you're dating—just make sure you're doing it for the right reasons."

She left when Grace began to nod off and I thought about what she'd said. I know she means well, but I know what's best for me. I think.

Monday, August 8

Got into work and there was an e-mail from Lucy!

From: Lucy Jacobs
To: Phoebe Henderson
Subject: Hello!

It's 28 degrees over here muthaaafuccckkkaaa! Hotel is superb—right on the beach and I might never come back. I'm drinking a pineapple cocktail right now and it's only eleven in the morning. Don't bother replying. I only wanted to brag about the weather—I won't be checking my email for a whole week now.

Byee! xx

I walked into the conference room, trying not to feel jealous that Lucy was living it up somewhere sunny while I was stuck here.

The morning meeting went like this:

1. Frank announced Lucy was on vacation. Kelly would be running reports.
2. Kelly tutted and shuffled some blank paper.
3. Frank went over sales figures for the week. Kelly moaned that Lucy was on vacation and now her workload had doubled.
4. Frank told Kelly to stop complaining, as she only had to push three buttons at quarter to five.
5. Kelly tutted. Frank exhaled.
6. Brian's stomach made a noise like a cat. I laughed until I couldn't breathe.
7. Frank left the room.

I have no idea how we all manage to function on any level. We're hopeless.

This evening was reserved for pampering, given that I had two dates at the end of the week. I had to do my eyebrows, give myself a facial, and do something about the hairs that had appeared on my big toe. I had just applied a face pack and begun painting my nails dark blue when the phone rang.

"Hello. What's happening?"

"Hello, Oliver. Not much. Just stuff."

"Stuff? Sexy stuff? I want details."

"No. I'm painting my nails and preparing my sagging face for my TWO dates this week. Is that enough detail?"

"Are you using that green stuff on your face? Man, that stuff is scary. When it cracks you look like Dana escaping from that demon dog in *Ghostbusters*."

"Don't make me laugh," I snorted. "It's still drying."

"Hang on, two dates?" asked Oliver. "You mean business."

"Indeed." I nodded. "I'm paying for this—I intend to get my money's worth." I put the phone to my other ear and continued painting my nails. "But I was thinking—we still have the bondage challenge left to do and a final role play. Any thoughts?"

"Nope, I'm now thinking of all the dastardly things I'm going to do to you in the bondage challenge."

"Like what?" I asked. "Don't do anything weird like punch me or drip hot wax on me."

"You'll see." He laughed. "Anyway, you're not the only one who has plans this week—Ruth has decided to stay on for a few days."

I stopped painting. "Don't you feel bad about having her there and arranging this with me?"

"Not at the moment, no."

"So you'll be off-limits until when? That woman is ruining my sex life, Oliver. Where is she just now?"

"At the shops. She's heading back for a shoot on Saturday, so just a week. I'm working on Sunday so e-mail me Monday."

"Will do. Hang on . . . Is this getting serious with Ruth?"

"Speak later."

He hung up without answering. We're going to have to do these challenges soon before he marries that Ruth girl and she spoils all my fun. Now he's busy all week as well as Lucy being on vacation? Fuckssake. I have really inconsiderate friends.

Friday, August 12

Oh, just kill me now. Tonight was awful. For my first date I found out I was being taken to a midnight showing of some hypnotist act with a shit name, my idea of hell, but Matthew wasn't to know that. He thought it was inventive, but unless it's Derren Brown I really have no time for showmen.

Matthew was a stereotypical lad, another thing that's high up on my list of pet hates (just below hypnotists). But he had a cool jacket and complimented my hair, which was enough to win me over sufficiently to hope he'd get me pissed at the bar. No such luck. We walked straight past the bar (damn him) and got settled in our seats. At least I had an aisle seat so I could make a dash for it if it came to the worst. Forty-five minutes into the show I was politely laughing at some poor bastard who was acting like a chicken onstage, when the hypnotist turned his terrible mustached attention to the fat guy beside chicken boy pretending to be asleep.

"When you wake up on the count of three, you'll think you're Superman, racing to save a damsel in distress. . . . One, two, three!"

My polite laughing face quickly changed to one of sheer horror as Superman raced up the aisle, threw me over his shoulder in some kind of gymnastic fireman's lift, and carried me back to the stage, during which my skirt was hitched up and my underwear revealed to the entire audience. Being laughed at by two hundred people because a fat man picked me up is not my idea of fun. Neither is being told by the middle-aged hypnotist that he "definitely would" while my date almost pissed his pants laughing and then proceeded to go to the bar afterward and talk about my underwear to other men. He continued snorting all the way home, by which time I'd made it clear there would be no second date but thanks for a humiliating evening. Stupid hypnosis.

I now cannot believe I thought it was a good idea to arrange another date with a different man tomorrow. I might not have fully recovered from this one. What was I thinking?

Saturday, August 13

I made a point of asking my second date, Craig, where we were going tonight—I wasn't taking any chances after last night's fiasco. We agreed to meet in a small but trendy bar in town and I arrived there ten minutes early so I didn't have to be the one walking around on my own like a tit, looking for someone who resembled a photo I'd once seen. Unlike Alan, his picture was recent but he'd lied about his height, and his build. He was around the same height as me and twice as wide. Not the six foot, slim build he'd lied about online. However, determined not to be so freakin' shallow, I accepted a drink and we sat down. Craig was forty-one, a stockbroker who absolutely loved the sound of his own voice. That man went on and on and fucking on for hours about himself, what he did, what he thought, and only asked me questions so he could then disagree and tell me his reasons for doing so. His love of whisky meant he got hammered extremely quickly and then started prattling on about some twenty-five-year-old politics student called Mia who had rejected him and he couldn't understand why. By the time I'd finished my third drink it was time to go.

"Why are you going? I thought we were getting on," he slurred.

"No offense, Craig, but you've been going on and on about this Mia girl all night. I think perhaps you should get her out of your system before you start dating."

"Oh. OH! I see what this is! I see what's happening here," he announced as I put on my jacket. "You wish you were Mia."

"What?" I asked, totally confused. "What are you talking about?"

"You're jealous. You wish you were Mia."

"I fucking wish YOU were Mia, babe. At least she sounds vaguely interesting."

I actually made a sort of frustrated yelp out loud as I left the pub and caught the last train home with all the other losers.

This is tougher than I anticipated. So far I've been out with a shouty man with an eating disorder, a man who laughed at my underwear, and a boring man who was pining for someone else. I'm clearly a terrible judge of online character. At least with Oliver I know exactly where I stand. Why aren't all men like him?

Monday, August 15

Lucy is back! She was sitting at her desk when I walked into work this morning, wearing a summer dress and sporting at least seventeen new freckles.

"I've missed you!" I shrieked. "How was it? When did you get back?"

"My flight got in at one last night so I'm shattered, but it was brilliant. Total 'me' time: I slept late, sunbathed, hardly spoke to a single person all week, and ate the most amazing food. You'd have loved it. I'll e-mail you pictures once I get around to downloading them."

Frank also looked happy to see Lucy, given that Kelly had been nipping his head about admin the entire week.

He wandered over, carrying a green coffee mug. "You look well," he said graciously. "If you want to come into my office at ten, I'll run through last week with you."

"Blimey! What have you done with the real Frank?" She laughed.

He frowned at her.

"Oh. There he is," she added quietly.

"Let's get on, shall we, girls?" he requested, leaving the coffee cup on her desk and walking away.

"No problem, boss," she replied, lifting his cup and dropping it into her bin. "It's good to be back."

Around three I remembered I'd said I'd e-mail Oliver. Today was the day that Ruth would be making her way down south, leaving him free to continue his sterling work on my list.

From: Phoebe Henderson
To: Oliver Webb
Subject: Hello

My dates were awful. Ghastly. Is Ruth away now? Did your week go well? Please say no and make me feel better.

P x

From: Oliver Webb
To: Phoebe Henderson
Subject: Re: Hello

My week was awesome. Yeah, she's gone back down to London. Ruth's great. I'll definitely be seeing her again. Re. Dates: I hate to say it but I TOLD YOU SO. Internet dating is weird—you don't need it.

From: Phoebe Henderson
To: Oliver Webb
Subject: Re: Hello

Awww, that's nice! Is she moving in? Do you love her and want to marry her?

From: Oliver Webb
To: Phoebe Henderson
Subject: Re: Hello

When have I ever been in love? But now she's away we can do the bondage challenge. K'TSH! That was the noise of a whip btw.

A whip? What the fuck does he have planned?

Tuesday, August 16

9 p.m. I'm sitting here looking into this bondage lark and have no idea where to begin. The Internet is full of leather-clad women looking grumpy and men looking frightened, which doesn't help. I don't want Oliver to think I'm going to tie him to the bed and break his ankles. So I'm about to watch some bondage porn and hope I get some ideas.

9:15 p.m. Argh! CLAMPS!

9:45 p.m. Right. Forget it. I am NOT doing that.
  I called Oliver. "Jesus, what the fuck are you watching? What? No, Phoebe, I don't want to clamp your labia. Listen, just calm down and stop watching S&M videos. I'll find you something else."
  Half an hour later he sent me a link to a video that was much, MUCH better. No pain, no gagging and no damn

clamping. We've agreed that he's going to be submissive for once in his life, and I'm going to be the dominatrix. I get to be shouty. I LOVE BEING SHOUTY!

Wednesday, August 17

As I got dressed for this evening's challenge, I realized two things: (1) Attempting to put on a corset by yourself is a challenge in itself, and (2) I was very excited about getting to play with Oliver again. I applied a second coat of bright-red lipstick before rushing around to get my bedroom ready, occasionally pulling at the black thong that was annoyingly riding up my bottom every few minutes. My raspberry-pink bedsheets had been replaced with borrowed black-satin ones, and I'd dotted black candles around the room for a gothic feel. Just as I finished zipping up my knee-high boots, the doorbell rang. I answered, blindfold and restraints in hand.

Thank fuck it was Oliver.

"Wow, Phoebe, you—"

"Shut up and go to the bedroom," I demanded forcefully. Scaring even myself a little.

Once in the bedroom I ordered him to undress slowly while I watched. I must admit, seeing him strip while looking a tad nervous was a total turn-on. He stood there naked. God, I love his cock.

"Phoebe? PHOEBE? What now?"

"Hmm? Oh yeah. Lie on the bed. Close your eyes."

I tied both his hands to the bedpost, covered his eyes with the blindfold, and hastily adjusted my thong. "Lie there. Don't fucking move."

Then I went into the kitchen and had a cigarette, pretending it was part of the game but really I had no idea what

I was going to do next; I needed a better game plan than blow jobs and yelling. That, and I really wanted a cigarette. My brief but eye-opening look at bondage videos had made me realize that I was never going to be an ass-whipping, ball-crushing, face-sitting dominatrix, but I could give it my best shot. I brought back a cup of cold water and a cup of warm water and set them down on the bedside table. I could see him squirming slightly, wondering what the hell I was doing. I then gave him a hot and cold blow job which went: mouthful of warm water followed by mouthful of cold water. I saw it on the net. Good, eh? Well, it must have been as I've never heard him moan so loudly. Then I ran my tongue over every inch of his body, telling him what a filthy, dirty boy he was. He started to struggle with the restraints.

"STOP IT!" I shouted, and then leaned in to whisper in his ear. "Listen," I said, "I get to do whatever I like. You don't even get to touch me." Then I kissed him hard and straddled him. I fucked him slowly and he even let me put my finger up his ass. Which felt weird but I coped by not looking directly at it, like the final scene from *Raiders of the Lost Ark*.

When we'd finished he said, "Undo my wrists. I need to feel you." So I did and we lay down in bed and cuddled and listened to Johnny Cash. Fucking cuddled? Dominatrixes don't cuddle and listen to Johnny Cash; we are complete bastards and we listen to Rammstein.

Friday, August 19

Today dragged on. Every customer I called was either on vacation or had already left for the day, leaving me twiddling my thumbs and counting down the minutes until wine o'clock. Lucy and I planned to go for half-price cocktails in Merchant City. I grabbed a seat in the courtyard while Lucy fetched our drinks. Relieved to no longer be at work, I kicked off my shoes and happily wiggled my toes under the table, savoring my half-price mojito. I was listening to her yabbering on about her latest man, a tree surgeon who can hold her up with one arm while they're screwing, when I felt a tap on my shoulder. It was James: baked-bean-phobic James. I couldn't believe it! With nearly 600,000 people living in Glasgow, you'd think I'd be able to avoid bumping into the ghosts of boyfriends past. "Phoebe! I can't believe it. God, it's been forever. Are you good?"

It'd been ten years since we went out, but he hadn't changed. Well, perhaps grayer, but that's not a bad thing. Our relationship was fun at times but it finally ended when I realized that behind the gorgeous exterior lay a man with no discernible personality and a tendency to refer to his "sack" a lot. Beyond annoying. "How are you, James?" I asked, rising to hug him. "Wow. What are you up to these days? Sorry, this is my friend Lucy."

He lowered himself into the empty chair beside Lucy, shaking her hand. "Still in the building trade, but I took over the company after Dad retired. You?"

"Newspaper sales. It's dreadful. So, are you married?"

"No. You?"

"No."

"Good. We should catch up properly. How about dinner tomorrow? My place?"

From the corner of my eye I could see Lucy grinning, so mostly for reasons of nostalgia and curiosity I agreed.

"Great. Here's my number. Text me your address and I'll pick you up. Sorry to run, but I'm already late to meet a customer. Nice to meet you, Lucy." And with that he was off.

"He's cute. You'll bang him," Lucy observed, taking a sip of wine. "Big windaes, Phoebe; I can see that one coming a mile off."

"Not necessarily," I replied. "We broke up for a reason, remember?"

"Well, I didn't know you or him back then, but from what I've just seen, he's fucking fit. I would."

"He did look good, didn't he?" I grinned stupidly.

I've certainly changed in ten years. How could he not have? Maybe this is a sign?! I said I wanted a boyfriend, I didn't stipulate it had to be a new one. . . . Why did we break up again?

Saturday, August 20

James picked me up tonight, we got a takeaway and spent the entire car journey to his place chatting about old times and unashamedly eyeing each other up. Despite thinking that he'd been a twat all those years ago, I couldn't see any evidence of it now; perhaps I'd been too harsh. I still found him enormously attractive. I went into his tiny kitchen with him to help plate up dinner and as I reached up to get a glass from the shelf, he took me by surprise and kissed me. It was awful—wet, sloppy and it felt like he was tonguing my entire face. I gingerly moved away from his mouth and wandered back into the living room, wondering whether he used to kiss like that and I'd just known no better at the time or blocked the experience from my memory. We began to eat and it took exactly fifteen minutes to remember the rest of the reason why dumping him was the smartest move I've ever made. He said "sack" seven times (I counted), ate with his mouth open, and when he started to tell me that his girlfriend of three years was at a wedding in India I practically had a fit and left promptly with a "fuck you" and the prawn crackers. WHY DO I BOTHER?

Monday, August 22

I had flowers delivered for me to the office today. Me! Flowers! A huge bunch of pink lilies, smelling like heaven and wrapped in a bow. This has never happened before and I'm sure the look of confusion on my face was apparent to the rest of the office.

Kelly stood up at her desk. "Are they for you? Who sent them? They're a bit much."

"They're gorgeous!" squealed Lucy. "Do you have a secret admirer?"

"I have no idea!" I answered excitedly. "Let me read the card."

I'm sorry. Alex xx

My heart sank and my face began to flush. The entire office stared at me, waiting for me to announce the sender. "They're from my mum," I said. "No mystery man. Just my mum."

Lucy walked over and took the card out of my hand. She read it, and then placed it back in the tiny envelope.

"How very thoughtful." She smiled. "I'll just go and put these in some water for you."

That was the last I saw of those flowers.

When Oliver came over this evening, I was so annoyed we ended up fighting.

"It's not my fault he sent you flowers. Why the fuck are you shouting at me?"

"Because there's no one else here and I'm angry about this whole sorry mess. I thought they were from you. Why the fuck couldn't you have sent me the flowers?"

"Why the fuck would I send you flowers? You're insane. And sweaty in that jumper."

I made a frustrated groan and pulled the jumper over my head, leaving me standing in my bra and jeans with my hair messed up. "Happy now?"

"You're a sexy bitch. Shut the fuck up," he said, and threw me on the floor, where we had really angry sex. Afterward I apologized. Not for being a sexy bitch, for being a dickhead.

"He's just playing mind games with you. Do you want me to have a word with him?"

"No, don't, Oliver. I don't want to give him any reason to get in touch with me."

"Don't let him mess with you. Not again, Phoebe. You're far too good for him, I hope you know that."

"I know," I said, looking at Oliver. "Sometimes I wonder if the big love of my life was that weasel. What a depressing thought."

He remained silent for a while, and when I got up to use the bathroom he said, "What happens when you finish your list? Do we just stop this?"

"I suppose so."

And for a fleeting moment I hoped he'd come up with a reason not to stop. But he didn't. Why would he? He has Ruth now.

Thursday, August 25

So I texted Alex telling him, once again, that I'm not interested. I've been tempted to tell Miss Tits what he's been up to, but I know he'd say that I sent the flowers myself and I'll end up looking like a psycho. This year was supposed to be about getting rid of the old and starting anew, but that bastard won't let me forget him.

Tuesday, August 30

Things are looking up! I had a BRILLIANT date tonight with a guy from the Internet called Barry. I'm still stunned and spent the evening expecting that freakin' hypnotist to appear, click his fingers, and turn him into a moron.

We went for dinner, then cocktails, and then he kissed me at the station before I caught my last train home, texting me ten minutes later to ask when he could see me again. KEEN! He was shy, funny, has a sensible job, and is pretty much the complete opposite of the guys I usually go for, but I'm feeling quite smitten.

Oliver called me as I walked home and I told him all about it. "Barry? How can you be passionate about someone called Barry?"

"What the hell is your problem, Oliver? I have my first brilliant date in ages and all you can do is make snide comments."

"I'm only kidding, Phoebs. Christ, have we met? Every date I've ever had you've taken the mick out of! Pedro? That Sandra girl, Ruth . . . and remember Tash in high school? What was it you used to call her?" He waited for a response.

"Gash," I replied quietly.

"That's right, and when I went out with Joanna a couple of years ago you said I couldn't have sex with someone whose name rhymes with banana. This is what we do, Phoebe, so don't go getting all bitchy on me now."

"OK, I'm sorry, but you never took any of your girlfriends even remotely seriously, so how the fuck was I supposed to? I like this guy—just leave the jokes until later, yeah?"

"Fine. Whatever. I'm off anyway. Safe home."

I feel stupid now. I don't know why his comment bothered me so much. I just wish he could have just been happier for me. I'm also bothered by the fact that I didn't feel like dragging Barry back home after the date, but my sensible side thinks taking things slow for once could be a good thing. My current liberal "free boobs for all" attitude is a far cry from the old Phoebe, who would never have considered screwing on a first date, but she's still in there somewhere, telling me that boys don't want to have relationships with women who give it up so quickly.

Will I be able to control my urges and take it slowly with someone? I might have to have my libido removed with tweezers like in that "Operation" game if there's any hope of me pulling this off.

SEPTEMBER

Thursday, September 1

I have another date with Barry on Saturday. Now every time I say "Barry" I try to make it sound sexy just to prove Oliver wrong. I'm sure he's extremely sexual, but I intend to play it cool and not jump him and ride him like a stolen BMX.

Lucy and I discussed my plans for self-restraint over toasted sandwiches in the canteen at lunchtime. "I don't see the point in waiting," remarked Lucy, pushing her pitiful side salad around on her plate. "What if you fall in love with this guy, sleep with him and it's a disaster? Do you want my tomato?"

I nodded and stabbed it with my fork. "Fuck, Lucy, I'm only planning on waiting a bit, not until my wedding night."

"Well, don't wait too long," she said very seriously. "Your vagina will close up."

"Enough about me. What's happening with your love life? Tree surgeon still on the scene?"

"Kyle? Yup. I'm seeing him again on Saturday."

"Kyle is a good name," I said wistfully. "It's better than Barry."

"Most names are." She smirked. "Kyle's just hot as hell. He says I'm a force of nature."

"Like a tsunami?"

"Probably." She laughed. "Listen, I once dated a Nigel. That's worse. I tried to just call him 'N,' but he wouldn't let me. Call him Baz or B or something if it bothers you that much."

"It didn't until Oliver made fun of it, but now it's stuck in my head."

"You two are like children! Stop listening to him and go and enjoy your date. If you really like him, it won't bother you one iota. What time is it?"

I looked at my phone. "Almost one. I suppose we'd better head back." Lucy gulped down the last of her Diet Coke and grabbed her gray jacket from the back of her chair. "I expect details on your date tomorrow, even if it doesn't involve anything salacious."

"It won't. I'm going to be very well behaved. I can totally do this."

"What if he makes the first move? Are you going to push him away and tell him you want to wait?" She placed her hands on her chest and cried dramatically, "NO, BARRY. WE MUSTN'T. NOT HERE! NOT NOW!"

"Maybe," I replied, embarrassed that everyone was now staring at us. "I could make him wait."

"Liar!" She laughed, propping open the canteen door for me. "You'd be bouncing on him like a 1970s space hopper the second he made a move."

She knows me so well. After work I got to play the exciting game of "where the fuck are my keys?" outside my apartment in the pissing rain. Once I'd angrily emptied the contents of my handbag onto the doorstep I finally found them in the lining of my coat pocket.

One long, hot shower later, I was snuggled up on the sofa eating strawberries and laughing loudly at a Dylan Moran DVD that Oliver had left at my apartment ages ago. The man is a genius and has confirmed my affection for funny dark-haired Irish men. I should have put that in my dating profile.

Saturday, September 3

For some reason I thought having a quick nap before getting ready for my date was a good idea. I lay down on the couch at three and woke up at six, groggy and with cushion imprints all over my face. We were due to meet at seven, which only left time for a quick shower but no leg shaving or hair washing. Still, I figured that by remaining hairy I'd eliminate any chance of sleeping with him, regardless of how much I drank.

Roughly seventeen seconds after leaving the house it started to rain, leaving me with no option but to hide in a bus shelter and call a cab from there. There was no way I was turning up to this date smelling like bus.

I got there five minutes late but he hadn't arrived either so I had time to run to the bathroom and check my hair for rain-induced frizzing. Luckily it had survived the downpour but my dress was damp. I attempted to dry it under the hand dryers while reapplying my lippy at the same time. One final check in the full-length mirror revealed toilet paper clinging to the heel of my boot and lipstick on my teeth. I am perfection.

I returned to the bar, ordered a Jack and Coke, and sat down at a table on my own like a soggy loser.

By seven thirty he still hadn't appeared and I was on my second Jack Daniel's. I was almost dry and also starving. I called him but his cell just rang out. I thought about buying some overpriced Pringles and then decided against it when I realized I'd look like a sad case, sitting eating chips on my own in a bar on a Saturday night. Eight arrived and I knew I had been officially stood up. Two of the chairs at my table had been swiped by people who actually had friends and I felt like a complete idiot—no—a totally humiliated idiot. As I rang him one last time I felt a tap on my shoulder. "Been stood up then?" I swung around and there was Alex. My heart leapt into my mouth, then landed in my stomach with a massive thud.

"Oh for God's sake, what are you doing here? Following me now?" I snapped at him.

He rolled his eyes. "Hardly. I'm here with Rob. Remember Rob?" he asked, pointing at a drunken man in tight jeans propping up the bar. Freakin' Rob, I had always disliked him. He was a music writer, a total snob who pretty much hated every band except Radiohead and would bore us all rigid, practically jizzing himself over Thom Yorke. He only put up with me because I liked the Flaming Lips and he could "tolerate" them, like I should be grateful for his acceptance.

"Sure, I remember Rob," I replied with very little enthusiasm. "What do you want, Alex? I've already told you I'm not interested. I don't want your flowers or your e-mails, so what the hell do you want?"

He sat down in Barry's seat, or at least it would have been Barry's seat had he shown up. Damn him.

"Just to talk, Phoebe. Just give me five minutes and then I'll go if you want me to."

"No."

"Please. Look, it'll pass the time until your friend gets here."

Stupidly, I hesitated. Five minutes turned into three hours. We chatted, we argued, more drinks were bought, and Rob disappeared, no doubt up his own bottom.

"Where is she, then? Your fiancée?" I asked, slurring my words, "Tits weighing her broomstick down?" He looked down at the table.

"She's in Manchester on a hen night. Actually things aren't going—"

"Oh, I freakin' knew it!" I shouted triumphantly. "That's what all the e-mails have been about! What, she's not enough for you now?" I waited while he finished his pint.

"It's not that . . . I mean, ever since I saw you in the shop that day. You're so different now. Look, Phoebs, I miss you. I was an idiot. I know I can't undo what I did, but if I could I would, and, well—"

I cut him off in midsentence. "Stop waffling, Alex. What's done is done. We've both moved on."

"Have you moved on, Phoebe?" he asked, looking me straight in the eye, "because I don't know if I have. Not really."

He touched my hand and I didn't pull away. I wanted to cry. Partly because I was so very drunk and fucking starving, but there was another part of me that had secretly hoped one day he'd miss me, just like he was claiming to now.

Of course, being me, this should end with me putting on some sunglasses, picking up a suitcase, and declaring, "Sorry, Alex, I have to go. My country needs me," before swanning off. Oh no, I did what any confused, pissed girl would do. We went to a hotel and I slept with him—hairy legs and all.

Sunday, September 4

I woke up next to Alex this morning. He was still peacefully asleep, facing away from me with one leg hanging out of the bed. I stared at the back of his head for ages. His brown hair was now much shorter, his shoulders still wide and freckled with a single annoying hair sticking out below a new tattoo. Some sort of Chinese writing. I went through possibilities of what it might say: "Warrior," "Peace," "Eater of souls" . . . "Susan"? I felt my stomach start to churn at the realization that I was now just like her. *I* was the other woman. My level of disgust for both of us overwhelmed me and I sat up.

"Eurgh," Alex groaned. "Where are you going?"

"Get up," I said sharply. "It's time to go."

He reached down and picked up his watch from the floor. "We don't check out till eleven. It's only half eight. We have ages yet."

"Do what you like. I'm leaving now."

I stood up and walked to the bathroom, stepping over last night's tangled clothing. Hazy flashbacks of him undressing me, kissing me, touching me, came creeping into my head as I closed the door behind me and turned on the shower. There was a knock on the bathroom door.

"Feel like some company?"

"No."

He strode in anyway and finally I understood Hazel's annoyance at not being able to shower in peace. He put his arms around my waist and whispered: "Last night was phenomenal."

"Was it? I was too drunk to recall."

"Well, it was and I'm so glad you've finally forgiven me."

I pushed his arms away. "I'm not sure I have. Last night was a result of too much alcohol. Now, can you let me shower, please?"

He pulled me in again, the shower running beside us. "Nah, last night is something we'll both remember for years to come."

Again, I pulled away. "I don't want to remember this for years to come. I don't want any new memories of you! Do you know how hard it's been to deal with the old ones?"

He lowered the toilet seat and sat down. "Phoebe, we're good together. This past year has made me realize that I made a huge mistake—not just my affair—the fact that I didn't even try to work things out with you. I just never imagined just how much I'd miss you."

And then he started to cry. He fucking cried, and I just stood in silence as the bathroom began to fill with steam, not knowing what to do. So I cried too.

I got home at twenty past twelve, feeling completely drained. I'd left Alex in the hotel, telling him I had to think things over, and caught a taxi home. My phone had died during the night so I plugged it in to charge and almost immediately it began to ring. It was Barry.

"I'm so sorry, Phoebe. My sister went into labor and I had to take her to hospital because she's on her own. I forgot my phone and I feel terrible. I hope you didn't hang around for too long."

"No," I lied. "I thought something must have come up, don't worry about it."

"You sure? I feel awful about this."

I took a deep breath and said, "Of course. New baby, eh? How exciting!"

"She did well. Listen, I'm just going back over with some clothes, but I'll call you later if that's OK? We can rearrange then."

I used the last of my fake cheery voice to say, "No problem. Speak soon!" and then threw myself onto my bed. So while Barry was off helping to bring new life into the world I was trying to raise an old life from the dead, one I thought I'd left behind. I have no idea what I'm going to do.

Monday, September 5

I decided to have everyone over for a roast this evening. I made up an excuse about having some lamb I had to use up, but really I just didn't want to be on my own. Lucy was the first to arrive, with homemade dessert. She plonked it down on the kitchen worktop before searching my cupboard for a wineglass.

"Voilà! Lemon and beetroot pie. I got the recipe online. I made it on Saturday—had a couple of unsuccessful attempts but I think this one worked." It looked like someone had stepped on a lung then dusted it in icing sugar.

"Wow," I said. "Just wow."

"I know, right?"

Oliver and Hazel turned up just as I was basting the asparagus in butter. I impress myself sometimes. Oliver threw his jacket on my bed and plonked a second bottle of red wine on the table.

"Phoebe, that smells amazing. I don't think I've ever had a roast on a Monday night."

"Me neither." I laughed. "Sit down, everyone, and I'll bring it over."

We began to eat, and any hopes I had of forgetting Alex for the evening were dashed when Hazel asked, "How did the date go? Barry, wasn't it? Was it fun?"

"He couldn't make it. His sister gave birth and he had to help," I spluttered. "I sat waiting on him for an hour like an idiot though, until . . . Never mind, I'm seeing him again on Wednesday, though."

"Until what?" Oliver grinned, pouring more wine. "What are you not telling us, girl?"

My face went red and I stood up. "Until Alex showed up and we screwed in a hotel."

The room was silent. "HA!" Lucy laughed. "Nice one. What really happened then?"

The look on my face must have said it all.

"Oh fucking hell, Phoebe!" cried Lucy. "What were you thinking? Where was his girlfriend?"

"I wasn't thinking. I was drinking and I thought I'd been stood up and he said he missed me and . . . I really don't want to talk about it."

I ran into the kitchen, followed by Oliver. "You really make things hard for yourself Phoebe, don't you?" he said, placing his glass on the worktop. "That guy turned you into a wreck, and what? You suddenly forget all that when he clicks his fingers? The man says 'dance' and you start tappin'?"

"It wasn't like that!" I insisted, thinking that it pretty much was exactly like that. "It was just a mistake. And anyway, why the hell do you care? You're not my boyfriend."

He looked hurt. "No, I'm not, Phoebe, heaven fucking forbid. I don't get you. You're sleeping with me, trying to start something up with this Barry fella and now you're screwing Alex again? It's self-destructive and completely fucked-up; even you must see that."

I opened my mouth but couldn't think of a reply. He was right. He left the kitchen, briefly turning back to look at me. "We've been friends for a long time, Phoebe. Don't you dare ask me why I care. Just be really careful I don't stop." And with that I was left feeling about two centimeters tall and Oliver went home.

Lucy and Hazel didn't know where to look; they were both silent until Hazel finally asked, "So . . . was it good then?"

I sighed. "You have no idea how much I wish it had been crap. I mean it wasn't great but it didn't matter—it was Alex."

I walked back into the living room and Lucy gave me a hug. "I hope you know what you're doing," she said quietly. So despite my culinary efforts, this evening was a massive flop. Lucy and Hazel went home at ten and I'm now sitting up in bed, trying to work through the million thoughts all whizzing around my head at the same time. I need to focus. At the start of the year I felt like I knew what I wanted and where I was going; now everything is fucked up and I've lost direction again. I have another date with Barry on Wednesday. God, at the moment I feel like canceling and staying in bed forever. I hope tomorrow is a better day.

Tuesday, September 6

Lucy bought me a latte this morning and we had a quick chat before the morning meeting.

"They didn't have any vanilla syrup so you've got caramel. How are you feeling?"

I shrugged. "OK, I guess. I'm supposed to have that date with Barry tomorrow. I think I'm going to cancel. I don't think that's what I need right now."

Lucy laughed. "Oh, I think it's exactly what you need. He's a clean slate! You haven't slept with him, you have no history and, most importantly, he's never hurt you. I say you put this whole Alex business down to a momentary lapse in sanity; go out with Barry and see if he's one of the good guys. Christ, he's practically a saint already."

"Saint Barry?"

"Well, maybe not, but I think it would be a shame not to see where this goes. Don't you?"

I pondered this all afternoon, but as usual she's right. I'm going to approach this sensibly with an open mind. Anyway, it's only our second date. I should at least get to know him properly before I write him off.

Wednesday, September 7

My second date with Barry started positively, as he actually turned up. We met at the Italian Kitchen on Ingram Street, a cozy little restaurant I've been to a million times before. We sat in the upper dining area, near the window, just far enough away from a sixtieth birthday party that already was in full swing.

I nursed a glass of wine, determined not to get tipsy before I'd even ordered, and glanced over the menu, already sure what I wanted: lobster ravioli followed by king-prawn linguine.

"I never normally like Italian restaurants," said Barry, signaling to the waiter that we were ready to order. "I always feel like I can throw a carbonara sauce over some tortellini at home, so why pay a tenner for it? But this place is divine. Their king-prawn linguine is outstanding."

"That's what I'm having!" I exclaimed excitedly. I was just grateful I was with someone who actually enjoyed eating. "I love seafood!"

"Me too." He laughed as the waiter reached our table. "Go ahead, you order first."

We had a lovely dinner, and talked about everything, including his boring job and my dreadfully dull one.

"So you call up companies and get them to place adverts?"

"Yep. That's pretty much it."

"What if they say no?"

"They usually do. I just move on to someone else. God, my job is dull. What about you? What exactly does a chartered engineer do?"

At this moment half the restaurant began to sing "Happy Birthday" to sixty-year-old Mary, who looked pissed as a fart.

"Basically, I make tubing."

"What? Sorry, it's loud in here. You make tubas?"

"Ha, no, tubing. Tubing to go 'round wires for planes, cars . . . that sort of thing. I'm not making it sound very interesting, am I?"

"Is it interesting?"

"No."

"So we both have dull jobs." I smirked. "We should have some tiramisu to celebrate our terrible career choices."

After the meal Barry helped me on with my coat and we had another glass of wine at a pub nearby, after which he walked me to my train and kissed me good night. Again, no invites back to his . . . nothing. But this is fine. THIS IS HEALTHY. This is part of the courting ritual—unlike Alex, who I banged on our second date—this is the proper way to do things. We've arranged to meet again on Tuesday. I texted Oliver earlier but he hasn't replied. He's always the one I think of speaking to first when I've had a nice evening, but it seems I've really pissed him off. More than usual, I mean.

Thursday, September 8

Lucy followed me into the restroom at work this morning, dying to know how things went on my date with Barry. I barely had time to wash my hands before she bombarded me with questions.

"How did it go? Did you call him B? Have you heard from Alex? Is Oliver speaking to you yet? TELL ME THINGS!"

"Fuckssake, Lucy, how many coffees have you had this morning?"

"A million."

I stuck my hands under the dryer and yelled, "Date went well! Haven't heard from Alex or Oliver, and before you ask—no, we didn't do it. We had Italian food and conversation."

"Pah. Vincent and I had sex all over his apartment last night. Totally dirty."

"Who the hell is Vincent? What happened to Kyle? I cannot keep up with you!" I exclaimed, fluffing my flat hair in the mirror.

"Kyle is off to Perth for work and I'm not waiting around for any man. Vincent is one of those professional conspiracy theorists, which I wouldn't mind except that this morning I couldn't even brush my teeth without a lecture on Nazi fluoride use in prison camps. He still used the fucking toothpaste after me though."

"Oh God. Next he'll be going through the contents of your fridge, holding up cheese triangles and saying they're secretly made by the Illuminati."

"I know. He's annoying but he's covered in tattoos. You know how I love a tattoo sleeve. Also, huge cock. We've both got the day off tomorrow. I'm going to ruin him."

"God, it's too early for this." I sighed, heading for the door.

"IT'S NEVER TOO EARLY FOR COCK!" I heard Lucy shout as the door closed behind me, startling five other people loitering in the corridor. I love her.

Saturday, September 10

I called Oliver twice this evening and left voice mails before calling Lucy to whine that he was still ignoring me.

"He's gone away with Ruth. Amsterdam or Africa or something, I've forgotten."

"How do you know this? Did you see him?"

"Yeah, in the coffee shop yesterday. Sorry, I assumed you knew. He asked after you, if that helps?"

"Did he? Well I've been calling him for days and he hasn't picked up."

"He's sulking. Fuck him. You know he'll come around, don't worry. Anyway, you have that Barry fella to seduce. Hurry up and do it—I'm bored waiting for the sordid details."

"Barry makes tubing."

There was a pause. "I don't even know what that means."

"Me neither."

"Why do you keep meeting on weekdays? What's wrong with a Friday or Saturday night? Wait, isn't this going to be your third date?"

"Yep!" I said enthusiastically. "Third-date rule, baby! He's coming to mine. I'll give him a little dinner, a little wine and then—"

"Demand he bang you?" she interrupted.

"I was going to say 'attempt to seduce him,' but your plan might work too."

"'Course it will. He's probably as frustrated as you are by now. It'll happen."

I'm excited about Tuesday now. I haven't had sex since that night with Alex and I've managed to convince myself that the next person I sleep with will cancel that out. I'm hoping the fact that Alex hasn't been in touch means he's realized it was a mistake too.

Monday, September 12

I had an optician's appointment this morning so I didn't get into work until eleven, just in time to see Kelly throw a book at Brian's head and storm into Frank's office.

"Jesus! What's going on?" I asked, unbuttoning my jacket.

"Brian made fun of Kelly's fringe," Lucy answered. "Kelly didn't take it too well."

"I could sue her for assault," moaned Brian, rubbing the back of his head. "She's a fucking nut case."

I looked into Frank's office and saw Kelly in tears. Real tears, not her usual dramatic wailing. This was different.

"I was only saying that it was too short for her massive forehead." He laughed. "It's true."

"After you'd said her ass was too big for her skirt," mentioned Lucy, not amused. "You really can be a bitchy little fucker, Brian. All she did was ask you to stop watching porn on your cell in the office. It's a reasonable request."

"Fuck off," he snarled. "She's a fat bitch with saggy tits who thinks she's better than the rest of us."

At that Lucy picked up a pen and launched it across the room at him. "You're a chauvinist little prick, Brian. She might not be the easiest woman to get along with, but I'll be fucked if I'm going to sit here while you vomit that kind of bile all over the place."

Then Frank came out and called Brian into the conference room and Kelly made her way through to the staff restroom, avoiding catching anyone's eye. Stuart and I looked at each other in disbelief. I turned to speak to Lucy but she'd taken a call and was smiling like nothing had ever happened.

Ten minutes later Brian appeared, flustered but saying nothing. Frank called me into his office and asked me to close the door.

"What the hell is going on today?" I asked in astonishment. "The office is usually so uneventful."

"I've put Brian on a warning. He's been told to apologize to Kelly for his inappropriate comments; whether she'll take it up with HR I don't know. I've also had complaints about his Twitter account from clients. Apparently he's been tweeting racist remarks at soccer players."

"What the hell was he thinking?"

"Heaven knows. He's only twenty-three, he'll learn. Honestly, Phoebe, sometimes I hate this job."

"Really? And you're telling me all of this because . . . ?"

"I don't really know." He smiled. "Because you're a good listener and there's no one else in the office to vent to?"

"But Frank, surely it's not appropriate to be discussing this with a junior member of staff?"

"Oh, any boundaries we're supposed to have vanished a long time ago. Wouldn't you agree?"

"This is true." I nodded, remembering the first time we screwed in his office. I'm pretty sure he was too. "But it's lunchtime and I'm starving."

"You were supposed to work through lunch. You were at the optician all morning."

"Yes, but that was before you told me you hated your job and discussed Brian's personal business," I said slyly.

He frowned at me. "That's blackmail."

"Oh. So it is. Welcome to my world, Frank!" I got up to leave. "I'll bring you back a Danish. Deal?"

"Get out." He laughed. "And that would be great. Thank you."

I think we might have become friends. How odd.

Tuesday, September 13

Just before lunch Frank called me into his office to say Kelly has decided not to take the Brian matter any further.

"It's a relief for me, actually. I have no idea how I'd explain to my boss why he was watching porn in the office while I was here."

"Because he's a dickhead," I replied.

"True. Anyway, I'm hoping he won't be my problem for too much longer."

"Oh? What does that mean?"

"I can't say, but you'll find out soon enough."

"Is he getting fired?"

"Stop fishing. I can't say. Right, back to work, you."

"You're a terrible gossip." I smiled, closing his office door behind me.

I returned to my desk to find an e-mail from Lucy.

From: Lucy Jacobs

To: Phoebe Henderson

Subject: TONIGHT IS YOUR NIGHT BRO!

Looking forward to it? What time is he coming over?

From: Phoebe Henderson
To: Lucy Jacobs
Subject: Re: TONIGHT IS YOUR NIGHT BRO!

Not coming until eight, which is good as I still have to tidy up. Will let you know how it goes xx

I've made sure the house is super-tidy, lit candles, and even changed my sheets in the hope that I'll be happily rolling around on the clean ones later on, throwing my freshly shaved legs over his shoulders.

12 a.m. He was ten minutes early and seemed delighted I'd asked him for dinner. I took his suit jacket, carefully hanging it over a chair instead of throwing it on my bed, like I do with Oliver's. He sat on the couch while I chatted to him from the kitchen.

"It's only pizza and salad, I'm afraid," I said, wishing I'd actually cooked. "I hope you weren't expecting something drizzled with au jus."

"Hmm, a fan of *MasterChef*, I see. Nope, pizza works for me," he replied, looking around my living room. I thought to myself, I bet your place is nicer than mine. Please don't notice that weird stain on my couch; even I don't know what that is.

I brought over the food and we sat at the table smiling politely at each other, both doing our best to avoid any awkward silences or annoying table manners. The dinner part was successful, but once we moved to the couch (and I got close enough to kiss him) he suggested putting on a film. My mouth said, "Of course!" but my head said, ARE YOU SHITTING ME? But he was probably nervous, so I let him choose from my DVDs while I opened another bottle of wine.

A quarter of the way through *Salem's Lot*, he finally put his arm around me and kissed me. It was sweet. He was gentle and stroked my face, but he wasn't exactly all over me. If this had been Oliver, he'd have had one hand down my bra and the other undoing his fly. Finally, I suggested going through to the bedroom because (1) I have no will-power; (2) life is fucking short, and (3) dammit, I wanted to sleep with him.

He pulled back and ran his hand through his hair. "I have to be going. School night and all that."

I composed myself and looked at the clock. "It's only eleven! Have I said something to offend you?"

"Oh no! Of course not. I'd love to stay longer, but I really do have an early start. We'll do this again though. Cinema tomorrow?"

"Sure. Yes, OK," I replied, stunned that he was now actually putting on his jacket to leave. Before I could convince him otherwise, he'd kissed me, thanked me, and left the building.

I stood at the window and watched his car drive off, wondering what had just happened. Had I come on too strong? No, because he kissed me first! I was so confused. It was third-date night and he didn't want to sleep with me! Why? My first thought was to phone Oliver to help me get to the bottom of this, and even though I knew he wouldn't pick up, I still called him.

But he actually answered! "Oliver! It's me!"

"I'm not speaking to you," he said, speaking to me.

"We both know I'm an idiot. Please don't be mad any longer. I have a problem."

"Put some cream on it, Phoebe. I'm kind of busy. Ruth's here."

"Well, you can't be screwing or you wouldn't have answered your phone. Barry's just left and—"

"Left?" Oliver interrupted. "It's only just after eleven! What happened? Does he hate you like I do?"

"That's the problem—I don't know! We watched a film, he groped me on the couch . . . well, saying that, I did have to physically put his hand on my boob . . . but all I did was ask him if he wanted to go through to the bedroom and he ran away. What's wrong with me? Am I that repulsive?"

"Yes. Yes, you are."

"I knew you'd say that."

"So let me get this straight," said Oliver, beginning to laugh. "You had to force him to grope you and you basically offered him sex and he went home."

"Yes . . . that's about right."

"Who kissed who first?"

"He did."

"Oh. Well, that's my homosexual theory out of the window, I guess. Did you make fun of him?"

"Nope. I save that stuff for my friends."

"Maybe you're just too good for him and he knows it . . . or perhaps he thinks you're a beast. Maybe you remind him of his mother."

"You're not helping." I laughed. "I'm now dressed up and alone with no one to admire my tits."

"Afraid I can't help you there, and I really do have to go, Ruth's waiting downstairs."

"One more thing . . . we good now?"

"We're good. I'm sorry too. Speak tomorrow."

Suddenly I didn't mind so much that Barry hadn't
wanted to sleep with me, because my best friend and I were
speaking again. Suddenly everything felt just a little bit
brighter.

Wednesday, September 14

From: Lucy Jacobs
To: Phoebe Henderson
Subject: WELL????

You've been at your desk for 18 minutes and you haven't spilled
the beans on your date. I want details.

From: Phoebe Henderson
To: Lucy Jacobs
Subject: Re: WELL????

NOTHING. I made some moves and he went home. MY MOVES
ARE LEGENDARY. So fucking frustrating. He's taking me to the cinema tonight, so all is not lost.

From: Lucy Jacobs
To: Phoebe Henderson
Subject: Re: WELL????

Weirdo. Him, not you. If he doesn't at least finger you this evening, dump him.

So the evening arrived and I was ready for either an evening
of cinema and sex with Barry or a showdown that would
make me look like a desperate sex pest. I slipped into a
short black skirt in the hope that when I crossed my legs

during the film he might take it as a sign to place his hand on my thigh. My makeup was faultless, the small tear on my pink sweetheart top had been temporarily mended, and I was ready on time, waiting for him to text and say he was on his way to collect me. Just as I lit a cigarette my cell beeped. Excitedly, I scrolled to my inbox.

I can't stop thinking about you. Let's give this a go. Alex x

With one text I swung from happy to nauseous. I replied:

I can't live like this. We need to talk but not tonight.

My phone beeped almost immediately.

Be 10 mins. Barry x

I turned my phone off and stood at the window, watching for Barry's car and finishing my cigarette. I was not going to let Alex ruin this night for me. I was perfectly capable of doing that on my own.

The film began at eight fifteen and we made it just as the trailers were finishing. Barry chose seats in the middle, which meant no back-row groping and the only time he touched my thigh was when his hand missed the popcorn tub I held on my lap (he apologized). Ugh. As hard as I tried to pay attention to the film, my thoughts wandered from annoyance that Barry was possibly the most frigid man I'd ever met to Alex's suggestion that we "give this a go." Was he serious? Did he expect me to get back together with him properly? Could I?

As the end credits rolled we left the cinema and walked back to Barry's car.

"So, my place or yours?" I smiled as he opened the passenger door of his Volvo.

"Neither, I'm afraid," he replied. "I work early during the week. But another time?"

That was the final straw. As we drove out of the car park I blurted out, "Are we ever going to sleep together? We've had four dates now. What's the problem? Do you just not like me?"

He stared straight ahead. "There's no problem, Phoebe. Of course I like you! It's just . . . I mean—"

"What?"

"I just don't see the big deal about sex. There's no rush. I'd rather wait for a few months until we . . . It's not that important, is it?"

And there I was, driving home from the cinema with myself from a year ago. I wanted to stop the car and show him just how important it could be if you did it right, but I didn't. I said, "Of course not," and we drove home. I texted him a few minutes ago and called it all off. Shame, he's a lovely guy, but without that spark there wasn't any point carrying on and, God help me, I need that spark. I've experienced passion this year and I'm not willing to return to an existence where that's not viewed as important. I texted Oliver:

Barry was a stupid name anyway.

Thursday, September 15

Hazel called me at work today, just as I was getting ready to leave for my appointment with Pam.

"Just booked you in to get a facial with me on Friday at six."

"Oh great, my skin could use an overhaul. Where are we going?"

"That natural-beauty place on Bath Street. I'll meet you after work; Kevin's picking up Grace for me."

"Great stuff. Listen, I'm just running out of the office but I'll see you on Friday. You're a star!"

Pam Potter's consulting room is located above a betting shop in the middle of town. It looks like it was once a bed-sit, as it's only one room with a toilet and a small kitchen, where I imagine someone, penniless and lonely, has at some point quietly made beans on toast and wept for their youth. Despite Pam's fondness for weird ornaments and purple seat covers, it's a very relaxed environment. Although the double glazing is basically nonexistent, so occasionally your train of thought can be brought to a screeching halt by shouts of "Get me twenty smokes, ya bastard" or "Fuck off, ya fag" from the gamblers smoking outside the bookies' below.

"How are you, Phoebe?" Pam asked, stirring my tea. "We haven't had a session since July. Has this been a problem for you?"

"I think I've coped rather well on my own." I laughed. "Who'd have thought it?"

"I'm glad to hear that. Anything in particular you want to discuss today?"

"I'm feeling disheartened. You know, romantically," I admitted, feeling like I should come up with a better reason. "I've decided I'm ready to have a relationship again, but Jesus, it's slim pickings out there."

We had a lengthy discussion about what I felt I wanted from a new partner and a relationship and by the end I felt like I had no idea what I wanted.

"What about this Oliver chap you've mentioned before? Aren't you involved with him?"

"Oliver? God no. Well, we sleep together, but that's all. We're friends. He'd never date me anyway."

"Why not?"

"I've seen the way he is with women. He tends to date more compliant women than me. And well, better-looking. He has a type, you know? Like his new girlfriend Ruth. The model. He tries to pretend that stuff isn't important to him, but it is. Besides, he messes women around a lot and he knows me too well. He knows all of my flaws and the kinds of hideous things that friends forgive and boyfriends dwell on."

"So you'd rather have someone who didn't know the real you?"

"Yes. What? No, of course not. I'd just like to meet someone who isn't already aware of every aspect of my life. Oliver is one of my best friends. That's all we need from each other."

She had a look in her eyes that said, *Who are you trying to kid?* but she didn't say anything. She just nodded and looked at her notepad and then her watch.

"That's our time up. I've scheduled you in for October, but if you need any additional support before then, just call."

And with that I left Pam's office and headed back to the station, musing over what she'd said. Oliver as a boyfriend? With his track record? Not a chance.

Friday, September 16

Hazel was waiting for me after work and we grabbed a quick glass of wine in the Drum and Monkey before making the short walk to Bath Street.

"Do you think they do threading?" I asked as we stood in reception.

"Your eyebrows are fine."

"Not my eyebrows. The sunlight caught the little hairs on my chin this morning and I looked like Gandalf."

"Stop it." She laughed. "Here come the beauty therapists."

Two girls in their early twenties—Amy and Annie—welcomed us, took our coats, and led us through to the treatment rooms. Hazel choose an anti-aging facial and I chose one that would supposedly get rid of the open pores I wasn't aware I had until Annie pointed them out. She pulled back my fringe and began cleansing my skin to within an inch of its life.

Forty-five minutes later I emerged into daylight with a sticking-up fringe and a freshly scrubbed pink face.

"Oh, of all the days not to bring my makeup bag," I moaned, keeping my head down.

"You could have borrowed some of mine," said Hazel, who'd reapplied both foundation and concealer before leaving the salon. "Might have taken a bit of the redness away."

"It's OK. Given a choice between wearing no makeup or having a face three shades darker than my usual skin tone, I think this was the lesser of two evils. I'm getting a taxi home though. I'm not sitting on the train like this."

By the time I got home, my face had calmed down and felt smooth and wonderfully clean. I put on some comfy clothes and settled down to watch *Mulholland Drive*, probably the only David Lynch movie I haven't seen.

10:51 p.m. God, that scene between Betty and Rita was a total turn-on and now I need to get laid or I'm going to die. But everyone I know seems to be happily screwing someone else: Frank has Vanessa, Oliver has Ruth, and Stuart's still seeing his girlfriend. It's not that I'm envious; it's more like I'm JEALOUS AS HELL. I've had the feast and now the famine is slightly harder to swallow.

11:48 p.m. I'm lying in bed, trying to take my mind off my own sad, sex-free existence by listening to Ludovico Einaudi and reminding myself that my birthday weekend is coming up and I'll be able to relax with my friends and forget about everything for a while, under a blue sky and a cloud of cigarette smoke. I need some normality.

Saturday, September 17

"Would you mind if I bring Ruth along to Skye?" Oliver asked. "She's never been and I think it'd be fun for her to meet everyone properly."

Meet everyone? Properly? Was this serious? I was completely taken aback and blurted out, "Sure, if you want to. Why not? Hooray!" and then mumbled something about having bread in the oven (bread?) and got off the phone. Paul is bringing his boyfriend, so I couldn't really tell Oliver not to bring his girlfriend, could I? Will this be awkward? It's not so much that he has a girlfriend, it's more the fact that I'm not going to get any damn sex on my birthday now, am I? For the first time it occurred to me that my time with Oliver might have finally come to an end.

Sunday, September 18

Today is a day of action. I woke up with a plan to overhaul my bedroom and start taking control. My room is a mess— neglected, and clearly the bedroom of someone who isn't coping very well with life. I texted Alex and told him to come over on Wednesday so we can talk, and now I'm off to B&Q to choose paint and a new lightshade, then Marks & Spencer to buy new bedding and curtains.

9:14 p.m. With a lot of hard work I have finally finished transforming my bedroom. My lovely dark-red "feature wall" has turned my bedroom into a boudoir and I'm pleased with myself. It looks sexy. Not that I have anyone to show it to.

10:45 p.m. I've decided that when I get back from Skye I'll get back on track with the dating plan and I'll be happily involved with someone awesome by Christmas. Part of me is still annoyed at Oliver, but he's met someone he wants to spend time with and I should be happy for him. I guess I'm just miffed that he found someone more quickly than I did.

Tuesday, September 20

Holiday meeting tonight! Guests invited to Skye: me, Lucy, Hazel, Paul, Dan, Oliver, and, of course, Ruth. We've arranged to take two cars, as there are seven of us (boys in one, girls in the other). The fellas have agreed to bring the booze, the girls are bringing the food. This is actually a cunning ploy, as (a) booze is more expensive, and (b) if the boys bring the food we'll be living on chips and toast for two days. Lucy has been politely banned from making anything with her own two hands and must only buy from supermarkets, and Hazel is bringing the cake. I made it clear that if anyone puts thirty-three candles on my cake, I'll blow them out using spit.

Wednesday, September 21

Son of Satan arrived at my door this evening carrying a bunch of flowers. More freakin' flowers. Why couldn't he have brought gin?

"Thanks for coming, Alex," I said, letting him in. "We really need to sort this out like grown-ups."

"The flowers are for your birthday, since I won't see you," he said, taking off his coat and handing it to me before swanning into the living room.

"Make yourself at home," I mumbled, dropping his coat on the hall floor.

"I'm leaving her," he announced. "Is that grown-up enough for you?"

"What? You're leaving her?"

"I am, Phoebe, I'm leaving her. Listen, I don't know how things got so bad between us, but I'll make it right." He pulled me in for a kiss but I pulled away.

"You'll fuck me about, Alex, because that's what you do, and I don't think I could take it again."

"I won't. I promise I won't." He sounded so sincere, just like he had in the hotel room.

We sat and talked for hours about everything. It was like when we first met, as cheesy as that sounds. There's part of me that still believes he loves me and another part that remembers what a complete shit he is. We ended up in bed and he noticed I'd been in training for the sexual Olympics. "It was never like this before," he grunted while on top of me. "We're so good together."

For a time we were good together, and I wonder if it could be like that again. But could I ever trust him? I told him I'd have to think about things and would see him when I got back from my vacation. Once again I've got no idea what I'm doing. God, I hate women like me.

Friday, September 23

BIRTHDAY TRIP!

This morning I was the first one into the car, with my sunglasses on and half a croissant stuffed in my mouth.

"You do realize it's pissing it down?" said Lucy, who still had her pajamas on, her glittery flask of coffee in hand, "and not sunny."

"Well, you still have your pajamas on. I might look odd, but you just look crazy."

Lucy looked down at her pajamas, then reached into her bag and pulled out some massive sunglasses and put them on.

"Now I look crazy. Let's go!"

2 p.m. We're almost there! We'd probably be closer if Hazel didn't have to stop for the toilet every few miles ("Shut up, I have IBS and that bacon sandwich is killing me. Unless you want me to shit myself, you'll stop"), but the sun is shining, the sky is blue, and I just know it's going to be the best weekend ever! I have nothing to do but eat, sleep, get drunk, and think about where my life is going. I should do that before I get drunk.

4 p.m. We still haven't arrived. The boys are there, of course, way ahead of us and are no doubt picking the best bedrooms and showing each other their muscles. Ruth has been eating the same bag of chips for an hour and the rustling is driving me crazy. I inhaled mine within twenty seconds and am now on to my second sandwich.

5 p.m. We're here! I drove the last half hour and we all sang along to *The Immaculate Collection*, except Ruth—"I don't know the words to 'Vogue.'"

Who the fuck doesn't know the words to "Vogue"? Even my dead goldfish knows the words to "Vogue." Despite the GPS telling us we had arrived at our destination twenty minutes ago (a field with one unimpressed bull staring at the car), Hazel managed to remember where the house was.

6 p.m. I get my own room 'cause I'm the birthday girl. Hazel and Lucy are sharing, the happy couples are also sharing and probably doing perverted things to each other as I write this. Going down for dinner soon and then it'll be wine o'clock. The house is small but gorgeous and it's pretty much surrounded by nothing except some friendly sheep and a *Blair Witch*–style wood I'm sure I'll end up exploring when I'm drunk.

4 a.m. Tonight was all about the booze. We played drinking games, sang drinking songs, and when we'd run out of those we just drank. It felt strange watching Oliver with Ruth, and a couple of times he had to remove my hand from his leg when I drunkenly forgot I wasn't allowed to touch him. She really is beautiful. We had my birthday cake just after midnight (one big candle) and then we all went outside and did some terrible dancing in honor of me being old. Oliver stepped into the middle of our little circle and made a speech:

"Everyone, please raise your glass, well, your tumbler . . . whatever you have in your hand . . . to Phoebe! Whom I've known since we were seventeen. Who has no idea just how beautiful she is, but makes some cracking jokes about her own face so we all laugh anyway. Who, in fact, makes me laugh like no other person I know and who is, without doubt, my best friend. To you, Phoebe!" Of course then I had to say a few words. "To my lovely friends, old and new," I said, trying to point to where Dan and Ruth were. "Thank you for celebrating my birthday with me and for generally putting up with me and my exploits this year. It's been quite a year, eh, Oliver?" I laughed and I could see Oliver glaring back at me, with a "don't say any more, Ruth doesn't know" look. I continued:

"In other news, I might also be getting back with Alex, but this hasn't been confirmed yet . . . But I think I love him. Again. Anyway, you're all fuckers but be assured that I love you all more than Alex."

I remember the stunned looks on everyone's faces. Now it's four a.m., I've sobered up, and all I can hear is moaning coming from both Oliver's and Paul's rooms. I wonder if Ruth is better than me in bed? If I don't get some sleep soon it's going to be a long day tomorrow.

Saturday, September 24

11 a.m. Happy Birthday to me! Thirty-three and I don't look a day over thirty-three. I woke up feeling surprisingly well, considering I drank almost an entire bottle of Jack myself last night. Mum and Dad called after lunch.

"Happy birthday, darling!" they both yelled over speakerphone. "Are you having fun?"

"Thank you. I am, actually! How are you both?"

"Oh, fine," said Dad. "We're just off camping."

"Why?" I asked, screwing up my face at the very prospect. "Jesus, you're both in your sixties. Go and lie down or something."

I heard Mum shouting in the background, "Tell her we're going to look for trolls." Dad continued, "She's not kidding, you know. We're going to have some nature time. There's nothing quite like waking up in the morning beside a lake and skinny-dipping by moonlight. You know how it recharges your mother."

"Oh God, ENOUGH!" I yelled, dying inside at the prospect of my mother and father howling at the moon, dressed in nothing but Jesus sandals. "I remember you used to do that by the loch. Well, until the police told you to stop."

"We've got to go, darling, but we just wanted to wish you lots of fun on your birthday!"

"Recharges." Yuck, I just know that is hippie code for "arouses." Still, it could have been worse. Oliver's parents are the same age and they never leave the house. They sleep in separate beds and watch the world through twitching curtains. I'd take my crazy parents over them any day.

The seven of us spent a couple of hours this afternoon exploring the island and pretending to have adventures, like characters from an Enid Blyton novel, but a really warped one filled with swearwords, smoking, gay men, and characters who screw at the drop of a hat. When we got back from exploring we all congregated in the garden to sunbathe. Ruth looks amazing in a bikini; even I couldn't take my eyes off her. I played it safe with a sarong over my bottom half to avoid giving the entire troop nightmares. We all had a playful joint while listening to "Rainy Day Women" and giggled hysterically at fuck-all. Ruth just read her book. "Let's have a bonfire tonight!" announced Hazel with great gusto. "It'll be brilliant. We can get wood from trees!" I giggled again.

Oliver stood up, stoned as hell. "Right, I will go and collect wood and Henderson will come as my wingman."

I scowled. "Don't tell me what to do. YOU'RE NOT MY REAL DAD."

Ruth looked up from her book. "I can help you, babe," she said quietly.

"With those nails?" Oliver laughed. "Finish your book, honey. It's about time Phoebs did something around here other than drink." I made a face but tied my sarong around my waist and threw on some flip-flops: "Right, into the trees we go."

Hazel shouted, "There's rope in the shed for the twigs, makes them easier to carry!" We grabbed the rope and walked the short distance to the woods behind the house. "So . . . Ruth is nice then," I said, kicking a stone out of my shoe. "Nice and thin and pretty and—"

Oliver cut me off midsentence. "You're getting back with Alex? Phoebe, don't do it. Please. You know how I feel . . . how we all feel about this. I couldn't bear to see you hurt again, none of us could."

"Oliver, I know. I don't know what I'm going to do. I'm confused. He says he still loves me and, well, everyone needs someone, don't they, and you have Ruth . . . and I don't have a Ruth and . . . what was I saying again?" Truly the ramblings of a stoner.

Feeling woozy, I sat down and Oliver lit two cigarettes. "Ruth is great, Phoebe, but it's nothing special," he mumbled. "She is nice—and really clever—but she doesn't make me laugh. It's strange."

"You're strange," I said, smiling at him. "I heard you guys last night, even with my drunken ears. What's the problem?

2

88   **Joanna Bolouri**

Sure she doesn't know the words to 'Vogue,' but she's probably been on the cover and you hate that song anyway. Impressively, she manages to stay thin and eat chips and she . . . Ouch!"

I had dropped my cigarette on my thigh. Oliver hurried to brush the ash away but I was left with a small red blister. He blew on it, very gently at first, gradually moving his mouth closer and closer. I closed my eyes. The next thing I felt was his mouth kissing the inside of my thigh. I opened my eyes again. "Oliver, we—" but he stopped me.

"Remember the bondage challenge? It's your turn now."

I looked at him. My heart raced. "Here? Now? But what about Ruth?"

Oliver didn't answer. Instead he picked up the rope we'd brought for tying the twigs and stood over me. "Get up," he said quietly, and I did what I was told. He pushed me back toward the tree and began to loop the rope around me, making sure my arms were restrained but leaving my legs free. To be honest, a five-year-old Girl Scout could have undone the knot he tied, but I didn't struggle. He carefully pulled down my bikini bottoms and began licking me, so slowly I felt my knees buckle and my face flush. He undid his jeans, wrapped my legs around his waist, and held me up. I could feel the tree scratching my back as he went faster and faster and then he stopped, looked into my eyes, and kissed me. I mean really kissed me, and all I could do was kiss him back. It was passionate, and as he started to move inside me again I cried out it was so intense. "The thing about Ruth," he breathed as we fucked, "is that she's not you, Phoebe."

I stared back at him, trying to think of something clever to say in response. But by then I was so close to coming I couldn't focus properly. He let me come before he did and then kissed me again and pulled up his pants.

"Why did you bring Ruth here?" I asked as he untied me.

He sighed. "Why do you think, Phoebe? I hoped actually seeing me get serious with someone else would make you realize you wanted me too. In my own twisted way I hoped you'd be jealous."

I rubbed the tops of my arms where the rope had been. "On my birthday? I don't get you. We agreed no strings, you've never once shown an interest in me in that way, Oliver, and—"

He looked annoyed. "Oh, I have, believe me I have. You've been so wrapped up in your own world and your stupid list of challenges you just haven't noticed. It's been getting more and more difficult hearing about you with other guys. I thought maybe after taking you to that hotel, and that moment we had at the beach, you might realize . . . but now this thing with Alex again. I've never heard anything so foolish, even for you."

"You're foolish," I said quietly, like a four-year-old who's just been told off. "And Alex and I have a history. It's not that simple—"

"I give up," he said. "Get back together with Alex. Do whatever the fuck you like. Christ, Phoebe, I'm standing here telling you I love you and it doesn't make any difference to you. Fuck you."

I watched him walk away.

"What about the sticks?" I shouted.

"Fuck the sticks!" he yelled back. Then he was gone.

I managed to gather some up and walked back to the house, wondering what the hell to expect. But there was Oliver, sitting beside Ruth, having a beer with everyone else.

"You took your time, Phoebs." Lucy laughed. "Did you find a gingerbread house in there?"

"Sorry I was too stoned to help," said Oliver flatly before putting his shades on, kissing Ruth and lying back in the sun. I just smiled and dumped the sticks at the front of the house before retreating to my room to cry.

11 p.m. Oliver and I haven't spoken much since this afternoon, just enough to make it seem like everything's normal. I faked a headache an hour ago and left them all beside the bonfire, dancing around it like *Tales of the Unexpected*. Hazel came in about half an hour ago. She's smarter than a lot of people give her credit for. She sat on the bed and brushed my fringe from my eyes. "What a mess, Phoebs. I know Alex is the Antichrist, but if you decide to get back with him, that's your choice." I nodded. "And if a certain Irishman really loves you, he'll accept that too." I looked at her, wondering how the hell she knew. "Oh, that's been coming for a while," she laughed. "Now, come downstairs and finish your birthday. Please, I insist." She got up and, before closing the door, she added, "You've spent almost a whole year taking no shit, Phoebe. Don't give up now."

I'm just about to head back down. I need a drink.

Sunday, September 25

I'm just home and feeling rather fragile. Lucy drove and I stared out the window all the way down. So far I haven't allowed myself to actually stop and really think about what's going on, but I'll have to at some point, undoubtedly at three in the morning, when I'm obsessing over this instead of sleeping.

Monday, September 26

When asked by my colleagues how my birthday trip was I smiled and said, "It was the best time ever, thanks!" because telling them that my best friend ruined it all by telling me he's in love with me wasn't something I cared to share with them.

I got through the day by throwing myself into work and trying to ignore the voice in my head that kept telling me I should have handled the Oliver situation differently. Finally, on my way to the station, I gave Oliver a call, hoping to meet up and sort this mess out. It rang once and then went to voice mail, which I'm assuming was him rejecting my call. We've been friends for sixteen years—surely we can get past this?

Tuesday, September 27
As Oliver won't answer my calls I've sent him thirty-two texts today, begging him to speak to me. He'll either cave in or get the police to caution me for harassment. It's a chance I'm willing to take, as this is driving me crazy. I need to speak to him. I miss him.

Wednesday, September 28
At work this morning I must have looked at my phone fifty times in the hope that Oliver had texted me back. Nothing. So I tried e-mailing.

From: Phoebe Henderson
To: Oliver Webb
Subject: Hi

Look, we need to sort this out. Can you blame me for being surprised at what you said? You're the one who told me you didn't "do love," and look at your track record with women. There are millions of them, most of them much more fanciable than me. I'm a mess, Oliver, and you'd get bored with me (you know you would) and our friendship would be fucked. I don't want that. Can't we just go back to the way things were? Come over soon and we'll talk. Please?

Staring at the computer screen for forty-five minutes seemed to generate a response, albeit not the one I was hoping for:

From: Oliver Webb
To: Phoebe Henderson
Subject: Re: Hi

Phoebe, there's nothing more to say and I think it's best we don't see each other for a while. You're absolutely right about my track record with women and that I would get bored with you, lord knows I'm getting close already. Anyway, I'm with Ruth—as you pointed out, she's probably more my type physically anyway. Good luck with Alex, you're going to need it.

Ouch! That was below the belt; nothing like hitting a neurotic girl where it hurts. I feel so sad about this. I tried clicking my heels, wishing I'd never started anything with Oliver, but it didn't work. I guess now I know where I stand.

Friday, September 30

Alex called me this morning while I was on the train to work.

"I've told her it's over. I've resigned and she's moving out. We can be together now. Can I come over tonight?"

"If you break my heart again, I'll fucking kill you," I said in a low voice, aware that everyone on the train could hear me. "But fine."

"I won't. I promise. I'll see you tonight."

7:53 p.m. He's on his way now. Of course I'm nervous about the whole thing, and it's dawned on me what a life-changing move this is. No more Oliver, no more challenges . . . but on the other hand, no more horrendous dating and no more missing Alex. I hope I'm doing the right thing.

OCTOBER

Saturday, October 1

This time last year I would have happily smothered the man sleeping next to me to death and now I'm about to get up, make him coffee, and give him a blow job in the shower. How did that happen? Actually I don't care. I'm just glad that it did. We talked again for a long time last night. I think things will work out this time. I can't help feeling a sense of relief deep down that he realized he was wrong and still loves me. He wants me to move back in with him but I've told him no. I want to take things slower, get to know each other again. If he wants to give us another chance he's going to have to make the effort too. If it all goes well, we can look for somewhere new together. Too many memories in the old place, and it would smell of her and have her ass imprint in the mattress. On top of all this I feel incredibly sad about Oliver and me. He's the last person in the world I thought would ever use the L word with me (or tell me to fuck off and actually mean it) and I wish he hadn't. Why did he have to change things?

Sunday, October 2

My neighbor brought over some post that had been delivered to her house by mistake. It was an orange party invitation with a pumpkin on the front.

Dear Phoebe and Partner,
You are invited to Lucy Jacobs's Halloween Party on Saturday
October 29th. Please come suitably dressed and with booze.
Adults only—don't bring any children as entry will be
refused and booze confiscated. RSVP.

Hurrah! The last Halloween party I attended was held in my school gym hall. I dressed as Madonna and I won a Bros record for being the best dancer in the universe.

Alex looked at the invitation and sighed. "I suppose you'll want to go to this."

"HELL YES! Let's go as Che and Eva Perón!" I said excitedly.

"Do I have any say in this?" asked Alex.

"Nope. You'd make us dress like Bert and Ernie if you had your way."

"What's wrong with that? Anyway, I'm not sure about going at all. Your friends hate me. It's not the best idea."

"They don't. Not really, and it's a good time to see them again. After all—it's a party!"

Actually, I think they might lynch him. I'll have to have a word in their ears beforehand. Alex hasn't left my apartment since he got here on Friday. It's odd having him here; I'd become so used to having an Alex-Free Zone that now I feel quite uneasy in my own home.

"You should have your hair cut," he suddenly announced while I was showering. "Get something more traditional maybe, more feminine. You look a bit emo with that fringe."

I ignored him. "So are you going to go home at any point? You don't have any stuff here."

"Yeah, I'll bring some things over later. Why don't we go to that barbecue place tonight for dinner? I hear it's delicious."

"Oh, not there. I went with Oliver for his birthday. . . ." I started to laugh. "Let's just say I became unwell."

"I never liked Oliver much. He loves himself, thinks he's God's gift."

"Don't slag him off, Alex. He's a good guy and he doesn't love himself."

No, I thought. He loves me.

Monday, October 3

Frank can be surprising sometimes. He e-mailed me today after the morning meeting.

From: Frank McCallum
To: Phoebe Henderson
Subject: Quick e-mail

Phoebe,

Couldn't help but hear (and read) that you're back with your ex. None of my business of course, but since you've been helpful with your advice, I'd like to offer some of my own. Don't. You weren't half the woman you are now when you were with him. I like this Phoebe much better and I'd hate to see you return to that sad place you were in for so long. You can do better (not with me,

I hasten to add—that ship has sailed). Ignore this if you wish, but it's written with no agenda.

Frank

Of course I'm annoyed that he thinks he has the right to continue reading my e-mails and comment on my private life, but also sort of touched. It'll get easier having Alex around again, even though he is everywhere I turn at the moment. Maybe when he gets a new job, things will be easier. He seems to want to carry on like we've never been apart, which I don't. I rather want this to be like a new relationship, but I know, with our history, it can never be exactly like that. The one area he hasn't changed AT ALL is in bed. I'm pretty sure the sex is only better because I am. Working through my list has made me actually pay attention to sex and he's obviously still ignoring it. I bet he thinks he's great in bed. I think I'll add another challenge to my list: Make Alex more adventurous in the sack.

Thursday, October 6

Last night I woke up with Alex's penis digging into my back and hands on my breasts. Excellent, I thought. Now's my chance.

I started to grind against him and whispered, "Is there anything you've always wanted to try?"

"You mean in bed?"

"Yeah . . ."

"No."

He moved my ass up and slid inside me, not caring whether I was actually ready or not. "Oh, come on, there

must be something—against the wall, holding me down . . .
sex toys? Being tied up?" No response.

"Come on my tits? . . . Finger up your ass?"

My suggestions were met with silence, but he still continued to bang me with a firm but monotonous stroke.

"Alex? . . ."

"No, nothing. Now, stop talking, you're putting me off.
I'm nearly there."

So I remained silent for the next fifty-four seconds and
resigned myself to the fact that sex for Alex was all about
him and not about us. Can I live like this?

At work Stuart announced that he's asked his girlfriend,
Laura, to marry him and she's said yes. I congratulated
him, thinking, Would your girlfriend have agreed if she
knew you banged me in April? But maybe she does know. If
this year has taught me anything it's that (a) I'm hopeless at
understanding relationships, and (b) sleeping with someone else's partner is a really shitty thing to do. I thought it
best to decline the invitation for celebration drinks after
work and went home, dying to take a bath and chill out.
Alex had arranged to meet Rob, so I had the place to myself.

I brought the phone into the bathroom so I could chat to
Hazel on speakerphone while I soaked.

"Hi, Phoebe. I'm just about to get Grace to bed. How are
you? How's Alex?"

"Good," I said, unsure whether that was a lie or not. "It's
been exhausting, actually, but we're getting there."

"Hmm, you sound a bit flat. Want me to come over?"

"No, I'm fine! I'm just having a soak, then I'm going to
watch some TV and get an early night. I think Alex will
crash at Rob's tonight."

"OK, I have to run, but call me back if you need to talk."
She hung up and I lay in the bath for twenty minutes, turning into a giant raisin. Just as I got into bed, Alex appeared, shit-faced and stinking of pakora sauce.

"Rob went home and I got food but I ate it on the train, so NO PAKORA FOR YOU!" He laughed. "You don't need any more pakora, do you, Phoebe?"

I didn't even ask him what he was slurring on about. I just turned off the light and went to sleep.

Friday, October 7

The postman arrived with my Evita costume. A red-and-black suit and a blond wig, which, admittedly, looks like the scalp of an elderly woman, but who cares. Alex's costume will be instantaneously recognizable and it shouldn't be too hard to put two and two together.

I rushed into work, excited to tell Lucy.

"That sounds genius! I think I'm dressing up as Wonder Woman. I found an online shop that rents out the outfits."

"Boots and everything?"

"Yup!"

"You're going to look sexy and I'm going to look like a politician. No fair."

"Behave. There will be food, booze and bobbing for apples. It'll be a night to remember!"

I had dinner out with Hazel tonight. It felt like ages since I'd last seen her. No one's been round to my apartment in days. I put on a new dress I hadn't had the chance to wear yet and sashayed into the living room.

"How do I look?" I asked Alex, giving him a twirl.

He looked up from his magazine. "Good. I wish you'd dressed like that the first time we dated. You sure you're meeting Hazel?"

I bit my tongue. "I'll be back late; will you be here or at yours?"

"Here. You have the good sports channel."

"Wrong answer," I said. "The correct answer would be: I'll be waiting here ready to hump the shit out of you when you come home."

"I wish you wouldn't talk like that, Phoebe," he sighed. "It's just not like you."

Hazel was already there when I arrived. I gave the waiter my jacket and sat down.

"So how's married life then?" she inquired, looking over the wine list. "Everything rosy?"

"Yes," I said quickly. "It's great." My face obviously told a different story.

"Hmm. What's wrong?"

"I know Alex is . . . well, Alex," I said sipping my water, "but the trouble is—"

"He hasn't stopped being THAT Alex. Has he?" she said.

"Yes," I replied. "No." That was exactly it.

"Well, you can either see how it goes or you can finish it. There's no law that says you can't dump the same man twice."

"I've only just got back together with him! No, I made my decision, I'm not admitting defeat. Not yet. It was bound to be tricky at first."

"Isn't this normally the honeymoon stage?"

"Ugh, there's nothing normal about this. Can we talk about something else, please?"

"Have you heard from Oliver?"

"Not that either. Something else."

"OK. Well, I was thinking about getting my tits done."

She smiled.

"We have a winner! Tell all."

The waiter appeared and we ordered wine, two starters, and three desserts, then Hazel told me about her floppy boobs and I laughed. A lot. It was a good night.

When I got home Alex was in bed sleeping peacefully and I looked at him with puppy-dog eyes, thinking how handsome he was. Then I walked into the living room and wanted to scream. He'd rearranged all my furniture and left his shit everywhere—socks on the floor, unwashed plates in the sink, and empty lager cans all over the place. My eyes were no longer puppy-dog eyes; they were big, red Cujo-the-psychotic-dog eyes. I moved back all my furniture, snarling. He was starting to take over already.

"Don't be stupid," he said when I woke him up to demand an explanation. "The place looked better my way. There was more space."

"Alex, this is my place. At least ask before doing something like that. I prefer it this way."

"Suit yourself, Phoebe. It's not important."

"Stop being so dismissive. It is important. To me. This is my home."

"You hate this place. When we get a nicer place together, things will be better."

I let him fall asleep again before I got into bed beside him and realized there was no way in hell I was moving back in with this man.

Sunday, October 9

Alex went to the gym first thing this morning. I lay in bed, watching him pull on a pair of jogging pants that clung to his penis like a shroud.

"Want to come with me?" he asked, stuffing a spare T-shirt into his rucksack.

"No, I'm going to move from the bed to the couch. Then have croissants and coffee."

"Do you remember that yellow summer dress you had?" he asked. "The one you used to love wearing?"

"Oh yes! It's hanging in the wardrobe, although I can't fit into it anymore," I laughed. "Why? Do you want to borrow it?"

"Very funny." He frowned. "I'm asking because I'd like to see you in it again, and maybe if you lay off the croissants and come to the gym with me, I will someday."

I threw the covers back and got out of bed. "That was fucking low, Alex, even for you," I snarled, pulling on my robe. "I've gone up exactly one dress size since we split and this bothers you?"

"No, I thought it would bother YOU," he replied, surprised at my reaction. "It doesn't bother you that you've gained weight?"

"No, YOU bother me," I snapped. "Who do you think you are?"

He followed me into the kitchen, "Look, I'm sorry if I offended you. I just thought you'd want to look good again. Forget I said anything."

"'Look good again'? So, what, I don't look good now?"

"Of course you do; you're pretty. You carry the weight well."

"Oh, do fuck off," I said, filling up the kettle. "I'll see you later, unless I've eaten myself to death while you're gone."

I sat nursing my coffee, now too angry to eat my croissants. He's such a pig. Oliver would never have spoken to me like that.

He came back late in the afternoon while I was reading on the couch and apologized, telling me he only wants me to be healthy and was trying to be supportive. I accepted and got back to reading my book, but I spent the remainder of the evening with a sinking feeling in my stomach. Maybe, and despite his protests, Alex hasn't changed one bit.

Monday, October 10

Work was the usual mixture of inane chat from Kelly and occasional bursts of song from Lucy, who's now seeing tree-surgeon Kyle again.

"He decided not to go to Perth. It might have had something to do with the fact I'm irresistible. His words."

"Wow. You happy about that?"

"Surprisingly I am," she said happily. "It's early days, but I fear I might be entering into an actual relationship. I do believe I'm turning into you, Miss Henderson."

"Fuck, don't say that. You know I only want good things for you."

"You're either joking," she said, furrowing her brows, "or you think you've made a mistake with Alex. Which is it?"

I shrugged. "When I've made up my mind I'll let you know."

At five I saw Alex talking to Miss Tits outside his office and felt anxious. I hate this feeling. I think it's entirely possible to forgive someone for cheating, but I'm finding it impossible to forget. Am I going to spend the rest of my days wondering if, or when, he'll do it again? We've only been back together a matter of days and I'm already starting to struggle, but if I admit that, I'll just prove everyone right and look like a fool.

Tuesday, October 11

During the morning meeting, Lucy interrupted to tell Frank he had an emergency phone call. He took it in his office and then rushed out without saying a word. Everyone looked at Lucy.

"Don't bother asking, I have no idea where he's gone. It was some woman called Janet."

He called me an hour later.

"Phoebe, can you ask Maureen to run things today?" he asked solemnly. "And tell Lucy to cancel my meeting with that agency. I can't remember who it is, but it's in my appointments on my PC."

"Yes, OK. Is everything all right?"

"Vanessa's mum died. She's a mess. I'm here with her and her sister Janet. I can't leave her. I've spoken to Hugo, so he knows I won't be in for a couple of days."

"I'm so sorry to hear that. Go and take care of her. Things will be fine here."

"Thanks, Phoebe."

He hung up and I called Maureen to let her know what had happened, then e-mailed Lucy to let her know too. I didn't want to announce Frank's business in front of everyone. Poor Vanessa.

I got home to find that Alex had been for a job interview at a chiropractor clinic on the south side of Glasgow.

"Guy who runs it is pretty nice. Smaller than Susan's place, but the pay is almost identical. He's letting me know next week."

"That's excellent news. Fingers crossed, then!"

"How was your day?" he asked, running his fingers through my hair. "Another day feeding the corporate machine, eh?"

"Frank had some bad news, but apart from that it was OK."

"I always liked Frank. He's very well educated. No idea why he's working in sales. It's such a ghastly profession. Sales people are morons. Well, apart from you. I didn't mean you."

"Keep digging. You're lucky that I'm too tired to argue with you. I'm having a shower and an early night."

"It's only six. Have a nap and I'll wake you up for dinner in a while."

I lay down in bed and closed my eyes, quickly drifting off to sleep, grateful that I had some alone time. But Alex woke me up again only a few minutes later by getting into bed beside me and kissing my neck, which got my attention. We began to have sex, and for the first time ever, I closed my eyes and imagined it was someone else. I imagined it was Oliver. Oliver used to know exactly when to go slowly and when to speed up and how close I was by the sound of my breathing. He'd spend a ridiculous amount of time going down on me and . . . God, I miss his face. Our conversations. Lying with him in bed. Being without him is killing me. Oh Christ. Hello, feelings for Oliver! Do come in and completely screw up my entire life, won't you? I really miss him! I miss his curly hair and his smell and his accent and the way he laughed at my jokes and the way he pulled me up when I was being a dick and I love him. Oh God. I. Love. Him. Fuck. What have I done?

Wednesday, October 12

Thank God I had a session with Pam Potter already booked for today. Yet again I was totally confused about what I wanted and needed and, well, about everything really. I marched into her office, dismissing the offer of tea before she'd even made it. Twenty minutes later I hadn't stopped talking.

"So I'd already started something with Alex again when Oliver told me how he felt, and it was too weird and confusing so I said no."

"You rejected Oliver in favor of Alex?"

"Yes. What an idiot."

"OK, I'm going to put something to you. I think, after your split with Alex, you view relationships as you plus a man who will inevitably hurt you, and I don't think you consider Oliver to be one of these men. So how could you consider Oliver in terms of a romantic relationship at all? If you did, you'd start to view him differently and that would mean he'd be like every other man. You never really got Alex out of your system and you still craved his approval—so, when he announced he still loved you, this made you feel safe and wanted again."

I left Pam Potter's office feeling clearer than I had done in a long time. She was absolutely right. How am I going to fix this? I told Alex to spend the night at his place. I need some time to myself.

Thursday, October 13

Frank returned to work today and I had a quick chat with him at lunchtime while the others went to the pub downstairs. I brought him a coffee in his office.

"I'm really sorry to hear about Vanessa's mum," I said, handing him the mug. "What happened? How is she?"

"Devastated," Frank replied. "But she'll be OK. Her sister is dealing with most of the arrangements. It was a heart attack."

"Well, it's good that she has you there too. Regardless of previous comments, you're a good guy, Frank."

He smiled. "Thank you. It's made me realize how special she is to me, and I'd never have got to know her properly if it wasn't for you. So I guess we're both awesome."

"Did you just say awesome?"

"Go to lunch. You're not allowed to pick on me today. I'm emotionally drained."

"I'm kidding. Listen, if there's anything you or Vanessa need, let me know."

He nodded and I left to meet the others downstairs, feeling like a worthwhile member of the human race. Maybe I'm not so useless after all.

Friday, October 14

"Can you come over tonight?" I asked Lucy as we got ready to go home. "I need to talk."

"I said I'd meet Kyle, but if it's urgent I'll cancel."

I shook my head. "Not urgent, I just wanted to have a chat about something. It can wait."

"Meet me downstairs," she said, pulling her cell out of her jacket and placing her red bag on her desk. "I'll be one minute."

I stood outside watching everyone leave work, wondering who was going home to partners or children or bad relationships, who was just going home alone. I didn't notice Lucy until she tapped me on the shoulder.

"I'm meeting Kyle at eight instead of seven, so let's grab some chips and take them back to your house. Won't Alex be there?"

"No, he's out with his friends tonight. Thanks, Lucy. I appreciate it."

We got to mine and I turned the heating on. We sat on the couch and ate chips from the paper.

"So, what's up?" she asked. "Aw, you got a pickle. I wish I had a pickle."

I bit the pickle in half and handed it to her. It was so sour my face practically turned inside out.

"Well . . . I'm in love," I gushed.

"Yes, we all know you're in love with Alex, Phoebe. Oh God, you're not getting married, are you?"

"Fuck no!" I exclaimed. "It's not Alex I'm in love with. It's Oliver."

"I freakin' knew it." She laughed. "I wondered how long it would take. When you got back with Alex, I thought I'd got the whole thing wrong, but that wouldn't be like me, now would it? Have you spoken to Oliver yet?"

"He won't speak to me. I've been trying, believe me. I've blown it, Lucy, and now I have to get rid of Alex too. I don't want to hurt him as well. It's such a mess."

"Hurt him? Come on, Phoebe—that guy almost finished you last year and you're worried about hurting his feelings? You tell him you've made a mistake and it's over. ONCE AND FOR ALL."

"Oh, that easy is it?" I snapped.

"Actually, it is. I don't know what it is about that sanctimonious prick that turns you into a fucking mouse, Phoebe, but I'm fed up with it. You've just admitted you don't want to be with him anymore, so do something about it. He'd be quick enough to do it to you; in fact, he was quick enough to do it to you. Remember that."

"Don't be angry with me—I gave you half my pickle," I mumbled.

"I'm frustrated, Phoebe. For you. You let Alex back into your life, not because it was the right thing to do but because it was easier than missing him. Now you've finally realized that he isn't the man for you because Oliver is and he always was. I'm not saying you have to be cruel to Alex, that isn't your style, but do not let that man stand in the way of your happiness any longer."

"When he gets back tonight I'll talk to him," I said, wondering how the hell I was going to break it off with him. "I'll do this and then I'll figure out how to get Oliver to talk to me."

"Good girl." Lucy smiled. "I think you're amazing and brave and Oliver is a very lucky man. One who deserves you. Not that Alex fucker. Now, I have to run and see my boyfriend because I have a boyfriend now."

"You look happy." I grinned. "Go and have fun."

I watched her skip out the door and prepared myself for Alex's return so I could end things.

He didn't come home.

Tuesday, October 18

I woke up with a very sore throat. With no Alex there to go and get me painkillers I had to call in sick to work and then drag my unwell ass to the chemist, feeling sorry for myself.

The lady behind the counter gave me some ibuprofen and made a motherly "you look awful face" face at me as I handed her the money. Just as I was shuffling out the door, who walks in? Miss Tits. I averted my gaze and pushed past her, but she grabbed my arm.

"Can we talk for a second, Phoebe? I just need a minute."

"Oh, this should be good," I said, standing on the pavement beside her and letting the door close. "What could you possibly have to say to me?"

"That I'm sorry. I know I did a shitty thing to you and I'm sorry."

I was dumbstruck.

"After Alex cheated on me, I wanted to kill that fucking waitress, but then I realized, I'd done exactly the same thing to you and—"

"What waitress?" I snapped. "When?"

"Few months ago. I tried to forgive him, I even believed getting married would change him, but then I found out he was still sleeping with her. I dumped him and I moved out of the apartment. The guy is a cheating shit; he always will be."

I could feel the rage building up inside me. "You. Left. Him?" She had no idea we were back together. "Where is he now?" I asked.

"Oh, he'll be back in the apartment, I'd imagine, looking for the next sucker. He's scared of being alone. He doesn't know how to be on his own. Anyway, I'm sorry and that's all I wanted to say."

"Thank you," I said. "I can't say I'm sorry it didn't work out, but I appreciate that. You've no idea how much." I walked back home in a daze.

HOW COULD I HAVE BEEN SO STUPID? Oh, I'll kill him when I see him, I'LL FUCKING KILL HIM!

Wednesday, October 19

OK, so I didn't kill him, but I did throw him out. That was the easy part.

"She's making that up, Phoebe! She's just hurt. There was never anyone else. I decided it wasn't working and asked her to leave. That's all there is to it."

"Oh, shut up. Just shut up!" I said, fed up with hearing the sound of his voice. "I cannot believe I fell for your bullshit AGAIN. You don't want me. You're just frightened that no one else will put up with your lies and—"

"I'm not lying, Phoebe."

"Of course you're lying!" I shouted. "You just can't stop lying—you're like the Lord of the Lies!"

I threw some of his stuff into a carrier bag and handed it to him on the way out.

"It's that weight-gain thing, isn't it?" he snarled, finally showing his true colors. "I called you on being fat and you just can't hack it."

"Do you know what?" I shouted, forcing his bag into his hand. "I was concerned about my weight for a while and a very good friend of mine pointed out that whether I lost or gained, no else gave a shit. I was still me."

"Well, Lucy would say that," he scoffed. "Women always say that crap."

"Oh, it wasn't Lucy," I said, moving closer to him. "It was Oliver. Oliver, who happily fucked me and my extra ten pounds for months. So it seems not all men are as superficial as you."

He stopped smiling. "You slept with Oliver?"

"Many, many times," I said, smiling.

"Well, if he was so happy about it, why isn't he fucking you now? Maybe he found someone thinner."

"No, that was my mistake. We would still be sleeping together if I hadn't LOST MY FUCKING MIND! How did I EVER think you were good enough for me? Now, fuck off."

"Look, can I just say something?" he yelled as he was leaving, desperate to have the last word.

"No," I said, and firmly closed the door.

And now the hard part. Here I am. Back to square one. No partner, no sex life, and, what pains me the most, no

Oliver. Out of all the mistakes I've made this year, it's my only true regret.

Thursday, October 20

Oh for the love of God, I feel awful today and it has nothing to do with that miserable toad Alex, although he has been pestering me with texts all morning. I have a temperature, my throat is killing me, and I don't even want a cigarette. This must be serious. The selfish part of me wishes I'd kept Alex around to run after me and then infected him with this stupid mystery illness before I kicked him out.

Friday, October 21

One emergency appointment at the doctor's later and I've returned home with a two-week antibiotic prescription for tonsillitis. What am I, twelve? Still, I'm happy to get a few days off work, but no one will come look after me for fear of getting the bug. I want my mum, but she's in Canada. It's usually the kids who move as far away as possible from their parents, not the other way around. All the rest of the family went to Canada too, so at least they'll have someone handy if they get sick. Pah. Oliver would have looked after me. I want a pity party complete with emotionally unstable dancing girls and whining.

Saturday, October 22

My tonsils are the size of golf balls, but I've managed to eat noodle soup and drink tea. I had a fever last night and could have sworn I was having sex with Oliver in my pajamas. I had one cigarette, which made me feel ill to my very soul. I can't find the remote and I want to watch *Criminal Minds*. Nothing is going right. Oh, WHY have I been forsaken?

Wednesday, October 26

I'm finally feeling better and made it back into work, which, weirdly, I was actually looking forward to. But then I got the news: Frank has resigned and is going on leave at the end of the day.

"Can I see you for a moment, Phoebe?" he called from his office.

I walked in and closed the door. "Nice to see you back. Feeling better?" he asked.

"Much, thanks," I said, trying to cut to the chase and find out what the fuck was going on.

"You've heard I'm going, then? Vanessa is setting up a new business in London and I'm going with her. It's nearer her sister and she has no family left here now. Be a new start for both of us. We fly down tomorrow."

"Wow. So that's what you meant when you said you hoped that Brian wouldn't be your problem for much longer! Sneaky."

He smiled at me. "Yes. I didn't want to jinx things by saying anything too early."

"Good luck with everything. I mean that."

"You too, Phoebe. You too."

"Oh, before I forget, thanks for that e-mail. You were right. I've dumped Alex, but not because of what you said, before you get all conceited and smug. And that will be the only time I ever admit you were right about anything."

He left at five, with a bottle of scotch and a knowing smile we both shared as the door closed behind him.

Friday, October 28

I was going to take the weekend to recover properly, but then I remembered Lucy's party tomorrow. Shit. I've got no time to organize another costume. I'll have to wear my half of the Eva/Che costume, even though it really requires Che to be there in order to work out who the fuck I'm supposed to be.

Reason number 1,232 to hate Alex.

Sunday, October 30

Feeling much better, I arrived at Lucy's party last night in my fabulous outfit, armed with two bottles of Champagne and intending to get seriously pissed and ignore the fact I'm still on antibiotics and could fall into a booze-induced coma at any point.

The apartment was packed with guests and I spotted Lucy straightaway, dressed as Wonder Woman.

"PHOEBE! Why have you come as Margaret Thatcher?" she asked, doing a little spin.

"I'm Evita, you ridiculous cow. I'm a legend. Is Kyle here?"

"No. He's up in Thurso or somewhere. Not back till Tuesday."

"That's a shame. I was looking forward to meeting him!"

"Oh, you will! Soon. Now, get some booze down you, Maggie." She laughed. "Everyone's here already." And so they were. I looked around the room, smiling: Paul and Dan had come as Sonny and Cher, Hazel and Kevin had come as Morticia and Gomez, and Oliver . . . fuck . . . Oliver was there and he had come as a man who was going to ignore me all evening.

I grabbed Lucy. "You didn't tell me Oliver was coming!"

"Of course I didn't," she agreed, grinning. "You wouldn't have come. But he knew you'd be here and he still came."

"Is Ruth with him?"

"No. Now relax, Mrs. Thatcher, and if my milk disappears I'll know who to blame."

And off she went, leaving me to hide in the kitchen and drink my Champagne. It took me three glasses to pluck up the courage to speak to Oliver. "What have you come as then?" I asked, looking at his pirate costume and wishing I hadn't asked such a stupid question.

Thankfully, he smiled. "Nice to see you, Phoebe. How have you been?"

OK, I thought. Polite, but he's talking. "Not well, but I'm better now. Medicine's good, isn't it?" (What was I saying?) "But, yeah, it's nice to see you too!" We both smiled at each other and then someone at the other side of the room called him over and he walked away without another word. So what did I do? I did what I do best: I drank and flirted outrageously. On Champagne I flirted with Dracula, on gin I flirted with a cowboy, and on Jack Daniel's I came on to James Bond, Al Capone, and even a mermaid called Dave—although I'm not sure; I was pretty hammered by then. When the world started to spin, I went to Lucy's spare room to lie down. I was in there about ten minutes, and feeling a bit better, when I heard the door open and close. Then I heard Oliver's voice. "How's Alex? I hear he moved in. I'm glad things are working out for you." I sat up too quickly and then fell back down again with an "urgh" sound.

"No. Nope. Alex is gone. Away . . . away . . . You were right about him. Even my stupid boss was right about him. In fact, I was right about him until I decided to become an idiot and take him back. So go on. Tell me you were right. Make fun of the crazy lady," I ranted, waving my arms around in the air above my head. There was no reply.

I felt his weight on the bed beside me. Then he lifted my head into his lap and stroked my hair. "I'm not saying anything," he replied, "but I'll feel better in Chicago knowing you're not with that piece of shit."

"You still care? Oh, that's nice. We had sex in my pajamas, you know," I slurred. Then his words actually managed to bypass the booze and penetrate my brain. I sat up again and managed to stay up. "Chicago? Again? You're leaving?" My stomach did a huge somersault. "When?"

"Next week. Just for two months initially, and if it goes well I'll stay on. I'll be living with Ruth."

I suddenly felt sober. "Gosh," I said, not really knowing what else to say. "Hope it goes well then."

He just smiled, said, "Thanks," and gave me a hug. And as I hugged him back it hit me: He was leaving. OH FUCK HE WAS LEAVING. WITH RUTH! Panic set in. The thought of losing him completely made my head spin and my mouth go dry. "Don't go," I whispered. "Oh fuck, please don't go. What will I do without you?"

"What you've always done, I imagine. Meet some guys, maybe go out with a few, invent some new challenges if you're bored." He grinned. I couldn't let him leave. I had to think of something.

"WE STILL HAVE CHALLENGES LEFT!" I shouted in a panic, grabbing his face with both hands. "Remember? We still have a role play to do!"

"Phoebe," he began, "I don't think—"

"No. Listen." I sat up properly and made sure he was looking at me. "Here's an idea. What if we role-play that we're a real couple? What if we pretend we're in love? I mean, what if we pretend none of this shit ever happened and we pretend I'm not a selfish bitch who couldn't see what was right in front of her. What if you pretend, just for a second, to believe every word I'm saying and know that I mean it?"

He just stared at me.

"I fucking adore you, Oliver. I love you. I didn't realize until recently, but I do. I'm in love with you."

He didn't say anything. He walked to the door . . . and then he stopped. And locked the door.

We made love right there on the bed. There was no shouting, or gymnastics, or laughing. We were slow and quiet and we never took our eyes off each other. He was so gentle, and the moment he entered me I was so happy to have him back inside me again, to feel him moving his hands over my thighs and to feel his mouth on mine. It was so intense and I came before he did. It was beautiful.

This morning when I woke up he was gone.

I called him on the taxi ride home but he didn't pick up. He returned my call about half an hour ago. "I'm glad you called, Oliver. Are you coming 'round?"

"No," he said quietly, "I'm not."

"What? Why not? I thought last night . . ." And then it dawned on me. Last night was his way of saying good-bye.

"I've loved you for a long time, Phoebe, but you were right. What you said in that e-mail after we slept together— you were spot-on. I would get bored with you because I get bored with every woman I'm with, and I couldn't bear to hurt you, and I know that you'll fuck up my mind, more than you have already. We're both messed up and that's not a good combination. You went out of your way to date pretty much every man in Glasgow when I was right in front of you, spending all that time with you, sleeping with you, and you never once considered me. That says a lot about both of us. And after Alex again . . . I don't think you know what you want, Phoebe, but I don't think it's me. I don't know what will happen with Ruth, but she doesn't confuse me, and that's good enough for now."

I tried to find the words to tell him how wrong he was about me, about everything, but the only thing that came out was a pathetic sob.

"I didn't want this to happen, I really didn't, and I wish I could go back to just not giving a fuck what you do. But I can't. Let's just leave it at that. Take care, Phoebe."

I didn't think I was capable of getting my heart broken again after Alex. I guess I was wrong.

NOVEMBER

Thursday, November 3

The shops in Glasgow have already started putting up their Christmas window displays, which reminds me that this freakin' year is almost gone. I started it with such enthusiasm and now all I want to do is start it all over again.

I'm still pining for Oliver, but I think I'm getting near the stage where I can go two minutes without wondering what he's doing. Maybe. Still, work today was interesting. Dorothy from the London office took over for Frank as head of sales and she arrived all bright-eyed and bushy-haired; I like her. She looks like she doesn't take any shit, but she secretly listens to Paloma Faith on her iPod and walks around her office with no shoes on, admiring her own feet. Also, she took us all out for drinks, which is a clever way to get the troops on your side. She's given me the entertainment section to work on, as she feels it will excite me a bit more than the damn auto pull-out, and I agree. I need a change.

Friday, November 4

I resisted the urge to send Oliver an e-mail and pour my heart out because I know he won't reply. Everyone is trying to cheer me up, but it's not working. I want to go outside, throw my hands in the air, and wail at the sky, but Lucy reminded me how disturbingly weird that would be so I won't. For now, anyway. Tonight I rearranged my underwear drawer, occasionally looking at pairs of panties I wore when I had sex with Oliver and creepily hugging them. Enough is enough. He's not fucking dead, Phoebe, get a grip.

Saturday, November 5

OK, back to business, I am fed up crying over this. Oliver is clearly an idiot and a distraction I don't need; besides he's made his choice—he obviously wasn't as in love with me as he made out. So screw him. Any kind of self-respect I had at the beginning of the year has been lost. I have to get it back and remember that when life gives you lemons, add them to gin and stop fucking moping. I'm perfectly capable of putting this to the back of my mind and getting on with another challenge. I said I'd follow this list through to the end and I intend to do so. Voyeurism. Bring it on.

I'm not sure why I'm so drawn to this, but maybe it's because I like porn. I like watching people have sex. The sight of two slightly vacant, hairless people screwing each other senseless can turn me on. Not all porn, mind you. I prefer stuff where they actually kiss each other and smile, rather than the ones where they just look like they want to kill each other while they're screwing and shouting. Sex excites me, and the thought of another couple having sex excites me—but would I actually get turned on watching a real-life couple have sex right in front of me? I've placed an ad for a couple who'll help me find out. Get me, all businesslike and not thinking about Oliver's stomach and that "treasure trail" line of hair that leads down from his belly button . . . Nope, not at all. Oh, who am I kidding?

Monday, November 7

"Morning, Phoebe. What's your opinion on performance poetry?" asked Lucy as soon as I walked into the office. I hung my green winter coat on the back of my chair and shrugged. "Um. I don't have one. Why?"

"Because last night Kyle told me that he goes to open-mike nights and reads his poems to strangers and I have the feeling I'm dating a hipster."

"Ha, did he read one to you? Did he woo you with his rhythm and meter?"

"He didn't, but the fact you know what that means leads me to believe you're a hipster too," she sniggered.

"What's the problem with hipsters?" I laughed. "Sam was one, with his guitars and his tattoos and his silly straight hair."

"Sam was young—he'd have grown out of it. Kyle is thirty-nine. It's too late for him now. I don't hate hipsters; I just hate the automatic pretentiousness that goes with being one."

"Go and see him perform before you start being all judgy about it. It might be fun."

"Fine, but if I do, you're coming with me. I'm not sitting alone in some beatnik café surrounded by girls who have mustaches tattooed on their fingers and no shoes on while he recites a sonnet about losing his iPhone."

"Deal. Even if his poetry is crap, it'll be fun to watch you silently implode."

The afternoon was typically uneventful, but I'm almost enjoying my new section. Bar, club, and restaurant owners are far chattier than the grumpy car dealerships I'm used to dealing with. I also managed to kick Oliver out of my head whenever he popped in there, being all sexy and distracting.

As soon as I got home, I logged on to my special e-mail account with the false name and actually had a lot of replies to my "let me watch you do it" ad; (twenty-three, in fact) and have duly sifted through them. The majority of them have been sent by complete maniacs, old-timers, and people who compose their e-mails in text-speak:

Prof Cpl who have done this b4 but would love 2 do again LOL!

Why are you laughing? Stop pretending to text me.

I replied to a few with very specific conditions, like "must not be uncontrollably hairy" and "no toilet activities," and now all I can do is wait and see. Knowing my luck, I'll get to watch Mr. and Mrs. Missionary, who'll stare at me during the whole thing.

Wednesday, November 9

I received two e-mail replies back today. One from a couple who said they'd be happy to let me watch but only after their child was asleep (ARGH! I considered calling Social Services) and one from "Jamie and Lisa," who seemed to fit the bill—photogenic, midthirties, married, and as new to this as I am. We've arranged to meet up. It's kind of nice to know that I'm not the only one into trying this stuff. Sometimes I feel wrong in so many ways.

"You sure you want to do this alone?" asked Lucy. "It sounds sketchy."

"I know it does, but they seem fine. And no, you're not watching with me, before you ask."

"Well, I'll wait in the hotel bar for you. Just to be on the safe side."

That would make me feel better, although knowing Lucy she'll have had four cocktails and be showing her boobs to the bartender by the time I come back downstairs.

Thursday, November 10

I've taken next week off work, as I'm totally burned out. Dorothy couldn't care less, as I've met my targets and I told her I liked her toe ring. I think this entire year has suddenly caught up with me and I feel drained. A week of relaxation and reflection is just what I need. In other news, I got an e-mail from Jamie of "Jamie and Lisa." They've booked the hotel for Saturday and I'm beginning to feel nervous. What if it's too weird? What if I giggle? What if they don't let me leave? What if . . . what if they hold me down and burst into an a cappella version of "Brand New Key"?

I should have thought this through more.

Hazel, Kevin, and Grace have gone to Aviemore for the weekend, but she texted me on her way to the airport:

Good luck with your final challenge. You're almost there! xx

I'm glad someone's rooting for me.

Saturday, November 12

The big night. I met Jamie and Lisa in the hotel bar as planned. They were already sitting at a table when I walked in, trying not to stumble in new red heels. Lisa noticed me first and smiled, showing perfect teeth hidden behind adult braces. Jamie, tall and boyishly handsome, politely stood up to shake my hand.

"Phoebe?" he asked. I took his hand and it was sweaty. He must have been as nervous as I was.

"I got you a glass of red—hope that's OK?" asked Lisa, tucking a brown curl behind her ear. "I tried the Chardonnay and it was hellish."

"Perfect," I replied, feeling like I was there to interview them. I took a sip of wine just as Lucy wandered into the hotel. She walked past my table, winked at me, and perched herself at the bar.

Although the conversation wasn't awkward, I still felt tense. Was I going to see something that would give me nightmares in bed forevermore? I steeled myself and made my move.

"Shall we do this then?" I asked, downing my wine.

"Yep!" chirped Jamie eagerly.

He hadn't had any alcohol, whereas Lisa, like me, had inhaled her drink. As we all headed for the elevator, I turned around to make sure Lucy was still there and—surprise, surprise—she was chatting to a man at the bar and paying no attention to me or my impending doom.

Once upstairs, Jamie closed the curtains and they both sat on the bed. I sat on a great big chair like Ronnie fucking Corbett, wishing that I'd worn my contacts instead of my glasses to make it less obvious I wanted perfect vision for this. But when they began kissing I started to feel like a big old pervert and wondered what the fuck I was doing. Would it be rude to run away screaming? I was very conscious of my presence in the room, and I had a million questions popping into my head: what should I do with my hands? If I can't get a good enough look should I stand up, or is that just taking the piss?

At one point I did almost laugh out loud, but purely because my mind was in overdrive and from a certain angle Jamie's cock resembled a root vegetable and I started reciting *"One potato, two potato . . ."* in my head over and over. Thankfully, aggressively biting my lip stifled any giggles.

I must admit that the more they got into it, the less it did for me. I don't know how much of the act was for my benefit, but they fucked like pros and even genuinely seemed to be enjoying themselves, but it left me cold. I wasn't aroused, I just felt stupid. I didn't touch myself or even speak, and my initial embarrassment was soon replaced by a desire to get the hell out of there. However, I stuck around and watched silently until they finished.

They tumbled onto their backs in bed, smiling at each other. Not wanting to appear awkward or insensitive, I mumbled something about keeping in touch and sheepishly backed out of the room. I mean, keep in touch? What? Are we going to be pen pals now?

Maybe I'd have felt differently if Oliver had been there, but equally I know there's no way he'd have been able to sit still and resist the urge to whip off his clothes and jump in. One thing is certain, however, I will never look at a potato again in the same light.

I rushed back into the hotel bar, face flushed, wondering if somehow everyone knew exactly what I'd been up to.

Lucy nearly fell over a chair, rushing to get all the details. "How was it? What happened? Did you join in? TELL ME!"

"It was fine," I said with a shrug. I think I was in shock. Apart from the final role play with Oliver that would now never happen, my list was complete. Halle-fucking-lujah. Game over.

Sunday, November 13

I met Lucy and Hazel (and baby Grace) for coffee this afternoon.

"I still cannot believe you did that," said Lucy, scooping the froth off her cappuccino. "It's so insane. He was really hot as well. I'd have jumped him."

"Should we be talking about this in front of Grace?" asked Hazel, glancing over at the stroller.

Lucy rolled her eyes. "Oh, she's already seen it all with you and Kevin. You've scarred her for life—this conversation won't matter a jot."

"We've never done it in front of . . . Oh, actually there was that one time where I looked over and she was staring at us, but she was only a few weeks old. They can't even recognize color at that stage, never mind"—she dropped her voice to a whisper—"cock."

Lucy smirked.

"Oh!" Hazel continued. "Before I forget, ladies, New Year party at the Royal Hotel—I've booked the tickets. You can pay me later, Kevin got them on his credit card. Anyway, was that your final challenge, Phoebe?"

"There was one more role play to do with Oliver, but that's not going to happen now anyway, so . . . um, yeah . . . I guess it was!"

"Excellent work, young Henderson," said Lucy, raising her oversized mug. "You finally followed through on a resolution. You've gone from suburban shagger to Mick fucking Jagger! I'm very impressed."

I wasn't. I'd completed my challenges, but I'd lost Oliver. I smiled, silently congratulating myself on being the stupidest person alive.

Monday, November 14

9 a.m. Vacation week! I'm up and ready. This is going to be a good week. I'm going to catch up on some reading, clean up this hellhole, dance around in my slippers to quirky music, and make cocktails while watching '80s movies.

11 a.m. I'm going back to bed for a nap because doing nothing remotely strenuous for the past two hours has made me sleepy. I also killed a spider on purpose. What a complete bastard.

5 p.m. I'm still in bed and have wasted the entire day. I don't even feel like masturbating. My sex drive is at zero and I can't be bothered to find new batteries for my vibrator anyway. There's a sentence I never thought I'd say.

10 p.m. I've ordered curry and I'm now waiting for the delivery man in old jogging bottoms, no makeup, and my slippers on the wrong feet. Lucky boy.

1 a.m. Still awake and listening to Kate Bush. She and Florence Welch make me feel like I should be running around a pretty field with a floaty dress and bells on my toes, instead of lying in bed, bloated, wondering where the fuck my life went. I need to sleep.

Wednesday, November 16

I'm in a funk and not a Bootsy Collins kind of happy funk. I feel lost. So utterly hopeless and lost. I need to have a party. A big one that will spill out on to the street and end with a massive Mardi Gras–style conga. I need my friends. I need a hug. I need loud music and balloons and streamers and a '70s ice bucket shaped like a pineapple. I need to throw pretzels at folk and drink Advocaat (even though I've never tasted it and it might kill me). I need poetry, and braids in my hair and feminist rantings from a woman in stupid pointy glasses, and most of all I need to know that at some point I'll be happy again. Because I'm not. This whole journey of self-discovery has been pointless because regardless of who I'm fucking, and regardless of whether we spend the night together, I'm still going to bed and waking up completely alone. I never thought that one little list would turn my entire life upside down.

Thursday, November 17

Hazel phoned me first thing. "You all right, Phoebe? I got a really random voice mail from you last night. Something about pretzels and pointy women? I couldn't quite make it out."

I began to cry—sob uncontrollably is more accurate—and still had the phone in my hand fifteen minutes later when she appeared at the door. "Oh my goodness, Phoebe," she said quietly, putting her arms around me. "It'll be all right."

I wiped my eyes with my robe sleeve and sniffed. "I've fucked everything up. I'm such an idiot. He won't even speak to me."

"Don't be so hard on yourself," she whispered in my ear. "This was bound to happen. Oliver didn't stand a chance while you still had those feelings for Alex, and you can't be blamed for feeling them. But it's time to move on, Phoebe, you can't spend the rest of your life wishing things were different. If you love Oliver then keep telling him that and don't stop until he realizes what an idiot he's been."

Lucy came 'round after work armed with flowers and we talked for ages. She was predictably more blunt than Hazel.

"So you fucked up. Big deal. Nobody died, Phoebe. This year has been good for you. This was the year you stopped being so numb to everything and actually chose to experience your life instead of just muddling through, waiting for things to change. You changed them, so hallelujah to that!"

Despite the fact I'm three days into my vacation and have spent a third of that pissed and crying, I don't feel quite so desperate anymore. Sure, my eyes are puffy, but I feel incredibly clear. I'm starting to feel like me again.

Friday, November 18

Going out with Lucy tonight and I'm going to avoid gin and anyone with a penis just to be on the safe side. It will be the first time in ages that I've gone out with the intention of not hooking up. I feel liberated.

Sunday, November 20

FOR THE LOVE OF FUCK I'M HORNY! I was wondering when my sex drive would show up again. So far I've made my way through half a ton of crappy porn, and completely soaked my sheets twice. I'm now sitting here wishing someone would just come to my house and lie on top of me. I should place an ad for that: "Emotionally challenged woman seeks man for lying-on-top duties and possible thrusting." Knowing my luck I'd get that swinging Stormtrooper I saw online turning up and banging his head on the doorframe.

Wednesday, November 23

From: Lucy Jacobs
To: Phoebe Henderson
Subject: Tomorrow night

Hello. I don't care what you've got on this evening, you're coming to watch Kyle perform at his spoken-word event in town. I've managed to dodge two so far and he's insisting I go to this one. 7pm at the Gallery of Modern Art. You have to come.

From: Phoebe Henderson
To: Lucy Jacobs
Subject: Re: Tomorrow night

Oooh, OK. I'm dying to meet him. If it's terrible, I'll lie.

Thursday, November 24

I met Lucy outside the Gallery of Modern Art on Queen Street. She was waiting beside the Duke of Wellington statue, which for once didn't have a traffic cone stuck on its head. She waved me over.

"Are you ready for this?" she chuckled. "It's going to be dull as hell."

"Probably," I said, sticking some chewing gum in my mouth, "but I've never been to one before. It'll be an experience."

"Skydiving is an experience. This will be more like a punishment from God."

We went downstairs to the gallery library, where they'd set up an area of around twenty chairs in front of a small podium. The seats were beginning to fill up with the oddest group of people I've ever seen. There was a woman in her forties with a teacake in her hand, alternating between staring at it intensely and slowly tonguing the creamy filling. Then there was an elderly gentleman who wore a cravat, tapping his foot gently to music only he could hear. A crash from the back revealed four tipsy women in their twenties who couldn't quite master the art of sitting down and, finally, several nervous poets clutching their notes. A fella wearing jeans and a black T-shirt with leather bands wrapped around his wrists began to move toward us and I heard Lucy say behind me, "So what are you reading tonight, sexy?"

He smiled and opened the paper in his hand. "I'm doing a sonnet and a haiku. Is this Phoebe?"

"Yes," I said. "Lovely to finally meet you!"

"She's a hipster too." Lucy smiled. "I have no idea what a haiku is."

He laughed. "Pleasure to meet you, Phoebe. A haiku is a short poem that follows a syllabic structure, Lucy, and if you call me a hipster once more I'm never taking you to Urban Outfitters again."

I think I'm going to like Kyle.

The first person up was the organizer, thanking everyone for coming and reading a poem he'd written about a bus journey he'd once had and how the scenery reminded him of pompous ghosts (or something to that effect). Next was a tiny woman who'd written a poem to a man she hadn't seen in thirty years—after hearing at length about her "empty chasm" it was easy to understand why he'd fucked off. But when Kyle appeared onstage, everyone seemed to pay attention. He spoke beautifully, and although I'm not entirely sure what his sonnet was about, his haiku was beautiful and I remember every word:

When I look at her
My heart starts to see her in
Ways my eyes cannot

When it was over, Lucy clapped so hard I thought she'd damage her hands. "I didn't expect him to be good! Shit, I might like him even more now."

We politely stayed until the end, enduring poets of all shapes and sizes, some with obvious talent and some who just shouted words out in no apparent order and called it free verse while Lucy and I silently shook with laughter.

I left Kyle and Lucy kissing in the library and made my way home feeling both excited that my friend was embarking on a journey with someone like Kyle, and sickened that I was going nowhere except home alone.

Sunday, November 27

I'm kind of glad November is almost over. It's been an emotional one, to say the least. Couples have been watched, tantrums have been had, and tears have been shed on more than one occasion, but I feel better after my latest meltdown. Not having Oliver around has been strange, but I hope he's happy whatever he's doing. What I mean by happy is: miserable as sin and missing me terribly, but I'll send good thoughts anyway.

Monday, November 28

I grabbed an elevator with Lucy into work and I felt so much brighter and happier than I have in ages. I also didn't think about Oliver once all morning. Breakthrough! But by the afternoon, he was all I could think of and the inevitable e-mail was sent:

> **From:** Phoebe Henderson
> **To:** Oliver Webb
> **Subject:** Hi
>
> Hope Chicago is treating you well and the job too. The weather is now freezing here and, actually, fuck that—what I really want to say is that I miss you. I miss you terribly and I wish things were different and that you'd even reply to this to tell me to piss off. I know we haven't discussed the last night we saw each other, not properly, but I meant every (coherent) word I said. I love you. Very much.
>
> Phoebe x

So far no reply. This has to be the last attempt. I don't want to still be e-mailing him in ten years' time like some bunny boiler. Anyway, drinks with Paul, Dan, and Lucy planned for tomorrow, which should be fun, and if I pretend I'm still depressed/suicidal I might be able to persuade them into taking me for sushi to ease my pain.

Wednesday, November 30

I've been sick as a dog all day, so had to cancel drinks with the team last night. I feel so yucky, what the hell is wrong with my immune system? First food poisoning, then tonsillitis, and now some freakin' tummy bug that is keeping me away from my daily Bounty fix. Bah. I feel awful and I'm so stressed out, and my period is late and usually that's a good thing as it—

Wait a minute . . . My period is late? My period is late! FUCK!

DECEMBER

Thursday, December 1

"I'm late."

"You're fine. It's only just gone nine," said Lucy from behind her desk, "the boss doesn't . . . Oh. Wait. Late? As in . . . ?"

I nodded.

"Oh SHIT."

"I know. Just a few days . . . but I'm never late! Stress? Don't you think it could be stress?"

"When did you last have sex?" asked Lucy quietly. "Do you remember?"

"Of course I do! It was at your Halloween party. With Oliver. But I'm on the Pill! I can't be pregnant—I always take my pill for this VERY REASON!"

"You were also on antibiotics at the time, Phoebe, and stop shouting at me. I didn't knock you up."

"Antibiotics? Oh. Hmm . . . I'd forgotten about them. Oh shitshitshit!"

"Stop panicking. Go and get a test at lunchtime, we'll do it together."

And so we did. I bought my overpriced test from the chemist and peed on it in front of Lucy. We stood in the toilets and waited. It was negative. "Panic over." Lucy winked. "Now, stop being such a stress bunny and it'll appear. Then you'll moan to me about that instead of this. Trust me."

Saturday, December 3

Still no sign of my period and I'm still feeling rough as dogs. I'll see the doctor on Monday and get something for this. I've been looking up my symptoms online and, having ruled out pregnancy, I'm either going through the menopause or it is just stress and my diet, which is probably much more likely. Maybe my ovaries are broken?

Monday, December 5

I went to the doctor and she doesn't think it's anything to worry about, probably stress, but she took a blood sample to check my hormone levels and so on. Apparently menopause is rare in women my age BUT not impossible. I don't know what's worse—the thought of being pregnant or the thought of never being able to become pregnant. I should have the results on Wednesday, which means two days of acting like a massive hypochondriac. Mum was due to call tonight but I texted her to say that I wasn't feeling well so I'd speak to her later in the week. Of course she called anyway.

"Feeling sick? Are your boobs sore?"

"I'm not pregnant, Mum, I've checked. The doctor took some blood to check my hormone levels anyway." I started to laugh. "She's even checking for early menopause. I'm only thirty-three!"

"Well, I did go through the change at thirty-nine."

"What?"

"And your grandmother, too."

"What?!"

"Oh, and your great-aunt Helen. She was also about that age. So it might not be such a wild theory."

"ARE YOU KIDDING ME? Why on Earth didn't you mention this earlier? That's only six years away!"

"Didn't I? Sorry, love. I'm sure it's not that. I always put mine down to the copious amounts of drugs I took in the '70s. Something had to give."

After I hung up, I threw up.

Tuesday, December 6

I'm feeling fine today. No period but a couple of cramps and the nausea has gone. I feel silly for panicking so easily. I made my way into work, stopping to get tea and a bacon roll from the café across the street. I felt ready to embrace the day.

Dorothy has decided that daily morning meetings aren't productive and so she scrapped them, saying she wants us to "hit the ground running at nine a.m." Ugh, it seems that despite her endearingly quirky ways, underneath it all she's still an evil saleswoman.

Hazel texted to say she's received our booking confirmations for the New Year party at the Royal Hotel, which reminded me I haven't bought a dress. I spent most of the afternoon on eBay looking for one and wondering why the hell people sell makeup online that's already been used. Bleurgh. "I have a rare but contagious weeping skin condition that this concealer wouldn't cover up. I tried. Yours for only a tenner!" Yeah, I'll pass, thanks, scabby.

Wednesday, December 7

I called the doctor's office, but again the stupid receptionist wouldn't give me my test results over the phone so I have to go in and see the doctor first thing tomorrow.

"After what your mum said, it probably is the menopause," Lucy laughed. "If you were of noble blood you'd be Barren Von Henderson."

"That's not funny! I bet my iron levels are down or something, due to the millions of periods which have arrived ON TIME over the years. Maybe I've run out of blood. Is that possible?"

"You need to calm down. Come over to my place tonight. We can eat cake and watch *The Good Wife*."

"Did you make the cake?"

"No, Kyle brought it the other night."

"OK then."

"He said that he wanted me to lick cake off the end of his—"

"LALALALALA!" I shouted, covering my ears. "If you finish that sentence I won't be going anywhere near your dirty little dessert."

"I was joking," she chuckled. "Got your mind off your results, though, didn't it?"

"I don't believe you, but thanks. I'll be over at eight."

I popped in to see Dorothy and tell her I needed to see the doc in the morning. She twirled around in her chair to check the vacation board. "You still have a day to use up. Take it tomorrow if you like."

So I've got the day off tomorrow and I get to eat cake tonight. Things are looking up.

Thursday, December 8

I crashed at Lucy's house last night. We managed to demolish the remaining three-quarters of a chocolate cake (which I checked first for penis imprints) and watched five full episodes of *The Good Wife*.

"I could totally be a big-time lawyer," said Lucy, admiring Josh Charles in his suit. "I'd be all 'OBJECTION!' The judge would sustain it and then the case would fall apart because of things that happened. Then I'd sleep with Josh Charles."

"He isn't a real lawyer, you know."

"I don't care. It's my destiny."

I left her place at half eight this morning and drove over to the doctor's office to get my test results. Regardless of what it might turn out to be, I felt utterly and completely grateful that at least I wasn't pregnant. THAT would have been a fucking disaster. The doctor saw me right away.

"From the date of your last period, you'll be about six weeks along," she said with a bright smile. "Would you like me to book you in for your first appointment?"

I sat there stunned.

"I'm pregnant?"

"Yes."

"I'm pregnant?"

"Well, yes."

"But I took the test. It said I wasn't. I don't . . . I mean . . . how can this . . . ?"

"It's not uncommon for tests to come back negative, especially in the early weeks. So, shall I book you in to see the midwife?"

"No . . . I mean, I don't know. I'm on my own. I don't know if I can do this on my own. What would you do?"

"Erm, I can't answer that. OK. Take some time to think— it's still early, and you have options."

I know what my options are, and I can't bear to even think about that. Not yet, anyway. I went straight home and sat on the couch for, oh, about four hours. Lucy called four times but I didn't answer. Fucking pregnant? I'm thirty-three and single. Oh God, what do I tell Oliver? This is bad. This is very bad.

Friday, December 9

The commute this morning was a blur. I remember sitting next to a woman who smelled like she was wearing all of the perfume ever made and the next thing I remember is Lucy picking up my coat, which had fallen from the back of my chair to the floor.

"You're a sleepyhead today!" she chirped. "You didn't call me back yesterday. Was it bad news? Are you going to get hot flushes and chew on calcium tablets all day long?"

"I'm pregnant."

I saw the smile evaporate from her face. "How? We took that test. I saw you pee. There was only one line! Two is for yes, one is for no."

"The test was wrong," I sighed, putting my head in my hands. "This is a nightmare."

Lucy pulled over a chair and sat down beside me.

"It doesn't have to be," she whispered. "You don't want it, and . . . It's not a baby yet, you know, it's a bunch of cells."

"I can't think right now. I'll try to get through today nor-mally and then take the weekend to try to start processing this."

"You call me if you need me," said Lucy. "Promise?"

"Promise."

9:40 p.m. I've had a bath and I'm feeling calmer. I think I need to have an abortion. I'm not remotely religious and I'm practical. I have no partner, my family lives in Canada, I have no savings, and most important I know nothing about kids! I've never been maternal. Maybe I want them one day, but not like this. I would make a terrible mother. Children scare me—they're noisy, uncooperative little rat bags AND I'd have to stop smoking. I'm too selfish for this. There's no way I'm having a baby.

Sunday, December 11

I've had a lot of time to think about things. In fact, I haven't thought about anything else. I have a million questions, like: What if I did have this baby? What if this is my one chance, only I don't know it and I have an abortion and it's too late? What if I spend the next twenty years waiting for Mr. Right and he doesn't turn up? Also, how much will it hurt and will giving birth completely destroy my lady parts?—which aren't as important but still crossed my mind. I haven't told Hazel because I worry that telling another mother (not my own—God, not yet) would make it seem real, and at the moment it still feels like it's happening to someone else. Good plan, Phoebe: head in the sand. I wish it were happening to someone else. I'd arranged to see Hazel tomorrow anyway. I'll tell her then.

Tuesday, December 13

I went 'round to Hazel's for dinner, even though I wasn't remotely hungry, and we sat in her kitchen. I watched in silence as she fed Grace —who's now one and very sweet—in her high chair. Grace watched her mummy intensely, got really excited about her pudding, then threw the whole fucking lot onto the floor.

"So what's new with you?" Hazel asked innocently.

"I'm pregnant."

I waited for the shrieks of happiness and the joyous tales of how wonderful motherhood is, but they never came. Instead she said, "Right, OK. How do you feel about it?"

"Scared," I mumbled, and I could feel the tears starting. "I don't know if I can do this."

She hugged me for a minute. "Listen, Phoebe, I'm no expert, but I know how you feel, believe me. Being a mum is hard work and it'll change everything. You'll lose sleep, your body will change completely, you'll be demented half the time; you'll realize you actually know nothing about hard work and you'll pretty much spend every second worrying."

"So, what?" I sniffed. "You're saying don't do it?"

"No," she said, looking at Grace. "I'm just telling you the facts. But what I will say is that, for me, having my baby was the single greatest move I ever made. Think you love Oliver? Try multiplying what you feel by ten million and it won't even come close. It's astonishing what you can do when you love someone that much."

"On my own?"

"Yes, on your own! You're not incapable, Phoebe, and I have no doubt that you'd cope very well. Women do it all the time. Besides, you have all of us. You won't be alone."

And that was the moment I decided to keep my baby.

Thursday, December 15

The dress arrived from eBay and it fits, despite a huge amount of boob squashing, but I can live with that. Apart from the nausea and tiredness, I don't *feel* very pregnant, but then again, I have no idea what pregnant is supposed to feel like. What I *am* feeling is highly emotional and annoyed at Oliver, which unfortunately got the better of me this morning before work:

From: Phoebe Henderson
To: Oliver Webb
Subject: Some news

Dear Oliver,

Hope you are well. A lot has been going on here and we really need to talk. I know I've tried several times with no success and perhaps you've blocked me or changed your identity (or something less dramatic) but it is imperative that we speak. Imperative's a good word, isn't it? Anyway, I miss you, I hope you miss me and OH, JUST STOP DICKING AROUND AND PHONE ME—WE'RE HAVING A BABY, YOU MISERABLE BASTARD!

The e-mail ended up in my deleted items. I'll try again when I'm less irrational and less inclined to write something hideous.

When I got into the office I made an appointment to see the midwife. This is just too weird. Then I was reminded that it's the work Christmas night out tomorrow: drinks here followed by drinks in the pub downstairs and the compulsory wearing of silly paper hats. It would be less painful if I could actually partake in any of the above drinking. Dammit.

I had lunch with Lucy in the canteen and told her I'd decided to keep the baby.

"Are you sure this is definitely what you want?"

"It's not ideal, but my heart is telling me yes. So, yes."

She squealed and threw her arms round me. "I get to be Auntie Lucy! This is so exciting!"

"I'm not telling anyone until after the holidays, so keep it quiet. But yes, you get to be Auntie and I get to be Mummy. Fuck. I'm going to be a mummy. Holy shit."

"An amazing mummy. Your kid will adore you as much as I do. Have you told Oliver yet?"

"He won't return my calls or texts, but to be honest, I'd rather do this face-to-face."

"I'm starting to dislike him," she said, biting into a banana. "He needs to know, but if he won't pick up, what the hell else are you supposed to do? Skywriting? Carrier pigeon?"

"Carrier stork?" I suggested before making a groaning noise and placing my head in my hands. "He's going to freak, I know he is."

"Stress isn't good for the baby, Phoebe. Or the embryo or whatever the fuck it's called. It needs a calm place to chill out and grow feet and stuff. The Oliver thing will work itself out. Trust me."

Friday, December 16

I've been trying not to smoke, but this morning I had one and it smelled and tasted as vile as my guilt, so the rest of the packet got binned—I bought some nicotine patches and a year's supply of chewing gum on the way to work.

My dysfunctional brain meant I'd forgotten to bring a change of clothes for the work do tonight, so while everyone else got glammed up, I was left borrowing Lucy's makeup in the hope that heavy eyeliner would distract from my boring gray work suit.

"Is Kyle coming to the New Year party?" I asked Lucy, inspecting the various shades of lipstick she had in her bag.

"No, it's sold out," she replied with a sigh. "And he's going to see his family for Christmas."

"So you'll be just as miserable as me, then? Excellent. I hate to wallow alone."

"Yes, although I'll be drunk for the entire fortnight and Skyping him naked."

"You're so lucky. When is this freakin' party going to start?"

When five p.m. hit, Dorothy popped open the Champagne, Brian put some shitty Christmas playlist on YouTube, and Kelly handed around the mince pies, fluttering her new press-on party lashes in Stuart's direction. I declined a pie and ate some salty crackers instead, washed down with milk for my heartburn. Rock and fucking roll.

"Not drinking, Phoebe?" Dorothy asked when she saw my untouched glass of Champagne.

"Um, no," I said, scrambling around in my brain for a reason why. "It's just . . . I'm on antidepressants."

"Oh. Right," she said, not knowing how to respond. "I'll get you some Coke."

Antidepressants? Oh fuck it, I'd rather the office gossiped about my mental health than know the real reason. They'll find out when I want them to.

At nine everyone made their way downstairs, where friends and partners had already arrived. By eleven I'd had three glasses of fresh orange and was feeling increasingly annoyed by everyone's various states of drunkenness. I decided to call it a night. I grabbed Lucy on my way out. "Have a good night. I'm going home now; turns out I'm a thundering bore when I'm sober."

She laughed and hugged me. "You, Phoebe Henderson, are remarkable. I'll call you tomorrow."

I made my way to the taxi rank, stopping to get a fried pizza, and chips with curry sauce, on the way, vowing that from tomorrow I'll make an effort to eat more healthily.

Wednesday, December 21

Bored with my own company, I drove over to Hazel's tonight to help her wrap Christmas presents.

"Are you feeling any happier?" she asked, fiddling with the end of the Scotch tape roll.

"I think so," I said, considering things for a second. "I imagine it's like being in prison: all my pleasures and privileges have been revoked, I'm spending a lot of time thinking about my life, and I know that very soon some woman is going to make me spread my legs and inspect my chocha."

"Oh hell, Phoebe." Hazel laughed. "Any positives you'd like to share?"

"Yeah. My tits look great in this top." I stuck a bow on Hazel's perfectly wrapped present and giggled. "I'm already wondering if it's a boy or a girl and what I'd prefer. Do I want to know or just wait and get a surprise when it pops out?"

"They don't 'pop out,'" remarked Hazel. "It's more like a feeling of pressure, then a whoosh, and they flop out."

"Oh, so it's just a feeling of pressure? That's good!"

"Well, you feel like you're being ripped in half and that your rectum might also make a guest appearance, but yeah. Pressure."

"ARGGH. That's it, you're having this baby for me."

Thursday, December 22

Work was manic today, with everyone trying to sell any advertising space we had left before we finish tomorrow for the holidays. Luckily for me, this is a busy time for bars and restaurants so I was sold out and left twiddling my thumbs, wondering what I'd like for Christmas. As much as I'd like Santa to bring me Ryan Gosling, what I really want is my mum. I feel vulnerable, confused, and very much in need of a hug. I've left two messages for her and Dad but I think they've pissed off somewhere for Christmas week. They're probably visiting my hippie aunt Kate and her mystical offspring. I hope she calls me back sooner rather than later, I don't want to get to the Christmas Day phone call and have to explain what's happening through a mouthful of Brussels sprouts.

Friday, December 23

Last day of work. There was nothing to do, the phones were blissfully quiet, but still we had to hang around the office and wait for London to tell us we could piss off. Dorothy gave us each a £10 M&S voucher, which was very thoughtful and will no doubt go toward a decent maternity bra. It's finally starting to mentally sink in, but I still don't physically feel like I'm with child. Perhaps that starts when you get booted in the ribs by an invisible foot. Still, there are some benefits:

1. My acne has cleared up.
2. My boobs are getting bigger.
3. There's no chance of my being sacked from work unless I deliberately kill everyone during a particularly impressive mood swing.

And some drawbacks . . .

1. I can't dye my hair. A gray-hair mutiny is taking place.
2. I can't smoke or drink—possibly the only two things in life worth getting out of bed for.
3. I throw up at least twice a day, sometimes more if I smell coffee.
4. I nap constantly and am becoming a giant bore.

Kelly is going to Paris for New Year with her boyfriend and she's hoping he proposes. Normally I'd be snarky about this, but I gave her a hug and wished her luck. It would be nice if someone got a happy ending this year.

Saturday, December 24

I ventured out to get some last-minute shopping done today. At the moment I want to grab every pregnant woman I see and shout in her face, "I'VE GOT ONE OF THEM IN MY STOMACH TOO! IT'S VERY SMALL, YOU KNOW!"

I got home, had a bath, lay on the couch, and put the TV on. That was it. Of course I also went online for the millionth time to see what exciting things my fetus was up to. Apparently it's the size of a blueberry now. That's ridiculous. I'll be at Lucy's for Christmas dinner and, knowing my condition and not wanting to poison me, she and I have agreed that we'll just buy prepared food and she won't be involved in any attempts at cooking. After dinner, Hazel, Kevin, Paul, and Dan are coming over in the evening, which will be fun until they all get drunk and boring and I make myself sick on wafer-thin mints.

Sunday, December 25

7 a.m. I woke up feeling sick so spent half an hour sitting on bathroom floor beside the toilet, not being sick but making an impressive low-pitched moaning sound. Then I went back to bed.

12 p.m. I got woken up again by the phone:

"Merry Christmas, darling! How's my favorite girl?"

"Merry Christmas, Dad. I'm fine. How are you? How's Mum?"

"She's here—we're both fine, leaving shortly for an eleven-hour drive to Vancouver so thought we'd catch you beforehand. I'll put your mum on."

"Hi, Mum. Merry Christmas!"

"Phoebe, Merry Christmas, how are you? We've put some money in your account, so buy yourself something nice. Just doing some last-minute packing so I can't stay on long. We're visiting your aunt Kate—she's finally finished her Reiki training. She uses crystals, you know. I've been looking forward to this for weeks. Not the most conventional Christmas, of course, but your dad's sacral chakra's been all out of whack since that camping trip. It's like living with John Wilmot. I need some calm back in my life. What about you, darling?"

Oh, brilliant. I can't tell her now, can I?

"Going to Lucy's for dinner, nothing too exciting. Same old, same old here, Mum." Yes, except I'm a monumental idiot and soon-to-be single parent. Would you mind giving up your life in Canada and popping back here for eighteen years, please?

"Good for you, have a wonderful time! Oh, before we go, we'll be over for a visit in January—I'll let you know when later. Bye, love."

"Bye, Mum. Say bye to Dad for me."

I'll tell them in January. Face-to-face is better—at least then I can see their tears of disappointment up-close.

2 p.m. I arrived at Lucy's house for dinner and her place looked very festive. I had one glass of cava and orange juice and we opened presents. Lucy loved her earrings and I got my first pair of maternity jeans.

"I could fit into those now."

"Nonsense. In a few months you'll be wishing to fuck you had the figure you have now."

She saw the look of sheer horror on my face.

"No, I just mean that you're not fat now. But you will be. I'm not helping, am I? Erm, Merry Christmas!"

3:30 p.m. Dinner eaten, we moved into the living room and I promptly fell asleep on the couch from food exhaustion.

7 p.m. I woke up on the couch with a party hat on my face and Lucy, Paul, and Dan all giggling in the kitchen.

"Sorry," I said, walking through. "How rude of me. Merry Christmas!"

"Don't be silly!" replied Paul. "Get all the sleep you can now. You'll be constantly exhausted once the baby's here."

"Why does everyone feel the need to tell me how crap my future's going to be? I hope you have presents for me, otherwise this will be a long night."

It was a good evening and surprisingly I lasted until well after one in the morning. Paul and Dan bought me an electronic cigarette and some cartridge things that don't have any tar in them.

"I thought at least pretending to smoke might help," Paul said conspiratorially. "It has water vapor so it looks like you're smoking. I wouldn't use it in public, though—the dirty looks might tip you over the edge."

Finally I wandered off to crash in Lucy's spare room, the very room I conceived in, in fact, and dropped off to sleep, thinking about Oliver and wondering if he was thinking about me.

Thursday, December 29

I attempted to call Oliver at his office today, with the notion that I'd just tell him about the pregnancy and get it over with.

An American girl answered his phone: "I'm sorry, Oliver's not here. Who's calling?"

"It's Phoebe. When will he be back?"

"Oh, I'm not sure; I think he's staying with friends over the holidays."

"Can you tell him I called?"

"Sure will, Fifi. Bye."

Fifi? Oh, genius. Just brilliant.

Friday, December 30

So this horrendous year is almost at an end but I still have the New Year party to look forward to. Being pregnant has actually taken all the social pressure off going out: I have no sex drive or inclination to hook up, and the lack of booze in my diet has ruled out the possibility of any drunken mistakes. I can just arrive, eat, dance, then go to bed early like a bore and no one will talk about me for being a big drip.

Saturday, December 31

4 p.m. Arrived at the hotel and made it to the room just in time to throw up all over the lovely clean toilet, which I then had to clean up and it made me sick again. Lucy promptly left the room, swearing she'd sleep in the lobby if they couldn't find her somewhere else to stay. I sat on the bed and ate crackers I'd brought in my suitcase, cursing every penis I've ever encountered and swearing I'd never go near one again except for castration purposes. I also swore at Oliver for not being here to support me, even though I haven't actually told him yet.

5 p.m. Naptime before the pointless dinner I've already paid for. I'm considering not going, as the thought of food is almost too much to bear. I don't want dinner. I want crackers. And ice cream. Oh, and pickled onions.

5:30 p.m. I woke myself up by rolling over on my sore boobs. I was so hungry I ate some shortbread before running the shower to get ready. Then I stood under the shower for twenty minutes, singing Bruce Springsteen songs and rubbing my belly, wondering who's in there.

6:30 p.m. I got dressed for dinner and became bewitched by my growing chest, which looks great in my new black dress. I ate another biscuit on way downstairs to meet everyone.

"How are you feeling, love?" asked Hazel, pretending to act concerned, but secretly pleased at my condition.

7 p.m. The main hall looked beautiful. New Year balloons sat patiently in a big net on the ceiling, waiting to bounce off everyone and reminding me that I'll soon resemble one. We all sat down to eat—I managed to make it through the meal perfectly fine, until dessert, when the texture of my perfectly lovely chocolate mousse made me gag, and I had to run to the bathroom, leaving my friends to explain to onlookers that I'm pregnant and they should carry on and enjoy their meal. I returned in time to devour Kevin's oat-cakes and sip a glass of red wine while the lady at the next table looked at me disapprovingly through tiny glasses. So I then had a puff on my fake cig (she got up and left).

9 p.m. The ceilidh began. Usually my favorite part, but this year I sat and watched, almost pissing my pants when an overenthusiastic twirl from Kevin revealed he wasn't wearing anything under his kilt. I did try a few of the slower, less whirly dances, but my feet began to hurt so I went up to my room to change my shoes and lay on the bed like a big sweaty lump.

11 p.m. On the way back down I noticed a tall, kilted man with brilliant legs at Reception. It made me miss sex for a moment, and as I walked past the man with his sexual legs said, "Phoebe?"

I knew that voice. That Irish voice. I turned around, and standing there on those very legs was Oliver, looking so handsome I could have just leapt on him from across the room. "Oliver! How . . . What . . . what are you doing here?" I stammered.

"Wait for me inside. I'm just going to dump my case. You look deadly, by the way."

I rushed through to the hall, thankful that I'd changed my shoes, and grabbed Lucy, who was doing shots with Kevin.

"He's here! Oliver is here!" I blurted out.

"I know." Lucy smiled. "I invited him. I was worried he wouldn't make it."

"What? Did you tell him? Oh, Lucy, please tell me you didn't tell him."

"Of course not. That's your job. I just made him realize that he should be here for New Year, with the people that love him. Like you."

And with that Lucy was dragged off to dance by some old fella in a gray suit and I sat down at the table. God, I was nervous.

Oliver came in five minutes later and sat down beside me.

"So, how are you?" he asked. I could tell he didn't have a clue what to say to me and noticed that his gaze had moved from my face and was now transfixed on my boobs.

"Why are you back, Oliver? All those e-mails and texts I sent, and you never replied. To any of them. I felt so stupid."

"I'm so sorry," he said, looking down at the table. "I behaved so badly—I just didn't know what to say to you. I'm a cunt, I know."

I took a sip of my orange juice and tried to figure out what to say next. "Orange juice?" remarked Oliver, like he'd just watched me drink bleach. "You're not pacing yourself, are you?"

"No. Well, yes . . . long night ahead, you know."

We sat in an awkward silence for a moment as the ceilidh ended and the band began. "Want to dance?" asked Oliver, taking my hand.

"Sure," I said, not really wanting to, but we made our way to the dance floor anyway, Oliver waving at people as we walked past. We both danced stupidly to the band's terrible rendition of "Billie Jean," but I wasn't having fun. At all. Half of me wanted to grab him and kiss him and pretend like none of this was happening and the other half wanted to sit him down and ruin his life.

"Oliver!" I shouted over the music. "We need to talk."

"What?" he said, straining to hear me. "What did you say?"

The music dimmed and: "Ladies and gentlemen, one minute to go, please have your glasses ready!" the bandleader announced.

Lucy ran over with lemon soda and orange juice for me and a glass of Champagne for Oliver and I saw everybody make their way over to join us. Both Hazel and Lucy glanced in my direction as if to ask, *Have you told him?* but I shook my head and took another sip of my drink.

As I watched my friends count down to the New Year, I suddenly felt horribly alone. They had no idea what lay in store for them, but I knew exactly what was ahead for me. The only thing I didn't know was if Oliver would be part of it.

"HAPPY NEW YEAR!" So we all kissed and hugged and sang that traditional freakin' song and then danced to the band like maniacs. Half an hour later I decided it was time.

I took Oliver by the hand and led him up to his room. I'm sure the poor guy must have thought I was taking him there for make-up sex, but he was in for a shock. He went to kiss me and I kissed him back for a second, remembering how much I missed his kiss and his touch and his . . . "Wait," I said, pulling away, "I need to talk to you. It's important and might rule out any future kissing."

"Oh fuck, you're not seeing someone, are you? Lucy didn't mention anyone and I thought—"

"No, I'm not seeing anyone, Oliver, it's just—"

"You're not still doing those challenges, are you? I mean it's fine if you are, but don't involve anyone else. Please. I don't want you to be with anyone else. Can you do that? For me?"

"Well, I do have one more challenge," I said. "An unplanned one, shall we say . . . and it will involve another person—"

"A girl?" he asked, suddenly becoming interested.

"Or a boy," I replied. "I don't know yet."

"I don't understand, Phoebe."

"Oh Christ, I'm not explaining this very well. Just sit down, Oliver." He sat on the edge of the bed looking totally confused.

"Oliver, I'm pregnant. That night at Halloween . . . my antibiotics fucked up my Pill and I'm pregnant. Yes, it's yours, and, yes, I'm keeping it. So there will be a new challenge. Fuck, this will be my biggest challenge yet. And I'd love for you to kiss me and be excited and want to be involved, but I'll also understand if you don't. There's no pressure from me at all."

He just stared at me. I could see his mind working overtime.

"So what I'm going to do is this: I'm going back to my room because I'm exhausted. If you come to my room later—Room 202—come only if you want this too. You have to be sure. But if you don't come, I'll know the answer and

I'll see you at breakfast and we can talk about what's going to happen when you go back to Chicago. Deal?"

Sounds which resembled "Fuck" and "OK" were made, so I turned around and made my way back to my room. Which is where I am now. In bed and waiting. It's been two hours.

I know it's a lot to take in; perhaps a few hours isn't enough time for anyone to make this kind of decision. If he doesn't come, I'll manage somehow, but I'm hoping he loves me enough to show up. . . .

Sunday, January 1

I was woken by the sound of Lucy and Hazel knocking at the door at around four in the morning.

"PHOEBEEEEE. WAKE UP!"

"Go away," I grunted, annoyed it wasn't Oliver.

"Phoebe. Play with us. Come play with us . . . forever . . . and ever. . . ."

"I'm sleeping, you bastards. I'll see you tomorrow."

"FINE!" shouted Hazel. "But we brought you back something from the bar. If I leave it out here someone will steal it."

I got up and dragged myself to the door, and when I opened it, there was Oliver, looking completely disheveled and tipsy, with Lucy and Hazel on either side, smiling like lunatics. He stepped forward and placed his hand on my stomach.

He grinned. "Let's fucking do this."

Acknowledgments

I'd like to say a massive thank-you to the following people:

My spectacular agent, Kerry Glencorse, at Susanna Lea Associates and my fabulous editor, Kathryn Taussig, at Quercus, who believed in my novel from the beginning and who have guided and supported me throughout. Also, to everyone who read my novel at various stages and gave me invaluable feedback.

My wonderful parents, Yvonne and Hassan, and my sister, Claudia, for their love, understanding, and support and who never once doubted that I'd get there in the end, even when I did. Also to my friends who have encouraged and supported me regardless—I'm very grateful to you all.

Finally to my precious, beautiful daughter, Olivia, who makes every single day just that little bit brighter and who is never, ever allowed to read this book.